TITANS

TITANS

Leila Meacham

G|C

GRAND CENTRAL
PUBLISHING

NEW YORK   BOSTON

Copyright © 2016 by Leila Meacham
Reading group guide copyright © 2016 by Leila Meacham and Hachette Book Group, Inc.

Cover design by Anne Twomey. Cover photo b y Elizabeth Watt. Cover copyright © 2017 by Hachette Book Group, Inc.

Grand Central Publishing
Hachette Book Group
1290 Avenue of the Americas, New York, NY 10104
grandcentralpublishing.com
twitter.com/grandcentralpub

Originally published in hardcover and ebook by Grand Central Publishing in April 2016.

First Trade Edition: April 2017

Grand Central Publishing is a division of Hachette Book Group, Inc. The Grand Central Publishing name and logo is a trademark of Hachette Book Group, Inc.

The publisher is not responsible for websites (or their content) that are not owned by the publisher.

The Hachette Speakers Bureau provides a wide range of authors for speaking events. To find out more, go to www.hachettespeakersbureau.com or call (866) 376-6591.

Library of Congress Cataloging-in-Publication Data
Names: Meacham, Leila, 1938- author.
Title: Titans / Leila Meacham.
Description: First Edition. | New York ; Boston : Grand Central Publishing, 2016.
Identifiers: LCCN 2015044430| ISBN 9781455533831 (hardback) | ISBN 9781455566013 (large print) | ISBN 9781478932727 (audio download)
Subjects: | BISAC: FICTION / Family Life.
Classification: LCC PS3563.E163 T58 2016 | DDC 813/.54--dc23 LC record available at http://lccn.loc.gov/2015044430

ISBNs: 978-1-4555-3384-8 (trade pbk.), 978-1-4555-3381-7 (ebook)

Printed in the United States of America

LSC-C

10 9 8 7 6 5 4 3 2 1

In loving memory of Sara Lynn Leck Robbins,
paleontologist, irreplaceable friend

Coincidence is God's way of remaining anonymous.

—Old saying

TITANS

Prologue

From a chair beside her bed, Leon Holloway leaned in close to his wife's wan face. She lay exhausted under clean sheets, eyes tightly closed, her hair brushed and face washed after nine harrowing hours of giving birth.

"Millicent, do you want to see the twins now? They need to be nursed," Leon said softly, stroking his wife's forehead.

"Only one," she said without opening her eyes. "Bring me only one. I couldn't abide two. You choose. Let the midwife take the other and give it to that do-gooder doctor of hers. He'll find it a good home."

"Millicent—" Leon drew back sharply. "You can't mean that."

"I do, Leon. I can bear the curse of one, but not two. Do what I say, or so help me, I'll drown them both."

"Millicent, honey . . . it's too early. You'll change your mind."

"Do what I say, Leon. I mean it."

Leon rose heavily. His wife's eyes were still closed, her lips tightly sealed. She had the bitterness in her to do as she threatened, he knew. He left the bedroom to go downstairs to the kitchen where the midwife had cleaned and wrapped the crying twins.

"They need to be fed," she said, her tone accusatory. "The idea of a new mother wanting to get herself cleaned up before tending to the stomachs of her babies! I never heard of such a thing. I've a mind to put 'em to my own nipples, Mr. Holloway, if you'd take no offense at it. Lord knows I've got plenty of milk to spare."

"No offense taken, Mrs. Mahoney," Leon said, "and...I'd be obliged if you *would* wet-nurse one of them. My wife says she can feed only one mouth."

Mrs. Mahoney's face tightened with contempt. She was of Irish descent and her full, lactating breasts spoke of the recent delivery of her third child. She did not like the haughty, reddish-gold-haired woman upstairs who put such stock in her beauty. She would have liked to express to the missy's husband what she thought of his wife's cold, heartless attitude toward the birth of her newborns, unexpected though the second one was, but the concern of the moment was the feeding of the child. She began to unbutton the bodice of her dress. "I will, Mr. Holloway. Which one?"

Leon squeezed shut his eyes and turned his back to her. He could not bear to look upon the tragedy of choosing which twin to feast at the breast of its mother while allocating the other to the milk of a stranger. "Rearrange their order or leave them the same," he ordered the midwife. "I'll point to the one you're to take."

He heard the midwife follow his instructions, then pointed a finger over his shoulder. When he turned around again, he saw that the one taken was the last born, the one for whom he'd hurriedly found a holey sheet to serve as a bed and covering. Quickly, Leon scooped up the infant left. His sister was already suckling hungrily at her first meal. "I'll be back, Mrs. Mahoney. Please don't leave. You and I must talk."

PART ONE

Nathan

Chapter One

On the day Nathan Holloway's life changed forever, his morning began like any other. Zak, the German shepherd he'd rescued and raised from a pup, licked a warm tongue over his face. Nathan wiped at the wet wake-up call and pushed him away. "Aw, Zak," he said, but in a whisper so as not to awaken his younger brother, sleeping in his own bed across the room. Sunrise was still an hour away, and the room was dark and cold. Nathan shivered in his night shift. He had left his underwear, shirt, and trousers on a nearby chair for quiet and easy slipping into as he did every night before climbing into bed. Randolph still had another hour's sleep coming to him, and there would be hell to pay if Nathan disturbed his brother.

Socks and boots in hand and with the dog following, Nathan let himself out into the hall and sat on a bench to pull them on. The smell of bacon and onions frying drifted up from the kitchen. Nothing better for breakfast than bacon and onions on a cold morning with a day of work ahead, Nathan thought. Zak, attentive to his master's every move and thought, wagged his tail in agreement. Nathan chuckled softly and gave the animal's neck a quick, rough rub. There would be potatoes and hot biscuits with butter and jam, too.

His mother was at the stove, turning bacon. She was already dressed, hair in its neat bun, a fresh apron around her trim form. "G' morning, Mother," Nathan said sleepily, passing by her to hurry outdoors to the privy. Except for his sister, the princess, even in winter, the menfolks were discouraged from using the chamber pot in the morning. They had to head to the outhouse. Afterward, Nathan would wash in the mudroom off the kitchen where it was warm and the water was still hot in the pitcher.

"Did you wake your brother?" his mother said without turning around.

"No, ma'am. He's still sleeping."

"He's got that big test today. You better not have awakened him."

"No, ma'am. Dad about?"

"He's seeing to more firewood."

As Nathan quickly buttoned into his jacket, his father came into the back door with an armload of the sawtooth oak they'd cut and stacked high in the fall. "Mornin', son. Sleep all right?"

"Yessir."

"Good boy. Full day ahead."

"Yessir."

It was their usual exchange. All days were full since Nathan had completed his schooling two years ago. A Saturday of chores awaited him every weekday, not that he minded. He liked farm work, being outside, alone most days, just him and the sky and the land and the animals. Nathan took the lit lantern his father handed him and picked up a much-washed flour sack containing a milk bucket and towel. Zak followed him to the outhouse and did his business in the dark perimeter of the woods while Nathan did his, then Nathan and the dog went to the barn to attend to his before-breakfast chores, the light from the lantern leading the way.

Daisy, the cow, mooed an agitated greeting from her stall. "Hey, old girl," Nathan said. "We'll have you taken care of in a minute." Before grabbing a stool and opening the stall gate, Nathan shone the light around the barn to make sure no unwanted visitor had taken shelter during the cold March night. It was not unheard of to find a vagrant in the hayloft or, in warmer weather, to discover a snake curled in a corner. Once a hostile, wounded fox had taken refuge in the toolshed.

Satisfied that none had invaded, Nathan hung up the lantern and opened the stall gate. Daisy ambled out and went directly to her feed trough, where she would eat her breakfast while Nathan milked. He first brushed the cow's sides of hair and dirt that might fall into the milk, then removed the bucket from the sack and began to clean her teats with the towel. Finally he stuck the bucket under the cow's bulging udder, Zak sitting expectantly beside him, alert for the first squirt of warm milk to relieve the cow's discomfort.

Daisy allowed only Nathan to milk her. She refused to cooperate with any other member of the family. Nathan would press his hand to her right flank, and the cow would obligingly move her leg back for him to set to his task. With his father and siblings, she'd keep her feet planted, and one of them would have to force her leg back while she bawled and trembled and waggled her head, no matter that her udder was being emptied. "You alone got the touch," his father would say to him.

That was all right by Nathan and with his brother and sister as well, two and three years behind him respectively. They got to sleep later and did not have to hike to the barn in inclement weather before the sun was up, but Nathan liked this time alone.

The scents of hay and the warmth of the animals, especially in winter, set him at ease for the day.

The milk collected, Nathan put the lid on the bucket and set it high out of Zak's reach while he fed and watered the horses and led the cow to the pasture gate to turn her out for grazing. The sun was rising, casting a golden glow over the brown acres of the Barrows homestead that would soon be awash with the first growth of spring wheat. It was still referred to as the Barrows farm, named for the line of men to whom it had been handed down since 1840. Liam Barrows, his mother's father, was the last heir to bear the name. Liam's two sons had died before they could inherit, and the land had gone to his daughter, Millicent Holloway. Nathan was aware that someday the place would belong to him. His younger brother, Randolph, was destined for bigger and better things, he being the smarter, and his sister, Lily, would marry, she being beautiful and already sought after by sons of the well-to-do in Gainesville and Montague and Denton, even from towns across the border in the Indian Territory. "I won't be living out my life in a calico dress and kitchen apron" was a statement the family often heard from his sister, the princess.

That was all fine by Nathan, too. He got along well with his siblings, but he was not one of them. His brother and sister were close, almost like twins. They had the same dreams—to be rich and become somebody—and were focused on the same goal: to get off the farm. At nearly twenty, Nathan had already decided that to be rich was to be happy where you were, doing the things you liked, and wanting for nothing more.

So it was that that morning, when he left the barn with milk bucket in hand, his thoughts were on nothing more than the hot onions and bacon and buttered biscuits that awaited him before he set out to repair the fence in the south pasture after breakfast. His family was already taking their seats at the table when he entered the kitchen. Like always, his siblings took chairs that flanked his mother's place at one end of the table while he seated himself next to his father's at the other. The family arrangement had been such as long as Nathan could remember: Randolph and Lily and his mother in one group; he and his father in another. Like a lot of things, it was something he'd been aware of but never noticed until the stranger appeared in the late afternoon.

Chapter Two

The sun was behind him and sinking fast when Nathan stowed hammer and saw and nails and started homeward carrying his toolbox and lunch pail. The sandwiches his mother had prepared with the extra bacon and onions and packed in the pail with pickles, tomato, and boiled egg had long disappeared, and he was hungry for his supper. It would be waiting when he returned, but it would be a while before he sat down to the evening meal. He had Daisy to milk. His siblings would have fed the horses and pigs and chickens before sundown, so he'd have only the cow to tend before he washed up and joined the family at table.

It was always something he looked forward to, going home at the end of the day. His mother was a fine cook and served rib-sticking fare, and he enjoyed the conversation round the table and the company of his family before going to bed. Soon, his siblings would be gone. Randolph, a high school senior, seventeen, had already been accepted at Columbia University in New York City to begin his studies, aiming for law school after college. His sister, sixteen, would no doubt be married within a year or two. How the evenings would trip along when they were gone, he didn't know. Nathan didn't contribute much to the gatherings. Like his father, his thoughts on things were seldom asked and almost never offered. He was merely a quiet listener, a fourth at cards and board games (his mother did not play), and a dependable source to bring in extra wood, stoke the fire, and replenish cups of cocoa. Still, he felt a part of the family scene if for the most part ignored, like the indispensable clock over the mantel in the kitchen.

Zak trotted alongside him unless distracted by a covey of doves to flush, a rabbit to chase. Nathan drew in a deep breath of the cold late March air, never fresher than at dusk when the day had lost its sun and the wind had subsided, and expelled it with a sense of satisfaction. He'd had a productive day. His father would be pleased that he'd been able to repair the whole south fence and that the expense of extra lumber had been justified. Sometimes they disagreed on what needed to be done for the amount of the expenditure, but his father always listened to his son's judgment and often let him have his way. More times than not, Nathan had heard his father say to his mother, "The boy's got a head for what's essential for the outlay, that's for sure." His mother rarely answered unless it was to give a little sniff or utter a *humph*, but Nathan understood her reticence was to prevent him from getting a big head.

As if his head would ever swell over anything, he thought, especially when compared to his brother and sister. Nathan considered that everything about him—when he considered himself at all—was as ordinary as a loaf of bread. Except for his height and strong build and odd shade of blue-green eyes, nothing about him was of any remarkable notice. Sometimes, a little ruefully, he thought that when it came to him, he'd stood somewhere in the middle of the line when the good Lord passed out exceptional intellects, talent and abilities, personalities, and looks while Randolph and Lily had been at the head of it. He accepted his lot without rancor, for what good was a handsome face and winning personality for growing wheat and running a farm?

Nathan was a good thirty yards from the first outbuildings before he noticed a coach and team of two horses tied to the hitching post in front of the white wood-framed house of his home. He could not place the pair of handsome Thoroughbreds and expensive Concord. No one that he knew in Gainesville owned horses and carriage of such distinction. He guessed the owner was a rich new suitor of Lily's who'd ridden up from Denton or from Montague across the county line. She'd met several such swains a couple of months ago when the wealthiest woman in town, his mother's godmother, had hosted a little coming-out party for his sister. Nathan puzzled why he'd shown up to court her during the school week at this late hour of the day. His father wouldn't like that, not that he'd have much say in it. When it came to his sister, his mother had the last word, and she encouraged Lily's rich suitors.

Nathan had turned toward the barn when a head appeared above a window of the coach. It belonged to a middle-aged man who, upon seeing Nathan, quickly opened the door and hopped out. "I say there, me young man!" he called to Nathan. "Are ye the lad we've come to see?"

An Irishman, sure enough, and obviously the driver of the carriage, Nathan thought. He automatically glanced behind him as though half expecting the man to have addressed someone else. Turning back his gaze, he called, "Me?"

"Yes, you."

"I'm sure not."

"If ye are, ye'd best go inside. He doesn't like to be kept waiting."

"Who doesn't like to be kept waiting?"

"Me employer, Mr. Trevor Waverling."

"Never heard of him." Nathan headed for the barn.

"Wait! Wait!" the man cried, scrambling after him. "Ye must

go inside, lad. Mr. Waverling won't leave until ye do." The driver had caught up with Nathan. "I'm cold and…me backside's shakin' hands with me belly. I ain't eaten since breakfast," he whined.

Despite the man's desperation and his natty cutaway coat, striped trousers, and stiff top hat befitting the driver of such a distinctive conveyance, Nathan thought him comical. He was not of particularly short stature, but his legs were not long enough for the rest of him. His rotund stomach seemed to rest on their trunks, no space between, and his ears and Irish red hair stuck out widely beneath the hat like a platform for a stove pipe. He reminded Nathan of a circus clown he'd once seen.

"Well, that's too bad," Nathan said. "I've got to milk the cow." He hurried on, curious of who Mr. Waverling was and the reason he wished to see him. If so, his father would have sent his farmhand to get him, and he must tend to Daisy.

The driver ran back to the house and Nathan hurried to the barn. Before he reached it, he heard Randolph giving Daisy a smack. "Stay still, damn you!"

"What are you doing?" Nathan exclaimed from the open door, surprised to see Randolph and Lily attempting to milk Daisy.

"What does it look like?" Randolph snapped.

"Get away from her," Nathan ordered. "That's my job."

"Let him do it," Lily pleaded. "I can't keep holding her leg back."

"We can't," Randolph said. "Dad said to send him to the house the minute he showed up."

His siblings often discussed him in the third person in his presence. Playing cards and board games, they'd talk about him as if he wasn't sitting across the table from them. "Wonder what card he has," they'd say to each other. "Do you suppose he'll get my king?"

"Both of you get away from her," Nathan commanded. "I'm not going anywhere until I milk Daisy. Easy, old girl," he said, running a hand over the cow's quivering flanks. "Nathan is here."

Daisy let out a long bawl, and his brother and sister backed away. When it came to farm matters, after their father, Nathan had the top say.

"Who is Mr. Waverling, and why does he want to see me?" Nathan asked.

Brother and sister looked at each other. "We don't know," they both piped together, Lily adding, "But he's rich."

"We were sent out of the house when the man showed up," Randolph said, "but Mother and Dad and the man are having a shouting match over you."

"Me?" Nathan pulled Daisy's teats, taken aback. Who would have a shouting match over him? "That's all you know?" he asked. Zak had come to take his position at his knee and was rewarded with a long arc of milk into his mouth.

"That's all we know, but we think…we think he's come to take you away, Nathan," Lily said. Small, dainty, she came behind her older brother and put her arms around him, leaning into his back protectively. "I'm worried," she said in a small voice.

"Me, too," Randolph chimed in. "Are you in trouble? You haven't done anything bad, have you, Nathan?"

"Not that I know of," Nathan said. Take him away? What was this?

"What a silly thing to ask, Randolph," Lily scolded. "Nathan never does anything bad."

"I know that, but I had to ask," her brother said. "It's just that the man is important. Mother nearly collapsed when she saw him. Daddy took charge and sent us out of the house immediately. Do you have any idea who he is?"

"None," Nathan said, puzzled. "Why should I?"

"I don't know. He seemed to know about you. And you look like him…a little."

Another presence had entered the barn. They all turned to see their father standing in the doorway. He cleared his throat. "Nathan," he said, his voice heavy with sadness, "when the milkin's done, you better come to the house. Randolph, you and Lily stay here."

"But I have homework," Randolph protested.

"It can wait," Leon said as he turned to go. "Drink the milk for your supper."

The milking completed and Daisy back in her stall, Nathan left the barn, followed by the anxious gazes of his brother and sister. Dusk had completely fallen, cold and biting. His father had stopped halfway to the house to wait for him. Nathan noticed the circus clown had scrambled back into the carriage. "What's going on, Dad?" he said.

His father suddenly bent forward and pressed his hands to his face.

"Dad! What in blazes—?" Was his father crying? "What's the matter? What's happened?"

A tall figure stepped out of the house onto the porch. He paused, then came down the steps toward them, the light from the house at his back. He was richly dressed in an overcoat of fine wool and carried himself with an air of authority. He was a handsome man in a lean, wolfish sort of way, in his forties, Nathan guessed. "I am what's happened," he said.

Nathan looked him up and down. "Who are you?" he demanded, the question bored into the man's sea-green eyes, so like his own. He would not have dared, but he wanted to put his arm protectively around his father's bent shoulders.

"I am your father," the man said.

Chapter Three

Nathan frowned and cocked his head as if he'd heard an echo but could not determine its origin. "Say what?"

The man put up his hands in the gesture of one quieting a crowd. "I'm sorry to have to tell you like this. I'd hoped for...a less shocking introduction, but you're my son, Nathan. Mr. Holloway here"—he gestured to Leon—"is your stepfather, but *I'm* your father."

Nathan did not hold to violence. He was by nature nonconfrontational, but a surge of fury almost brought his arm back to drive a fist into the man's handsome face. Who did he think he was to come onto their land and make such a claim to set his father crying, a sight Nathan had never seen or expected to see? He had a good mind to run to the barn for a pitchfork to prod the fancy stranger into his carriage and on his way. For the confusion of a few seconds, he wondered why his father had not.

"Have you escaped from an insane asylum, mister?" Nathan said, breaching an innate respect for his elders that his parents had not needed to reinforce. "You must have to say something like that to me. Either that, or you've made a bad mistake." He pointed to Leon, who had straightened up and turned away to wipe at his wet face with his jacket sleeve. "That man is my father."

"He's the man who raised you, but you're my son," the stranger said. "Your mother can testify to it. Shall we go inside and discuss it? I for one could use the heat of the fire."

"I'm not discussing anything with you, and you can freeze your backside off, for all I care." Bigger than his father, taller, Nathan stepped in front of Leon. "Get off our property."

"Son...Nathan," Leon said, blowing his nose into a large handkerchief. "You need to listen to him. He has merit. We'd better go inside."

Nathan refused to budge. "Daddy..." His childhood address for his father slipped out on a note of panic. "What's he saying?"

"He's sayin' he's your father, son, and he is."

Nathan heard the words like the crack of a gunshot. Leon put a hand on his elbow to steady him. "I'm so sorry you have to learn...the truth," he said, his voice fading to sorrowful resignation.

The stranger made a move to take Nathan's other arm, but Nathan rejected the gesture and stepped away from both men. He looked over his shoulder at his brother and sister, heads stuck around the door of the barn, faces scared and worried. He was their big brother, their protector, a known and steady quantity in their lives. Nothing had ever happened to shake their faith in his permanence. Nathan knew it was his father's place to reassure them, but he called, "Everything's fine. You won't have to stay out there long. Settle Daisy down. She's nervous."

"All right," Randolph answered in a thin, doubtful voice. "But you'll...come get us soon?"

"I promise," Nathan said.

The three men started forward along with Zak, who'd sensed the tension and trotted close to Nathan's side. "I can tell you've been a good brother to your siblings, Nathan," Trevor Waverling said.

"Not have been. *Am!*" Nathan declared.

"Hmm, I can see you have a quick ear for nuances as well," Trevor said.

Nathan did not reply. His mouth felt so parched he couldn't have formed enough saliva to spit. *Nuances?* Who *was* this man, and why was his father going along with his craziness? When the man invited Nathan with a courtly gesture to go before him to follow his father up the steps into the house, Nathan thought of slamming the door and locking it behind him.

His mother sat on the hard Victorian couch in the front room used only for company. As he stepped over the threshold, Nathan halted sharply. He hardly recognized his beautiful mother's cold, bloodless face and had never seen her eyes so black. Ignoring him and his father, she directed her murderous gaze to the man behind him. "Get this over, Leon, so we can be done with him," she ordered without hardly moving her pale lips or taking her eyes from the stranger.

Nathan looked from one to the other helplessly. "Would somebody please tell me what's going on?"

"Gladly," Trevor Waverling said. "Years ago—almost twenty-one, to be exact—your mother and I had an...assignation—"

"In which you *raped* me, you son of the devil," his mother screamed.

"Millicent, I did no such thing. You were as willing as I."

"Please, please," Leon begged, flapping his hands. "Stop this! The boy don't need to hear every sordid detail. It's enough of a shock for him to learn that the man he thought was his father...isn't." He glanced at Nathan, tears springing again to his eyes. "This man is." Leon pointed a limp finger at Trevor.

"Can you deny it?" Trevor said, stepping to Nathan. "Look at us. But for the years I have on you, we could be brothers—same height, similar build, certainly the color of eyes. We get them from my mother. She's still alive and dying to meet you...your grandmother."

Nathan backed away from him. The man's lean facial structure, high, prominent cheekbones, sleek, fit build looked nothing like his. "I don't believe you," he said. Frantically, he gazed at his mother for affirmation that the man was some kind of evil prankster and this a cruel joke, but her glare was locked on the stranger. He turned to his father and felt his heart drop at the misery in his gaze. "Dad...?"

"He speaks the truth, Nathan. You are not my son...in a biological sense. Your mother was pregnant when I married her. By this man." Leon nodded toward the stranger. "Your mother knows it to be the truth."

"But I didn't know she was pregnant with you, or I would have come for you sooner, Nathan. So help me God, I would have," Trevor Waverling said.

Shock taking hold, Nathan lowered himself numbly to one of the prettily flowered chairs he'd rarely sat in. He glanced at his mother. "Mother? Is he telling the truth?"

"Only that you are his son. The rest are all lies. He raped me. I was never willing as he says, and he *did* know about you before now. Long ago the postmaster told me he'd been questioned about the older Holloway boy. That was when you were about fourteen, Nathan. This—this filthy excuse of a man sent somebody to find out if you were worth claiming. He didn't stoop to come himself." His mother flung a look at Trevor so scathing Nathan felt his scalp move. "Then, last year I ran into one of your high school teachers who told me a stranger spoke to her just before your graduation and asked what you were like. Did you get along well in school? Were you smart? Were you sound? The man gave as his excuse that he was investigating students to award scholarships to college."

Leon came alert. "Why didn't you ever mention these men and their questions?"

"Because, knowing you, I thought you might muddy the waters even more, figure you ought to tell the boy his father was looking for him, and then how could we have contained the scandal?"

Trevor turned a look of disgust to Millicent. "So the scandal was all you were thinking about? How typical of you, Millicent."

"Oh, don't use that moralizing tone to me, Trevor Waverling! Believe me, that man"—Millicent pointed at Trevor—"wouldn't be here now if you had been a disgrace, Nathan. He would have let you be Leon's and my problem."

Nathan shrank from her fury. Her thinly stretched lips had lost all color. In a moment of blinding clarity, he clearly understood the source of the faint ache that had nibbled at him since he'd been old enough to recognize the difference in the way his mother treated him from her other children. He had refused to acknowledge it as beneath the love and respect he felt for her. He was the oldest. More was expected of him for less praise. But now he knew. He was a reminder of the man she hated, a man Nathan's instincts told him she still had feelings for at some level beneath her skin.

Chapter Four

Nathan lifted his gaze to the man whose vague likeness to him he could not deny. "Why are you here?"

Trevor Waverling straightened his shoulders, the fine tailoring of his wool coat accentuating their power and breadth. "To claim you as my son. To take you home with me if you will go."

"Why?"

The rapid-fired question caught Trevor by patent surprise. His mouth opened before his mind could conjure an answer. "Why?" he repeated after appearing to grapple for a reply. "Because I would like to have you in my life, that's why. I want to give you a better one than the one you have here."

"There is no better life than the one I have here."

The man moved to stand over Nathan. "How do you know, Nathan? This place is all you've known. I'm a wealthy man, and I want to share my good fortune with you. If things work out, I'd like you to be my heir—"

"What if things don't work out?" Nathan challenged. "What then? Would I be fired as your heir?"

Again Trevor made to reply but appeared confounded for an answer. "This is all turning out badly. I'm implying things I don't mean and giving you a wrong impression. If you and I could just go somewhere and talk, let me tell you about myself...what I have to offer..."

Abruptly, Nathan stood up. "I'm not interested. This is my home, and these are my parents. I'm not going anywhere with you."

Trevor spread his hands imploringly. "Nathan, please. Don't you want to know about your father?"

"Did you want to know about your son before now?"

"No, he did not!" Millicent snapped.

"All right! All right!" Trevor said, his voice rising on a sharp note of impatience. "I admit it. I had you investigated. It's what has to be done when you're in my position, but I swear I did not know your mother was pregnant when I left her. I didn't know until one of my salesmen passed through Gainesville six years ago and reported that he's seen a boy in a general store who looked enough like me to be my son. He casually mentioned it to me, making a joke of it by asking if I'd had a one-night stand in a burg in Cooke County."

Millicent uttered a cry of protest and made to object, but Leon had gained control of himself. "Be quiet, Millicent," he said in a voice of quiet authority. "Nathan needs to hear this." Millicent cut a startled look at her husband but set her lips in a thin line of silent defiance.

Trevor continued. "So I sent a trusted employee here to look into the situation. He took your picture…" Trevor withdrew a money case from an inner pocket and removed a photograph he offered to Nathan. It was a shot of him standing by the road fence, and he remembered the afternoon a man asked if he could take his picture against the background of the flowing wheat field behind him. He had told Nathan he was a photographer shooting scenes for *Progressive Farmer* magazine.

"When I saw that picture, I knew instantly that you were my son," Trevor said, taking back the photograph. "I looked just like you at fourteen. I didn't come for you because…well, how could I? You were still in school, apparently happy here with your mother and…the man you thought was your father. I didn't want to break that up, but then, once you were a couple of years graduated from high school, I thought it my right and obligation to show myself, so I waited until today, your twentieth birthday, as an appropriate time to make myself known."

Nathan stared at him. *Today was his birthday?* It should have been a day he remembered. Turning twenty was an important milestone to a boy, but he had forgotten, easy enough to do now that he was out of school and each day flowed into the next with no guidepost but seasons to mark important events.

But his family had forgotten, too. "How did you know today was my birthday?" he asked the stranger.

"I had your birth record at the county courthouse checked."

Leon turned to Millicent. "Did you bake him a cake?"

"I…forgot. I had my mind on nothing but that today was wash day…"

"And the day you planned to finish sewin' Lily's dress for that party she's been invited to in Denton," Leon said, his voice cold.

"God, Millicent!" Trevor's glare at Millicent was filled with loathing. "I see the way things are around here. Nathan is worked like a hired hand, but you make dresses for your daughter and scrape together every dime to send your other son to Columbia University." In his disgust, he looked as if he could have spat on the floor at Millicent's feet. She rebutted by folding her arms and turning her head to the fire in scornful disregard of his condemnation.

Leon addressed Nathan, who'd listened in dismayed wonder at the bitter revelations of which he'd been unaware. "It breaks my heart to say it," Leon said, "but it can't do no harm listenin' to the man, Nathan. He *is* your father."

Trevor gestured imploringly with his hands again. They were

large and powerful but smooth and well kept. "If there is some place we could go to speak privately..."

Stunned, confused, hurt, Nathan stammered, "There's no place. My brother and sister need to come in. It's cold in the barn, and my brother will want to study in our room."

"Then let's you and I go to the barn to talk," Trevor suggested. "Please, Nathan."

The stranger had said *please* twice, not easy for a man like him, Nathan figured. He felt disoriented, as if he'd been caught in a snowstorm where every familiar landmark had been blanked out. "Not tonight," he said. "I need time to think about...all I've heard, then I'll see."

Disappointment settled in the corners of Trevor's mouth and dulled his hopeful gaze. "I suppose I can ask for no more than that. In your position, I would do the same. All right, then." He opened the leather case again, inserted the photograph, and removed a printed card. "Here's the information you need to contact me when you're ready to hear me out. It contains my business address, or..." He extracted a pen and scribbled on the back of the card. "You can write to me at my residence. As you can see, they're both located in Dallas. You're welcome to come to my place of business, or if you prefer, I can meet you in Gainesville. I can even meet you here again, if you like."

"Not here, Trevor." Millicent glowered at him. "Never again on the soil of my family's land, you hear me? I'll shoot you if I ever see your face around here again." She swiveled her sharp gaze to Nathan. "And take that dog out of this room right now, Nathan. You know he's not allowed in here."

Nathan turned his attention to his mother. A stranger he'd never seen before had showed up on her doorstep to announce himself as his father, and she was mindful only of her hatred for the man and the forbidden presence of her son's dog in her parlor.

She had not shown the least concern for his shock, his disbelief, his pain. A heartsick truth merged with the other numbing revelations. His mother did not love him. She never had and never would. Under his quiet scrutiny, Millicent's expression altered. A faint awareness wafted across it as if she recognized he would never think of her again in the same way. Nathan patted his leg. "Zak, come with me, boy."

He left the parlor, and without a word of protest, as though conscious the boy had moved beyond any further attempt at discourse, his parents and the stranger let him go. Nathan walked out into the fading dusk, oblivious to the sting of cold air on his face. His hunger pangs had disappeared. The drop in temperature had no effect on him through his lightweight work jacket. The carriage driver's head popped up in the window of the coach, where he had gone to get out of the cold. "Is me boss coming soon?" he called.

"He has no reason to stay," Nathan called back without slowing down.

Randolph and Lily were huddled in a bed of straw under a horse blanket. They had taken turns drinking from the milk bucket. "Coast is clear for you two," he said before his voice broke.

Lily threw off the blanket and rushed toward him. "Nathan, what's wrong? Who is the man in the house?"

"I have no idea."

"Why is he here?" Randolph asked.

"He came on a family matter," Nathan said.

Lily peered uneasily into his face. "What's he done to you?"

"He…broke something that can't be fixed."

Only then did Nathan realize he still held the stranger's business card. He gazed at it, the name Trevor Waldo Waverling like a hot brand searing his eyeballs. Only then did the knowledge that he was not a Holloway fully hit him. It drove through him with such force he grasped the lodgepole to keep from keeling over. Tears cloaked his eyes. His windpipe closed. He was a Waverling. The blood of the man who had looked after him tenderly since he was born, who had taught him to walk, read, ride, farm, the man he loved and believed he took after, did not pump through his veins.

"Oh, my God! Are you crying?" Randolph squealed.

Lily touched his arm and asked in a plaintive key, "Nathan, what is it?"

"Leave him be, and you children go to the house. Your supper is waiting," Leon ordered from the doorway.

Randolph let out a huff of relief. "Finally," he said. "Do we have to bring the milk?"

"If you want any with your supper."

With a sigh of being put upon, Randolph grabbed the handle of the bucket, but Lily stood on tiptoe and kissed her big brother's ear. "It will be all right," she murmured softly and hurried to follow Randolph from the barn.

Chapter Five

But it would not be all right. Never again, Nathan knew. Leon shuffled toward him, shoulders hunched in his farmer's jacket, his hands plunged into the pockets of his overalls. "I wish I knew the words to say," he said. From outside came the clop of horses and the squeak of carriage wheels pulling away. The man had come by coach expecting to stow him and his things in it for the return trip, Nathan reckoned. Otherwise, he'd have arrived by train.

Nathan shrugged and brushed at his eyes. "This has to be as hard on you as on me."

Leon turned over a couple of buckets and set them on the barn floor. "In that I've lost a son as you have a father? Neither is true, Nathan. You've got to believe that. Kinship is not a matter of blood but of feelin's. You're my son. You always have been, and you always will be. And I'll be forever your father. Nothin' on God's green earth—no other man's claim—can undo that." Once more, Leon pulled out the handkerchief stored in the pocket of his overalls. He blew into it, his eyes watering again.

"Still..." Nathan said, accepting the seat Leon offered. "The truth changes things, doesn't it?"

Leon sat down on the other bucket. Zak took a vigilant stand between them. "Only things, not feelin's."

Nathan handed Leon the business card. "What kind of business is he in?"

Leon read aloud, "WAVERLING TOOLS. He told us his company primarily makes drillin' machinery for water and salt wells."

"As if I would know or care anything about that."

"He told us he'd been married twice, is divorced, and has one child, a retarded daughter named Rebecca, aged twelve. She lives with his mother—your grandmother. He's forty-six."

"Do you believe he raped Mother?"

Leon returned the card and leaned on a hip to push the handkerchief back into his pocket. "I believe your mother believes it. I've never known for sure. She was the belle of Gainesville as well as Denton in her youth. As the beautiful only child of well-to-do parents and the darlin' of your mother's childless, rich godmother, she was spoiled to the core and grew up thinkin' the world was hers for the asking, like she's gotten Lily to believin'. I fell in love with her in the fourth grade when she enrolled in school, the prettiest little thing you ever saw. I carried her books. Made sure no one bothered her. I was like her big brother. She could tell me anything and did. I went to work for her folks on this farm when I was eighteen. I watched as the boys made a beeline to her door durin' her midschool years, and they followed her here after her time in finishin' school, but she kept 'em all danglin' until Trevor Waverling showed up in town. He must have been around twenty-five."

Nathan had never heard any of this story before. "What brought him to Gainesville?"

"His aunt. She died and left him a saddle and tack shop she'd inherited from her husband. Trevor had no interest in runnin' a business in a small town like Gainesville, so he hung around until he sold it."

"And that's when he met Mother."

Leon got up and struck a match to the barn lantern. "Yep. I saw him only two, three times. He was a handsome devil. I heard the ladies were wild for him, but he had his sights set on your mother, at least accordin' to the way she tells it. He squired her about until the shop was sold, then vamoosed, leavin' her pregnant. Her daddy came to me. No decent man would have her, he said." Leon's attempt at a wry grin failed as he sat back down on the bucket. "That's what the man actually said to me."

Nathan had not liked his mother's father. Liam Barrows had no time for his first grandson and brushed him off like a pesky fly, but Nathan mainly disliked his grandfather because he treated his son-in-law like hired help. Today's disclosures had revealed the cause of the man's disaffection. He had died when Nathan was ten, succeeded by his grandmother who lived only a year afterward. The farm had then gone to his mother.

"Do you know if he was telling the truth when he said he didn't know that Mother was pregnant with me?" Nathan asked.

Leon plucked a piece of straw from a bale of hay and stuck it in his mouth. "Yeah, that part I believe. I'm not sayin' he'd have done anything about it, but I'm sure he didn't know."

"How can you be so sure?"

"Because your mother didn't know, not until Trevor had been gone for two months."

"So the reason she hates him is because he didn't marry her, baby or not?"

"That's the way I see it."

"Fancy a woman hating a man all these years when she has the best husband alive and three good kids."

"Trevor Waverling was the only man your mother couldn't have. She's never gotten over the insult. It's my view he wouldn't have had to rape her. Because of him, she was forced to marry a man beneath her and become a farmer's wife, a far cry from the life she'd expected to have, and she's never for-given him for it."

And gave birth to a son she didn't want, Nathan thought. So much was making sense now. It explained why his mother never looked directly at him but spoke to him from her profile. He gazed up at the open barn window where the first star of the evening had appeared. He could hardly stand the pain of admit-ting it, but he agreed with his father's view. He was not the child of rape, but he might as well have been for all the chance he'd had of winning his mother's love. "Wonder why the man has shown up now," Nathan said.

Leon chewed on the straw. "Could be it's like what he said. He wants an heir."

Nathan drew his jacket tighter around him. "Well, he's shown up twenty years too late, but I have a feeling there's more to his motive than that. Something else brought him here."

"Then why don't you go find out what it is?" Leon said.

Nathan looked at him in surprise. "Why should I? I have no interest in knowing the man. Like you said, you're my father. What do I need him for?"

Leon shifted his weight and looked uncomfortable, sure signs to Nathan that something was on his mind he was reluc-tant to talk about. He felt another level of unease. "What is it, Dad?"

Leon spit out the chewed straw. "Well, you might as well hear all of it, son. Take the blows all at once. The healin' starts faster that way."

"What are you talking about, Dad?"

"The farm, Nathan. It ain't comin' to you—or to me, but I married your mother knowin' that. The place is willed to Ran-dolph and Lily."

Nathan hopped up from the bucket. "*What? Why?* They don't

know piddling about farming. They hate the place. They'll only sell it!"

"I know that. You know that. Millicent knows that, but it don't matter."

Nathan plopped down again, too stunned to stand. "How could she, Dad? How *could* she? She knows how much I love the farm, that I live for it, that I'd be like a fish out of water anyplace else."

"It don't matter, son. I wish I could say it did, she bein' your mother and all, but your feelin's for the farm don't matter a drop of spit to her, not when it comes to makin' sure Randolph and Lily are taken care of financially, and that's why..." Leon pulled in his lip.

A shiver ran over Nathan's flesh. "That's why what, Dad?"

"Your mother is puttin' the farm up for sale. She wants it sold and a house bought in Gainesville 'fore Randolph leaves for college."

"*God!*" Nathan jumped up again, incredulous. He dragged his hand through his hair. "What will happen to you if she sells it?"

"She says I can go to work for the new owners or come live with her in town."

Nathan reeled. He could almost feel the ground move under his feet. His steady, certain world had suddenly collapsed, and everything he believed, trusted, loved, lay shattered around him like the aftermath of a tornado. He pressed his palms to the sides of his head. "She doesn't care a whit for us, does she?"

Leon answered with a mirthless chuckle. "Oh, Millicent cares for us, son. It's just that she cares more for Randolph and Lily. It don't matter about me. Let's talk about you—this opportunity that's landed in your lap."

Chapter Six

"O pportunity?"

"The one Trevor Waverling is offerin'," Leon said. "I'd like you to take it since there's no future here for you. You've got to realize that, too." As if on cue, Daisy let out a deep, melancholic bellow, and the two plow horses pricked their ears and turned their heads toward them over their stall doors. "Today you've had to take some mighty strong doses of the truth, son—too many for a boy to have to swallow on his twentieth birthday, but the facts are what they are."

Nathan sat down again, feeling drained. "How long have you known Mother didn't intend for me to have the farm?"

"I didn't know until I found a copy of her will a few weeks ago. Up until then, since the farm had been in her family for several generations, I assumed she meant to leave it to the three of you. You'd run it and share the profits with your brother and sister."

"My *half* brother and sister," Nathan corrected him, for the first time realizing he and his siblings did not share full family blood. Was it any wonder, then, that he had never felt entirely kin to them?

"I confronted Millicent about the will," Leon continued. "We had a terrible argument. She had the decency to look red-faced about it but said that originally she'd intended that nothing would change until her death unless a financial need arose. That's when I learned she planned to sell the farm."

"Did you ask her where that would leave me?"

Leon stroked his knee as he always did when considering how to go about imparting unpleasant news, misery sunk deep into the age lines of his weathered face. "I did. She said that if the sale had to come before her death, with your reputation, you could find work on a farm anywhere. They'd be glad to have you, probably make you manager."

Nathan felt compelled to move around to digest this information without choking on it. He went over to pat Daisy. Nearly every truth he knew, most of the knowledge and wisdom he'd gained, had come by paying attention to nature. At the moment, he remembered the clear blue stream he'd loved as a child. Butterflies and hummingbirds had played there. Eventually, the stream had dried up and left a depression in the sand. He recalled standing on its dry lip sad to his toes wondering how the most beautiful and essential things on earth could simply disappear. Like now. Only this morning, he'd gone off to the south pasture thinking what a lucky fellow he was to be doing what he loved to do on the land he loved and to have such a fine family and home waiting for him at the end of the day. In less than twelve hours, it had all vanished quick as morning mist before the rising sun.

He returned to the bucket and sat down again. "When were you going to tell me?" he asked.

"Soon's I could figure out how to go about it and to make other arrangements. I wadn't about to keep another secret from you."

"What other secret?" Nathan's ears perked for another shoe about to fall.

Leon reddened to the part in his sandy, thinning hair. "Aw, forget I said that. It don't pertain to you, so don't pester me about it."

Nathan didn't believe him. If the secret didn't pertain to him, why say he'd kept it from him? "What other arrangements?" he asked, convinced that whatever his father had almost let slip did relate to him, but he could worm it out of him another time.

"I've laid some money by, money your mother don't know about, money I saved for you. Old Man Sawyer plans to sell his spread one of these years, and I was thinkin' I'd have a word with him to say I'd be interested in puttin' a down payment on the place when the time came. I got good standin' at the bank, and I could borrow the rest. You and I could go on like we always had, only we'd have our own place. Your mother could come with us if she liked. Otherwise…" Leon shrugged. "That'd be up to her. It was the best I could do, son."

Nathan shook his head, the image of the dried-up stream reappearing. "So why don't we just go on with those plans?" he asked. "I've saved some money from my wages as well."

Leon leaned toward him. " 'Cause you've got a bird in hand right now, Nathan. We don't know what tomorrow will bring. You've just learned that you can be sure of nothin'. For two weeks, hopin' for a miracle, I've sat on your mother's intention to sell the place. I thought it might be she'd listen to her conscience and change her mind. I had no idea that the miracle would appear in the form of Trevor Waverling."

"I don't like him," Nathan said.

"That's no reason not to hear him out, son, to go see what he's offerin'. He's right, you know. You've never known any place but here."

"All I've ever wanted to know."

"Then, by God"—Leon whooped and slapped his knee— "go make sure this is the only place you ever want to know. Prove to yourself that you're not cut out for any other business but farmin'. Learn firsthand that you want nothin' to do with Trevor Waverling, but take it from me, son, if you don't find out now, a time will come when you'll regret not knowin' what else is out there."

Nathan nodded. "Like Mother," he said.

"She thinks about it ever' day."

Nathan looked again at the card. "If I go and hear him out and don't like what I hear, will you still be willing to put a down payment on Mr. Sawyer's land?"

"It's a promise, son."

Nathan stuck out his hand. "You'll always be my father, Dad. I could have asked for no finer or better."

Leon clasped it. "Or me a finer or better son."

In their bedroom as he undressed, Leon said, "I told Nathan about your will, Millicent. He had a right to know."

At her dressing table, his wife glanced at him sharply in the mirror. "You felt the need to do that, did you? I suppose now he hates me sure enough."

"He don't hate you, Millie girl. The boy don't have that in him, but I wouldn't expect him to feel the same for you again. The best you can hope for is that he don't realize he owes you nothin'."

Millicent's mouth twisted. "I suppose you'll make sure he does."

"No," Leon said, removing his boots. "You know me better than that, but I sure as hell won't block his vision like I've always done. I wouldn't worry about Nathan tellin' anybody what he's learned today, not even Lily and Randolph. He's as ashamed as you are. I assume you're not goin' to let them know Nathan is their half brother?"

"Certainly not. What good would come of it?"

Leon smirked. "Right. Now that it's open, you goin' to let the final cat out of the bag to Nathan?"

Millicent whirled from the mirror. She was wearing her night chemise, a long white garment with lace at the throat and ends of the sleeves. Her hair had been brushed from its daytime bun and hung in a lustrous mass about her shoulders. Not a thread of gray dulled its strawberry-blond sheen. At forty-one, Millicent Barrows was still the most beautiful woman Leon had ever seen, and her beauty could still grab him by the throat.

"Absolutely not, and don't you even *think* of telling him, Leon Holloway. You promised me. It's bad enough Nathan now knows you are not his father. He would have no reason to keep his silence if he learned we'd given away his twin sister. You've got to think what the scandal would do to Lily's chances of marrying well and Randolph's future as a lawyer if that secret got out."

"Well, you can certainly speak from experience on both those subjects, can't you?" Leon said, baring his teeth. "But to be clear. *You* gave the boy's sister away, Millicent. I can't let you shade the truth about that."

Millicent waved away the distinction, but she looked worried. "You *promised* me you would always keep our secret, Leon. I'm going to hold you to that promise to my dying day. You've never gone back on your word, and my feelings for you would alter completely if you ever did. I'm assuming my feelings for you still matter?"

Leon sighed. "Yes, they do, Millie girl, more's the pity." He came to stand behind her and began to massage her shoulders. "But don't you ever wonder about her? Where she is—if she's safe, well, happy—what she looks like?"

In the mirror, Millicent's gaze faltered. She closed her eyes and relaxed under the knead of Leon's hands. "I try not to. What good would come of it?"

"Yes, what good would come of it?" Suddenly feeling an impulse to inflict cruelty, Leon slipped his hands under his wife's arms and squeezed her breasts. "About those feelin's that somehow keep me crazy about you despite your black heart," he said. "Let's go do somethin' about them."

Samantha

Chapter Seven

Samantha Gordon looked down the long candlelit table at the guests invited to celebrate her twentieth birthday. The gathering consisted of her former classmates and the sons and daughters of fellow ranchers and their parents, all longtime friends of the Gordons. Samantha would have preferred the dinner party be held at Las Tres Lomas de la Trinidad to include the ranch hands, but her mother had insisted that the rustic great room of the main house was too informal for a milestone birthday. "For goodness' sakes, Neal," Estelle had argued to her husband, who'd made an appeal on Samantha's behalf, "knowing our daughter, she'd choose the bunkhouse for the party and have the guests served out of the chuck wagon."

Samantha had chuckled at the exaggeration when she learned of her mother's response, but it was close enough to the truth. Still, seeing the familiar faces, listening to the laughter and chatter of amusing childhood memories, Samantha granted that it was appropriate to be surrounded on her twentieth birthday by people who had known her all her life. Cowhands came and went. Only Grizzly, the ranch cook, and Wayne Harris, the foreman, had been around since she was placed in her parents' arms at four days old.

There were twenty squeezed in around the long-strung table. Each year Estelle Gordon added a guest to total the years of her daughter's life, pushing tables together and moving furniture about to accommodate the number in her town house. Her mother would be disappointed to hear it, but Samantha had determined that this would be the last of her birthdays celebrated in such a fashion. Twenty-one was the beginning of spinsterhood for a single woman, a state that Samantha saw looming and no need to honor since the only man she would have married sat across from this year's extra guest, a stunning beauty who was sure to become his wife.

But at the moment, Anne Rutherford was winning no points with Sloan Singleton, the Gordons' neighboring rancher and Samantha's one-time childhood playmate. Sloan's handsome face wore a trace of the scowl that Samantha's father was directing at her from his end of the table. Anne was holding forth on her theory—"from observation"—that certain human mannerisms, character traits, color of hair and eyes, and "proclivities" (a simper at the erudite word) can be credited to or blamed on one's bloodline. "I suppose that explains my penchant for public service," she concluded with a dazzling smile at the guest whose compliment of her charity work had initiated the discussion. "My grandmother always had an eye out for the unfortunate."

And you, an eye toward the gallery to see who was watching, Samantha thought, feeling a little thrill at Sloan's displeasure with Anne for discussing heredity in the presence of her and her parents. No blame or credit could be attributed to Samantha's bloodline, since she was adopted, a fact of which Anne was fully and artfully aware.

Adopted. The term had never bothered her. In her early years, her parents and their relatives had shielded her from the stigma. White children were "adopted" by the Indian tribes that had abducted them. Orphans were "taken in" by relatives. The terms suggested *captive* and *waif*, the implication being that the children were charity cases, never quite one of the family who'd accepted them.

But from the beginning, Samantha had been not only one of the family, she was the axis around which her adoptive parents' lives revolved. She had not known she was adopted until she was six years old, when a cousin of her mother's not seen for a decade came to visit from New York City. Cousin Ella had come presumably to admire the Gordons' recently built town house. By then, in 1886, the cattle industry, over which her father was a reigning force in North Central Texas, was flourishing, and Fort Worth had emerged from the economic severities of the Civil War, Reconstruction, hard winters, and drought to become known as "Queen City of the Prairies."

Her father's prosperity and the city's relative civility had warranted his wife to insist on the construction of a house in town where their daughter could attend school and "be near the more cultural aspects of life," as Samantha recalled her mother explaining to Cousin Ella when she stepped from the first-class coach of the Texas and Pacific Railway.

"And who is this?" Cousin Ella had demanded of the shy little girl peeking around her mother's skirts. "Where in the world did she get that strawberry-blond hair?"

Her mother had taken Samantha's hand protectively. "This is Samantha, our daughter."

"Daughter? I didn't think you could have children, Estelle."

Holding Samantha's hand tightly, her mother had slipped her arm through Cousin Ella's. "Yes, well, that's true," she said and lowered her voice. "We'll talk about it when we get home."

So it was that Samantha gradually came to understand that she'd not actually been born *physically* to her mother and father. She'd been *given* to them as a miracle from heaven, a difference they said made her even more special. Even so, to avoid any unpleasantness that could develop, friends and family never referred to the adoption, so that in time the fact of it was almost forgotten or never known. But Samantha always remembered whose loving hands had rescued her from what could have been a terrible fate.

She became aware that Todd Baker, a recent graduate of the Jackson School of Geology at the University of Texas and former classmate whom she'd known since her cradle days, had begun to regale the group with stories of their school experiences at Simmons Preparatory School in Fort Worth, where Samantha, the only girl in their science courses, had "given the boys a licking." She had hardly been listening to the conversation that had turned from genetic theory to geological science.

"Exactly what is paleontology, Samantha?" Anne Rutherford was asking. Samantha perceived that her polite query was a ploy to earn back Sloan's favor. It failed. His countenance grew darker. All faces but his and her parents' turned to her inquiringly. Samantha's special interest in the history of the Earth through the study of rocks and fossils and plant life was another subject uncomfortable to the couple who had raised her.

She gave a brief answer from her long-ago textbooks. "It's the study of life-forms existing in prehistoric times," she said.

"And they can be determined from old rocks and fossils?" Anne asked, smooth brow rising skeptically.

"Surprising as it sounds, yes," Samantha answered. "For more than a century, geologists have extracted a remarkable timetable from rocks of how Earth has evolved. You might say they are documents and records of the past." Samantha turned to another guest. "Marcia, tell us about your trip to San Francisco," she invited, annoyed at Todd for prompting another line of conversation he should know her parents wished to avoid.

Marcia's reply never penetrated her thoughts. Her mind was on Sloan and the understanding wink he'd given her at her adroit turn of the conversation. She'd averted her eyes lest he rightly interpret the flush that warmed her cheeks. It was the only secret she'd ever kept from him, her feelings for the boy-grown-man who had romped with her through childhood. She was doomed for spinsterhood, little doubt about it. How could she ever love another man when her heart belonged to Sloan Singleton?

Dr. Donald Tolman read aloud the letter he'd just written. Hearing his words rather than reading them in silence lent a different perspective. He could better place himself in the position of the man to whom he would be mailing them. How would he feel if he were Neal Gordon reading this letter? Would he tear it up, burn it to ashes with no one the wiser of its contents? Or would he lock it away to be found with his papers after his death? Show it to Mrs. Gordon? To Samantha? No, no, he believed he could say with certainty that Neal Gordon, that tough, rugged, ruthless rancher with a heart gentle as a lamb for his adopted daughter, would never, ever show the letter to Samantha. Neal Gordon was known as a man who jealously guarded what was his, and of no one was he more protective and vigilant than the young woman he'd taken and raised as his own flesh and blood.

Donald Tolman was certain of that fact. He had kept tabs on the Gordons and the baby he'd left with them twenty years ago. He would have called the couple on it straight enough if they hadn't been the people he'd judged them to be—decent, caring, starved for a child. This he'd known from a late sister who lived in Fort Worth, a friend of Estelle Gordon. She'd died ignorant of the little bundle her brother had surprised the Gordons with at midnight one late March. When Mrs. Mahoney, his midwife, had come to him with the rejected twin, an adorable baby girl, he'd known exactly with whom to place her. No papers were drawn up. No rules of adoption followed. Back in 1880, registration of orphaned or abandoned infants on the Oklahoma frontier was slack at best. It had been a clean handoff to the Gordons with no government agency involved.

Now, though, he couldn't die without some record left behind of the child's parentage in case it might be of interest to someone down the line, presumably Samantha. She was aware the Gordons were not her parents. How could they be, they being rangy, dark, big-framed, the direct opposite of their fair, delicately boned daughter with hair the color of an autumn sunset.

Dr. Tolman read the letter again, silently this time, to make sure he'd not left out the few details he knew. He'd stated the names of the parents as Leon and Millicent Holloway, and the place of birth as their farm, but he wasn't sure of its location near the Red River. He listed Bridget Mahoney as the attending midwife. According to Bridget, she'd been visiting her sister in Gainesville, another midwife, but she was out on a call when she was summoned to the farm, so Bridget had gone in her place to assist in the birth. Bridget was a closemouthed sort, so as far as Dr. Tolman knew, he, Mrs. Mahoney, and the Holloways were the only people, besides the Gordons, who knew Samantha had not been wanted. His midwife had come to him in Marietta in the Oklahoma Territory with the child, bearing only the skimpy information that the mother refused to nurse her. Dr. Tolman decided not to include that information in the letter. Perhaps the child's parents had been unable to care for her and depended on his midwife to find their daughter a good home. He'd been so happy to have a normal, healthy child to present to the Gordons that he'd asked few questions of Mrs. Mahoney, and the Gordons had asked even fewer of him. Beggars could not be choosers. In the letter, Dr. Tolman stated that he could give no further information except the little girl had been born with a twin brother.

His conscience satisfied, Dr. Tolman licked the flap of the envelope and sealed the letter. The post office was located not far away. He threw a couple of pills down his throat, gulped a glass of water, took up his cane to assist his weakening frame, and made his way to the door.

Chapter Eight

The fifth day after her twentieth birthday, Samantha awoke from a nightmare that had not reoccurred in years. In it, she was a waif abandoned miles beyond escape before the door of a dark, forbidding house located in a landscape as barren as a moon crater. Heart racing and mouth dry, ears still holding the cry that had awakened her, she blinked at the abrupt reality of the morning sun pouring through silk-draped windows into her French-inspired bedroom, lighting the rose-papered walls and graceful furniture and the canopied bed in which she lay. Its benevolent warmth fell upon her like the reassuring smile of an angel. It's all right. You're in your mother's house. You're safe. With her heartbeat steadying and a sense of rescue, Samantha burrowed deeper into the downy comfort of the bed as the last vestiges of her dream faded away.

She could blame Anne Rutherford and Todd Baker for the return of her nighttime horror—Anne for bringing up her bloodline theory at her birthday party to make a point of Samantha's lack of one, and Todd for trotting out stories of her laboratory experiments from their school years. Those strands of conversation had led to her mother asking over the menu at Tea and Crumpets yesterday, "Now that you've turned twenty, darling, have you any regrets about...anything?"

It was like Estelle Gordon to couch possibly painful subjects in vague terms. "Anything" referred to the question of whether Samantha regretted her choice of avocation. Did she regret staying behind to learn the business of ranching over her opportunity to study natural science at the Lasell Seminary for Young Women in Massachusetts? And...was she ever curious about the family and roots from which she came?

"No, Mother, I have no regrets about anything," Samantha had answered. "I wouldn't change my lot for anything in the world."

"Lot" meant her home, her parents, her situation in life. Samantha was noted as one for not hedging the truth. Don't ask if one did not wish a straight answer. Her mother had looked at her over the rim of her teacup with a gratified smile in her gaze.

Samantha wondered if her father, alone at the ranch while she spent the week of her birthday with her mother in Fort Worth as she did every year, was asking the same question. At twenty, did Samantha have regrets about anything? He wouldn't ask out of pride and maybe a secret fear of the answer, but that didn't mean he didn't question whether she was as happy as she might have been if things had worked out differently.

Darn Anne and Todd for causing them to wonder even a trifle if Samantha had regrets! She didn't. It took only the image of that little girl in her nightmare and the terror it evoked to make her realize how lucky she was. Her mother was so easily readable. It was clear that Todd's reminiscences had triggered a memory of the time the Gordons, unbeknown to Samantha, had been asked to meet with the headmaster of Simmons Preparatory School. Samantha, too, had been called from biology class and walked into the headmaster's office to find her parents and Mr. Latimer, the chairman of the science department and her favorite teacher, seated before his desk. She was sixteen years old and in the final months of her schooling before graduation.

"What's the purpose of this meeting, Headmaster?" Neal Gordon had demanded. "Is our daughter in trouble?"

The headmaster had exchanged a grin with the chairman of the science department. "Absolutely not," he said, and pushed a letter across his desk for the Gordons to read. "Your daughter has been accepted at the Lasell Seminary for Young Women in Massachusetts to pursue a degree in science." He tipped his head to his colleague. "You have Mr. Latimer here to thank for sending Samantha's résumé listing her outstanding credentials to the school. It only remains for you to fill out the application form to make it official, Samantha."

Samantha remembered woodenly intercepting the letter before it could reach her parents' hands. She was aware of the prestigious, highly respected institution known for its radical and innovative approach to women's education, especially in the field of sciences. She had followed the career of Annie Montague Alexander, a Lasell graduate whose work with fossils and the study of paleontology was internationally recognized. Sensing her parents' stiff dismay, Samantha read the glowing reply to Mr. Latimer's request for enrollment, then pushed the letter and its attached application form back across the desk.

The two academics regarded her with puzzled expressions. "Uh, Miss Gordon, perhaps your parents would like to read the letter," the headmaster suggested.

"It is for me to decide whether I wish to attend Lasell Seminary, and I decline," Samantha said. "May I now return to class?"

Mr. Latimer shifted his flabbergasted gaze to the Gordons. "Mr. and Mrs. Gordon, your daughter is the most brilliant student I've ever taught. She is a natural scientist. Surely you support this opportunity for Samantha to fulfill her calling and contribute her gift to the world. It's a rare privilege that will not be extended again once she's out of school."

Neal Gordon had stood up, offering his arm to Estelle. "My daughter knows what she wants and doesn't," he said. "That's how she's been raised, and as she says, it's not for anyone else to decide."

Later in the day, Mr. Latimer had approached her. "Miss Gordon—Samantha—I beg you. Don't give up your dream to become a scientist for the sake of your father. You know how much you love research and the study of plants and animals."

"Which I'll have plenty of opportunities to do at Las Tres Lomas, Mr. Latimer, and an interest is not a dream. I've made my choice."

"Your father made your choice."

"I'm devoted to the ranch. Ranching is in my blood."

"How can that be? You're devoted to your *father*'s passion for the ranch, not yours. If he owned a chain of candy stores, you'd feel the same loyalty."

"Probably," she'd admitted, "but I wouldn't feel the same about candy that I do about cattle."

Mr. Latimer had hardly spoken to her again.

Todd's birthday present to her had been a pair of tickets to a lecture given by a noted paleontologist who was to speak on structural and sedimentary aspects of fossil strata as a means to identify possible oil traps.

"Were you being thoughtful or provocative, Todd? What's the point of either?" Samantha had scolded him later in a private conversation when everybody had adjourned to the parlor for ice cream and cake.

"No point at all," he'd said. "I thought you'd like an opportunity to keep up with the times. Petroleum exploration is the next great archeological dig, Sam. Ginny and I are going to the lecture, and my boss will be there. I want my future wife to meet him and learn what her geologist husband will be doing. I thought you could bring along a friend, and we could make it a foursome."

She'd handed back the tickets. "Thank you, Todd, but I've no idea who I would invite. You and Ginny enjoy the use of these with another couple."

He'd taken the tickets, but she'd later found them in the calling card tray in the foyer.

Todd, two years into his geological studies at Jackson, had been as upset as Mr. Latimer, almost outraged, when he learned she'd given up her place at the seminary. She could not convince him that it was *her* decision to stay behind.

"Because your parents make you feel you *owe* them, Sammy!" he'd yelled.

"I *do* owe them!" Samantha had shouted back. "If you'd seen what I saw—"

She'd pressed her lips together. Never would she divulge to anybody the sights that had sent her running home to her adoptive parents to throw herself gratefully into their arms.

"Saw what?" Todd asked.

"Never mind," she'd said.

The scene was one Samantha had never been able to forget and had come back to haunt her in her sleep through the years. She was ten years old. Her Sunday school teacher, a well-meaning soul, had thought it a great idea to take baskets of Christmas treats to the unfortunate children who had been left without parents, either through death, misfortune, or abandonment. She proposed a trip to the Millbrook Home for Orphaned Children. On a gray and cold Sunday morning, in lieu of the lesson, her charges piled into a wagon in their warm coats clutching their holiday-decorated baskets and headed off to their destination. Samantha had never forgotten the ugly, forbidding house that loomed into view at the end of a muddy country road. Barren, treeless fields stretched for miles around the dark, sinister-looking structure that proclaimed itself A HAVEN FOR THE HOMELESS in a sign over the fortress of the front door.

Samantha hung back close to her teacher immediately upon entering. The first memory never to leave her was the rancid smell overlaid by the heavy odor of cooked cabbage. The second was the shocking realization that looks could be deceiving. The woman who bustled toward them to introduce herself as the head matron looked as if she could have been the wife of Santa Claus. Rosy cheeked and round as an apple, her gray hair done up in perky braids that framed a cheerful face, the woman personified sweetness and light until Samantha saw how quickly the merry eyes could freeze to ice, the smiling mouth form a trap of steel. She did not fail to notice the ring of jailers' keys dangling from the matron's belt, the sharp metal tip of a rod in her pocket, and how the children cringed from her hand upon their shoulders meant to demonstrate affection. The Sunday school teacher had pronounced her a lovely person on the way home, and Samantha had wondered how adults could be so fooled.

One gaze had stood out from all the other pinched faces and blank stares that eyed the members of the Sunday school class as they distributed the baskets. It belonged to a small girl her age. "Thank you," the girl said, looking at Samantha out of shy hazel eyes when she handed her the basket. Samantha wanted to cry. The little girl, like the other children, looked hungry and under-nourished. Her thin face and arms and hands appeared to have been washed, but not enough to wipe away the grime of long neglect. Her golden hair hung limp and greasy, and a rim of dirt was under her fingernails.

"You're welcome," Samantha said. "What is your name?"

"Susie," the little girl said. "What is yours?"

"Samantha. I will come again, Susie."

"I hope so, Samantha."

Samantha never did. Her mother forbade another trip to the orphanage and was furious with the Sunday school teacher for arranging the visit and with her husband for allowing it while she'd been away on a weekend shopping trip.

"I thought that by now she would have forgotten that she wasn't born to us," Samantha overheard her father defend his action to her mother.

"Samantha may have forgotten, but how could you think that mean, snobby Anne Rutherford would forget? Anne asked Samantha on the way back if she was aware of what she'd been spared. The child is traumatized. I had hoped her *never* to know what her life might have been like if she hadn't come to us."

"So what do we say when Samantha asks about her parents and how we got her—and she will, Estelle. They are inevitable questions only normal to an adopted child. We have to tell her the truth. Her parents didn't want her and they gave her away. Plain and simple. The truth will keep her with us, Estelle. If her parents come looking for her, she won't want to go with them. She'll stay with us."

"We are *not* going to tell her the truth. We're going to let her believe her parents are dead," Estelle said. "Why would those awful people come looking for her anyway, since that doctor told us she wasn't wanted? Neal, dear, you must stop living with the fear that we're going to lose her. Our love, not truth, will hold Samantha fast to us."

"I can't seem to shake the fear that they'll show up someday and take her from us, honeybee. Blood can be stronger than a court order saying she's ours…stronger even than love."

Samantha, deeply upset and not wanting to let her parents out of her sight, had gone in search of them and caught the conversation huddled outside the door to the library in the ranch house.

Up until then, she'd simply assumed her real parents were dead. It never occurred to her that they were alive and she'd been given away because they didn't want her. Now, even more terrified at what could have been her fate, she'd backed away and gone to her room before the people to whom she owed her life could discover her presence. She loved them so much. They never had to be afraid she'd go with her real parents if they came to take her back. She'd run away and hide until they were gone.

In her childish hand, Samantha wrote a letter to Susie explaining that she'd been forbidden to come see her again. She addressed it simply "To Susie" and hoped there was only one by that name at the Millbrook Home for Orphaned Children. Whether she received it, Samantha never knew. When she was thirteen and was presented Pony, a quarter horse, for her birthday, her first sprint of freedom was to the orphanage to visit Susie. Susie was no longer with them, the merry-faced matron informed her. She had died of tuberculosis the preceding winter.

Chapter Nine

Did she have regrets about anything? Absolutely not, unless it was Sloan Singleton's infatuation with Anne Rutherford. Samantha adjusted her pillows against the headboard to indulge in a few more minutes of thought and reflection. Todd Baker and his like had no background or experience to understand her willingness to accept the future laid out for her by virtue of loyalty and obligation. Todd came from a family of academics. He was the son of the president of AddRan Christian University located in Waco, approximately ninety miles south of Fort Worth, and had grown up in a liberal home where all four children had been encouraged since birth to follow their own star. His parents were not native born. They had arrived in Texas from Pennsylvania fifteen years after the Civil War, Professor Baker to spearhead the fledgling AddRan Male and Female College, then situated in what became Fort Worth's notorious Hell's Half Acre. Neal and Estelle Gordon, like their parents before them, were Texas born and bred. Todd couldn't begin to understand the life-blood connection of men like her father to the land their ancestors had settled and fought to keep against every adversary that would have taken it from them. Todd's father would never expect his children to follow in his footsteps, while in the world of the Neal Gordons, offspring were reared from birth to fill their fathers' shoes.

Also, Todd Baker had not lived with the knowledge that, but for the loving people who had raised her, she could have been Susie. Samantha *did* owe them, and that was the end of the argument. She was the only heir to all her father and mother had worked for. To go off to pursue a degree in science—paleontology, to be exact—would have been a betrayal of their caring and giving. What would happen to Las Tres Lomas de la Trinidad— the Three Hills of the Trinity—once its mighty owner died? How could Samantha allow her father to live out his life knowing that all his sacrifice, work, and devotion to the land of his family and heritage would pass into other hands at the time of his death? No other passion was worth it.

When she was sixteen, Todd had asked her if she ever wondered about her birth parents, who they were, where they lived, if they were still alive. *"Of course not!"* she exclaimed, like one jumping back from a spitting fire.

But that was not entirely true. Around her fifteenth birthday, an incident occurred that caused Samantha to question briefly the fragment of fact about her adoption she'd overheard at ten years old. She was in her workshop cataloging her find for the day, when she heard a moan of animal distress outside the window. Looking out, she saw a mother cow in agony, her unweaned calf beside her. Samantha ran out and discovered the cow had swallowed a crab apple too deep to be extracted from her throat. The animal had wandered far away from the pasture into human territory, and Samantha, peering into the dying Hereford's brown eyes, wondered if the cow had not intentionally brought her calf to her laboratory workshop where she spent her spare time.

"Do you suppose she led her calf here for me to look after?" Samantha asked Wayne Harris, the foreman, her father's long-time and most essential hand. Hurriedly, he'd helped her prepare a concoction of milk and mash for the calf to suckle from a "banana bottle," so named because of its curved shape. It was a glass container with two openings at either end, one smaller for attaching a rubber nipple and the other larger for adding food. It was perfect for feeding motherless calves, and a large improvement over the awkward and unsanitary nursing contraptions used in the past.

"Wouldn't surprise me none," Wayne said. "Ain't no denyin' a mama's natural instincts when it comes to her offspring, be she human or animal."

That drew Samantha's startled attention. Her father's words— *Her parents didn't want her, and they gave her away*—stuck with her still, if banished to the netherland of memory. A thought flashed in her head never considered before. What if...like the mother cow, circumstances beyond the control of her real parents had forced them to give her up? There could be many reasons...poverty, illness, approaching death, an excess of offspring. Maybe it wasn't that her natural parents hadn't wanted her; they'd simply been unable to provide for her. It wasn't uncommon in hard times for parents who couldn't care for their children to leave them by the wayside in hope that somebody would come along who would give them a good home. Maybe...her real parents missed her and would like to know that she was loved and well looked after.

"Wayne, do you recall anything about my birth?" she'd asked. She had never gone to her parents with those "inevitable questions only normal to an adopted child."

A wary look had crossed his face. "Can't say I do, Mornin' Glory. I just remember the morning the bunkhouse was informed a baby girl had been delivered to the Gordons in the middle of the night."

"Why in the middle of the night? Was I a secret?"

"Well, now, if you'd been a secret, the news of you comin' to us wouldn't have been shouted to the whole world the next mornin', now would it? Why do you ask?"

"Just curious."

"Well, it'd be a good idea to keep your curiosity between you and me. Your folks might not understand it." He'd squinted an eye at her. "You comprehend what I'm sayin'?"

Clearly, Wayne was right. Her father would feel threatened and betrayed, her mother rejected. They would interpret her curiosity as dissatisfaction with them, and Samantha wouldn't have them feel that way for anything in the world.

"I understand," she'd said, rubbing the ears of the baby steer. He had finished feeding and was bawling for his mama. "Wayne, I don't want this little fellow ever sold. He's to be allowed to live out his life on the ranch eating all the grass he wants."

"I imagine your daddy will have a say about that, Mornin' Glory. He ain't one to offer free grass and water without somethin' in return, and this little fellow is money on the hoof."

"He'll understand."

Her father had heard her out in silence and finally, after considering her carefully from behind his massive oak desk, cleared his throat of something rough that had stuck there. "All right, daughter," he said. "It'll be done. But how will you identify that dogie from the rest of the herd?"

"I'll paint the tips of his horns red."

"I suppose you'll give the critter a name."

"Yes," Samantha said. "I'm going to call him Saved."

Her father smiled in understanding and approval of her choice. He nodded. "Saved. That's a fine handle. I'll let the boys know."

That had been the last time Samantha had spared a thought to the questions of her birth. At fifteen, she'd been almost grown. She remembered thinking that she was too old and it was too late for the people who'd given birth to her to come looking for her. Her life was set. She had her parents and wished for no other. Neal Gordon no longer had to worry that she'd be taken from him.

Samantha watched the sun spread its light in her bedroom. No, she had no regrets. Las Tres Lomas de la Trinidad was the place where she was meant to be, no matter that her "fit" for it did not come from inherited blood. The wide-open range, where the wind blew fresh and unobstructed and the only smells and sounds were natural to the country, was for her a vast laboratory that offered plentiful opportunities for scientific exploration and analysis. Land and livestock management required paleontological skills. Samantha had rigged up an outdoor workshop with basic tools for testing water, soil, grass, even animal urine and fecal matter, and seeds for fodder production. It was in her workshop that she kept her rock collection that recorded the geology of Texas and a growing accumulation of ancient sea relics found on the ranch while she went about her daily duties. Central Texas was proved to have been covered by an ocean millions of years ago, and Las Tres Lomas was a virtual treasure trove of prehistoric marine life. A shelf in her "lab" boasted a fragment of a fossilized turtle shell, an imprint of a sea urchin preserved in rock, an intact tip of a partial horn that might have belonged to a mammoth, and—her prize: the full impression of an ocean scallop discovered when she was baling hay.

She felt at home on a horse, with cattle and cowmen, and when her father discovered she had a head for making judicious financial decisions, she became indispensable to the business operations of the ranch. Samantha had heard him tell her mother, "We were blessed, Estelle. The good Lord gave us the whole package in Sam. No man's son has a better head or pair of hands for running a ranch than our daughter."

Samantha had studied her hands. They were small with slender, tapered fingers and barely visible knuckles. One of her science teachers had commented their shape was "just made" to slide plant specimens under a microscope and to examine bits of rock through a loupe. She'd told the teacher that her hands were also perfect for aiding prolapsed cows in distress.

"Prolapsed cows? What in the world are they?"

"It's a condition that occurs most often at calving time," Samantha had explained. "It happens when a cow expels her uterus in giving birth, and it hangs outside her body, sometimes almost to her hocks. When that happens, the uterus has to be cleaned and inserted back inside the cow or she will hemorrhage to death. My father's foreman thinks the size of my hands are just right for the job."

"How…interesting," her teacher had murmured, turning pale.

In her canopied bed, Samantha chuckled, remembering.

Chapter Ten

Samantha threw back the covers. She'd lain in bed long enough indulging in past memories. Time was burnin' itself, as her father would say. She must get back to the ranch. Many of the heifers—females having their first babies—were calving now, and they needed more help than birthing cows. This was also the last week of the month, when bills had to be paid and profits and losses tallied.

She dressed in the work attire she'd brought along to wear back to the ranch: denim pants, long-sleeved flannel shirt, leather vest, and high-topped boots. Buttoning the fly of the "blue jeans," designated such because of their color and style, Samantha anticipated her mother's sniff of disapproval. It was Estelle's opinion that "Levi Strauss never meant for women to wear his copper-riveted work pants when he created them," leaving her daughter to wonder if her mother had forgotten she'd worn men's trousers in the early years of helping her husband run the ranch.

There were so many things her mother wanted to forget from that time. She'd been the daughter of a poor dirt farmer in 1867 when Neal Gordon came calling and married her the same year. In becoming Mrs. Neal Gordon, Estelle had gained a proud family name. The Gordons were landed gentry. In 1820, the patriarch of Las Tres Lomas de la Trinidad had come to what was then a province of Mexico and established a ranch he stocked with a breed of cattle native to the region known as Longhorns. In 1867, Neal, along with his father and two younger brothers, owned the beginnings of what would become one of the largest ranches in Central Texas, but prosperity was nearly fifteen years away. Comanche raids and Reconstruction were wreaking financial havoc, and that year Neal's father and his two unmarried brothers succumbed to a yellow fever epidemic that swept up through Texas from the coastal city of Galveston. Estelle was left to fill the boots of the depleted labor force. Not until the end of the Indian Wars and Reconstruction when the Texas and Pacific Railway arrived in Fort Worth did Estelle enjoy the lady-of-the-manor life she'd dreamed about during her courtship. By then, at thirty-six, she was middle-aged.

Samantha had long figured out that her mother had hoped to live vicariously through the little girl she took to raise. Impoverished as a child and a far cry from beautiful, Estelle Gordon would experience through Samantha what it would have been like to be pretty and graceful, to wear fine clothes, and to enjoy the frilly feminine amusements she'd longed to know growing up. Samantha was sensitive to this side of her lanky, rawboned mother and did her best to satisfy her yearning.

For a while, Samantha had wished that it was possible to be two daughters, one for her mother and one for her father, but then she'd matured to realize she could be only one, so Estelle Gordon had lost the daughter she would have preferred to see in lace and silk to leather and denim. There had been no division of loyalties when both her parents had lived at Las Tres Lomas, but when her mother came to live in town, visiting the ranch only occasionally and her father remained behind, Samantha had begun to be pulled in two directions. Her mother wished her to take her place in society. Her father wanted her to learn the business that sustained their livelihood.

"She's the heir to Las Tres Lomas, Estelle. Can't you understand that the only way for Sam to learn the workings of the ranch is to *be* there?"

"She'll get old before her time, Neal. The land will sap the youth right out of her. Like it did me," Estelle said.

"Why, you're as pretty and youthful as the day I met you, honeybee," her husband declared. "What are you talking about?"

"Oh, Neal! You're as impossibly blind as you are stubborn!"

"I'll encourage her to wear a hat and gloves when she's on the range, Estelle. I promise."

In the beginning, her mother had hoped her daughter's attendance at Simmons Preparatory would give her a taste for city life, but it had not, and with reluctant grace, Estelle had let her go. Samantha had been relieved. She was accommodating only to a certain point and would not live in town with its mud streets, uneven boardwalks, raw sewage in the gutters, drunken cowboys shooting up the place on Saturday nights, lack of a water system, and *flies*! In the summer, it was nothing to see them swarming like a hive of bees around crates of fruit and meat hanging in grocery markets or in restaurants where the pests were so numerous, the help would tack two-inch strips cut from newspapers onto broomsticks and wave them over the tables to keep them off the food.

Samantha would have dressed this morning in her fashionable three-piece riding habit with top hat and veil she usually wore when arriving and departing the town house, but the costume was meant for sidesaddle, and she'd brought along Pony, her quarter horse, for the ride back to the ranch. Immediate and dirty chores awaited her upon return, for which she'd already be dressed.

Samantha intercepted the housekeeper taking her mother her breakfast tray. "I'll carry that in, Mildred," she said.

"You up awful early, Miss Sam, and already ready to leave us, too. Does your mama know you're going so soon?"

"I'm not sure. That's why I want to take the tray in so that I can break it to her gently."

The housekeeper widened her gaze and swept it over Samantha's seasoned work wear. "You ain't going to break it to her gently in that gear," she said. "Your mother was hoping you'd stay at least through luncheon." Mildred was half American Indian, half white. Her mother had been abducted by a Comanche raiding party in 1864 and impregnated by one of its warriors. Mother and daughter had been rescued and returned to her mother's family by the Texas Rangers in 1871, when Mildred was six years old. As a young woman, she had come to live at Las Tres Lomas as a kitchen maid when Samantha was two. When Estelle moved to the town house in Fort Worth, she had brought Mildred along as housekeeper.

Samantha took the tray with the familiar thought of feeling like a rope tugged between two giant oaks. "I can't, Mildred. Will you please tell Jimmy to saddle up Pony for me?"

Awful early. It was past eight o'clock. At the ranch, long before now she'd already have had breakfast with her father and begun her duties for the day. He would be anxiously waiting, glad for Estelle to have had their daughter's undivided attention for the traditional yearly week of her birthday, but pawing at the ground for her return.

Her mother's sudden, happy smile at Samantha's entrance with the breakfast tray melted when she noted her ranch attire. "I can't entice you to stay another day?"

Samantha positioned the bed tray over her mother's lap. "You know I can't, Mother. The boys will need my help with the heifers, and I've got the books to do this afternoon. Daddy is expecting me."

Estelle spread the napkin over the bodice of her nightgown. "Well, we can't have your father disappointed, now can we?"

"Mother..." Samantha's sigh warned Estelle not to start with the old resentment.

"I know, I know." Estelle's tone conceded defeat. She placed her hand over the lid of the silver pot and poured a steaming cup of coffee. "But speaking of your father, I have a concern that I must mention before you leave."

Samantha drew up a chair and set her wide-brimmed, high-crowned hat on the bed, feeling a clench of alarm. Was this about the whistling sound back in her father's chest she and her mother had heard at her birthday dinner? It had come and gone for years. Neal Gordon declared it normal for a man shot in the lung by a Comanche arrow. "What concern?"

"Sloan Singleton."

"Sloan Singleton?"

Estelle blew on the surface of the hot coffee. "Don't say his name and look as if you don't know who and what I'm talking about."

Samantha forced a blank stare. "No, Mother, I'm afraid I don't."

"Is he going to marry that supercilious fraud?"

"How would I know?"

"Don't you two talk anymore?"

"Not for a long time."

Estelle sipped her coffee. "That's what your father and I were afraid of."

"What were you afraid of?"

Carefully, Estelle set her coffee cup in its saucer. "That you two have grown apart. Neal says you don't invite him to supper anymore and decline invitations to the Triple S. That's opening the door for Anne Rutherford to waltz through, Samantha. And she will, too, and lock you out. That girl's got her sights on Sloan as the man she intends to marry."

Samantha felt a sudden loss of air from her lungs. "Even if Sloan and I were still close friends, what makes you think she wouldn't waltz in anyway? Sloan has never thought of me in any way but as another sister."

"Good friends make the best spouses, Samantha, and you and Sloan were made for each other. Don't deny it. What other beautiful woman does he know that fits to ranching like you do? Good God! Anne Rutherford doesn't know the back end of a cow from a pig's snout." Stirring sugar into her coffee, Estelle made a face. "Seth Singleton, God rest his soul, will turn in his grave if his son marries that holier-than-thou piece of fluff. From the time you and Sloan were children together, your father and Seth were dead-set on the two of you marrying and combining the ranches as one."

"That must have gotten by me," Samantha said wryly, surprised by this new information. "By Sloan, as well." She reached for her mother's coffee cup and took a hot swallow to loosen her tight throat. "Daddy's main concern wouldn't be that if I don't marry Sloan, I won't marry at all, would it?" She did not add: *And have those heirs he wants?*

A blush bloomed on the flat, weathered planes of Estelle's cheeks. All the face creams now on the market and easily affordable to her mother's budget had not effectively bleached years of her skin's exposure to the sun. Estelle looked disconcerted. "What other man is out there that you would consider, Samantha?"

"You mean what other man is out there to *be* considered?" Samantha said.

Estelle sighed. "Why did Lawrence Hendrick and Tom Bedford have to go off and get themselves killed in the Spanish-American War, a conflict the U.S. shouldn't even have been in?

Who in the world ever heard of Cuba? Those boys would have been knocking each other out for your hand."

Samantha pushed back the chair and stood. "I'm only twenty, Mother, not an old maid yet. A candidate wearing the right spurs might come along for my affections yet."

"I've heard as much confidence in the song of a dying bird. You love Sloan Singleton and might as well admit it."

Samantha picked up her hat. "So what if I do? He'll probably marry Anne, and who can blame him? She's stunning, and he's convinced she has a heart to go with her beauty. Maybe she does—for him, at least."

"Oh, good heavens! Anne Rutherford's beauty is surface deep, not like yours that shines from the soul. And those noble causes of hers..." Estelle buttered a slice of toast with a furious swipe of her knife. "Only a show to make herself appear superior to everybody else. You'd think someone of Sloan Singleton's common sense wouldn't be taken in by her. His mother certainly wouldn't have been, God rest *her* soul."

Samantha bent down and kissed her mother's cheek. "You've just never forgiven Anne for suggesting to Miss Sims that she take her Sunday school class out to Millbrook Orphanage when I was ten years old," she said.

"And I never will, either. Anne did it deliberately to make you feel bad."

"She succeeded. Now I must be going. Thank you for a beautiful birthday party and a wonderful week."

"I hope you enjoyed yourself," Estelle said, doubt in her look. "I know I enjoyed having you here. I so wish you'd have had one of the boys come collect you in a ranch wagon that's easily recognized. I worry so when you ride back alone. Those drovers that come into town with the herds...nothing but a bunch of rowdies, and on horseback, they have no idea who you are."

"I'm safer on a horse than I'd be in a wagon, Mother. Pony can outrun anything on four legs, and you know I'm not bad with a gun, either."

Samantha could see the unease that image implanted. Was it the way of mothers that they were always anxious about their children's happiness and safety? Would she ever have reason to know for herself?

Mildred met her in the foyer as she was tying on her hat before the hall mirror. "You'll go by the post office to collect your father's mail? And what do you want to do about these?" The house-keeper had picked up Todd Baker's birthday present from the calling card tray where Samantha had left them.

Samantha took the tickets from Mildred's hand. The date of the lecture was in eleven days, scheduled on Saturday, when she'd return for the weekend to attend a christening on Sunday. She knew no one to give them to. Who but a scientist would be interested in hearing a paleontologist speak on the process of ex-tracting oil from fossils?

Todd had spent a tidy sum for the tickets, Samantha read on the stubs. A shame not to make use of them. When she returned, she'd contact the Simmons Preparatory School. Perhaps a student or teacher in the science department might like to attend. "I'll just leave them here," she said, depositing the pair in a drawer of the hat stand.

Chapter Eleven

Pony was saddled and waiting for her, the toss of his head and twitch of his tail irritably informing Samantha that he was eager to escape the restrictions of his stall. For a week he had been denied his daily work with cattle. "He's rarin' to go, Miss Sam," Jimmy, the wizened stableman, said. "If yore goin' into town, keep a tight hold on the reins. Lordy, the traffic we got these days. A sorry sight. I 'member the days when Fort Worth was so quiet, it wadn't nothin' for a panther to crawl into town for a nap."

Samantha smiled. How many times had she heard Jimmy, who had been with the Gordons since she was a child and described by her father as "a little slow in the head but mighty damn good with horses," refer to the incident in his youth that had resulted in Panther City becoming the nickname of Fort Worth. Because of the devastation to the cattle industry by the hard winter of 1873 and the termination of the Texas and Pacific Railway thirty miles short of Fort Worth, the town had become so sleepy that an article in the *Dallas Herald* reported a lawyer seeing a panther asleep on its courthouse steps. Fort Worth's prosperous rival meant it as a dig, but the city thumbed its nose at the insult and enthusiastically adopted the panther as a symbol of its survival and indomitability.

"I'll keep a firm grip, Jimmy," Samantha said, climbing up.

Lord, it felt good to be in the saddle again wearing comfortable clothes. The morning was bright with sunshine and fresh from the last of winter's chilly rains that had fallen during the night. Spring was on the way. She wished she could hit the open road to the ranch right then and avoid the trip to the newly built post office situated on the other side of town. Except for Friday, when the carrier made morning rounds in her mother's neighborhood, mail was not delivered until late afternoon. The modern structure and boast of the city had replaced a convenient general store for collecting letters and packages at any time of the day, one of the many signs of progress offering mixed benefits to the no-longer sleepy town of Fort Worth. Samantha shared the neighbors' irritation at having to make the trek this morning when she was in a hurry. She patted the horse's muscular neck. "One more stop, Pony, then we'll head for home."

On the ride into town, as she noted the paved streets and new buildings that had gone up, Samantha's thoughts returned to the surprising revelation of her father and Seth Singleton's hopes for her and Sloan to marry. She'd thought of Seth Singleton like an uncle, as her father was fond of Sloan like a nephew. From her first steps, siblingless, she'd considered Sloan, almost four years older, as a big brother, a role he'd played ever since, but no place beyond that. It was not so much a surprise that she'd missed her father's romantic hopes for them as that her father had overlooked Sloan's lack of romantic interest in her. The union of Las Tres Lomas de la Trinidad and the Triple S would never be. The daughter of Neal Gordon ignited no amorous spark in Sloan Singleton.

Which was just as well, Samantha thought. She and Sloan were definitely not a good match. As time had gone by, their differences in opinions, attitudes, and beliefs had arisen. Prejudices had developed. Had circumstances granted Sloan an ordinary adolescence, allowed him time and range to reach adulthood, perhaps the towhead she'd grown up secretly loving through the boy stages of changing vocal cords, acne, and awkward growth spurts would not have developed such a hard edge and an inflexible outlook. A turn of events had cut his youth short when Seth Singleton died unexpectedly, and his only son at seventeen was forced to take over the Triple S, become head of the household, and assume responsibility for his two older, unmarried sisters.

"He's got what it takes, but he'll have to prove it," Samantha remembered her father saying. "It won't be easy ordering men around two, three times his age, making decisions for a ranch the size of the Triple S. The boy will have to earn his spurs, and God almighty, he'll have a job showing those older sisters of his who's boss. With the death of their mother, they've pretty much had free range to do as they please."

Sloan had proved he had what it took. With the help of her father's mentoring and the impression that Seth Singleton's son had been born fully mature, with nary an irresponsible bone in his body, he had picked up the fallen reins of his father and held them firmly. At nearly twenty-four, deep-voiced, clear-skinned, and a graceful six foot two, Sloan was regarded as one of the most respected and influential ranchers in the state, and his sisters, Millie May and Billie June, had been left with no doubt who was in charge. Samantha's disenchantment with their brother began when he refused to allow Billie June, the younger of his sisters, to continue seeing a man he deemed unsuitable.

"He's a drifter, Sam, and five years younger than Billie June," her father had argued in defense of Sloan's action when Samantha had voiced her objection at Sloan's high-handedness. "The man's got no established means of earning a livelihood."

"Mr. Chandler says Daniel Lane is the best assistant he's ever had."

"Assistant to a smithy? What kind of recommendation is that?"

"It recommends him as a hard worker. Claude Chandler is not an easy man to please."

"Daniel Lane's got no background, Sam. No education, no breeding. He's certainly not the kind of man Seth would have a daughter of his marry. Sloan did right to exert his authority and put an end to it."

Exert his authority? How was it right for a brother to have "authority" over the heart of a sister? How was it right for a man to exert any control over a woman at all? The world had entered the twentieth century. Could Sloan, so willing to embrace the latest and most modern methods of cattle raising, not see that the cultural landscape of women was changing? The Civil War had forced female members of the household to undertake the responsibilities and make decisions formerly the province of their late menfolks. Such freedom and independence, according to what Samantha read, was spilling over from the domestic scene into occupations such as law, journalism, geology, medicine, and engineering. Women's labor unions had formed, and the suffragist movement was gaining momentum. All over the nation, the "new woman" was replacing the "ideal woman," challenging male dominance.

Everywhere but in Fort Worth, Texas, it seemed.

"But Billie June loves him," Samantha had protested.

"Makes not a whit of difference, daughter, and you must get it out of your head that it does."

Yes, indeed, Anne Rutherford was the perfect mate for Sloan Singleton, Samantha would not argue. Content to bask in his light, seeking none of her own but a slice to illumine the complement of her good works to his status—having no *mind* of her own—Anne would make a splendid wife, mother, mistress of the house, charity organizer, hostess. Samantha saw herself as none of those things exclusively. She was well aware of her father's hopes for her to marry a man of his ilk, someone who understood the ranching business, but he thought she failed to see that, while he'd leave the ranch in her hands, he assumed her husband—someone like Sloan Singleton—would control the reins with her permission. It was the way things were done in Texas, but Samantha was determined such would not be the case when she inherited Las Tres Lomas. If she was to be groomed to take Neal Gordon's place, then she would take her position with no thought of sharing the driver's seat unless as an equal partner, another reason that she and Sloan could never be.

The stench of the stockyards and the Fort Worth Dressed Meat and Provision Company assaulted her as Samantha tied Pony in front of the new post office. The Ladies' Society, of which her mother was secretary, had urged the city council to encourage the structure be built farther south where the finer residential areas lay. The powers that ran the stockyards and the Swift, Armour, and Libby's meat-packing plants soon to come to Fort Worth had won the debate with the United States Postal Department. They claimed that access to mail service was essential to their businesses.

Samantha noticed the fine workmanship of the hitching rings that were crowned with the city's logo, a reclining panther. Daniel Lane, a miracle worker with iron, was responsible for the design. The blacksmith's shop where he worked had been commissioned to forge the rings, and Samantha wondered if Billie June Singleton had seen them. She did not come to town as often since her brother had put a stop to her affair with Daniel Lane in a showdown before the whole community.

"She's become somewhat reclusive," her mother had said of Billie June to Samantha in a discussion of the scandal that had quietly exploded with the fireworks when Daniel escorted Sloan's sister to the Fourth of July picnic last July. "What a shame. Daniel

Lane is likely to be the only suitor Billie June will ever have, plain as she is, but the girl asked for her brother's wrath when she paraded that smithy's helper in front of the whole town. She should have known better."

"Sloan should have known better," Samantha had said.

Mildred had inserted her opinion into the rehash. "Young Sloan better watch himself with that ironmonger. Daniel Lane ain't one to forget the injury he suffered that day. Nothing sets deeper or burns longer in the human gut than the shame of public humiliation. The master of the Triple S has sowed the seed of revenge."

To this day, Samantha winced at the memory of Sloan's public threat to Daniel Lane and Billie June's humiliation before her friends and neighbors and the townspeople at the Independence Day gathering. As Billie June was unloading her picnic basket, Sloan had arrived on horseback behind the family carriage. The men riding alongside him and driving the team were two of his top ranch hands, formidable bronc busters to whom people gave a wide berth. Calmly, Sloan had dismounted and approached the spread blanket. Without a word to his surprised sister and her companion, he'd loaded the fried chicken, deviled eggs, and lemonade back into the basket, picked up the blanket, and handed them to his riding sidearm. He then offered his hand to Billie June, his jaw set hard as stone, and stared a message into Daniel's face that could be read by every eye in the crowd.

Billie June, poppy-red to her mouse-brown hair line, ignored the offered hand and marched to the carriage, the door held open by the driver, and once inside yanked the window curtains closed. Still without a word spoken, Sloan and his ranch hand remounted, and the entourage ambled off toward the Triple S, followed by the gazes of a rigid Daniel Lane and the scene's thunderstruck witnesses. All understood that dauntless Billie June had gotten into the carriage, not out of fear of her brother, but for Daniel Lane. She knew her disobedience would result in severe consequences for her lover if she did not. Sloan Singleton had publicly flexed his muscle.

"Obviously, Billie June had been warned about seeing Daniel Lane, and Sloan did what he had to do to get her attention," her mother had argued in favor of Sloan's behavior and of the man she had once dandled on her knee as an infant. "We all know that Billie June can rub raw the horns of a bull moose."

"Not anymore," Mildred had said.

Her father's post office box was crammed full. A postal clerk, sorting mail, helped her to dislodge it. "Glad you stopped by today, Miss Sam," he said. "Nobody's been sent for almost a week, and there wouldn't have been room for more."

"No wonder," Samantha said. "It's hard to spare someone during calving season."

Samantha glanced through the bundle, looking for business envelopes containing invoices that her father would hand to her without opening. One of her responsibilities was to see to the payment of Las Tres Lomas's bills. Most of the collection appeared to be periodicals related to the ranching business, but there were several letters, one from an army buddy who had served with her father in Hood's brigade during the Civil War, and another of heavy cream vellum from a doctor marked "Confidential." *Confidential?* From a doctor? Samantha felt the spike of apprehension her father's wheezing had caused at her birthday dinner, but the imperceptible shake of her mother's head at Samantha's worried look had said there was no cause for concern. Her father was only agitated at the conversation.

The doctor's name was Donald Tolman and the return address listed a post office box in Marietta, Oklahoma Territory. Samantha had never heard either the name or place mentioned. Perhaps the writer, too, was an old army comrade getting in touch, but thirty-five years after the war? And why write and underline "Confidential" in bold black print as if a warning against anyone but the recipient from opening it? Disturbed, Samantha stowed the bundle in her saddlebag and set Pony to a gallop before she could be delayed, now even more eager to get home.

Chapter Twelve

Pony was at the crossroads to the pasturelands of Las Tres Lomas and the Triple S when she heard a fast-approaching horse behind her and the cry, "*Samantha, wait up!*" The voice quickened her heartbeat, but not enough to throw it out of rhythm. It had been trained against racing at the sight of Sloan Singleton some time ago. Samantha reined Pony around to observe her neighbor pounding toward her on his sleek Thoroughbred, halfway wishing she'd pretended not to have heard him. She felt the letter from Dr. Tolman burning a hole in her saddlebag.

As horse and rider drew closer, Samantha wondered if Sloan had been aware of his father's hopes for them. He had never given any sign of it, but he had learned a few tricks of demeanor, had Seth Singleton's son. It was necessary for a boy making his way in the world of tough, sometimes cunning and ruthless men to adopt the artifice of camouflage to conceal his thoughts and feelings. It was true that they no longer saw each other as they once had. The diversions of childhood they'd enjoyed together were relics of the past.

"Yes, Sloan?" Samantha greeted him as he reined up.

It was an unintentionally cool greeting, and Sloan's blue eyes tightened with surprise. If ever there was a man who looked bred straight out of the cow land of his heritage, it was Sloan Singleton. Tall, slim, straight as a Comanche arrow, brown as river rock, hardened by wind and sun, saddle seasoned, he could have passed for none other than what he was—a son of the range.

"That had a little ice in it," he said.

"Did it? I'm sorry. I'm in a hurry, and I've got a lot on my mind."

Sloan shifted in his saddle. "Like what?"

It was a question Samantha once would have answered without a second's thought. They used to tell each other everything. She gave him a tepid smile. "No time to tell." He was dressed in a business suit, and Samantha remembered that this morning had been the monthly board meeting of the bank of which Sloan was chairman. The bank was owned by Noble Rutherford, Anne's father. Samantha unbent a little. "You must be coming from your board meeting," she said. "You didn't stay for your usual luncheon with Anne?"

"Wasn't in the mood for it today. As a matter of fact, I went by your mother's town house to see if I could take you to the Worth for a bite, but Estelle said you'd already left."

Samantha doused a flicker of joy before it lit her face. Sloan had preferred *her* company to Anne's for luncheon? Her mother would be dancing a jig in the foyer. "Well, then, I'm sorry I missed you, but Mother must have told you I need to get back to the ranch. Daddy is expecting me."

"Can you spare a few minutes for me to apologize for Anne's unfortunate topic of conversation at your birthday party?"

"No need for that, Sloan. Really."

"Yes, there is. I think she did it to impress without once thinking how it might affect you and your parents."

Of course she did, Samantha thought, but a man in love would not see that. "Think no more about it. The subject was informative. Well, if there's nothing else..."

"There is," Sloan said, moving his horse a trifle into her path. "It's about Billie June. She's still…well, she's still mad at me."

"After almost a year? I'm sorry to hear it."

"I can't get her to understand that I had to do what I had to do. It was the only way I could get her to stop seeing Daniel Lane."

He wanted to talk as they had in the old days when no trouble went unshared between them. Samantha could see he was deeply bothered by the rift between him and Billie June. Sloan adored his sisters. Five and seven years older, Billie June and Millie May had been maternal substitutes after the death of his mother when Sloan was four, but the girls, especially Billie June, had given Seth Singleton fits. His daughters were for nearly everything their father had been against: Prohibition, women's suffrage, the Society for the Prevention of Cruelty to Animals. Their list of rebellious acts to support their causes had become the stuff of Fort Worth family legend. Among them was the girls' emptying of Seth's bottles of prized bourbon into the Trinity. Another time, they arranged the escape of two suffragettes arrested for disturbing the peace, and on another occasion, they marched onstage to break up a performance by Wild Bill Hickok to protest the mistreatment of his horses in his Wild West Show. They set animals dangerous to livestock free from their traps, released quarry captured for the hounds to tear apart in the Triple S's famous hunt breakfasts, embarrassed their father at dinner parties by espousing beliefs contrary to the guests, and could be relied on to take the side of every controversial figure in society.

While his father had been alive, Sloan had thrown his support to neither faction. Once head of the household, he had continued to assume a live-and-let-live policy, until Billie June's affair with Daniel Lane.

Sloan had no one to talk to about personal matters such as how to get out of this pickle with the remaining members of his family. Neal Gordon would unequivocally agree with his protégé's quashing the only possibility for marriage Billie June might ever have, and no confidants like Grizzly and Wayne Harris were on the Triple S payroll. Anne Rutherford worshipped him like a king, and since kings did not confide in subjects, Sloan Singleton stood virtually alone with no one in his life to lend an objective ear and offer an unbiased opinion.

Unless it was Samantha.

"Do you think I'm a bastard for what I did?"

Pony nibbled at his bit. He wanted to go home. "Are you looking for affirmation or denial?" Samantha said.

"You know better than to ask. The truth will do. I can always get it from you, painful as it is sometimes."

"Was there not some other, less public way to express your disapproval of your sister's friend?" Samantha asked. "It was awfully brave of Billie June to appear at the picnic with Daniel Lane, and she did it to show her love for him."

"She did it to defy me."

"I doubt she was thinking of you at all."

"Daddammit, Sam—" Sloan pushed back his Stetson, and a shock of sun-bleached hair sprang forward. "Billie June knows damn well Dad would never have allowed her to see a man like him. He's not worthy of her."

"How do you know?"

"Oh, come on, Sam! What would a man like Daniel Lane see in my sister other than her trust fund? Lane's a good-looking guy, years younger than Billie June, not a nickel to his name while Billie June is…well, not to be unkind, but plain as a tin plate."

"Your sister is smart, funny, and interesting, Sloan. Perhaps Mr. Lane has the intelligence to see beyond the plainness of the plate to its worth." Unlike you, who can't see beyond Anne Rutherford's décolletage to her little black heart, she thought.

Sloan looked aghast at her. "You're as blind as Billie June if you believe that of him."

Samantha patted Pony's neck to quiet him. "You may be the blind one, Sloan."

Sloan remained silent for a moment, his eyes thoughtful upon her. "I'd hoped you'd agree with me and talk some sense into her."

"I can't speak against a man I do not know. If I were to talk sense into anybody, it would be you. You're lucky to have siblings, Sloan. I wish I did."

"You're telling me to make my peace with Billie June, is that it?" Sloan said, disappointment souring his voice. He reset his hat firmly. "Well, I can't if it means giving her my approval to continue seeing Daniel Lane. I'm doing what my father would have done. I'm protecting her from hurt." He nudged his horse closer, the brim of his hat shadowing his eyes. "And what is this...wistfulness I heard in your tone just now? You have a sibling, Sam. You've got me. I've always been a brother to you and will continue to be. These last years...if I haven't been around as much, it's because I've been so occupied just keeping my head above water. The Triple S takes so much of my time—"

"And of course, Anne," Samantha said, too quickly.

"She's been taking a part of it, yes." Sloan gave her a searching look, and Samantha bent down to pat Pony's neck to disengage from it. Sloan had an uncanny way of reading her thoughts. He could detect trouble in her as clearly as he could spot a fish in clear water.

"No need to explain," she said. "Sometimes Las Tres Lomas is more than Daddy and I can handle together." She straightened and turned Pony's head toward his home. "I've got to get on, but keep in mind my comment, Sloan. Billie June misses her brother, too."

She was about to dig her heels into Pony when Sloan called softly, "Sam…"

"Yes, Sloan?"

"I meant what I said—about being your brother. You do believe that, right?"

"I believe that, Sloan. Trust me, I do."

Chapter Thirteen

It was the moment she relished the most when returning home, the instant Pony crested the small rise that gave a far-reaching view of the grazing acres and ranch compound of Las Tres Lomas de la Trinidad. A thrill of pride nearly always raced through her at first sight of the sweeping, cattle-studded pastures, corrals, and paddocks, the sprawling ranch house and outbuildings and threads of the Trinity River that wound through the valleys of the three small hills that had given the ranch its name. Nearly always, because there had been seasons when the view from the rise had been more heartbreaking than breathtaking, years of "brown springs" when not a drop of water had fallen and the tributaries had dried up. Samantha wished she could pause to take in and savor the spring lushness of her father's empire on this bright, rain-washed morning when the green of the fields and the russet hides of the fat, grazing Herefords were almost blinding.

But she could not tarry. Samantha had learned that truth, good or bad, was the best counter to worry. Most worries were based on uncertainty, and she could handle anything as long as she knew the truth. It might take a little working it out of her father, but eventually Samantha would get him to reveal the content of Dr. Tolman's letter, for better or worse. He could not keep anything from his daughter, but from his wife, yes. *Tell Estelle anything, and she mounts her horse and rides off in all directions*, he was wont to say, *but not you, Sammy girl. Thank God for your cool head and bridled tongue.* Samantha could be worrying for nothing—*pole-vaulting over mouse turds*, as her father would say—and the letter could certainly be from an old army comrade. But then, why would the author write "Confidential" across the envelope and underline it in a strong, dark hand?

Samantha heard the one o'clock bell summoning the ranch hands to the Trail Head, Las Tres Lomas's dining hall, when Samantha turned Pony under the crossbars of the ranch and tethered him in front of the main house. The quarter horse was fractious, nibbling at his bit, snorting. The raucous sounds of men and horses and bawling cattle in the birthing pens came from half a mile away, and Pony was demanding in horse language why he wasn't a part of the activity. "Soon, Pony, I promise," Samantha said, scratching the area between his ears while she withdrew the mail from her saddlebag. The poll was the only part of his face the horse allowed to be stroked.

She found her father in the ranch library at the far side of the great room, the main living area of the house. At its dining end, the table had been laid with plates and cutlery for two. They would be having their noon meal alone together in the main house, then, rather than in the Trail Head with the work crew. Samantha was relieved. Because calving mothers required someone be with them constantly, the men would come in shifts smelling of blood and placenta to sit down at their meals. Samantha could abide the birthing odors in the barns and corrals, but not at the dining table.

"*Samantha!*" Neal Gordon's greeting boomed from a barrel chest beginning to slope toward the onset of a thickening waist, but there was still a strong suggestion of the raw physical power

that had made him a legendary figure among men who worked
with cattle and horses and ropes and guns. He came from around
his desk with arms outstretched to pull her into a hearty embrace.
"I cleaned myself up just for you, so give your old man a big hug.
I was expecting you earlier."

He smelled of Ivory soap and freshly ironed cotton. He had
changed out of his range wear into creased woolen trousers and a
white shirt fastened at the collar with a string tie and silver clasp
fashioned in the brand of Las Tres Lomas de la Trinidad.

"I ran into Sloan at the crossroads and stopped to chat for a
while. He was going home after his board meeting at the bank,"
Samantha said.

Interest, and a wisp of hope, sparked in Neal's eyes. "Good!
You two haven't had a chance to visit for a while. That Ruther-
ford gal had him tied up like a roped calf at your birthday party.
What did he have to say?"

"Just the usual." Samantha handed him the mail, studying his
leathery face for signs of illness. She saw none.

"You should have invited him here for Grizzly's fried steak. It
would have been great to see him."

"It didn't occur to me," Samantha said. "Did you have to pull
many?"

His chagrined expression said, *Well, it should have*, before he
answered. She was referring to the risky procedure of extracting
a calf from the birth canal of its struggling mother, another life-
threatening problem that Samantha's small hands had often corrected. "Only a few, thank goodness, since you weren't here,"
Neal said. "We've had a strong, healthy crop so far. How's your
mother?" He placed the stack of correspondence on his desk
while he put on his reading glasses. Samantha had arranged it so
that Dr. Tolman's letter was the last in the group. His reaction to
the sender would tell her if there was anything to worry about.

She would not get a straight answer if she asked him how he was feeling. *Fine*, he would say even if he was dying.

"Probably lonely by now, I expect," she said. "She'd gotten used to having me around."

Neal sniffed. "She doesn't have to be lonely, you know. Her choice. Mind goosing up the fire a bit while I look through these? There's still a chill in the air."

Samantha took the stoker to the logs while watching her father stack the newspapers and periodicals in one pile and set the bills in another for her attention. He let out a grunt of surprise when he came to the letter from his Civil War comrade and said, "Well, what do you know? Here's one from my old buddy from the First Texas Infantry Regiment. I hope he's not writing to tell me he's dying. Oh, and what is this…?"

Neal adjusted his spectacles and brought the letter closer to his eyes. It could have been her imagination, but Samantha thought he paled slightly beneath the deep, burned color of his skin.

"I see you have a letter there from a doctor marked 'Confidential.' Is there something you're not telling me, Daddy?"

He glanced at her, startled. "Like what?"

"That you're sick."

"Oh, good God, no!" Neal's guffaw made light of her concern. "If I were sick, I'd go to our old Doc Madigan in town. Nothing's wrong with me. Never felt better. No, the letter is from a…a veterinarian. They're called Doctor now, you know. He must be writing in reply to a letter I wrote him some time ago about his article on cattle ticks. He's developed a compound that wards off the buggers. I'm surprised he answered."

"I don't recall the article."

"That's because you probably didn't read it."

His terse tone told Samantha that Neal Gordon had said the last on the matter of the letter. She was not to push further, a rare stance for him to take with her. Now she *was* worried. She reviewed every article pertaining to the cattle business that he read and then they discussed it. In none of their periodicals had she read of a compound for treating cattle ticks developed by Dr. Donald Tolman. Further, if the contents of the doctor's letter were as her father claimed, why did he not read it at once and share its information with her? But if he had written away for information about a health issue, why to a doctor in a small river town in the Oklahoma Territory? Marietta was located a few miles inland from the Red River, not exactly the likely home of a physician her father would consult for medical counsel.

"You'll probably want to have a wash before we eat, so why don't you run up, and I'll have a couple of drinks poured when you get back," Neal said. "We'll have time for a snort before we eat. There's something I want to discuss with you."

He was getting rid of her so that he could read the letter in private, Samantha thought. No matter. Should he not show it to her, she knew where her father kept his private papers and the location of the key if it should be locked. She *must* find out what was in that confidential letter and why he was so secretive about it.

Washing her hands and face in the bathroom, Samantha studied her facial features in the mirror above the basin. Did Sloan Singleton find her the least bit attractive? She could not recall one compliment he'd ever paid her appearance. She would have remembered. Her hair was her best feature, of course, but her gray eyes were clear and well shaped, her nose small and pert, and the rest of her features suitable to her face. She had good skin and a pleasing figure, all pretty enough, but sparrow plain compared to Anne's peacock beauty.

The trace of depression that had hung over her ever since awakening from that dream this morning had now formed into a full overhead cloud. *Never be afraid of your thoughts and feelings, no matter how scary*, her father had instructed her. *Face the buggers like you would any other threat to your person. Examine 'em. Question 'em. Find out where the hell they came from, what they're doing in your head and heart. Sooner or later, understanding will come.*

Understanding had come. Life expectancy for a woman in 1900 was forty-eight, and she was almost halfway through her allotment of years upon the earth. Her ship was firmly underway on an unalterable course, and there was no setting it in another direction. Inevitabilities loomed in the future. The correspondence from Dr. Tolman had sparked a fear she'd not allowed herself to dwell on. Her parents would get older and one day die, and she would be left to run and preserve one of the biggest ranches in Central Texas, not her first choice of a life pursuit. The man she loved would marry someone else, and she had little hope for another to come along who would win her heart.

Well, so be it, Samantha thought, drying her hands. She would take life as it came and make the best of it. There could still be surprises. No sea stayed unchanging.

Neal handed her a glass of sherry when she returned to the library and settled down with his bourbon in his "papa bear" chair, as Estelle called it, while Samantha took her usual seat on one end of a deep leather couch. She glanced at the desk. Neither letter was visible. She would wait until he brought up the subject of their contents in his own good time.

"What did you want to talk to me about?" she asked.

"At our poker game Monday night, Buckley Paddock told me about a wheat farm going up for sale in Cooke County—140 acres. Buckley says that the owner's ad will appear in the classified section of the *Gazette* starting this Monday, and from the description, the place appears to be within proximity to La Paloma." Buckley Paddock was the publisher of the *Fort Worth Gazette*; La

Paloma was the name of a cow camp, home to a portion of Las Tres Lomas's herd.

"In what direction and how much?" Samantha asked.

"North," Neal said, "and the ad doesn't say."

Samantha understood the meaning of the twinkle in his eyes. Las Tres Lomas ran five thousand head of cattle on ten thousand acres in Cooke County. It was a large operation overseen by another foreman who had been on the Gordon payroll half his lifetime. The camp was situated seven miles from the Red River, an ideal location from which to move the herd at market time across the river to the Missouri-Kansas-Texas Railroad's loading ramps in Marietta for transport to the Kansas stockyards. The only hitch was the intervening wheat farm that cut off direct access to the river, requiring that the herd be driven around the farm ten miles out of the way to reach the ford crossing. Samantha had never been to La Paloma. The camp lacked amenities suitable for a lady.

"It could be the farm that smacks right up next to our holding," Neal said. "Years ago when I bought La Paloma, I approached the owner about buying his place, an irascible old goat named"—he thought a moment—"Barrows. Liam Barrows, but he informed me that farm had been in his family since before statehood, and that his two boys would make sure it stayed. He didn't care if I had to drive the herd to hell and back to get across the river."

"Sounds like a nice neighbor," Samantha commented. "So what are you proposing?"

"That we—you—check out the place. What harm can it do? Buckley says it won't stay on the market long. We'll get all the details in Monday's paper, and I propose that we immediately contact the owner by telegram and set up an appointment to look over the place. You can take the train to Gainesville."

Samantha did not ask why she should be the one dispatched. Why not her father to look over the place? His answer would have embarrassed him. Neal Gordon was ashamed of the phobia that made it impossible for him to endure the close quarters of a train compartment. To go by horse would take the better part of three days and risk the chance the farm could be sold by the time he arrived.

Samantha thought the idea worth considering. In regard to acquiring land, her father had sometimes failed to show good judgment, but in 1890 he had wisely purchased 160 sections to add to the 166,400 acres of grazing land of La Paloma where he could permanently establish a part of his herd. Before the purchase, when the summer heat of Central Texas dried up grassland, Las Tres Lomas had enjoyed open access to drive three thousand head of cattle north to Cooke County to relieve the number of bovine mouths to feed at the home ranch.

If we don't make a move now, Estelle, Samantha remembered her father saying in a family discussion, *it may be too late in a few years. Prices will rise, and fences between here and our summer range are going up faster than a maple sheds its leaves in fall. It won't be long before passageway to drive our cattle up to La Paloma will be blocked, and then what will we do? You know that in summer, the whole herd can't be sustained on the grass we have here, and there's no land contiguous to ours going on the block anytime soon to fix the problem.*

Neal was warden of the ranch's purse, but Samantha was keeper of the books, and it was her job to play devil's advocate when it came to spending proposals. Her father, bent on becoming a titan in the cattle industry and making Las Tres Lomas de la Trinidad one of the biggest ranches in Texas, sometimes had to be reined in, especially if there was a bulging surplus in the bank—the Cattleman's Bank, rather than the Rutherford City Bank.

"I suppose it will all depend on the price the place is going for and if the owner is not opposed to the family farm being converted to a ranch-to-market road," she said. "I wouldn't want Las Tres Lomas changed in character."

Silbia, the Mexican housekeeper who saw after the domestic management of the main house, came in to announce that *la cena*—dinner—was on the table. She prepared breakfast and supper for *el patrón* and his *hija*—daughter—but the noon meal was carted to the main house from Grizzly's kitchen unless her boss and his daughter ate with the ranch hands.

"Ah, Grizzly's fried steak," Neal said, rising. "I hope he sent over plenty of gravy."

A look at her father betrayed no sign of illness, just bright anticipation of enjoying a good meal, but as Samantha rose, she glanced toward the fireplace, and her heart caught. Fallen from the softly glowing embers into the grate was the burned corner of a cream-colored letter.

Nathan

Chapter Fourteen

Five days after his twentieth birthday, on the tail end of a bright, crisp Wednesday, Nathan rang the doorbell of his father's town house, which was situated in an elite enclave of other distinctive homes nestled on a tributary of the Trinity River in Dallas, Texas. The cabbie who had picked him up at the train station immediately recognized the address Trevor had written on the back of the business card that Nathan showed him. "Oh, yes, that's in Turtle Creek," he said, giving Nathan's barn jacket and faded jeans a skeptical look. "You goin' to do some work on the place?"

"My father lives there," Nathan said.

A black maid wearing a frilly white cap and lace-fringed apron over a dark dress opened the door. It was made of ebony, lacquered to a glossy finish, and bore a shiny brass knocker. "Deliveries go to the rear door," she said, frowning down at Nathan's knapsack at his feet.

Nathan removed his cloth cap. "I'm not a delivery boy. My name is Nathan Holloway, and I'm Mr. Waverling's son. He asked me to call on him."

The maid's mouth opened like a gawping fish. Nathan heard the toot of several horns from the street before she spoke. "Well, I never in all my life expected to hear such a thing. Get out of here before I call the police."

"You do that, and you'll hear from Mr. Waverling. I'll wait here until you telephone him at his office to inform him I've accepted his invitation. I imagine an establishment like this has one of those inventions."

The maid backed away, eyes bulging, and closed the door. Nathan could hear the hard click of the lock. He put his cap back on and sat down on the front step of the round brick stoop to await the result of the maid's threat or the call to Trevor Waverling's office. Leon had advised that he write to his father to warn him of the date and time and place of his appearance.

Show up at his office, not at his home address, Leon had said. *I didn't hear that option extended, and when you introduce yourself, say simply that you're Nathan Holloway from Gainesville, Texas, and you have an appointment with Mr. Waverling. Don't mention anything about bein' his son. That way things'll get off on the right foot with no embarrassment for anybody, 'specially for you if there should be…well, some awkwardness.* He also advised Nathan to dress in his best and only suit. *Shows respect*, he'd said.

Nathan had listened and disregarded. He was Trevor Waverling's son. If the man was ashamed of that fact or preferred to ignore it, Nathan figured that by declaring who he was up front to any who asked, he would know soon enough if Trevor Waverling was sincere in his wish to claim his son. Back entrances were not for Nathan. If his father thought him good enough to visit him at his office, he was good enough to meet him at his home before his front door dressed as he was every day with the exception of his cap.

Nathan pulled a copy of Jack London's *Son of the Wolf* out of his jacket pocket. Though rare, his idle moments were spent reading, and his spare money went for books he bought in a general store in Gainesville. He couldn't abide sitting doing nothing, like Lily could. He didn't have enough to think or dream about to fill his mind as his sister did, so he let in worlds and people and events through used copies of the classics and dime novels of detective stories and frontier tales and medieval romances he could think about during his long, solitary chores.

"Hello."

Nathan turned his head toward the sound of the childish voice. He'd been so engrossed in the tales of the unforgiving Alaskan wilderness and the Klondike gold rush that he had not heard the approach of footsteps. At first he thought his mind was playing eerie tricks on him. A little girl's head had bloomed among the masses of blue hydrangeas in one of a pair of hedges that flanked the flight of steps, her hair ribbon the same color as the tightly compacted florets. She blinked at him, her long lashes like crescents of feathers above shy, deep brown eyes.

Nathan laid down his book, spread open to the pages he was reading. "Hello," he said, his greeting softened with a smile. "Who are you?"

"I'm nobody. Who are you? Are you nobody, too? Then there's a pair of us—don't tell! They'd banish us, you know."

Nathan slowly rose from the step. Her singsong words sounded familiar. He was sure he'd heard them before, and then he remembered. They were a verse from one of his sister's poetry books she'd read aloud to the family one evening. "I suppose you'd call me a nobody," he said, addressing her across the hedge.

"How dreary to be somebody!" she quoted. "How public, like a frog, to tell your name the livelong day to an admiring bog!"

She was not quite right in the head, Nathan perceived immediately. Leon had mentioned that Trevor Waverling had a retarded daughter. There was something otherworldly about her gaze. She was staring straight at him but without really seeing him, and her lip twitched involuntarily as if pulled by an invisible puppet's string. He had come expecting to meet her and his grandmother, too.

"What is your name?" he asked.

The question puzzled her. "Rebecca!" she sang after a moment's struggle to remember.

He thrust his hand across the hedge. "I'm Nathan."

Slowly, she reached across the blue haze and shook it. "Nathan...Are you nobody, too?"

"I reckon I am to those folks who think they matter," he said.

Nathan heard an approaching *tat-tat-tat* that sounded like the strike of steel against the flagstone path that ran alongside the house, and within a few seconds out from the trellised entrance stepped an elderly woman wielding a cane. The expensive scent of a floral fragrance reached him before she spoke.

"Well, for heaven's sakes," she said. "You did come."

Nathan yanked off his cap. "Ma'am?"

"I'm your grandmother, Mavis Waverling," the woman said. "There's no denying it. You've got my eyes." She peered at him as she drew closer. "Your father's, too, of course, but there's something in yours missing in his. I see you've met Rebecca." She placed her arm around her granddaughter's shoulders. "Rebecca, dearest, this is your...brother." She glanced at Nathan. "Do you mind if we dispense with the half part of it?"

"Not at all," Nathan said.

Rebecca's eyes grew round. "My...brother?"

"Yes," Nathan said. "You're my sister."

Rebecca turned to her grandmother. "He's nobody, too," she said proudly. "There's a pair of us—don't tell!"

"I won't," Mavis Waverling whispered conspiratorially into her ear.

Nathan was afraid he gawked. So this was his grandmother. She looked wafted from a flower box, perhaps one stored away in an attic yellowing and growing brittle with age but exquisite just the same. Nathan thought she must have been extremely pretty at one time. He had wondered about her, what she would look and be like, if they possessed anything in common. She was the main reason he had come. Indeed, they must be related, for they shared the same color and shape of eyes, the flesh around hers finely webbed. Beyond those features he could claim no identity to her fine bone structure and head of diaphanous white hair and a stature hardly as tall as the border of hydrangeas she stood behind. An odd sensation filled him as he realized he carried her blood. "You're...my grandmother?" he said.

"I am. We have a lot of time to make up for, don't we? Let's go inside. Your father's on the way, but we'll have a little time to get acquainted before he butts in. Come, Rebecca, darling."

They came from around the hedge, the girl so spindly and the woman so fragile a puff of his breath could have blown them away. Yet the little girl skipped with the bounce of youth and her grandmother stepped with a will of such strength that Nathan thought he might cause offense if he offered his arm. "Is that your only luggage?" Mavis asked, poking Nathan's knapsack with her cane.

"Yes, ma'am," he said.

"There doesn't look enough in it for a change of clothes."

"I don't plan to stay long."

"Really? Well, we'll see about that. You'll lodge with us, of course."

"Oh, no, I couldn't do that, ma'am. I saw a boardinghouse on my way here."

"Nonsense. I'll have a guest room made up for you. No grandson of mine is staying in a bedbug-infested boardinghouse. Rebecca, why don't you run and tell Lenora to report to me in the parlor and to bring us tea with plenty of sandwiches. Your brother looks hungry. Don't forget your book, Nathan."

Deeming it pointless to argue, Nathan picked up the book and his knapsack and followed the two slight figures in their pretty pastel dresses into the house. They had made his acquaintance outside in case he proved to be too unsuitable to be invited in, he realized. He must have passed muster, but closing the ebony door behind him, he wondered what he was entering into and if it was a place from which he could easily make his escape.

Chapter Fifteen

It was the grandest house Nathan had ever seen or hoped to see, not counting the fancy residence Lily hoped to inhabit someday as the wife of a rich man. "Sit over here next to me so you'll be close to the tea trolley, Nathan, and don't be afraid to sit on the damask. Your pants are clean enough," Mavis said, taking what appeared to be her usual spot before a softly glowing fire. "Besides, it's nice to have another male Waverling in my parlor in clothes that look to have done a day's work. Your uncle, my other son, was just such a fellow. I wish you could have known him, too. That's his picture there." She gestured toward the mantel where a portrait of a man who looked nothing like his urbane brother was positioned facing his mother's chair. There was a handsomely framed photograph of Trevor on the other end of its marble length as well, but the one of his brother reigned over the room.

"He's…deceased?" Nathan wondered if there was a picture of her husband anywhere around—his grandfather.

"Three years ago," Mavis said. "Mystery surrounds his death to this very day, but that's a story for another private moment." A large tabby jumped down from an embroidered seat on another chair and went immediately to hop onto Nathan's lap. "Well, well," Mavis said. "First Rebecca, now Scat seems to have taken to you, and they're not bad judges of character, either. Get down, Scat, before I take my cane to you."

The cat looked at her, yawned, and curled up in the nest of Nathan's cap before he could put it in his pocket. Nathan chuckled. "I don't mind. He's nice and warm. I'm sorry about your son. Were he and...my father your only ones?"

"My only ones. No daughters. Believe me, I am sorry my boy's gone, too. Jordan, his name was. Rebecca worshipped him. Jordan introduced her to poetry. It was a great love of his, and the reason Rebecca parrots it so. He read to her every night from his books of poems. Ah, here's Lenora with the tea tray. Lenora, this is my grandson, Nathan. He'll be staying with us awhile. Will you make up the blue room for him, please?"

"How'd do," Lenora said, her little curtsy accompanied by a sharp look of doubt that Nathan was who he claimed to be and a warning that he better watch himself. He acknowledged her meaning with a nod and small lift of his shoulders to convey that the invitation was not his idea.

"I'll try to be no trouble," he said.

"Be all the trouble you like," Mavis said. "You can tell a lot about a person by the trouble he causes. Lenora, take Scat to the kitchen so the boy can eat his sandwiches in peace, and keep Rebecca with you for a while so Nathan and I can talk. Nathan, heap your plate. I'll pour the tea. How do you like it?"

"Just plain will do, thank you," Nathan said, for politeness' sake, taking only two of the miniature-sized sandwiches. He was wolfishly hungry. His last meal had been supper yesterday. He'd not taken time for breakfast after he milked Daisy in order to catch the 7:30 train to Dallas. Leon had seen him off at the station and slipped him a dollar.

For breakfast, he'd said. *Get yourself some eggs and bacon at a stop along the way. It'll be a long, hungry ride to Dallas.* But, not knowing what he'd run into in the city, Nathan had saved the money to add to his meager store of cash, safely tucked into the tops of his socks.

Mavis handed Nathan his tea while adding more sandwiches to his plate. He sensed she could read and understand boys. He figured she was a good mother to her sons, though she didn't seem to like her surviving one very much.

"Let me tell you a little something about Rebecca," Mavis said. "Did Trevor mention his daughter to you?"

"Briefly to my stepfather," Nathan said.

"That figures. She's his daughter by his first wife. Because of Rebecca, the second one was afraid to bear him any more children. I took my granddaughter into my home to raise after Trevor's first divorce. Trevor lives here, too, but it's my house, like everything else, but I sidetrack." Mavis flicked away the digression with her pale, thin fingers. "The child is keenly intelligent, but her mind is manacled by some kind of nerve disorder. Doctors tell us her mental development will probably never mature beyond the age of eight or nine and she'll always be a little girl. As you noticed, her verbal skills are severely limited, but she can parrot anything she hears or reads back to you, and she can comprehend and write reasonably well for someone of her arrested mental growth."

"I would think it would take a good mind to fit the lines of a poem to a situation," Nathan said.

"One would think."

There was the sound of the front door opening and closing quickly, strong, rapid footsteps in the foyer, and the bustle of Lenora hurrying to intercept the caller. "Oh, Mr. Waverling, I was expecting Benjy to bring you to the back!" the maid cried, her frantic greeting pierced by a squeal of "*Daddeee!*" and the rush of small feet down the hall.

"Not now, Rebecca!" came the sharp rebuke. "Take her back to where she was, Lenora. I'll speak to her later."

"Yes, Mr. Waverling."

"Behold the arrival of my second son and father emeritus," Mavis said, her voice dry as a dead twig.

The double doors to the parlor flew open. "Nathan! What a surprise!" Trevor Waverling cried, striding forth to offer his hand. Nathan rose to take it, perceiving in his father's hale and hearty manner a clear attempt to hide his irritation at finding his son in his parlor. Where was the paternal enthusiasm he'd displayed at the farm? "I thought you understood you were to come to my office if you decided to accept my invitation."

"I decided to come here," Nathan said.

"And thank his good sense that he did," Mavis said. "We've been getting acquainted, a pleasure I may have been denied if he'd gone to your office, Trevor."

"Oh, well, I…yes…I see you've met your grandmother and…Rebecca?"

"He's met your daughter, Trevor," Mavis said.

"Then you see that we have an…interesting household. Where are you staying?"

"Here," said Mavis emphatically. "Your son is staying here in the blue room, until Nathan decides he can't abide us."

Trevor looked at his mother blankly. "Here?"

Nathan put up his hands. "Look," he said, embarrassed. He could feel his face turning red. "I came only for the day, actually, with no intention of staying. I planned to take the train back tonight after I visited your place of business and met my…grandmother and sister, so please don't go to the bother of putting me up."

"To look us over, in other words," Mavis said. "Very smart, but you can't do all that in one day, Nathan, and it's no bother to put you up."

"I agree to both," Trevor said, his composure restored. "Tomorrow morning is early enough for you to leave us if you feel you must get back. I've come to take you to the plant, and we'll lunch downtown, so don't expect us, Mother," he said, his tone rejecting any notion Mavis might have to the contrary.

"But I will expect you for supper, Trevor," Mavis said, her look forbidding any idea he might have otherwise.

"Come, Nathan," Trevor said. "Let your father show you the family business with the hope you'll see you didn't make the trip for nothing."

Nathan turned to his grandmother to thank her for her hospitality, his eye falling uncertainly upon his knapsack. "Leave it, Nathan," Mavis said. "It will be in your room waiting for you when you return."

Nathan drew on his cap. "Until then," he said, giving her a smile. "I really enjoyed the tea. The sandwiches hit the spot."

"If nothing else, the food is good here," Mavis said.

"Oh, Mother…" Trevor sighed resignedly. "Come on, Nathan."

Nathan followed the broad-shouldered figure of his father in his perfectly fitting suit out of the room. Glancing back at Mavis, he saw a look of yearning upon her porcelain fine face, but for who—for what? A pang of sympathy for her made him reluctant to leave. There was deep animosity in this house, he thought, but love, too—like two tigers circling in a cage. Which one would eat the other? Which one would win out? And why did he suddenly care?

Chapter Sixteen

Waiting in the circular courtyard before the town house were the same coach and pair of Thoroughbreds that had called upon the Holloways at their farm. At the reins was the circus clown. The Irishman hopped nimbly down and opened the coach door, his expression enlarging with recognition at Nathan's appearance.

"Benjy, this is Nathan," Trevor introduced him. "You didn't formally meet last time."

Benjy bobbed his head. "How do ye do? And the last name, sir?"

Trevor hesitated, and Nathan answered, "Holloway."

"Pleased to make your acquaintance, I'm sure," Benjy said, lifting his stovepipe hat.

An awkward silence settled in the coach to the sumptuous squeak of leather as Trevor and Nathan took their seats facing each other. Nathan had never been in such a conveyance but would not give his father the satisfaction of noting the fact by even a glance to admire the fine woodwork and velvet trappings. As they pulled away, Trevor said, "I gather you prefer to go by Holloway for now."

"I gather you prefer it," Nathan said.

"For your sake, I believe we should take things slowly. I don't want to push you into a family, business, or social situation you do not wish to be a part of."

"Or think I'm suited for," Nathan said.

"I'm merely remembering our conversation when we first met, Nathan, in which you made it clear that you were happy where you were and had no wish to enlarge your estate in life or assume an acquaintance with me."

Nathan nodded. "True enough," he said, feeling a little abashed.

"You've given me every reason to believe you're as reluctant to tell the world I'm your father as you believe I am to inform it you're my son, so do not attribute my consideration for your feelings to snobbery," Trevor said.

Nathan was tempted to apologize but personal judgment told him snobbery was exactly the reason Trevor Waverling was of yet no mind to make their family relationship known. All the luck to him keeping their connection under his hat, he thought. Other similarities aside, a stranger had only to look at their eyes to know they were related. Nathan allowed the reproach to go unchallenged and said, "So for the time being, I'm merely Nathan and you're...Mr. Waverling?"

"That will do," Trevor said. "We can spring the surprise later if all goes well, and you're amenable to becoming a part of the family and Waverling Tools." Trevor fixed him with an earnest stare. "I hope you will be, Nathan. I mean that."

"I haven't heard my grandfather mentioned. Is he dead?"

"He died five years ago, leaving my late brother, Jordan, in charge of Waverling Tools. Jordan drowned a couple of years later, and the business was left in my hands to run."

"But not to own, is that right?"

Trevor went still, and in the few seconds of his motionless silence, Nathan suddenly understood his need of an heir. His father had no children other than him and Rebecca, and Nathan assumed his brother, Jordan, had died childless. But why now and why him? "Who told you that?" Trevor asked.

"Your mother. She said everything belongs to her. I *gather* that means the business, too, huh?" Nathan leaned forward, vaguely aware of the fine brick streets over which the coach rumbled, the impressive buildings they passed, the congestion of vehicles, among them the phenomenon of several gleaming horseless carriages, the all-around commercial energy of this bustling city of Dallas. "Don't you think you ought to put your cards on the table and tell me why I'm here, Mr. Waverling? I'd just as soon believe you can get milk from a rock as think it's from a desire to unite with your son."

A tinge of color appeared above the wolfish hollows of Trevor's cheeks, then just as suddenly he laughed. "By God, Nathan, you're quite a boy. Little seems to get by you."

"I'd like you to spread your cards, Mr. Waverling," Nathan said, unamused. "Otherwise, I'm getting out of this carriage right now, walking back to your house, picking up my knapsack, and getting on my way."

"I so hope it will not come to that," Trevor said. "Your grandmother has taken a liking to your knapsack." A leap of respect shone in his sea-green eyes. "All right, Nathan, but not here. Let's get to the office where we can talk comfortably, and then you can decide whether to stay or go. Deal?"

"Deal," Nathan said.

Waverling Tools was located in a manufacturing district with direct access to the Southern Pacific Railroad. The belch of smokestacks and the odiferous smells from livery stables added to the industrial ugliness of loading docks and warehouses, foundries and storage buildings spread out close to the rail lines. That morning, Nathan had read a newspaper article describing

Dallas as becoming an industrialized city, leading the Southwest in the manufacture of tools, building equipment, and machinery. Nathan had wondered to what extent Waverling Tools contributed to the production statistics. A lot, he thought, judging by the impressive two-story building before which the coach-and-pair reined to a stop. The masonry structure had been erected apart from its wood-framed neighbors and stuck out in appearance from the other manufacturing establishments like little Lord Fauntleroy in a band of guttersnipes. Attention to aesthetics had gone into first impressions of Waverling Tools. A tall wrought-iron fence protected a water fountain, a canna-bordered brick walk, and an immaculate patch of green grass from wagon wheels and horses' hooves and the scraps of paper littering the dirt grounds of the other properties around it. Over the handsomely crafted doorway, WAVERLING TOOLS was announced in gold letters against a dark blue background, in contrast to the crude wooden signs nailed to posts or stuck into the ground of its neighbors.

"Is this the plant?" Nathan asked.

"The office," Trevor answered. "The plant is behind it." He pulled at a tulip-shaped instrument attached to a cord and spoke into its mouth. "Benjy, take us round to the back, please."

Nathan tried hard not to look impressed. What an amazing contraption, he thought. The idea of being able to speak to your coachman through a tube without having to leave your seat in the cab. What a world he had entered in Dallas, Texas. Something new, grand, and big on every corner.

He and his father had exchanged little conversation on the ride, but at one point, Nathan asked, "What was my grandfather like? What was his name?"

Trevor seemed pleased that he'd asked. His mouth softened. "My father? His name was Edwin. You remind me of him. I thought so the minute I laid eyes on you. Something about your"—he twirled a hand as if the word he desired could be spun from the air—"quiet but strong demeanor made me think of him. He was hard but fair, not an easy man to know. Most everybody feared him, including his sons, not out of fright but respect. Everything ran deep in him. Hardly anything ever rose to the surface, only the love he had for my mother."

"I'm glad to hear it," Nathan said. "She's a lovely woman. There was no picture of him in her parlor."

"That's because he didn't sit for many. He was not a vain man. The few taken of him are in her bedroom."

Nathan felt a surprising flush of pleasure to learn that the origin of some of his traits came from his paternal grandfather. He, too, was one to keep his feelings to himself, *down deep where the still waters flow*, so Lily called it, and he never sought notice for himself. Nathan would have liked to know if Trevor Waverling had loved his father. That would tell him a lot about the man who sat across from him.

Trevor had volunteered no more about the family, and they had jostled along in silence, broken only when he made some comment about the city or pointed out a landmark or milestone of progress, all offered with pride. "Dallas is the most populous city in Texas," he informed Nathan, "and someday it will be a metropolis to rival the great cities of the East. You mark my words."

They alighted in back of the building. Benjy opened the door, his droll look at Nathan curious, speculative, and Nathan wondered just how long the short-legged Irishman had been in his father's employ, the secrets to which he was privy. Somehow he had the sense the two of them were like pocket to pant, if not out of loyalty to each other, by virtue of the impression that Benjy knew where the bodies were buried.

Chapter Seventeen

Nathan heard the click of a typewriter as they entered the back passageway leading to offices beyond. The coachman was staying with the Concord. "How are you going to explain me?" Nathan asked.

"I'm the boss. I don't have to explain," Trevor said, "but I'll say simply that you're someone I've taken under my wing."

"A country bumpkin like myself? For a city man like yourself, that seems unlikely. For what purpose, will you say?"

"I won't. My people will figure it out soon enough from your looks if you stay. And if you stay, you won't look like a country bumpkin."

"This…job I assume you have in mind for me if I accept it…won't I be a thorn in the side of someone else you were priming for it?"

Trevor stopped and stared at him. "My God, but you're quick. Yes, there are a couple of employees vying for the position I'd like you to take eventually, but here's the difference. They're not blood kin. You are. The one and only who qualifies as an heir and might one day take over the throne after me."

They had arrived at a set of double doors, having passed a small office next to it with SECRETARY printed on the door. It was open, and a young woman glanced up from her work with a flash of surprise at Nathan. Another set of slightly larger offices appeared to be farther up the corridor, leading to a room that looked to be a reception area.

"I get that having no heir may be a problem for your company, but how is it you think I'm the answer to it? You've known of my existence all along. Why now am I all of a sudden in demand as your successor?"

Trevor sighed. "That's what I want to discuss with you. It's the reason I've asked you to come." He pushed open the doors. "Make yourself at home. I'll tell my secretary to bring us some coffee."

He was gone long enough for Nathan to take in the plush environment of his father's workplace. Rich woods, supple leather, thick carpets, velvet draperies, the telephone on his desk spoke of a prominent and prosperous company. Why would Trevor Waverling want to share it with a son he didn't know nor probably care to, a son who came with a BASTARD sign hanging about his neck? There was still time for him to beget and groom a legitimate heir. Nathan was standing at the large window admiring the fine view of the Trinity River framed by weeping willows and shady cypresses when his father walked in.

"I go fishing down there sometimes," Trevor said. "There's a small dock hidden by the trees."

Nathan turned, keeping his face impassive. "Nice place," he said. "Why am I here?"

Trevor gestured toward a chair before his desk and took his seat behind it. "You asked me to spread my cards on the table, Nathan, and I will. I'll hold nothing back."

I'll be the judge of that, Nathan thought. He suspected his father was a good one for holding things back. "I'm all ears," he said.

Trevor tapped a finger to his lips as if trying to decide where to begin. "I suppose I should start at a time when no clouds darkened the horizon of Waverling Tools," he said finally. "My brother and I worked for our father, who had us learn everything from A to Z about the company. Originally, we manufactured digging machinery, farm implements mostly, then we expanded to drilling equipment like cable tool bits and rigs to drill for water and salt. Profits were good. Work was steady, especially after the T&P came to town. The Waverling men were all on deck to move the ship forward into new waters in a city that was leading Texas into the new century. And then my father died unexpectedly. One night at supper he choked on a chicken bone and died before our eyes. There hasn't been a chicken served in the house since."

A knock on the door announced his secretary bringing in a coffee tray. "Put it there, Jeanne," Trevor said. "I'll pour for us."

Nathan caught the surreptitious glance of the young woman before she deposited the tray and left. He had the feeling the yokel Mr. Waverling had invited into his office would be a topic of discussion over the girl's noontime sandwich with her bookkeeper co-worker who occupied the office across the hall. Her door had been open as well. Trevor took the time to pour them each a cup of coffee, and when Nathan shook his head to sugar and cream, he continued.

"My father was one never to leave anything to chance. He was assiduous about dotting every *i*, crossing every *t*. He made sure the firm's contracts were legally flawless and that his business papers were always in perfect order." Trevor paused and a shadow crossed his face. "Except the one document that mattered the most upon his death."

Nathan had just taken a swallow of coffee. He gulped it down in surprise. "Oh, no, don't tell me. His will!"

Trevor nodded, his tight expression suggesting he still found it hard to believe. "His will. He had one, but in it, he left everything to my mother—the house, money, business, everything. It had been drawn up when they were first married before the children came. Edwin Waverling had never gotten around to revising it."

"So your mother controls the purse strings," Nathan said, thinking how similar Trevor Waverling's financial trap was to his stepfather's.

"That's right."

Puzzled, Nathan shook his head. "What does this family tale have to do with me? How does it explain why you asked me to come?"

"I'm getting to that, Nathan. Be patient. You wanted to see all my cards, remember?"

Nathan settled back in his chair with his coffee, and Trevor continued. "My brother and I were disappointed, but nothing particularly changed. Mother put Jordan in control of the company, but he and I had always seen eye to eye on most everything—"

Nathan held up a hand, interrupting him. "Wait a minute! Why? Why did your mother put your brother in charge over you? Why didn't she let you share the reins?"

Trevor contemplated his son over the arrested rim of his coffee cup, well-groomed fingers around the bowl. "I declare, Nathan, but you're a sharp one," he said, setting the cup in its saucer without drinking. "I'm going to have to watch myself around you."

"All I ask is that you tell me the truth," Nathan said. "I've lived with enough lies to last a lifetime."

"Yes, yes, you have," Trevor agreed. "So here's the truth, Nathan. At the time of my father's death, I'd fallen in disfavor with my mother. Jordan had always been her favorite anyway, not that she would have let that get in the way of fair play, but I'd definitely strained her maternal devotion. I'd been through a couple of scandalous divorces from women she didn't approve of from the start, and then there was Rebecca..." Trevor frowned. "I admit I'm not the father she thinks I should be to my daughter..."

Nathan watched him carefully. That last hadn't been easy to admit, and he could see regret in the man's grimace. "And then Jordan and I came to near blows over the direction of the company," Trevor said. "He wanted to stick with drilling water wells and salt mines, and I wanted to drill for oil. I foresaw the company converting its resources to that aim, and he was sorely against it. Said we couldn't afford it, and it was too risky. The horseless carriage would never replace equine power. Mother backed him up. And then he got engaged to a much younger woman, and I could see her popping heirs every nine months, and I would be nudged out of the picture. Mother was set on leaving the company in the hands of an heir who could beget heirs."

"Why couldn't that be you?" Nathan asked.

"Because I was divorced at the time with no intention of marrying again—not anytime soon, anyway. I was forty-three. By the time I deluded myself into thinking there was another woman out there who would win my heart forever—"

"In other words, a woman you could stay faithful to," Nathan said.

"If you prefer to put it that way," Trevor yielded the point wryly. "Anyway, by the time I fathered another child, it would have been too late..."

Trevor's voice faded away. Some of the vitality drained from his eyes. Nathan judged his father had come to a part of the story painful to talk about, but uncomfortable or no, he would hear it. He gave him a push. "So did Jordan marry and his wife pop out heirs?"

"No. He drowned a week before the wedding."

Shocked, Nathan suddenly understood why he'd been asked to

come. "And that left you in charge of Waverling Tools but without an heir," he said.

Trevor met his stare levelly. "And that's where you come in," he said. "My mother discovered the private investigator's report of your existence. At that time she was thoroughly disenchanted with me and was threatening to sell the company. Only my father's affection for me dissuaded her. When she learned she had a grandson, she sent me to find you with the stipulation that if I did not encourage you to come here and give the company and the family a try, I could kiss my position as heir apparent to Waverling Tools good-bye."

He'd asked for the truth straight and gotten it. Nathan was surprised only by the depth of hurt he felt. It settled among the others he'd known recently. "So you *did* know of my existence, and the only reason you showed yourself and asked me to come was to secure your inheritance."

"Not just an inheritance, Nathan, but the *company* my father— your grandfather—built and loved and would twist in his grave if it were ever sold, especially when he would have agreed to the heights I intend to take it. I want you to go with me, Nathan. *He* would want you to go with me. Believe what you like. I wouldn't blame you for despising me, but I honestly didn't think I had the right to claim you when I learned of your birth. Reports indicated you were happy, but then my mother gave me her ultimatum, and I had no choice but to seek you out and declare myself. Whatever you think of me and my motives, you are my son, and someday this place could be yours."

Nathan wanted to tell him he could cook in the stew of his own making, but he thought of the fragile woman and spindly little girl in the house on Turtle Creek and the strange but tender connection he felt to them. His grandmother had seemed genuinely glad he'd come.

"I can't believe your mother would deny you your rightful inheritance and go against what her husband would have wanted for you," Nathan said. "Why would she do that?"

Trevor pushed back from his desk, as if his next confession required space and distance should Nathan decide to lunge at him. He laced his manicured but strong hands together and rested them on his formidable chest. "Because she thinks I'm responsible for her other son's death," he said.

Chapter Eighteen

A swallow of coffee caught in Nathan's throat. "Were you?" he choked.

"Responsible for my brother's death? Absolutely not!" Trevor declared. "Jordan's death was an accident, and I mourn him as profoundly as my mother does. There's hardly an hour of the day I don't miss him. We weren't only brothers, we were best friends, confidants, hunting and fishing buddies."

Grief lanced through Trevor's sea-green glare. It would have been hard not to believe the man's sincerity. "What reason would your mother have to think you're responsible?" Nathan asked.

Trevor pulled back to his desk and picked up his cold coffee cup. "That's not what we're here today to discuss," he said. "I'm innocent, whether she believes it or not."

"*You* may not want to discuss it, but I do," Nathan persisted, refusing to offer mercy. "I'm not working for a man whose mother believes her son killed his brother. Why can't she believe you're innocent?"

"Because of who she thinks I am!" Trevor retorted. "And I'm not about to discuss that today with you except to say I'm to blame for my actions, attitudes, and decisions that would appear to confirm her opinion. But things are not always as they seem, Nathan, not even to a mother. Now if that's not enough for you,

I'll have Benjy drive you to the house to collect your knapsack, then to the station, and you can go back to the farm and that woman whose maternal love for you wouldn't fill a thimble. But you need to know that your grandmother is counting on you. I'm not using that as a stick to get you to stay. I'm telling you the way it is. And because of her, I want you to give it at least a try. Forget about me!"

"And if I come on board, you'll have a better chance of your mother leaving you all of this, is that it?" Nathan swept an arm to include the office complex and buildings beyond.

"She's made it clear that I'm to rescue you, build a father-son relationship, introduce you to the company with hope you'll want to become a part of it. At least, I'm to try, and if I don't succeed…"

"Then you're cooked," Nathan said flatly.

"Unless I can prove to her I didn't kill my brother, but…as you may have noticed, there's not a lot of time left for that."

Nathan set his coffee cup and saucer on the desk. "You're in one doozy of a ditch, aren't you?" he said.

His comment elicited a small smile. "That's another succinct way of putting it. So what's your decision? Benjy and your knapsack, or are you going to stay and let me show you around the place?"

"I need time to think about it."

Trevor got up. "The room is yours. I have to consult with my foreman. I should be gone about a half hour. Will that give you enough time to make your decision?"

"All I need."

When Trevor had left, Nathan refreshed his coffee from the pot and let himself out through an exterior door, cup in hand, to stroll down to the river. He could always think better under an open sky among growing things. A good flowing body of water helped, too. The hour had gone past noon, and the sun was warm through his barn jacket, but the air still held the last breath of a fading winter. He was downwind of the industrial fumes and odors that he'd expect to be pretty stifling during the hot, humid days of summer when the area's factories were going full blast. The smells would be a mark against his staying. He liked country air that a body wasn't afraid to breathe.

There would be plenty of bad air he'd have to inhale if he stayed here, Nathan thought, and he wasn't thinking only of the manufactured kind. He could almost hear Leon spouting his often-repeated philosophy that applied to the situation he was in now: *It's important for a fella to look at every knot and wormhole in a load of timber before buyin', or some night his house just might come crashin' down on his head.*

But in this case, Leon would push him to stay. *Lord'amighty, what do you have to lose?* he'd say.

Not anything but time, Nathan granted, and there wasn't much to gain by going back to Gainesville. He would have said *home*, but he couldn't think of the farm that way anymore. He'd given some thought to Leon's plan to buy Old Man Sawyer's land for the two of them to farm and decided that wasn't in the best interest of his stepfather. Leon was the other side of forty-five, too old to break ties with his wife and children and go into debt to start over on a farm that might or might not pay. Nathan couldn't let him do that for the sake of a boy not even his son.

So he was virtually homeless, Nathan had come around to thinking, and here in Dallas his real father had offered him a roof over his head and blood kin to boot. He might be flattering himself, but he did share the sense his grandmother needed him, his little sister, too, though he had yet to make up his mind about his father. Nathan had come prepared not to trust or like him, but somehow in the space of the hours he'd been in his company,

Trevor Waverling had shaken that mind-set a little. A sad thing about his brother, Jordan. Could Nathan believe him when he said he'd had no hand in his death? And would Nathan's own life be in jeopardy after a while if he should take to Waverling Tools like a fish to water, impress his grandmother, the holder of the keys to the kingdom, and turn out to be his father's competitor as heir apparent?

The sudden idea of being in personal danger from Trevor Waverling briefly unsettled him. The man was easy to fear physically. In his office, Nathan had noticed a couple of photographs on a bookshelf—not necessarily buried but not displayed for the world to see either—of his father in boxing gloves and shorts in his younger days. A narrow brass plate attached to the bottom of the frame read MIDDLE-WEIGHT CHAMP / DALLAS AMATEUR BOXING COMPETITION / 1876. Nathan had wondered at his father's obvious physical fitness, city and desk man that he was. Nathan admonished himself for his concern. He'd been reading too many Nick Carter detective stories of family skullduggery, and he was getting way too much ahead of himself thinking he'd be a contender for the Waverling crown. So far he couldn't imagine himself working in a stuffy tool-making facility or sitting in an office behind a desk. He wouldn't be able to draw a good breath. He was an outdoors man.

Besides, he would go nowhere where Zak wasn't welcome, and Nathan couldn't see his German shepherd getting along with his grandmother's tabby in her fine house of breakable things.

Nathan found the dock and walked to its edge. It was really a pier, for it extended a good length over what he could see was actually a fork of the Trinity that flowed through Dallas. Where had Jordan Waverling died? Here? Nathan was looking at a wide, long, deep expanse of water. Moored beside the pier, a sizable boat bobbed in the gentle swells under a covered slip, paddles

anchored within the hull. Was that boat the setting for the accident—or the crime? His grandmother had said the mystery of
her son's death was another story for a private moment. Away
from her surviving son's ears, Nathan had the feeling that if he
stayed, his grandmother would treat him to many private moments of family history. He did not know if he cared to listen.

But where else could he go for the time being? Nathan looked
out upon the water, finished his coffee, and reached his decision.
Zak would make or break the deal. If they'd accommodate his
dog, arrange it so he and Zak could be together, he'd stay. If not,
he'd go home, get Zak, and be on the road to California.

Back together in his office, Trevor Waverling looked at his son
with a frown. "That big German shepherd I saw?"

"Yes, and he eats a lot."

"He sleeps in your room?"

"Right beside my bed."

"Do you think he'd frighten Rebecca?"

"I couldn't say. He's gentle with Lily. That's my half sister."

"How does he get along with cats?"

"He's not crazy about them."

"Oh, God, Nathan—" Trevor combed a hand through his
graying, well-trimmed hair. "I know Mother won't go with your
suggestion to lodge apart from us. She expects you to live in the
house, become a member of the family. It's part of the arrangement she made with me, but with a dog? You absolutely must
have it with you? You can't leave it at the farm where it will have
lots of fresh air and space to run?"

"I absolutely must have Zak with me."

"And if we don't meet this…demand, you'll return home?"

"That's right."

"Then my mother won't have any choice but to agree to having
him in the house, but I must warn you, she's not fond of dogs."

"Zak knows to stay out of parlors."

Trevor regarded Nathan for a long moment in silence. "Do you ever budge on anything?"

"Not on what's important."

"And do you always know what's important?"

"To me, yes. It's other folks' ideas on the subject I have trouble with."

Trevor shook his head. "In that regard, you're Edwin Waverling's grandson, all right. Now let's go discover what else you may have in common with the founder of Waverling Tools." Trevor put his arm around Nathan's shoulders and walked him to his office door. "You may find it's where you belong," he said.

Chapter Nineteen

Nathan gratefully caught a ride to the Barrows farm with a neighboring farmer who'd come to the train station to pick up a crate of chickens. But for the neighbor, he'd have had to walk the two miles from the depot through the town of Gainesville, then another five to the farm. In the uncanny way of dogs, Zak sensed his arrival before the wagon turned into the gate of the Barrows farmstead and bounded full speed up the lane to the road. His excited barking set off the chickens, so Nathan thanked the driver and hopped down to walk the rest of the way to the house.

Zak's enthusiasm at his return nearly knocked him over, so he knelt to allow the dog his full expression of joy. Nathan had been gone four days, the only time in his life he'd been away from the farm. He had wondered how he would feel when he first viewed the wide acres he'd helped to tend since he was a child, the neat two-story house set in its grove of shade trees, the barn and pigpen, the chicken coop and orchard and grazing pastures. He'd gone off to Dallas thinking he'd left his heart behind—a broken heart, for sure, but one that would never fit in anywhere else. Now he realized that the sweetness of his labors had come from the satisfaction of knowing that the land he worked belonged to him. The truth that it wasn't and had never been still almost emptied his stomach, but it changed his perspective. The brown fields seeded with spring wheat by his own hands did not move him. They did not call to him, their one-time caretaker and friend, as he'd once imagined. A feeling of alienation swept over him like the time his mother's father had taken Randolph and Lily for a ride in his surrey and left him behind. "No room for you!" his grandfather had sung out as he sped off, and Nathan had stood there feeling severed from the family, an outsider, as if he did not belong. The brown arrow-straight rows eyed him as a stranger now. *Go on*, they twinkled in the late afternoon sun. *There is no place here for you anymore.*

Leon came out of the barn, spotted him, and hurried to greet him, the faded pants of his denim overalls flapping. Nathan's heart twisted. He would miss Leon most of all.

"I heard Zak's bark," he called, "and knew you were home. Good to see you, son. How did it go?" He indicated that they head toward the barn to discuss in private Nathan's decision. It was nearly time for the evening meal, and the savory aroma of roasting chicken trailed after them. Randolph and Lily would be at the kitchen table doing their homework, his mother at the stove. An ache burgeoned under Nathan's rib cage.

"Just in time for the milkin'," Leon said. "Daisy will be right glad to see you."

The cow, already at her feed but her back feet rooted firmly, lifted her head from the trough and bawled a greeting. Nathan dropped his knapsack and went to work.

"So you're going to give it a try," Leon said, when Nathan finished telling him about the events of the last four days, the people he had met, and his impressions of them all.

"Yessir. I'll be leaving in two days when Benjy comes for me in the coach. The train doesn't allow dogs in the passenger compartments. I'll leave everything behind but Zak and what I can fit in my knapsack."

"You'll take along a few memories of us, I hope. Don't let the last ones mar the good ones, Nathan. There were plenty of 'em."

Memories based on misassumptions, Nathan thought, but he would never hurt Leon by saying so. "I guess I'd better go tell Mother I'll be leaving," he said, leading Daisy back to her stall. "What'll we tell Randolph and Lily?"

"We've told them only that you went to Dallas to check out an opportunity the man in the coach-and-pair driven by his odd little driver came to offer you," Leon said. "Naturally, they were surprised. Randolph wondered what kind of opportunity you'd be qualified for other than farmin'."

Nathan grinned. "Sounds like him."

"Lily cried."

"Sounds like her, too. Will they ever know we're half related?"

"Your mother would die if the news ever got out."

"Uh-huh," Nathan said. "Sounds like her, too."

Millicent glanced at them from the stove when they walked in, then turned her face away quickly and went on with her stirring. "I see you're back," she said. "Go wash up. There's plenty, though we weren't expecting you. Children, put away your books, and Lily, set the table."

Lily leaped up from her chair. "Nathan!" she cried, hugging him. "We've missed you! Tell us all you did in Dallas. What's it like? Is it big—bigger than Oklahoma City?"

Randolph stood with a frown of annoyance at having to be pulled from his books. "Did you get lost in it?"

Nathan waited until they were through with supper to tell them he'd be leaving. Lily took the news with a cry; Randolph in wonder that his brother would be hired for any employment but farm labor. "You'll be working in a plant that makes oil drilling equipment?" he repeated in an incredulous voice.

"Working in a *supervising* position for a *company* that drills for oil, Randolph," Leon corrected him. "There's a difference."

"Mr. Waverling believes the economic future of Texas lies in petroleum," Nathan said, "so he's converting the plant to that end. They're already manufacturing oil field equipment, and he's got a notion for a rotary drilling bit with a hollow drill stem that could break up rock strata easier. He believes it would be a huge improvement over the repetitive lift and drop of heavy cable-tool bits used for water well and salt drilling."

"Sounds like Greek to me," Randolph said.

"That oil field they discovered over in Washington County certainly ushered in a boom for the Oklahoma Territory," Leon offered. "Maybe you'll be coming our way to drill your wells just over the Texas border."

"Maybe," Nathan said. "I don't know yet where I fit in the company. Mr. Waverling seems to have in mind my work may be more mental than physical, but whatever it is, it will have to be a job outdoors."

Randolph smirked. "How can drilling for oil be anything but physical?"

"There's brainwork involved in finding oil, Randolph," Nathan said patiently. "As a matter of fact, Mr. Waverling wants me to go with him Saturday to hear a lecture on paleontology. The speaker is going to explain what kind of fossils to look for that indicate the presence of oil."

Throughout the supper conversation, Millicent remained silent, her face no screen for her thoughts. Nathan had feared hearing the name Waverling would be repugnant to her, but he'd be a toad frog before he referred to him as "my father" in the presence of Leon. Finally, she rose to clear the dishes and said, "So you'll be going in two days' time?"

"Yes, ma'am. It'll take us three days to get to Dallas by coach, and Mr. Waverling wants me there by Saturday to attend that lecture."

"Then I guess I'd better wash your jeans in the morning so

they'll get dry," Millicent said. "We can't have you show up at the place in dirty pants."

"Thank you, ma'am."

Nathan did not tell her that hanging in the closet of the blue room he now occupied in Dallas were three new suits and a half-dozen dress shirts. On the floor were two pairs of "city" shoes, new boots, and the bureau drawers were filled with underwear still in their packaging. His father had offered to have his old clothes burned, but Nathan would not part with them. He stored them away should the situation ever arise that he would need them again. This last maternal gesture from his mother was nothing but a pat on the head, he understood, but Nathan felt moved by it, and he would not for the world deny her the opportunity to feel she'd sent him off with some token of maternal devotion.

In the next two days, the sun warmed the earth, and on his final morning to wake in his old room, he looked out the window to find a green blush over the brown fields. The wheat seeds had sprouted their first leaves. Up from the kitchen rose the smells of bacon and onions frying and biscuits baking. Nathan turned from the window and was surprised to see Randolph awake, watching him from his pillow. "We'll miss you, brother," he said softly.

Nathan tousled his hair. "Go back to sleep."

He finished dressing in the hall, passed through the kitchen to the outhouse without a word to his mother, then headed for the barn. Halfway through the milking, he set his forehead against Daisy's flank and cried.

The coach and Thoroughbreds arrived just before noon. Randolph and Lily had gone off to school voicing their protests. Even Randolph had whined to stay home to say good-bye, but Nathan was relieved his mother had not allowed it. "It will be hard enough for your brother as it is," she'd said. "Get on with you."

At last it was time to board the coach. The merry little Irishman, his stomach filled with the fried chicken and mashed potatoes and buttermilk pie Millicent had prepared for her son's last meal at the family table, had reins in hand. She and Leon and Nathan had gathered on the porch. Zak was already in the coach, observing them quizzically from the open window.

A palpable tension hung in the silence. Millicent rubbed at her throat, her eyes averted, Nathan stared down at his feet, Leon withdrew his handkerchief. *You can come home again, you know*, Leon had told Nathan in one of their private conversations in the barn. *We can still make it happen with Old Man Sawyer if you're not happy in Dallas.*

But Nathan knew he would never come home again. His farming days here were over. *That's good to know*, he'd said. On the porch, he stuck out his hand to Leon, "Well, good-bye, Dad. Thanks for everything. You've been the best father a son could ever have."

"You made it easy," Leon said, blowing his nose into his handkerchief.

Nathan turned to his mother. "Good-bye, Mother. I'll miss your cooking," he said.

Millicent responded with a flickering smile. She reached up and straightened a side of his collar, and for the briefest second, Nathan felt her fingertips touch his neck. "Take care of yourself," she said.

As the carriage pulled away, Nathan waved out the window, then settled against the leather seat and did not look back. Zak, whining, jumped next to him. "It will be all right, boy," Nathan said, wrapping his arm around his neck. But in his heart Nathan knew it would be a long time before it was so.

From the bed, Leon watched Millicent rub her elbows with cream from a jar on her dressing table. She had already spread the oily mixture on her face that she rarely exposed to outdoor elements. The stipulations of her parents' small trust fund allowed a monthly stipend that afforded such personal luxuries. The rest she set aside for Randolph's and Lily's wants.

"You didn't waste any time puttin' that ad in the paper, did you, Millie girl?" Leon drawled. "What made you think he wouldn't come back to stay?"

"Why would he? He knows there's nothing here for him anymore."

"I'm glad you didn't tell Nathan before he left. That was decent of you." Leon's tone dripped sarcasm.

"What would have been the good of it?"

"What newspapers did you put the ad in?"

"The *Fort Worth Gazette* and the *Dallas Herald*."

"And the ad will appear on Monday?"

"Yes, and run every day for two weeks. There'll be no need to run it longer. This place will be snapped up in no time."

"I hope the boy doesn't read the *Dallas Herald*."

His wife did not reply. After a long period of silence in which Leon observed the mesmeric rotation of her fingers, he asked, curious, "What are you thinking, Millicent?"

Millicent screwed the lid back on the jar and took up her hairbrush. "What makes you think I'm thinking anything?"

"This room is so thick with your thoughts there's hardly breathing room."

"I'm doing the right thing, Leon—for all us," Millicent said, her words underscored with brisk strokes of the hairbrush. "Daddy never meant for the farm to go to Nathan. You know that. I could not go against his wishes and will it to him, and his other grandchildren aren't interested in it. When my time came, Randolph and Lily would sell the place before my body turned cold, leaving Nathan high and dry when he's beyond his youth and too late to start over, like with this opportunity Trevor is offering him. Farm prices are at their highest now. What happens when the next tornado, or drought, or flood strikes, as one of them will eventually. You know it's the truth, Leon. Besides, you're getting too old to farm, especially now that Nathan won't be here to help you run things."

"Who're you trying to convince, Millicent?"

Millicent's jaw stiffened. She turned her head to glare at him. "We need the money *now*, Leon. Don't you understand that? College will be expensive. Randolph will need a new wardrobe for Columbia, and I can't keep making Lily's dresses. She needs tailor-made clothes…" She placed a hand at her throat, a habit when out of words, and turned back to the mirror. After a few more strokes of the hairbrush, she said softly, "He's a good boy, Leon. I never said he wasn't. I warned you when he was born that I would probably never warm to him. How could I when he looks so much like…him."

"Well, there's his winning traits of honesty and decency that might've won you over," Leon drawled.

Millicent shook her head irritably. "I know, I know, though where he gets it from considering the man who's his father—"

"—and the woman who's his mother."

Millicent laid down the hairbrush. Leon expected her to throw it at him, but she stared into the mirror, and he wondered who, what, she saw there. "Yes, that's right," she agreed. "Considering who fathered and birthed him, where does he get it all? I just hope he's not heading into the devil's den and that he'll be happy where he's going…that it's best for him." She turned the wick of the kerosene lamp, and the room was cast into darkness. "I mean that, Leon. As God is my witness, I really do." The mattress depressed under her slight weight. "Don't expect anything tonight. I'm not in the mood for it."

"Me, either," Leon said.

Samantha

Chapter Twenty

Samantha had no appetite for Grizzly's fried steak. She was feeling the pierce of sharp loss. Dr. Tolman's letter was now ashes in the grate, and she would never learn what it contained. Well, there was more than one way to pry off a boot stuck on a stubborn foot. Casually, she said, "From the way you're enjoying that steak, Daddy, your army friend must not be dying."

"Just the contrary, I'm happy to say," Neal said, sawing into a platter-sized sirloin. His voracious appetite did not suggest a hidden illness. "Cody and his wife have just sold their mercantile store in Charlotte, Virginia, for a large profit and are moving to the country to breed horses. It was a dream of his when we served together, and all these years later, it's come true. He wanted to give me his new address."

"What did Dr. Tolman's letter have to say about treating cattle ticks?"

Neal spooned more gravy onto his mashed potatoes. "No information we could use. The man wrote about a compound for dipping cattle that's a better product than Robert Kleberg's preparation. I'll stick with Bob's coal-and-tar concoction. What's good for the King Ranch is good enough for Las Tres Lomas."

His explanation, delivered with disinterest, was plausible enough, hard not to believe, but then why destroy the letter? It was a little thing and could mean nothing, but the bin beside the fireplace where scrap paper was collected for use as kindling was full and available. "Why did he write 'Confidential' on the envelope?" Samantha asked.

"Because he didn't want just any cowpoke reading it and copying his idea. He's filing for a patent on the stuff."

"And I'm just any cowpoke?"

Neal set down his knife and fork on their ends sharply. "The man's letter was not worth your time reading nor his product worthwhile, Sam, and that's all there is to it. You'd have given me grief over the price he was asking, and the preparation sounded dangerous to the cows. Something about carbolic acid. I threw the letter into the fire."

Perhaps that's all there was to it, Samantha thought, though an undeniable thread of doubt remained, underpinned by her father's unusual annoyance with her. Neal Gordon, however, was not a man with much tolerance for questioning his actions once they were done. He turned the conversation to the farm for sale in Cooke County.

"Buckley says the place has got its own underground spring as well as a good-sized house, garden, and orchard," he said. "Why, we could turn the place from a mere cow camp into a smaller version of Las Tres Lomas, nice enough for you and your mother to visit and to invite guests. The whole property doesn't have to become a livestock thoroughfare. We could grow our own hay against drought, and you could experiment with new grasses. We wouldn't be out a cent for a silo and barns."

Samantha had not seen Neal Gordon this excited in years. His eyes were bright, his color strong and ruddy. She had not heard the whistling in his chest. She saw no overt cause for concern about his health. In his mind, the deal was done. He relished the idea of owning another full-fledged ranch with the amenities of Las Tres Lomas: a main house, real bunkhouse and ranch kitchen, indoor privies, electric lights, running water, maybe even a telephone—which Las Tres Lomas did not yet possess, since the list of subscriber applicants in the Fort Worth area was long. A second ranch would get him a notch closer to becoming a titan among Texas cattlemen.

Her father would just as soon let slide recollections of his land-grabbing years, when he bought every parcel of acreage contiguous to his ranch that came on the market. Like now, they were times of overflowing watering wells and abundant grass and healthy herds—"the green years," he called them. *Buy now while the gettin' is good* had been his philosophy. But then "the brown years" had come, seasons of drought when most of the water sources and all the grasslands in Central Texas had dried up, and a financial crisis called the Panic of 1893 had struck the United States, casting its shadow on mortgaged ranches like Las Tres Lomas. Young as she was, Samantha's memory of those times was sharper than her father's, and they had bred caution in her so that now, even with ledger columns in the black and the mortgage long paid off, she was reluctant to part with an unnecessary penny. She believed in erecting impenetrable hedges against financial disaster.

"I declare, honeybee, your daughter is getting tighter than a debutante's corset about money," he'd said to her mother.

"Uh-huh, so now she's *my* daughter, is she? Well, maybe Samantha's never forgotten the deep worry lines on her papa's face or the tense discussions around the supper table when it looked like we could lose the ranch because we were one payment away from default. Samantha's just trying to preserve what Neal Gordon has worked so hard for so those worry lines won't come again."

Her mother had not needed to say it, but her accusing eye and tone had declared clear enough that Neal had been at fault for their near financial ruin. His zeal to become one of the biggest landowners in Texas had led him to buy grazing range for his ever-increasing herds. The Gordons had been left land rich but cash poor. Neal had learned his lesson, but it was still a dream of his to see the distinctive brand of Las Tres Lomas de la Trinidad—double *T*'s flanked by a pair of smaller *L*'s—spread throughout Texas. He wanted to become a titan.

"What's a titan?" Samantha, ten years old, had asked her father when he'd presented her with a book of Greek mythology as a birthday gift. Tales of gods and goddesses had been his favorite literature as a boy and—secretly—as a man.

"They were gods that once ruled the universe," Neal answered. "You can read all about them in that book. Today the word refers to people of great importance and power."

"And you want to be a titan?"

"God willing," Neal said.

Her mother had rolled her eyes.

As Samantha folded her napkin and excused herself from the table, the thought occurred to her that if she and Sloan were to marry and combine the two ranches, her father would have his wish.

Since Neal had cleaned up for the day, at her suggestion, she left him to his newspapers and a nap, since he was drowsy from the bourbon and heavy meal, and rode Pony to the birthing area where she was sure to find the ranch foreman, Wayne Harris. It must be the scientist in her that she could not let a thing lie once it piqued her interest. Her father looked and acted well, but he'd received a confidential letter from a doctor. It was uncharacteristic of him not to show it to her and even less so for him to burn it. He kept personal letters for months before they ended up in the kindling bin.

No season was more exciting on a ranch than spring when the

calves were born, but no time was more mentally and physically demanding for mother, calf, and cowhand. Certain pens were designated to hold cows giving birth so that their deliveries could be monitored and assistance rendered in case of difficulties. During calving season, Wayne was in charge of the birthing pens and a master at saving cows and calves in life-threatening straits, often with the assistance of Samantha. Samantha found him engaged in just such a struggle ten minutes later.

"Thank God you're here, Mornin' Glory," he said. "We can use your help. We've got a heifer in trouble."

"Is she going to make it?"

"Hard to tell. The calf's got problems, too."

The cow, her head held by two men and her legs tied to prevent her from suddenly leaping up in the middle of trying to save her, aborted her calf and hemorrhaged to death an hour later. Sickened by the agonizing ordeal, their boots, jeans, and shirts soaked in mud and blood and body fluids, Samantha and Wayne headed for a water tank to wash off the gore.

"You sure have to love ranching to witness that," the foreman said as he wrung out his shirt. "I don't reckon I'll ever adjust to the grief of it."

Samantha glanced at him. She appreciated that about Wayne—his sensitivity, despite that he gave the appearance and had the reputation of a man it was wise not to unduly provoke. He was not a tall man, but his wiry, corded frame toughened by years of ranch work and superintending cowboys gave the impression of a greater height. In age, he had looked the same to Samantha all her life, neither young nor old, simply durable and unchanging as post oak. She considered him and Grizzly her truest friends.

"I'm glad I didn't eat much of Grizzly's fried steak," she said. "Did everything run all right while I was gone?"

"Rawbone got into a saloon fight in White Settlement last Saturday night, and I had to go bail his sorry hide outta jail. Your pa put up the money and will dock it from his pay. Other than that, no mishaps."

"Daddy seem okay to you? Healthwise, I mean?"

Wayne raised an eyebrow. "Far as I can tell, MG. You have reason to wonder?"

Samantha flapped the water from her arms and hands to dry them. "Mother and I noticed Daddy wheezing a little at my birthday party. It's her opinion that someday he'll have to pay the piper for that Comanche arrow he took in his lung when he was young. Also"—Samantha rolled down her sleeves—"he received a letter marked 'Confidential' from a doctor in the Oklahoma Territory. He threw it into the fire before I could read it. I found that suspicious. I thought it might have to do with a reply to a medical question about himself, but Daddy said it was from a veterinarian in answer to a letter he'd written him about a dip he'd concocted to get rid of cattle ticks. He read about it in a magazine article."

"You can believe him, MG," Wayne said, buttoning into his shirt. "Fact is, Neal showed the article to me, and we both agreed the stuff wasn't for us. The ticks might've died but the cow wouldn't have lived."

Samantha blew out a little breath of relief. "Well, okay then."

"But the article wadn't written by no doctor."

Samantha stared at him. "Are you sure? A Dr. Tolman from Marietta in the Oklahoma Territory?"

"Sure, I'm sure. It was written by a rancher up in Denton County."

"Oh, God, Wayne." Samantha put her hands on her hips, anger peppering her concern. She'd been lied to, and so adeptly, too.

"Now, don't go gettin' mad at your pa, Mornin' Glory. He might'a had a good reason for keepin' that letter from you. The person who'd know is Grizzly. Neal can't keep nothin' from Grizzly, hard as he might try."

Samantha said, "Well, I believe I'll just go pay Grizzly a visit. You won't mention this conversation to Daddy?"

"Lips tighter'n a miser's pocket. I'll see if the magazine is still around. I may have it in my quarters in the bunkhouse."

Samantha removed Pony's saddle and set the quarter horse free in a paddock, then took off for the long log-timbered building that housed the kitchen and dining room of the ranch cook's domain. TRAIL HEAD was burned above its front door, named for the point of a cattle drive's conclusion. Grizzly ran a finely tuned staff of four that assisted him in feeding thirty cowhands three meals a day, six days a week. Sundays, his day of rest, ranch employees could fend for themselves, which they did by usually roasting a side of beef over a pit fire, with the more skilled among them stirring up deep-dish cobblers to go with the pans of biscuits and kettles of beans. On Sundays, Grizzly attended church in town, treated himself to dinner in the dining room of the Metropolitan Hotel, and spent the afternoon as a volunteer in the Masonic Widows and Orphans Home, erected the previous year, in 1899. Nobody on the ranch saw him until he reappeared in his own quarters Sunday night, where he could be observed reading by lamplight in his chair by the window.

Samantha found him in his small office next to the pantry tallying monthly receipts. Short in stature and bearish in build, he was teased as being almost as big around as he was tall, but wisely out of range of his rolling pin. When Samantha appeared in the open doorway, a frown was in place to bestow upon the intruder, but it cleared instantly when he spun around in his desk chair and saw his visitor.

"Mornin' Glory!" he cried, getting up to hug her. "Happy belated birthday! How did the party go? All we got from your pa was that you looked as pretty as a spring sunrise."

"Tell you the truth, it was just so-so this year, Grizzly."

Grizzly sat back down with a rueful grin. "Turnin' twenty get you down?"

Samantha chuckled at his quickness. "How'd you know?"

" 'Cause you're a woman turnin' twenty, that's why." *And unmarried*, Samantha was sure he was thinking. Not that her single state would be a cause of worry to Grizzly. He abhorred change. What if the man she married came in, threw his weight around, and upset things? He sniffed and looked her over. "You already been at the birthing barns?"

"I went out to talk to Wayne and got caught in a situation. We lost mother and calf."

Grizzly grimaced in sympathy. "Too bad."

"And now I've come to talk to you."

"Sounds dire. What about?"

"Daddy. Have you noticed anything or has he said something to suggest he's not well?"

Grizzly pressed his lips together, fleshy as plump plums. After a thoughtful second he said, "Nooo, not a whiff. What did Wayne say?"

"Same thing, but I'm worried, especially since he bald-faced lied to me when I questioned him about a letter he received from a doctor marked 'Confidential.' "

"What did the letter say?"

"He threw it into the fire before I could read it."

Grizzly leaned back in his chair. "Oh-oh, that's not good. Who was the letter from?"

"A Dr. Donald Tolman from Marietta, Oklahoma Territory."

Relief flooded Grizzly's bearded face. "Oh, Samantha, hon, there's nothin' wrong with your pa, thank the Lord. That letter was from the doctor who put you into your pa and ma's arms!"

Chapter Twenty-One

Grizzly's expression held the horror of someone who's accidentally swallowed a bone. Samantha stared back as if he had. The slip of his tongue penetrated slowly, like the return of feeling after a numbing blow.

Samantha said, drawing out her words, "The letter...was...from the doctor who delivered me?" She recalled her mother's mention of a doctor the time she'd held her ear to the library door at ten years old.

Grizzly flapped his hands as if waving a rebellious audience back to its seats. "Shush!" he rasped, glancing around at the open door. He got up and, with the duck-walk peculiar to short, corpulent men, swayed to close it against any of the kitchen crew who might be listening, even though most of them understood only Spanish. Then he waddled back and sat down heavily at his desk and clamped his temples between his thumb and fingers. "Lord have mercy, what have I done?" he moaned. "If your pa ever finds out what I just told you, he'll know the information came from me. He'll think I betrayed him, and I'd rather be flayed alive than have him believe that."

Samantha could feel a stirring inside her like a cat uncurling from a long nap in a corner of a forgotten room. "How do you know this Dr. Tolman?"

Grizzly shot her a miserable glance. "Please, Samantha, forget that name and what you just heard."

"Well, now, I don't know that I can do that, but I can give you my word that what you say here will never leave this office."

Grizzly looked alarmed. "What do you mean, what I say here? I've said all I'm goin' to say."

"No you haven't. Tell me about Dr. Tolman. How do you know him? Did you meet him the night he brought me here?"

Grizzly said sharply, "How do you know it was night?"

"Wayne told me—long ago. He said he didn't know anything else about that night."

"Neither do I."

"Please, Grizzly. What harm would it do for me to know?"

Obstinately, Grizzly fastened his gaze away from her, folded his arms and set them on the shelf of his belly. "Plenty, if your pa finds out."

"He won't. I have as much reason to keep this between you and me as you do. He lied to me about that letter and threw it into the fire, remember. He's obviously sworn you to secrecy and doesn't want me to know anything about Dr. Tolman, and I understand that. I know how he'd feel if he thought I was the least bit curious about the circumstances of my birth."

Grizzly cut her a razor-sharp glance. "Well, then, why are you all of a sudden? You've never been curious before."

Samantha frowned thoughtfully. "I really don't know. I was only this morning reflecting that I was way past the time for Daddy and Mother to worry that my real parents would show up. That was always a fear of theirs—Daddy's, especially—that they'd come looking for me. As for me, except for the one time when I was fifteen that I asked Wayne what he knew about my birth, I never thought about it again...until...this came up." Samantha looked at the cook entreatingly. "I'd do nothing with the information, Grizzly. Why would I? I'd just like to know…what you know, that's all, and then I'll be satisfied and mention it no more. Please, my friend?"

Grizzly let out the sigh of a cook who knows his pot roast is overdone and cannot be rescued. "The doctor came in the middle of the night with you. You weren't but a few days old. I heard the buggy drive up. Don't ask me how. I usually sleep sound as a hibernatin' bear, but that night I was awake. It was a good thing, too. It wasn't no time before Neal was bangin' on my door wantin' my key to the ice room. He needed milk but had no idea where the key was, or otherwise I'd never have known nothin' about you until the next day."

The cook paused, as if deliberating whether to go on.

"Please, Grizzly. What else?"

"Your pa said, proud as I've ever seen him, 'We got us a baby, Grizzly,' and I got the picture immediately. I told him to go on back to the house, I'd bring the milk."

"Then what happened?"

"I took the milk to the main house and the doctor, he had brought a baby feedin' tube, and he showed your folks how to use it, warm the milk, that sort of thing. He put a little honey in it. Oh, Lord, it was all somethin' to see, you no bigger than a man's hand, and your folks hoppin' all over themselves with joy. Your mother kept sayin', 'Oh, thank you, Dr. Tolman.' That's how I recognized the man's name."

Samantha sat mesmerized, picturing the scene. "And…did this doctor say anything about…anything else?"

"Nary a word, Mornin' Glory, and that's the truth. He came, he delivered, and he left. That's all I know, and it's more than your pa wants you to know. That's why he destroyed the letter. He wants no thread to lead you back to where you came from. You need to get that in your pretty head and leave it there."

"I have no intention of following a thread anywhere, Grizzly. I'm satisfied and grateful to learn that Daddy is okay, but I just wonder…why did Dr. Tolman write to him? What was in the letter?"

Grizzly sighed again. "Now see, it's that kind a' questionin' that can get you into trouble. One question leads on to another and then another, and before you know it, the bread crumbs have led you into somethin' you can't get out of."

Samantha rose and hugged the expansive breadth of the cook's shoulders. "Don't worry, Grizzly. I'm not following bread crumbs anywhere. My roots are here. The family and people I love are here. I want no other."

"Well, that's good to hear," Grizzly said, sounding unconvinced. He levered up from his chair and took down his badge of authority hanging on a peg. He slipped the neck of the capacious apron over his head and turned around for Samantha to secure the ties. "Just remember this, young lady. Your daddy loves you more than life, but there is no such thing as an unbreakable connection. There are some things in this world that unconditional, everlastin', endurin' love can't stand up to, and the biggest is betrayal. It's only natural for an adopted child turnin' twenty to be curious about where she came from, who her folks were, if she has any left, but I'm advisin' you to hold to your word and let the matter go."

Had she heard a faint echo of an experience in Grizzly's past that made him speak with such authority and caution? Grizzly possessed a Christian name, but Samantha had never heard it. As far as anybody knew, he had no relatives. He received no personal correspondence and had never introduced anyone as a member of his family. Hardly beyond a boy, he had been hired as the ranch cook's helper by her father's father and had lived on Las Tres Lomas ever since. It was assumed his kin were all

dead or he had forsaken them or vice versa. It remained un-
stated, but Grizzly considered the Gordons and Wayne Harris
his family; the ranch, his home. Samantha had never had cause
to wonder how it was that he had come to Las Tres Lomas
alone in the world, but now she was convinced he'd been orphaned or abandoned.

When Grizzly turned back around, a warning beam still in
his eyes, Samantha tugged his beard to make affectionate fun of
his needless concern, but it left her uneasy. She felt secure in her
adoptive parents' love, like a house with a strong foundation and
walls, but would the rafters hold in a storm? "Don't worry, Grizzly. I will heed your words," she said. "Now I have to get myself
washed up and then to the books."

Her father was awake and at his desk in the library when Samantha returned downstairs after a wash and change of clothes.
The day had warmed, and the fire in the great room had succumbed to ashes. Passing by the fireplace, she stooped and re-
trieved the scrap of cream-colored vellum that had escaped the
flames. It bore no writing, but the name of Dr. Donald Tolman
was imprinted indelibly in her memory.

Neal Gordon was not a patient man, and Samantha knew he'd
be hard to live with until Monday when Jimmy was to bring
the morning edition of the *Fort Worth Gazette* to the ranch.
The work crew was now so large that he and Samantha were
not called upon to assist in the day-to-day, hands-on operation of the ranch, but its length and breadth demanded diligent
overseeing. She and her father split duties and took shifts that
required that a good part of each day be spent in the saddle, but
in the intervening time before Monday, once his stint was over,
Neal could not seem to settle down to any other occupation. He
roamed the house, stalked the kitchen, pestered Samantha in

her workshop. "What's this?" he demanded, picking up a dark brown object that looked like a stone. Samantha hurried to rescue it from his casual handling.

"I don't know," she said. "I found it out at Windy Bluff. At first I thought it was a rock, but it's fossilized bone that must have belonged to some land creature millions of years ago. See the little holes that the blood vessels went through?"

Neal peered. "How do you know it's not a rock?"

"My microscope tells me. Because Central Texas was once covered in water, this area is favorable for preserving fossil evidence. That's why people around here are forever bringing me chips and fragments of unidentifiable animal life to analyze."

"Well, I'm glad you have a hobby at times like these," Neal said, his tone dour. "I wish I did."

Samantha laughed softly and patted his cheek. "Aren't you always telling me not to rush tomorrow, that it will get here soon enough?"

Neal shrugged. "Yeah, well, in this case, not soon enough. What if the place is sold by tomorrow?"

Monday came and Jimmy arrived with the daily edition of the *Fort Worth Gazette*. Neal had Silbia send a ranch hand to fetch Samantha from a pasture where she was overseeing the reunion of newborn calves to their mothers and keeping a lookout for cows that rejected their young. Neal had located the classified section of the newspaper and had it spread on his desk when she hurried in. The farm was indeed the Barrows homestead, for the ad read that "a representative of the Barrows farm" would meet a respondent at a place of his choosing in Gainesville and drive him to the land for sale. Contact and arrangements to meet could be made by telegram through Western Union.

"Halleluiah!" Neal cried. "I'll go into Fort Worth today and fire off a telegram to let 'em know I'm interested. I need to see your mother anyway. The seller can send a reply there and Jimmy can bring it to us."

For the next three days they waited. Finally, Jimmy, with the air of an emissary having come on an important mission, arrived with telegram in hand that he told Silbia he must deliver to "Mr. G" personally.

The housekeeper climbed the stairs to the widow's walk and rang a large bell atop a tall column whose peal could carry over a good portion of the twenty-thousand-acre ranch. It had been erected primarily as a summons. Silbia pulled the rope three times, the prearranged signal to alert them of the telegram's arrival. Two miles away, Neal and Samantha, called to consider what animal had attacked and killed a young steer, heard the funereal toll of the bell. "Oh, my God, it's come, Sam," Neal said.

In the great room, Neal snatched the telegram from Jimmy's fingers and let out an exultant cry at its message. He passed it to Samantha, who read that a representative of the Barrows farm would be happy to meet with Neal Gordon in the coffee shop of the train depot at two o'clock in four days' time. Neal snorted at the high-sounding tone of "representative." Why not just come out and name the member of the Barrows clan that would be meeting them? "Pack your bags, Sam," he said. "Looks like you're going to the Barrows homestead as a *representative* of Las Tres Lomas de la Trinidad."

Chapter Twenty-Two

So it was settled, the only question being who would go along as a companion and lady's maid—in reality, a bodyguard—to Samantha. Samantha said she didn't need a bodyguard, but her parents insisted. One woman alone was an easy target; two, a deterrent, especially if both were handy with self-defense weapons. Billie June's and Millie May's names came up, since the sisters were dead shots, but it was decided that Mildred would accompany her. The housekeeper's formidable countenance and bearing suggested a woman not to be fooled with. She was likely to be one who carried a knife in her garter and had the skill and fervor to use it. Neal believed that one look at Mildred and any ruffian entertaining unwholesome ideas about his daughter would think twice about implementing them.

The women would take the eight o'clock train to Gainesville, arrive by noon if it was on schedule, and meet with the farm owner at two. Since it was assumed the ride to the property and tour would take several hours, it was decided that an overnight stay in Gainesville was advisable. A return by train the same day would put the travelers in Fort Worth late at night—"when robbers are about," Estelle warned in disapproval of the whole idea of the women going. It was her notion that Neal should be making the trip. He could sleep the whole way and wake up when he got there. The women would stay in a Harvey House hotel and eat in its restaurant, one of a chain of such establishments built along railroad routes that was known for its clean rooms, fine food, and excellent service. Samantha used the Singletons' telephone at the Triple S to make the hotel reservation.

As she was returning the receiver to its hook, Samantha felt a presence behind her and turned to find Sloan Singleton leaning against the doorway of the great room, watching her. Her heart did a somersault—but only out of surprise, she thought, excusing her reaction. She hadn't expected him to be in the house that time of day. Millie May and Billie June had gone into town shopping. The housekeeper, a sweet-natured little Mexican woman who had been with the Singletons since before Sloan could reach the cookie jar, had let her in.

"I hope you didn't mind," Samantha said, gesturing toward the wall phone. "Consuela gave me permission."

"Why would you feel I would mind or that you even had to ask? *Mi casa, su casa*—always," Sloan said.

Not always, Sloan, Samantha thought. What an absurd word: *always*. And this house would never be hers. Once Sloan married, this house would belong to Anne Rutherford, and she'd never set foot in it again. To her humiliation, she realized that tears had sprung to her eyes.

"Good Lord, Sam! What is it?" In two strides, Sloan crossed the hall and took her by the shoulders.

"It's nothing," she said, stiffening. She knew what he would feel if she should suddenly burst out with her true feelings for him. First, embarrassment that the lifelong friend he thought of only as a sister was in love with him, and then pity that he could not return the "compliment" of it, he would say, or some such silly thing, because he would be inordinately kind. She would not have him look at her out of those blue eyes in the way someone would regard a proud cripple—bloody, but unbowed.

"Yes, I can certainly see that," Sloan said, dropping his hands. "What's wrong?"

What *was* wrong with her, welling up like that? "I'm just having…one of those days."

"Oh," he said, the simple statement full of understanding and a trace of embarrassment. To a man growing up with sisters, "one of those days" could mean only one thing.

"I've got a lot on my mind," she said to correct the misassumption.

"Oh," he said again, duly corrected. "You seem to have a lot on your mind these days. Melancholy things?"

"Yes, melancholy things."

"Like what?"

It was the same question put to her at the crossroads, and like then, Samantha thought that once upon a time she would have told him. She would have revealed her mild depression at turning twenty with maidenhood lurking around the corner, the letter in the fire, the haunting image of a tiny, unwanted baby girl left in the hands of strangers at midnight by a doctor who disappeared before dawn, and her sudden forbidden and traitorous urge to learn why she'd been rejected. But all that unburdening carried the risk that Sloan would recognize the real cause of her melancholia.

"I'm at a loss to say," she said, tamping at the overflow with the heel of her hand.

Sloan reached into his back pocket and withdrew a handkerchief. "Here," he said. "It's unused. Did you know I've seen you cry only once before?"

She dabbed at her tears and tried to smile. "Well, that's because I've never had much to cry about."

"That time you did."

"Oh? When was that?"

"The time you rode Pony to the orphanage and learned that the little girl you met there when you were ten—Susie, I believe her name was—had died."

Samantha studied him, speechless. Sloan's eyes were quiet upon her, patient, waiting.

"How...could you recall that after so many years?"

"Some things are hard to forget. Going on a trip?"

Samantha explained her upcoming mission to Gainesville. "You should have asked me to accompany you," Sloan said.

She chortled. "And what would Anne think of that?"

"Why would she think anything?"

Samantha handed back the handkerchief. Smart men could be so stupid. "She might have minded, Sloan. Women mind things like that."

"She'd be foolish to. Anne knows what you mean to me." He squeezed her elbow. "I've got to get on, but you'll be careful on the trip, won't you?"

She was close to tears again. "I'll be careful," she said.

Outside, as she mounted Pony, Samantha put it to her imagination that she could still feel the warmth of Sloan's squeeze on her elbow. He had gone out of the house through the kitchen, she assumed, but as the quarter horse cantered out the gate, she happened to glance back and saw that Sloan had come to the door of the ranch house to watch her leave.

"Now, you know what to look for, what questions to ask," Neal said in their final hour together before departing on her mission. Soon, a ranch hand would drive her and her portmanteau to Fort Worth in one of Las Tres Lomas's distinctive ranch wagons. "Make sure the place is as described with its own underground spring. Look over the house, make sure the buildings, corrals, and fences are as advertised. No need to tell that old coot Liam Barrows or whichever son is running the place now what we want the farm for, but try to find out why it's being sold. It'd be helpful to know. If the price is right and everything is as we hope, you can say it's as good as sold. Neal Gordon will be coming with check in hand." When the time came to go, he assisted Samantha up into the wagon and said, "Be sure to kiss the baby for me and tell your mother not to worry her pretty head over your safety."

"I might as well try to divert a charging Big Horn ewe with a tea towel, Daddy," she said. The baby mentioned was the infant to be christened on Sunday. Samantha was leaving on Saturday for Fort Worth because of the early baptismal service the next morning.

"You got some mail, Miss Sam," Mildred said when she arrived. "It's in the tree stand drawer. Two of 'em look like they're invitations to bridal parties for Mr. Baker and Miss Warner, and there's also a note from Barnard Laird hand-delivered this morning. You were asked to call him as soon as possible. It sounded urgent."

Samantha wondered what urgency would require her to telephone Barnard Laird. He was a former classmate who lived two blocks over and was a good friend of Todd Baker but not necessarily of hers. Samantha unfolded the message and read that Barnard had learned from Todd that he'd given her two tickets to a paleontologist's lecture Saturday night that she'd not be using. Might Samantha part with one of them? He was interested in the subject matter because, like Todd, he believed the next fortune to be made in Texas was in the discovery of oil. If she could let him have one of the tickets, would she mind sending it over to his house? As compensation, it would be his great pleasure to take her to a fine restaurant of her choosing at a time convenient for her.

Samantha refolded the message. Of course she'd part with a ticket, but that left an extra. When she sent Jimmy to Barnard's, she'd include the other with the suggestion he invite a friend to go with him. "Mildred, call the Laird residence and leave word to expect the tickets soon, will you? I've got to run up to see Mother."

"She's in a cross mood, Miss Sam."

The image of the Big Horn ewe crossed Samantha's mind.

Estelle was at her writing desk where she could be found every Saturday morning composing her correspondence. When Samantha bent to kiss her cheek, her mother pointed to two train tickets on a side table. "I bought them yesterday," she said, "but it was like buying tickets to purgatory. The very idea of your father putting his daughter in the way of train robbers and kidnappers. And there are still rogue bands of Comanche roaming about. They could recapture Mildred."

"I'd like to see them try," Samantha said with a laugh. "Gainesville is not purgatory, Mother. I'm not going to be kidnapped, and the Katy from Fort Worth to Gainesville wouldn't be worth robbing. It's a passenger train."

Estelle ducked her chin and eyed her over her reading glasses. "There's always a first time for everything, my girl. What if that ad is a nefarious attempt to lure pretty young women like you into a trap, and you go missing? It's been done before."

Samantha opened her other two pieces of mail as a distraction from her mother's harping. They were indeed prenuptial invitations to honor the coming marriage of her good friends Todd Baker and Ginny Warner. "I doubt the owner of the property had that in mind when he submitted his advertisement, since he's expecting a man to show up," she said. "Chances are he knows of Neal Gordon."

Samantha's logic missed the mark. Estelle continued. "Neal

should have his head examined. The idea of a grown man afraid of a train compartment, especially a man like your father who fears nothing. I'll be worried sick until you get home. So will your father, but he deserves to be." She glanced at the invitations that Samantha handed her and asked, "What did Barnard's note say? I was upstairs when it was delivered."

Samantha told her, then excused herself to send Jimmy off with the lecture tickets. As she slipped the pair into an envelope with her written suggestion, she thought, Why don't I go to the lecture instead of a friend? Barnard was as exciting as boiled milk, but he was a better choice to spend a Saturday evening with than her mother, who would trot out every reason against going to Gainesville until the world was flat. Samantha had to admit that she *was* interested in the lecturer's explanation of how oil could be derived from fossils. It was a theory she'd challenged at Simmons. She rewrote the note.

A reply came by telephone. Barnard was delighted she'd changed her mind about attending the lecture. He would pick her up in the family carriage at six o'clock. Also, if it pleased her, they would be joining Todd and Ginny for supper afterward at the Worth, where he would have the pleasure to treat her to that meal he promised.

Chapter Twenty-Three

The lecture was to be given in the auditorium at Polytechnic College, an institution established in 1891 by the Methodist Episcopal Church to promote Southern Methodism. The campus was located four miles east of Fort Worth and advertised itself as safe from Hell's Half Acre, the notorious mecca for gamblers, prostitutes, and outlaws that continued to be a thorn in the side of the city council. As a result, the liberal arts venue attracted guest lecturers of some renown and large crowds to hear them. The lobby of the auditorium was thronged by the time Samantha and her escort arrived, Barnard craning his neck to spot Todd and Ginny.

"There they are," he said, pointing at a group buried among the crowd.

Todd Baker and Ginny Warner were chatting with two men that Samantha took to be father and son based on their similar physical features and color of eyes, a remarkable shade of blue, she noticed when they drew to the group. The older man was speaking. As she and Barnard joined them, his eye lit upon Samantha, and he paused in midspeech. Todd's exclamations of surprised pleasure that Samantha had shown up—and with his best friend—covered the abrupt halt of the man's conversation. Introductions followed, Todd saying, "Mr. Waverling, may I present my best friends, Samantha Gordon and Barnard Laird. Sam,

Barnie, this is Mr. Trevor Waverling and his son, Nathan. Mr. Waverling is the owner of the drilling tool company where I'm happy to say I'm employed."

Samantha extended her hand to each of the men, a little disconcerted at the interest she'd attracted from the senior Waverling but who was too much of a gentleman to allow to linger. His son, too, appeared to make a conscious effort not to stare. Barnard addressed the older man as they shook hands. "I understand from Todd that your company is branching out into the manufacture of oil drilling tools, Mr. Waverling. That must be an exciting new venture for you."

"It is indeed," Trevor said and, with some reluctance, Samantha thought, turned his attention back to the subject under discussion when she and Barnard arrived. She withdrew mentally from the conversation to consider a possibility that had just occurred to her. Perhaps her emotional state of the last weeks was responsible for the idea, but cool logic would also have it that one day, somewhere, someone might stare at her and say, "You look so familiar, especially the color of your hair. Are you related to so-and-so?" One casually dropped comment—*You remind me of*—from an incidental encounter, and then those bread crumbs that Grizzly had warned her about might become whole loaves or at least a slice to lead to who knew where, what, or whom. Such incidences were not unheard of.

The sound of the gong announced that the lecture was about to begin, and as the group parted to seek their seats corresponding to the numbers on their tickets, Samantha had a moment to say boldly to Trevor Waverling, "I could not help but notice that you seemed to believe you knew me when Barnard and I joined you, Mr. Waverling, then decided not. Am I correct?"

"To a degree. The color of your hair reminds me stunningly of someone I used to know."

"Then I hope it evokes a pleasant memory."

"Unforgettable ones," he said and was gone.

Samantha felt oddly deflated. What had she hoped to achieve by her question to the man and why? *I have no intention of following a thread anywhere, Grizzly*, she'd promised the cook. So why had she hoped to find one?

Barnard took her arm, and they followed Todd and Ginny to their seats. The Waverlings were seated many rows down, near the stage, but Samantha had a good view of their heads, their squared shoulders, now and then the lean, high-cheeked profile of the father and more stolid one of the son, before she became lost in the speaker's fascinating lecture.

He began by identifying himself as a hound in search of fossil-fuel rocks. These were energy-rich substances filled with hydrocarbons that produce coal, fuel oils, and natural gas, he explained. Fossil fuels are formed when an animal or plant dies, and its remains are preserved within a protective shield of sediment such as sand, limestone, and organic matter like volcanic ash. Over time—thousands, millions of years—heat and pressure harden this covering of sediment into rock, trapping within it the decayed organisms that can generate oil or gas. It was his job as a paleontologist to search out and study specimens of this oil-producing phenomenon buried beneath the Earth's surface and report his findings. Why? Because, within the decade, America would become ever more dependent on oil and gas to fuel all forms of transportation, to heat homes, generate electricity, and provide mechanical power to factories.

Samantha listened, somewhat repulsed. When she had studied paleontology, the purpose had been to learn more about the animals and plants that had once inhabited the Earth. She could still remember the reverent thrill of her first analysis of a chunk of sedimentary rock where an animal's remains had decayed, leaving an empty space. Minerals had filtered down into this space and hardened into rock that formed a shape just like the animal that had died there. When she was in school, the process of fossilization had been studied for its own sake, not to inflate the pockets of investors drilling for money.

She was glad when the lecture was over and they were seated in the restaurant at the Worth, the city's first luxury hotel that also housed the town's finest restaurant. Sipping wine prior to the arrival of her pheasant-under-glass, Samantha listened without much interest to the others' eager discussion of the speaker's points. "Petroleum will displace agriculture as the principal locomotive of the state's economy, you mark my words," Todd was pontificating, as Samantha happened to glance over her shoulder and spot Trevor Waverling and his son at the hotel registration desk. She surmised that they were staying overnight, rather than taking the train back to Dallas so late. She did not wish to interrupt Todd's discourse, so Samantha waited until he had finished to alert him of his boss's presence in the hotel. Perhaps he'd like to invite him and his son to join their table, but when she looked again, the Waverlings were gone.

Monday fell on April ninth. "The original date for Fool's Day," Estelle announced at breakfast. "A proper date for the fool's errand your father is sending you on, Samantha."

Samantha exchanged a roll of eyes with Mildred, who was already dressed for the train they would take in less than two hours. The housekeeper was pouring the last round of coffee, a smock protecting the blouse and skirt of her gray mutton-sleeved traveling suit she'd bought especially for the occasion. She had never ridden on a train or spent a night in a hotel. Mildred's usually impassive face showed a hint of animation at the prospect of an adventure and amusement at her mistress's dire predictions of the doom that would befall it.

"You're making that up, Mother," Samantha said. "Fool's Day has always been celebrated April first."

"As the *beginning* date to celebrate *fooldom*," Estelle huffed. "Why in the world your father thinks we need another ranch is beyond me."

"He wants to become a titan."

"Well, he can forget it. He'll never catch Robert Kleberg and Dan Waggoner."

"He has to try."

Estelle insisted on seeing them off at the station, adding to the flurry of departure by pelleting them with questions too late to address when their feet were on the boarding steps. Did Samantha have her derringer in her purse? Had Mildred packed the sandwiches and hard-boiled eggs? Did the girls remember to bring their fans? Did they have their smelling salts? Their books?

Finally, they were away, seated in a Pullman car in the first-class section of the Missouri-Kansas-Texas Railroad, known affectionately as the Katy. With the deep stillness inherited from the race of her father, Mildred gazed out the window at the panorama of the rushing countryside, but after a while Samantha's silence drew her attention. Her mistress's daughter seemed indifferent to the original experience she was enjoying.

"What's the matter, Miss Sam? You seem down in your feelings."

"Just thinking, Mildred," Samantha said.

"Thinking or scheming?"

Samantha glanced at her, marveling. "Nothing gets by you, does it, Mildred? Yes, I suppose you'd say I'm scheming. Once our business is through in Gainesville, I'm going to leave you on your own for a while."

Mildred's dark eyes clouded with suspicion. "Where will you be?"

"On a little trip."

"Without me? I'm to stay by your side, Miss Sam."

"I don't want to involve you in what I'm about to do. What you don't know can't get you fired."

Mildred shifted uncomfortably in her seat. "Miss Sam, you're scaring me, and that ain't easy to do."

"All I ask is that you not tell my parents that I disappeared for a while."

"I ain't going to tell them nothing about nothing, but I'm sticking to your side whether you want me to or not, so you might as well tell me what you're up to."

Samantha hesitated. As with Grizzly and Wayne, she could trust Mildred to keep a secret. Of all people, the one-time kidnapped child of the Comanche would understand why she must do what she had to do with this opportunity so close at hand. She faced the housekeeper. "Swear to me that my answer will stay between us."

In the Comanche way, Mildred pressed a balled hand to the area of her heart. "I swear," she said.

"I'm going to take the ferry across the Red River into the Oklahoma Territory. There's a doctor I want to see in Marietta."

Chapter Twenty-Four

The train chugged into the station on schedule, allowing time for the women to register and deposit their portmanteaus in their rooms at the Harvey House, which was within walking distance of the depot. They forewent luncheon, having eaten their sandwiches and boiled eggs on the train. Samantha consulted the ferry schedule posted on the reception counter and made arrangements for transportation to the departure dock at nine o'clock the next morning. She should have her business over with in time to return to the hotel, collect their travel bags, and catch the two o'clock train home.

Samantha did not know what excited her most: the probability that at the conclusion of her visit to the farm, La Paloma would have a thoroughfare to the Red River or the possibility that the man she was going to meet knew and would disclose the full details of her birth. The latter, she thought, feeling a nip at her conscience. The women were sipping coffee at a table in the meeting place of the small café attached to the depot. They had chosen a spot that gave a view through the window of the street outside where the representative of the Barrows farm would likely appear.

"You have any idea what this Barrows man looks like?" Mildred asked.

"I figure I'll know him when I see him," Samantha said. "He'll have the manner of somebody looking for someone and will probably be in a hurry since he's late." In the time they'd been at the table, several possibilities had come and gone, but only to meet passengers. Samantha pulled at the chain of her lapel watch to check its face. It was an annoying ten minutes past the scheduled appointment.

The sound of a buckboard and mare clattering to a stop before the window raised her hope that he'd arrived, but the driver was a woman. Samantha and Mildred watched her alight. She was slightly built, ramrod straight in posture, and brisk in her movements. A calico neckerchief and a straw hat with a wide brim set just above her eyes almost covered her face. She wore a jacket with its sleeve ends tucked into the cuffs of work gloves and a sturdy pair of boots brushed by the hem of her skirt. Her footsteps when she reached the wooden porch were quick and purposeful, and Samantha found herself raptly watching the door when the woman barged in. She paused to survey the room, her mouth clamping tight in evident chagrin at not finding the passenger she'd come to collect. After a few more seconds, she turned on her boot heel and went outside to take a seat on the bench to wait, the high crown of her straw hat visible through the front window.

Samantha and Mildred traded looks, then giggles. The haughtiness of the woman had struck them as comical. "Now there's a woman whose husband has learned when it's wise to duck, I'll bet!" Mildred said.

Another hour went by, the coffee shop clearing of customers in the lull between the arrival and departure of the Katy but for a noisy family of six and two women at another table. Even the woman with the hat had disappeared in her buckboard. Samantha felt an emptiness fill her stomach. The seller wasn't coming. The farm had already sold. Her father would be devastated. After

another twenty minutes when the seller did not appear, she and
Mildred pondered what to do. They both agreed that the farm
had probably been sold or taken off the market and the owner did
not have the courtesy to let them know. "Nonetheless," Samantha said, "I can't leave here on only a guess that's what happened.
Daddy will expect me to make sure."

She left her seat at the table and consulted the stationmaster,
who had come in for a coffee. Did he know the location of the
Barrows farm? Absolutely, he said, and gave them directions.
With Mildred in tow, Samantha walked back to the hotel and
booked a ride to their destination with the cabbie of the same conveyance she'd arranged to take them to the ferry. They passed
fertile crop lands on the way, Samantha on the lookout for the
crossroads sign that would indicate the beginning of the Barrows
farm. Not long past it, she spotted a man in overalls and cloth cap
in a heated one-sided exchange with a mule hooked to a plow in
a field of new wheat.

"Stop here," she ordered the cabbie. "I'd like to speak to that
man."

The cabbie drew to the fence and Samantha stepped down.
The man in the field left his mule and plow and walked toward
her. He had a rather loping gait that suited his open, friendly face
despite his chagrin at the mule. "May I help you?" he called before he reached the fence.

"Good afternoon," Samantha called back. "Is this the Barrows
farm?"

"It is."

"Are you the owner?"

As the man drew nearer to the fence, he reached to remove his
cloth cap and his hand seemed to freeze on the bill. He stopped
in his tracks, and for a few seconds, he stood as still as a sculptor's
subject.

It's the hair, Samantha thought. They were all taken by the color of her hair.

"No," the man said, his response slow, his eyes thoughtful. "I'm the hired help."

"I had an appointment to meet the owner in town today to speak to him about buying his farm, but he didn't show up. Is the farm still for sale?"

The man reached the fence. "And your name, miss?"

"Samantha Gordon. I came on behalf of my father, Neal Gordon. He made arrangements by telegram to meet a representative of the Barrows farm at the depot coffee shop. Do you know anything about that?"

" 'Fraid not. I'm not told much." The man put his cap back on. "The farm, though, it's been sold. Went pretty fast."

Disappointed, Samantha said, "I figured as much when nobody showed up." She gazed out over the rows of healthy young wheat, straight as an army on parade. "I can understand why it sold so quickly. Well, thank you. I'll report to my father."

"You do that," the man said. "Good day to you."

"And to you," Samantha said, climbing back into the buggy.

Leon stood at the fence until the long stretch of road was quiet and empty. Not long ago, Millicent had pulled up to this very spot in the same mood as when she'd left—mad as a she-bear with a sore tooth. She rarely drove the buckboard, because the reins did not leave her hands free to hold a parasol, so she'd assumed that he would be the "Barrows representative" to meet Neal Gordon and bring him to the house, but Leon wanted no part in the sale of the farm. Fuming and fretting, covered from head to toe against the sun, Millicent had been the one to set off to collect the sender of the telegram come to buy her land.

"Damned man didn't show up," she'd barked.

"Well, then, it wadn't meant to be," he'd said.

And now Leon believed that was so. It wasn't meant for the father of the young woman just here to buy the Barrows farm. Leon still felt chills running through him. Jesus, Joseph, and Mary, at first sight of her, he'd thought he was looking at Millicent's long-lost daughter, then got ahold of himself. Fate wouldn't be so blackhearted, so downright mean, to bring her back to them in such a way, looking to buy unknowingly the farm where she was born and given away, but for a crazy moment there, seeing that hair…

Unbeknown to Millicent, not long after the twins were born, Leon had taken the ferry across the Red River and hitched a ride into Marietta, Oklahoma Territory, where Bridget Mahoney lived and worked for a Dr. Tolman. He got nothing from the midwife when he asked what had happened to the little girl. "You people have forfeited your right to know," she'd said, but Dr. Tolman had taken pity on him.

"I gave her to a ranching couple close to Fort Worth. She'll be all right," he'd said, and that was all Leon could weasel from him.

Leon had traveled to Fort Worth a few years after that and caught himself wondering if one of the little girls the age of Nathan he saw on the street could be his daughter, for he thought of her that way—as his own, as he would always believe that Nathan was his son. A child did not have to be of a man's flesh and blood to be counted as his own as long as he was part of his heart and soul. That was the connection that mattered.

Leon could guess exactly what had happened in the train depot coffee shop. Both women had gone expecting to meet a man. Neal Gordon's telegram had not said anything about sending his daughter, and Millicent had not wanted her name printed in the advertisement—"emblazoned for all the world to see," she'd said. No telling what sort of man might turn up if he thought her a widow eager to get rid of her husband's farm.

The shock of his first impressions of the girl had forced Leon to lie, a sin of which he was rarely guilty. Leon couldn't quite explain it to himself other than he could not see the farm going to a young woman with hair the color of what his daughter's might be—who, though her pretty face and figure were not cut along the same lines as Millicent's, could have been born from her womb. He turned to go back to his mule and plow. On second thought, he couldn't entirely discount fate's hand in the events of this afternoon. Fate was a strange customer. If old Mopey Dick, as Leon called his mule, hadn't gone into one of his blue moods and refused to budge, he would have been in the north pasture when that buggy went by.

Chapter Twenty-Five

The evening of April ninth, Neal Gordon dressed for his monthly Monday night poker game with no thought that it would begin the longest night of his life. He had planned to sleep like a well-nursed baby. His world had never looked brighter. The calf count was in, larger than anticipated, nearly all strong and healthy, and the fall calving season promised a bumper crop as well. Beef on the hoof was selling at top dollar. An order had come from the president of the Fort Worth Dressed Meat and Provision Company, for five hundred head, and another from the U.S. Army for two thousand, and more large drafts were coming. The grazing pastures had never looked thicker or greener. Watering tanks were running over, and the Trinity was flowing at full crest. Now if he could just nail down that farm for sale in Cooke County, his cup would runneth over.

The bomb that blasted his euphoria all to hell fell close to the end of the evening when the library was full of male good humor, tobacco smoke, and bourbon fumes. Seated at the card table were Neal's closest friends: W. A. Huffman, president of the Board of Trade; Jason Laird, president of the Fort Worth Union Stockyards and owner of the Texas Land and Cattle Bank; Buckley Paddock, editor and publisher of the *Fort Worth Gazette*; and Sloan Singleton.

Jason Laird, father of Barnard, said, "You're looking pretty pleased with yourself over there, Neal. You must have a good hand. Whatever happened to your infernal poker face?"

"Don't let that face fool you, Jason. He's probably got squat," Buckley said. "That pleased-as-punch look means he thinks he's got a land deal in Gainesville County sewed up."

"Explain, please," W.A. said.

Neal said, "You tell 'em, Sloan. I'm concentrating on my hand over here."

Sloan explained, to which Neal, studying his cards, spoke around the cigar between his teeth. "It's not a done deal until Samantha gets home and says it is. I had a little run-in with Liam Barrows, the owner of the farm, some years ago. With hope, he won't remember it or will want to sell his place so badly, he'll intentionally forget it. Either he or his sons, that is. I doubt Liam is still living."

"He isn't," Buckley said, throwing a few chips to the center of the table. "Neither are his sons, I reckon. It's the daughter selling the place, a woman by the name of Millicent Holloway."

Neal, about to contribute his own chips, paused with his hand over his stack. He sat back and slowly removed the cigar from his mouth. "Who did you say?"

Buckley, startled by the quiet, dead inflection of Neal's tone, repeated, "Millicent Holloway. At least, that's the person who sent the telegram and paid for the ad. I just assumed she was the owner of the place."

Sloan was sitting next to Neal. "The name resurrect a ghost, Neal? You look like you've seen one."

Neal felt a wheeze form in his chest. Before it could gather force, he took a hasty swallow of bourbon to discourage it. "Actually, yes, for a moment there, I sure did," he said, forcing a sickly grin. "Never mind. A story from long ago. Girl from my past by the same name. She's dead now."

"Then I can see how that would make your blood jump," Buckley said. He tapped the table with his finger. "Hit me."

Neal, the dealer, threw the publisher a card, aware that he was still in the corner of Sloan's worried eye, and he dared not make contact with it. The boy knew he could tap-dance around the truth if a tune called for it. The blood that had drained out of his head when he heard the name Millicent Holloway now returned. Dear God! He had sent Samantha straight to the farm of her birthplace and into the hands of her real parents. A surge of fear threatened to expel the contents of his stomach. Would they know each other by instinct—mother and daughter? He'd heard of that happening—parent and child recognizing a family connection through some intuitive sense. In their conversation, would one turn lead to another and then another and then…to the inevitable revelation? The horror of it brought sweat to his forehead.

Sloan touched his arm. "Neal? Are you all right? All of a sudden, you don't look well."

"I'm fine, Sloan. Really." With great effort, Neal directed a knowing smile to the older group at the table, men longer in experience with the ways of women than his younger protégé. They must not think him sick and leave his house too soon, leaving him the better part of the night to face alone. "I guess I just got struck in my breadbasket by a memory."

"Was she pretty, your Millicent?" Jason Laird asked.

The face and form of his daughter popped into Neal's mind. "Yes, very much so," he said and flipped a chip onto the table. "I'll raise you five."

It was midnight when the elite contingent of Fort Worth businessmen departed in the carriage that had brought them from town. All lived in imposing homes within a few blocks of one another. Sloan Singleton was the last to leave. He remained with

Neal on the porch to see the others off. "Neal, level with me," he said. "Are you feeling all right? Anything amiss with you besides the memory of an old girlfriend?"

Sloan was one of the few able to read him, not that Neal considered himself a complicated man. He just wasn't an open book. Things were basically either black or white with him, no areas of gray, no *if*s, *and*s, or *but*s. He and Sloan were no longer mentor and pupil. The boy had come into his own, and they had become, if not like father and son, like close uncle and nephew, only on an equal footing. Just the strong stance of him next to Neal, the moonlight pouring over Sloan's taller height and broad shoulders, drove home that point.

"Serious changes might be coming," Neal said, "and I'm worried how I'll handle 'em. I'm not one for compromise. I'll know more tomorrow, and that's all I care to say at the moment."

Sloan nodded in acceptance but clear dissatisfaction with his answer. They both had lines that required an invitation to cross. "And Samantha. Is she okay?"

A stomach muscle kicked. "As far as I know. You got a reason to think otherwise?"

Sloan shuffled a foot, as if thinking it was not his place to say. "She came by the house the other day to use the telephone, and...teared up about something, Neal. It was just a few trickles, but I was concerned. Samantha's not one to cry."

"No, she's not," Neal said, alarmed. "Did she give a reason?"

"Only that she had a lot of things on her mind...sad things, melancholy things, she said."

"Such as?"

"She didn't say, and I couldn't get anything more out of her. We don't talk like we used to. Samantha doesn't confide in me anymore."

Neal turned away to look up at the stars. Of course not, you

blockhead! She's in love with you, and you're in love with a pow-
der puff! "Well, you're a very busy man, Sloan. You've got a big
ranch to run, duties and responsibilities and…other interests besides."

"I'm never too busy to be available for Samantha if she needs
me, Neal. She can come to me anytime with anything. Remind
Samantha of that when she gets home, will you? I feel she's forgotten. I…care for her, you know. Always have, always will."

"I don't doubt it. Neither does she," Neal said, hearing regret
in Sloan's voice and the wish that it could be more, but it wasn't.
"You and Samantha have always been like devoted siblings, Sloan.
Speaking as her father and…feeling about you the way I do, I'd
hoped that…well, it could have gone deeper between you two."

Sloan pulled his hat brim lower, a prelude to departure. His
horse was tethered to the porch railing. The Thoroughbred gave
a soft snort. It was time for stable and bin. "Me, too, but it looks
like our feelings for each other didn't work out that way. Now, if
I can be assured I'm not leaving an old man to expire in his chair
tonight, I'll say good night."

"Be assured," Neal said. "Good night, son."

He'd have liked the boy's company longer but it was late
enough already, and Sloan was rotating a portion of his herd
to another pasture tomorrow and would be up before dawn.
Neal contemplated not going to bed at all. It was only six hours
until daylight, and his feet would hit the floor an hour before
that. What was the point of lying sleepless in bed imagining the
worst—that tomorrow afternoon when Samantha stepped from
the train, she'd look at him in a new light, for he intended to be
at the station with Estelle to meet her. She would be sensitive and
tender, as was her way, but she would be firm and fair, as he'd
raised her. *Mother and Daddy, you need to know that I met my real
parents at the Barrows farm. It all happened by chance…*

Where it would go from there, only God knew. What Neal knew was that he could not share his daughter with another set of parents and have things stay the same between them. It simply wasn't in his makeup. Whatever he gave heart and soul to must belong to him alone. One could not serve two masters. Loyalties could not be split. He became aware of this trait…this way of feeling…when he was six years old. He found an abandoned dog by the side of the road, brought it to the ranch, nurtured it to health and loved it, but the dog took up with the son of the foreman and divided his devotion. "Take him. He's yours," he said to the boy, and never so much as patted the dog's head again. It had been that way ever since. A terrible failing to have, but there it was. Estelle knew of it and accepted it.

That was not to say he wouldn't fight until his heart gave out to hold on to what was his, but what would he do if Samantha should choose to divide her affections? That would be the killing point with him. He could not imagine—it was unfathomable, unthinkable—that he would say to the people who, for one reason or the other, had given her up, *Take her. She's yours.* And, oh, my God, what would that do to Estelle?

He remained on the porch until the clip-clop of Sloan's Thoroughbred faded away. What had prompted Samantha to cry in the hallway of the Triple S? Neal had seen her cry only a few times in her life, none after childhood. She'd cried daintily, quietly, keeping her tears private, her pride and valiant restraint crushing his heart, elevating his respect for her. Estelle, now, she cried loudly, her face like the side of a mountain cracking open, all brown grooves and coursing rain.

Neal went back inside, a memory following, threatening to explode into tears. Samantha was five years old. Estelle was sick, in the feverish, infectious throes of influenza. Their old housekeeper, Mildred's mother, had fingers thick and rough as hemp ropes, fine for kneading dough and pounding steaks, but none too gentle when it came to combing and braiding a little girl's hair. Neal had come upon Mrs. Swift making the attempt and ordered, "Stop that!" when his daughter turned to him, too stoic to utter a sound but with her large gray eyes filled with tears. To this very moment, he remembered the wave of tenderness that had swept over him and a respect for her bravery that had left him weak. He had ordered Mrs. Swift back to the kitchen and taken over the job of making order out of the reddish-gold chaos of his little girl's hair. He'd set her on a footstool between his knees, a sprite on a lily pad in the shadow of a mountain. "You won't pull it, will you, Daddy?" Samantha had said, and he'd answered, "I would rather die than cause my little daughter pain."

And so he would.

His eyes felt gritty as he began to clear the library of the wreckage left after his Monday night poker party, a surprise for Silbia in the morning. He opened windows to let out the smoke and dumped trays of moist cigar tips and ashes into a bin. He cleared the table of leftover food and wiped it down after carrying plates and glasses into the kitchen and setting them in a pan of soapy water for tomorrow's washing, swept the floor, and put the card-playing paraphernalia away. The clock struck three as Neal climbed the stairs to his room with the thought of undressing and drawing a tub of hot water. He did neither. He stepped out onto his balcony, pulled a chair to the railing on which he propped his booted feet, lit a cigar, and spent the rest of the night looking at the stars.

Chapter Twenty-Six

The cabbie who'd agreed to drive them to the dock showed up as scheduled and delivered them to the ferry on time the next morning. "We're going to cross the river on *that*?" Mildred said, pointing at the crude wooden structure floating on water the color of a rusted nail. It was little more than a huge raft anchored by thick, heavy ropes to trees on each side of the Red River, presumably to assure a safe crossing and keep it from floating downstream. The only access to its deck was a makeshift pathway of wooden planks barely visible in the red mud. Samantha looked down in dismay at her handmade fawn boots stitched with flowers. Never mind, she thought. Her boots were worth the sacrifice and any discomfort if the ferry brought her nearer to learning the truth she'd come to find.

After an interminable wait while Samantha worried they'd not return in time to catch the two o'clock train, passengers were permitted to board. She and Mildred found standing space where they could among commercial cargo, luggage, crates of squawking fowl, and a team of mules and wagon. The "captain" was a tall, burly man with a long pole for a helm by which he directed the course of his ship. Not trusting the saggy rope railings to prevent a lurch overboard, the women stood as close to the center of the barge as they could among other passengers with the same concern.

"Are you eventually going to tell me why we're risking life and limb to see this doctor?" Mildred shouted over the wind when they were afloat.

"No," Samantha said.

"Does he know you're coming?"

"No."

"Do you know where he lives in Marietta?"

"No." The return address on Dr. Tolman's letter had listed only the number of a mailbox.

Mildred blew out her cheeks. "Then how you going to find him?"

"I've got a plan," Samantha said.

It was simple. Their cabbie in Gainesville had said there would be a number of his kind waiting on the other side of the river to transport passengers the five miles into Marietta. That worry satisfied, Samantha asked if he knew the name of a hotel in town. The Wayfarer Inn, he'd said. There was only one. A restaurant was next door. Splendid, Samantha had thought. She would deposit Mildred safe and sound in the lobby with access to a menu while she paid a visit to the doctor's office. The hotel manager would give her the address. In a small town like Marietta, he would know it.

Disembarking by a wooden pathway like the one on the other side, Samantha and Mildred climbed a flight of rickety wooden stairs that led to a large clearing that served as a waiting area for the ferry. Here people milled about or sat on benches, and cabbies were lined up with their teams and vehicles to collect fares. The women climbed aboard one and they were off to Marietta.

The manager of the Wayfarer Inn said that yes, Samantha's companion could wait in the lobby, and yes, he knew where Dr. Tolman lived—"that is, while he was alive," he said.

Incredulous, Samantha said, "I beg your pardon?"

"Our good doctor died a few weeks ago."

Sick with shock and disappointment, Samantha collapsed into a chair beside Mildred. The housekeeper prodded gently. "You going to tell me what this is all about? Maybe I can help."

Numbly, Samantha said, "Dr. Tolman is the doctor who placed me with my adoptive parents. I assume he also delivered me. He was... my only link to... my birth."

"Oh," Mildred said. Her face remained impassive, but a world of understanding was in her response.

Samantha glanced at her. "You've... never heard anything about how I came to be adopted, have you, Mildred?"

"No, Miss Sam, I never have. Now I understand why you made me swear to say nothing to your folks about this trip. It would kill them if they knew what you were about, but don't feel this is wronging them. Your curiosity is natural. I had plenty of it when I was in captivity. Even if my mama hadn't told me, I would have known in my soul I didn't belong where I was born."

"It's not that, Mildred. I feel I'm where I belong and was meant to be. I don't want to be anywhere else or with any other family. I'm not even sure why I'm curious about the situation of my birth. Before Dr. Tolman's letter came, I wouldn't have given it thought."

"What letter?"

Samantha sighed. "It doesn't matter. I've come to a dead end."

"Maybe not," the housekeeper said.

Samantha turned to her in surprise. "What do you mean?"

"There might still be somebody at the doctor's office who was around at the time you were born who would know something, maybe a nurse. A midwife? Since we're here, don't you think it's worth a shot to find out?"

Samantha hopped up. "Mildred, you're a genius." She approached the registration counter again. Fifteen minutes later, encouraged by the information the manager had given her, she left Mildred in the hotel lobby with their portmanteaus and walked the few blocks to Dr. Tolman's infirmary. His daughter had come in from Oklahoma City to get his house ready to sell and to clean out his office of his personal belongings before his replacement arrived. Samantha found the rustic, low-roofed log building easily enough. It sat next to a house of similar design posted with a FOR SALE sign in the front yard—Dr. Tolman's residence, Samantha presumed. Before the infirmary a bracketed physician's shingle with a black ribbon streaming from a finial swung in the brisk wind.

The small waiting room was empty except for a woman behind a counter industriously sweeping the floor with a large broom. She wore her hair bound in a kerchief, her dress sleeves rolled, and a voluminous apron around her stout, middle-aged figure. She glanced up at Samantha's entrance with the friendly but quizzical look reserved for strangers. Samantha hesitated. Dr. Tolman's daughter, she'd guess. Where did she begin to explain why she'd come? "Good afternoon, madam. I'm Samantha Gordon."

"Good for you," the woman said, an impish twinkle in her eyes. "I am Eleanor Brewster."

"Dr. Tolman's daughter?"

"I plead the Fifth until I know who's asking and why."

Put off a little, but thinking she liked the woman, Samantha said, "I have reason to believe your late father may have delivered me. I was given up for adoption, and I know that Dr. Tolman is responsible for placing me with the good people who became my parents."

Eleanor Brewster set the broom aside and wiped her hands on her apron. "Is that so? Well, aren't you the sweet one to come by and say so. I've been receiving such accolades of Dad's work ever since the funeral." She opened the gate to the reception area. "Come on in and sit a spell. I've got some coffee brewing."

A cup of coffee later, after explaining the reason for her visit, Samantha learned that Eleanor Brewster couldn't help her. She had grown up in Oklahoma City and was twelve years old when Samantha was born. Her father had come alone to the small outpost of Marietta in the Indian Territory of Oklahoma in 1878 to render his medical services to the Chickasaw Nation. Eleanor Brewster had no recollection of her father's mention of an infant for whom he'd arranged an adoption. "But then," she said, "I wouldn't have remembered if he had. There were so many stories of Dad finding homes for the orphaned and abandoned." His patients' records were still in his office, Eleanor said. They could look through them to see what they could find.

Samantha consulted her lapel watch. There was enough time if she hurried, she said. She had to get the ferry back to Gainesville in time to catch the two o'clock train. With an eye on the clock, together they scoured the records of names and details of girls born in late March 1880. They discovered four, but Eleanor could account for each of them. One had died and three still lived in the county. "Now, here's a name I recognize," she said, pointing to the signature of Bridget Mahoney that appeared in the birth records of the dates in question. "Bridget was Dad's midwife. Wherever Dad went, she went. She was indispensable to him. If Dad delivered you, she would have been there."

Samantha's heart lifted, but Eleanor's face fell. "Unfortunately," she said, "Bridget moved to San Francisco with her husband during the Gold Rush around 1889."

"Do you know where I can write to her?" Samantha asked.

"I'm afraid I don't, but leave me an address, and if I come across it, I'll mail it to you."

It was time to go. Hastily, out of courtesy for Eleanor's efforts but certain it was a lost cause, Samantha wrote down her mother's address in Fort Worth. The women hugged in saying good-bye. "Honey lamb," the older woman said, "if I may offer a piece of advice. If you're happy where you are, there are no greener pastures."

"I agree," Samantha said. She felt a strange peace and relief, as if she'd closed a book on a conclusive and satisfying ending. She'd done all she could do. She could go home now. There was no more to the story.

"Neal, for goodness' sakes! You're going to wear out the soles of your boots if you don't stop pacing. You've been at it now ever since we got here," Estelle said, speaking from a bench on the platform of the train depot. "I'm usually the worry wart."

Neal made no comment and peered beyond the station lights in the dark direction the train would arrive from Gainesville. The Katy was due any minute—finally! Samantha's face would tell the full story. The minute she set foot on the deboarding steps and her gaze lit upon him, Neal would know if he was to be consigned to heaven or hell. He had wrestled with the decision of whether to prepare Estelle for the darkest day of her life, but he chose to wait. He'd obeyed a personal rule that many times had served him well: Never show your hand until the other fellow lays down his cards. Sometimes you could get away with a bluff, but this time Neal doubted he'd be so lucky.

The train rushed into the station, whistle blowing and steam rolling, and Estelle, searching the compartment windows, joined Neal with the others awaiting the opening of the doors. Neal tasted something vile rising from the nether regions of his stomach. "There they are!" Estelle cried, spotting the golden roll of Samantha's hair under the brim of her spring hat. Samantha caught Estelle's wave and returned it through the glass, and

Neal's heart fell. Her face did indeed express it all. Despair, heart-sickness, disappointment written all over it. Neal waited until Estelle had embraced and released her, Samantha's glance at him over her shoulder flashing dismay.

"Hello, daughter," he said quietly when it was his turn, hardly able to speak for the grief swelling in his throat.

Samantha said in a voice mournful as a funeral dirge, "I'm sorry, Daddy, but the farm was sold by the time we got there."

Neal opened his mouth, but no sound came.

"Now, Neal, keep your temper," Estelle said, patting his shoulder. "It's not Samantha's fault that somebody else bought the place."

"The seller didn't even show up," Samantha said, "but I made sure the property had been sold. I spoke to a field hand who works for the Barrows, and he confirmed it."

Neal continued to stare speechless at Samantha, mired in an undertow of disbelief. Finally, he spoke. "You...never met the owner?"

"Didn't have the decency to even meet us," Mildred put in flatly.

"I'm sorry, Daddy," Samantha said again. "I can see how disappointed you are."

"You have no idea," Neal said huskily and drew her into a rough embrace.

Nathan

Chapter Twenty-Seven

In his office, Trevor Waverling stared at the notice in the week-old classified section of the *Dallas Herald*. Good Lord, it couldn't be. The farm advertised for sale was the Barrows place and Millicent was the seller. "What's your biggest dream?" he'd asked Nathan during one of their getting-to-know-each-other drives to the plant. Without hesitation, his son had answered, "Someday to buy my mother's farm." Trevor lifted his gaze from the paper. Damn the woman! What other ways remained for Millicent Holloway to break her son's heart?

He rotated his chair toward the window where he could see his personal swath of the Trinity River reflected in the April sun. The paper was dated April second—a day after April Fool's Day. No practical joke here. Trevor wished it were. Should he let the boy see it? Each week, to get a view of what was out there, Trevor pored over the classified ads from landowners wishing to lease their property for oil exploration. He'd jot down the details in the records he was compiling, keep an eye out for what leases disappeared after a few weeks and which ones stayed in the FOR SALE column. The information gave him an idea of the location of the most intense oil interest. Mainly, the advertisements were submitted by farmers from the Oklahoma Territory hoping to get rich because of the oil boom going on there, but petroleum speculators were now taking a look at land in Montague and Gainesville

Counties. Had the Barrows farm already been snapped up or leased to drill for oil and gas? Which offer would likely appeal to Millicent? She'd get more money up front if she sold it as a farm, but she might choose to lease her acreage for far less with the hope of bigger money if petroleum was found. Trevor had a feeling that she'd go for the bird in hand.

May Millicent Holloway burn in hell for what she'd done to Nathan! The boy had told him of her plans to sell the farm in order to grease her other son's start in life (Trevor's word, not Nathan's) and to finance her daughter's entry into society when they moved into Gainesville. *Society?* In Gainesville, Texas, for God's sake! Nathan didn't know she'd put up her place for sale the minute he stepped foot out the door. Well, his mother's loss was his father's gain.

Trevor swiveled back to his desk and reflected on the rarity of the boy who had slipped quietly with his dog into their lives. There was no noise about Nathan. You could almost forget he was there until he wasn't, and then the void shouted, as when he'd gone back to the farm for a few days. His daughter had been bereft.

Humpty Dumpty had a great fall, and all the king's horses and all the king's men couldn't put Humpty together again, she'd recited over and over, running despairingly about the house with her hands pressed to her head. Trevor had tried to soothe her. *It's all right, honey*, he'd said at least a hundred times. *Nathan will be back.*

But off she would go wailing again. *Humpty Dumpty had a great fall, and all the king's horses and all the king's men couldn't put Humpty together again* ... The rhyme ran through Trevor's head all through the days the boy was gone, and his heart wrung for his daughter. She thought of her father as the king. She believed him all-powerful. What would happen to Rebecca if Nathan remained at the farm and the king couldn't put Humpty Dumpty together again?

Trevor felt he should have been jealous of his mother's grow-ing affection for Nathan, but he wasn't. He was overjoyed. Things were working out better than he could have hoped. She had her grandson—a future heir—and his father was building a relationship with him. Trevor Waverling didn't have to worry about proving his innocence in his brother's death to her any longer. Mavis Waverling would never sell the company now. But aside from that, it was good to see her old, pretty face relaxed, at peace, contented now in the evenings. Before Nathan, he rarely saw her smile, and he hadn't heard her laughter in years.

Before Nathan. Trevor identified the former period in their lives in those terms. Before Nathan, he met people for supper or went to the gym or to his club most evenings following work, but after Nathan, he began going home with the boy to show his mother he was making an effort. Now they were quite a family group in the parlor after supper—he and his mother and son and daughter, the dog and cat. Another maid had been hired to give Lenora a hand with the extra mouth to feed—two, counting the German shepherd—and so Lenora was happier, too.

The boy was turning out to be an impressively quick learner. Trevor had put him under the wing of Jamie Foster, his foreman, who reported, "Your kid don't need to be told twice 'bout nothin'." Coming from taciturn Jamie, that statement spoke vol-umes and put the stamp of approval on him. Nathan had yet to be assigned a specific job. It was more important in these early days for him to become acquainted with the factory's workings and in-frastructure as well as the business transactions of the company. Surface grinders and auger drill bits, metal-cutting machinery, and other engineering tools were miles beyond the farm imple-ments of Nathan's experience, and the boy was finding there was a lot more to a company's books than a farmer's expense ledger.

To explain Nathan's heretofore unknown existence when introducing him, Trevor had come around to a clap on the boy's shoulder and a quote from the parable of the Prodigal Son. "This is my son who was once lost but now is found," he'd say and leave it at that. Brows were raised, glances exchanged, but Trevor's friends, colleagues, and employees knew his reputation for consorting with women and took Nathan as an *oh-oh* that happened. Which was exactly what he was. All shook hands and welcomed him graciously, if some could not resist a few winks at Trevor behind the boy's back, and some treated him with exaggerated courtesy like the kind shown a man missing a limb one took pains not to notice.

Within a week of their acquaintance, Trevor had decided upon the eventual right position for Nathan. The boy would chafe at working full-time in a factory. He'd fare worse learning the ropes of Waverling Tools behind a desk. The boy belonged on the land under the open skies. He'd make of Nathan a representative of the company to seek out and execute oil leases when the time came to drill its own wells. *Landmen*, they were called. There was no other formal name for them. The profession was as new as the petroleum industry and required no special education other than experience, but acquiring that took some time and doing. It was the geologist's task to find the right conditions where oil and gas could be found, but it was the landman's job to negotiate leasing terms for the mineral rights from the property owner. Along with that skill, which called mainly for handling people well, the landman had to know how to comprehend and write contracts and research public and private records to prove title and ownership status. Those sorts of things Nathan could learn, and Trevor had no doubt of the boy's ability to handle people. He did it simply— by being himself.

Trevor leaned back in his chair, considering. Should he tell Nathan about the ad? Was it better for him to learn the truth now rather than later? The news, coupled with the other sins of his mother against him, would wound him even more deeply, not that he'd show or express it. Other boys might stomp about and curse their mother, but not Nathan. Millicent, for better or worse, was the woman who had given him birth. Nathan would put his respect for that above his rage.

Now was the time, not later, Trevor decided. He'd promised Nathan that he'd put all his cards on the table when dealing with him. *Lie to me one time or keep one card up your sleeve, and I'm gone*, Nathan had said. *Zak and I will hit the road to California.*

At the time of the threat, the warning had no more impact than the bounce of a paper ball off his chest, but the last thirteen days had changed things, and now the thought of the boy leaving had the force of a well-landed right hook to his solar plexus. Trevor pulled a cord that rang a bell in his secretary's office. When she arrived, he said, "Jeanne, find Nathan and send him to me. He left before I did this morning, so he must be in the plant."

"Yes sir, he's here. Last I saw him, he was with Jamie when I took over the bill of lading for the latest shipment to England."

Trevor's eyebrows rose. Jeanne, hand-carry a B/L to his plant foreman when ordinarily she'd expect Jamie to pick it up at her desk? She fetched and carried for no man but her boss, she was pleased to say. But Trevor knew what was behind her sudden initiative. His secretary, young and single, had an eye for Nathan, but it would do her no good. His grandmother had other plans for the boss's son in the romance department. When Jeanne left, Agatha Beardsley, his longtime receptionist who had also warmed to Nathan, poked her head in. "You have two men here to see you, Mr. Waverling."

"Who?"

"The geologist, Todd Baker, and"—Miss Beardsley consulted her notepad—"a Daniel Lane. He says he's an ironmonger who presently works for a smithy in Fort Worth. He's come in answer to our want ad."

"Give them both some coffee and tell them to wait. I need to see Nathan."

Nathan appeared five minutes later, and Trevor thought as he walked in that he'd never seen a member of his gender so ill at ease in a business suit but so comfortable in his own skin. The observation confirmed his decision to put him in the field rather than behind a desk.

"You called for me?" Nathan asked.

Trevor didn't know how he avoided it, but once he'd disabused Nathan from calling him Mr. Waverling, the boy had never addressed him by any other name, paternal or otherwise, nor asked him what he wished to be called. He figured time would decide his son's handle for him. "You need to see this," Trevor said, pushing the classified section of the *Dallas Herald* across his desk with a finger pointed at the advertisement. "Is that the farm I think it is?"

Nathan read without comment. Only a tightening of his jaw gave away his inner reaction. "I see she wasted no time," he said finally.

"I'm sorry, Nathan."

"Me, too," Nathan said. "Anything else?"

Trevor wanted to say something to offer sympathy, but Nathan had shut him out. The boy's self-containment threw up a wall that made it impossible to comfort him. Further commiseration would be intrusive. Trevor felt a twitch of resentment, then recognized the feeling as a father's frustration with his inability to help his son. "Yes, there is," he said. "Step into the reception room and send Todd to me, will you?"

"All right."

Trevor swiveled back to the window, somewhat let down but buoyed, too. Another nail in Millicent's coffin. Another road closed to Gainesville, Texas. That was good.

Chapter Twenty-Eight

There's a good lad, Zak! There's a good lad!" Benjy sang out as the German shepherd bounded toward him to return a stick in his mouth the Irishman had thrown. It was noon, playtime for Zak while the plant workers brought out the contents of their metal "carryalls" to eat under the trees and enjoy the dog's romp in the fresh air and sun of the cool April day. Nathan was among them. Lenora always sent him off with a full lunch tin. Whether he partook of its thick sandwiches or not depended on whether Trevor invited him to join him for a luncheon business meeting. The generous slices of meat and bread did not go to waste. Benjy made thorough work of them along with his own fare, which he made for himself in the small kitchen of his apartment above the Waverlings' carriage house. Nathan had never seen anyone enjoy food as much as Benjy. The calories bypassed his thin arms and legs and long, skinny feet and headed straight to his expansive stomach that had the appearance of a perfectly round ball under his snug waistcoat. His inordinate relish for food—gluttony, Benjy didn't mind calling it—came from the tales he'd heard of family members starving to death during the potato famine in Ireland. "The power of the imagination is great, me boy," he'd say to Nathan. "Me mind conjures up pictures of the poor souls who wasted away, and me feels it's me duty to eat for them."

Played out, both dog and Irishman dropped next to Nathan by the cloth he'd spread on the new grass for their meal. The chance to expend his energy was a treat for Zak, which he enjoyed three days a week when he accompanied Nathan and Trevor in the carriage to work and spent the day with his master in the plant and office. On the other days, the German shepherd had to stay home, restricted to the small fenced backyard of the town house when let out of doors. Those days, because Trevor sometimes required the use of the carriage beyond normal working hours, Nathan rode his horse to the plant. When he'd first come to live in the town house, he'd wondered about transportation. Was he to ride in the carriage with his father to Waverling Tools each day? Nathan thought that might be a strain for both of them. Apparently, Trevor Waverling had thought so, too. The day after Nathan returned to Dallas from the farm, his father had taken him to a horse auction.

"Pick your choice, and I'll make a bid," he'd said. "You'll need your own mount while you're here."

While you're here. Did that mean he was on probation? Well, so was Trevor Waverling, for that matter, Nathan decided. Not so his sister and grandmother. They passed muster in every way. He would miss them if he had to leave, as he missed his whole family back in Gainesville, but so far he'd not felt the urge to sling his knapsack over his shoulder and hit the road to California with Zak if things soured. The only drawback was Zak's confinement, but his dog seemed happy enough to stay behind with the adoring attention of Rebecca and the dubious companionship of Scat, and nobody, not even Lenora, seemed to mind the hairs he shed, a relief to Nathan. They had been a constant complaint of his mother's. Nathan didn't have to worry that the long fibers of his dog's coat on the carriage leather might end up on his father's dark suits, either. Nathan trained him to occupy only one corner of the seat, and Benjy took care to wipe the spot clean on the days Zak rode with them to work.

"You've got yourself a mannerly mutt there, Nathan," his father said, commenting on Zak's seemingly good sense to know not to shake himself in the coach.

As Nathan became acquainted with the pattern of Trevor Waverling's daily schedule (every Wednesday after work, for instance, he took off for his gym), he realized his father had not bought the horse to avoid close contact with him in the coach but to give him the freedom to come and go without having to depend on him for transportation. Trevor actually tried to arrange his meetings and activities to give them a chance to ride together so they could talk business.

Nathan had to admit that in the three weeks he'd lived under his father's roof—his *grandmother's* roof—there was not much about his new life that he did not enjoy other than his natural reservation about becoming too trusting of it. He was especially enjoying his budding friendship with Benjy, whose residence in the carriage house apartment gave them opportunities to spend time together.

"How did you and my father meet?" he asked the Irishman one day.

"Well, now, me lad, therein lies a story."

"I'm interested in hearing it," Nathan said.

August twelfth, 1890, it was, Benjy said. He, an immigrant, had hopped a train from New York down to Texas without benefit of a ticket. New York City was dirty, crowded, polluted, and unkind to Irish Catholics. He wanted to live where there was space and clean air and a bloke could get a good start in life without people looking down their noses at him, and Texas was the place, so he'd heard. He didn't know to what city the train was headed. He just knew that when it got to Texas, he'd jump off at a stop that looked like it offered good job possibilities. That spot happened to be thirty yards from the front door of Waverling Tools, only he didn't have time to notice because he was jumped by two railroad peelers twice his size wielding billy clubs. He fought back but he was overpowered, and he figured he'd be meeting his mam and da in the great hereafter if the knacking went on much longer. Then all of a sudden the blighters were off him, and he was looking up through a film of blood and snot and tears into the face of Trevor Waverling. The man offered a hand. *Help you up?* he said and pulled him to his feet.

"I could hardly stand, and me head rung like a bell, and for a few seconds I thought I had died and gone someplace where men were clean-shaven and dressed in nice suits like Mr. Waverling was wearing," Benjy told Nathan. "But no, he was real and I was alive, and the peelers were out cold. 'Better get out of here before they come to,' he says to me, and I look around as if a place might exist where I could disappear. That's when Mr. Waverling told me to follow him, and I've been doing it ever since—wherever he wants to go."

"Quite a story," Nathan had said. "I guess the peelers met his boxer's fists."

"Aye. The man is a formidable fighter. You should see him in the ring."

"Does he still fight?"

"Not in competitions anymore, but that don't mean his hobnails are not in good order. I owe the man me life, me livelihood, me home, and…me family, Nathan. I'd do anything for your da and his mam and his little *inion*. Have not a doubt about that."

Nathan didn't. Benjy's loyalty to Trevor Waverling was rock solid. The Irishman had filled in one picture for Nathan, but it wasn't likely he'd answer the question he most wanted to ask. Did Benjy know how, where, and why Jordan Waverling had died, and did he believe that his father had a hand in his death?

Nathan bit into his sandwich and, with his usual amusement, observed Benjy carefully remove the ham from his two slices of bread, lay it on the tinfoil wrapper, and place the bread, lettuce, cheese, and pickles in a row beside it. Next he set out in order a boiled egg, an apple, and a cookie.

"Nay, lad, this is not for you," the coachman said to Zak, whose nose was sniffing closer to the ceremonial layout. "Now, don't bother me." He pushed the dog away and began to eat, first the ham and lettuce, then the bread; afterward, the pickles and boiled egg, followed by the apple and cheese, with the cookie as the finish to the meal. "Sandwiches go farther if you take them apart and eat the fillings separately as *courses*," Benjy maintained. "They stretch further that way than if you eat them as a *package*."

"I guess that works if your stomach doesn't mind waiting," Nathan said.

A tall, well-muscled man with a dashing air about him approached carrying a lunch pail. Nathan recognized him as the ironmonger his father had recently hired. He usually ate his sandwich while fiddling at his drafting table. No one knew much about him except that he was a bachelor and a wizard with metals. The man kept to himself and did not socialize, so Nathan had heard, much to the chagrin of the secretary when she wasn't flirting with him. "Mind sharing your spot?" the newcomer said.

"Not at all," Nathan said, moving over to give the man room in the shade of the oak tree. He held out his hand. "We've only met once, Daniel. In case you don't remember, I'm Nathan Holloway."

"Oh, I remember." The newcomer shook his hand. "Holloway? I thought you were the boss's son?"

"I am. I go by my stepfather's name."

Daniel Lane nodded. "I had one of those, but I wasn't too keen to hold on to his name. I shed it quick as I shed him. I go by my mother's, not that it was much better to be proud of."

"You know Benjy?" Nathan said. The man was remarkably handsome, but there was a hard bitterness about him. Nathan put him roughly in his late twenties.

"The boss's driver," Daniel clarified Benjy's place in the hierarchy. "Not had the pleasure. How'd do."

"How'd do," Benjy said. "Where do ye hail from?"

"Everywhere, but Fort Worth most recently. I quit my job as a smithy's helper over there. Atmosphere got a little…stifling."

Nathan bit into his apple. "How do you find the atmosphere here?"

"More to my liking. It's nice to be appreciated and paid what I deserve, not to mention respected."

"Sounds like ye got an ax to grind, if ye'll forgive the observation and the pun," Benjy said.

A grin at Benjy's humor improved the resentful slope of Daniel's mouth. "You could say that. I just need time and a little luck to get my own back."

"And what would your own be, if you don't mind my asking," Nathan said.

"I don't, since I brought up the subject," Daniel replied. "A woman. My own is a woman taken away from me because her brother didn't think I was good enough to be in her company. I intend to change his opinion about that."

"Well, good luck to you," Nathan said, packing away tinfoil and apple cores. "Let's hope she'll be waiting should you succeed."

"Oh, she'll be waiting," Daniel said.

"How can ye be so sure?" Benjy asked.

"Because nobody else will have her," Daniel answered. "Well, there's the gong. I better get back to work. I got a project I'm working on that I hope will impress the boss. Nice meeting you gents. See you around."

As Daniel walked away, Benjy mused, "For somebody known for hardly saying a word to anybody, me thinks that man talks too much."

Chapter Twenty-Nine

After two weeks, the advertisement of the farm for sale near Gainesville no longer appeared in the *Dallas Herald*. The last of April, Nathan received a letter from Leon telling him that Millicent had put the farm on the market right after he left and that it had sold almost immediately. They would be moving to Gainesville during May and be settled in when Randolph graduated from high school in June. Leon knew the news would be as heartbreaking for Nathan as it was for him. He had no idea what he would do as an idle city dweller. The new owner would take possession of the farm at the end of June, but not entirely to grow wheat, a fact that wasn't known until after Millicent had signed the contract.

Here he had to pause, Leon said, to give his mother just due. Early on, Millicent had been approached by a landman who wanted to lease a number of acres to drill for petroleum, but thank God his mutton-headed wife had refused. She didn't want her acres destroyed like other cropland in the Oklahoma Territory that had been leased to oil companies. She owed that to her folks and to her husband and to Nathan. Yes, Nathan, she included you, Leon wrote. Along came Mr. Burton (the new owner) and offered her twice the asking price if she included the mineral rights. Leon had insisted that Millicent keep them, but the offer was too tempting and his mother was eager to sell, especially after the man sweet-talked her into believing that he was a farmer first and foremost. It was only after she'd signed the sale papers that they learned he was a representative of John D. Rockefeller's Standard Oil Company. Part of the agreement, Leon went on, was that the Holloways would remain on the homestead until the end of June so they could bring in a final harvest and have time to sell off their equipment. Millicent had already bought them a place in Gainesville, the big, white-columned, two-story house she'd always admired. Leon didn't doubt that her decision to sell the farm was made when the owner of the house—a prominent lawyer—died and his home came on the market. Nathan was not to worry about Daisy's fate. She'd have a good home with their neighbor, who had agreed to buy her. Would Nathan be coming to Randolph's high school graduation the end of June? His brother had been named valedictorian of his class.

Nathan, sitting in a rocker on the front porch of his grandmother's town house, slowly folded the letter and tightly squeezed shut his eyes to hold in his sorrow. Recently, he had gone with Trevor to check out an oil drilling site on a cotton farm located near Nacogdoches in East Texas. The independent oil driller had bought his rig and drilling equipment from Waverling Tools. They arrived just in time to hear a noise that sounded like an oncoming freight train and to witness men hurriedly scatter from the vicinity of the latticework derrick. Within minutes, a horrific explosion shook the earth, and then, bug-eyed, their hands over their ears to save their hearing, they had watched in awe as an eruption of a liquid black as tar shot out of the top of the derrick a hundred feet into the air and spewed in all directions. The crew, having barely escaped the blast with their lives, danced and hollered and congratulated themselves on "bringing in a gusher." Trevor had looked at the escape of free-flowing oil and said, *Before I get fully into the business, I've got to come up with a cap to prevent this kind of blowout. A damned shame to waste that much oil before the hole is plugged.*

Nathan had stood back from the celebration. He had looked at the rows of healthy, stalwart cotton plants being drowned under hundreds of barrels of oil and felt sick to his stomach. While the men were dancing under the rain of "black gold," his heart had sunk at the fruits of the farmer's labor ground under by roads and draft animals and freight wagon wheels, the soil contaminated by the seepage from oil tanks and cement and mud-mixing troughs and the trash of cast-off equipment left to rust where it was tossed, the air polluted by flares from steel pipes erected to burn off smelly waste gas. The offal of oil production, Nathan had termed the detritus right then and there.

The same sickness curled his insides now as he imagined the golden acres of the Barrows farm laid to waste by a river of black crude like he'd observed flooding the fields that day, and he couldn't bear to think of the desecration of the underground spring and destruction to livestock, wildlife, and woods if an oil rig caught fire. A drilling site required two acres. Even if oil wasn't discovered, those two acres would be damaged beyond reclaim for at least a generation, if not forever.

His grandmother's two-wheeled trap came into view from up the street. Mavis had gone with Rebecca to a birthday party given for one of her granddaughter's friends, if Rebecca could be said to have friends. They waved gaily at Nathan in his favorite reading spot on Saturday afternoons, Scat and Zak lying on the porch floor beside him. Trevor was at his gym. In the one month Nathan had lived in the house, his father had never asked him to accompany him to his boxing workouts on Wednesday and Saturday afternoons. In the open-topped carriage, his grandmother and sister looked like garden flowers in their party dresses, Mavis a faded rose in her pink frock, Rebecca, with her long, noodle-thin arms flailing, a spider lily in her white-and-yellow creation.

Benjy turned the trap into the driveway, and presently "the girls," as Trevor called them, came from around the house to join him on the porch. Benjy, of course, had driven on to put away the carriage and have his afternoon tea in the kitchen with Lenora.

"Ah, Nathan, I see you've had a letter from home," Mavis said, tapping up the curved brick steps. The floating gossamer layers of her pink frock suggested the delicacy of a china tea cup.

"Let me see! Let me see!" Rebecca chimed, hopping up and down.

"No, Rebecca, dear. The letter belongs to Nathan," Mavis said. "Sit there on the swing, please."

"No! No! I want to see the letter!" Rebecca shrieked.

"Zak," Nathan ordered quietly, and the dog got up and went to nose Rebecca's hand.

Instantly, the little girl diverted her attention to the dog. "Zak..." she cooed, stroking the shepherd's head. Obediently, she sat down on the swing, Zak on his haunches before her, his muzzle on her lap.

"Extraordinary," Mavis marveled. "I've never seen anything like it. You and Zak are a godsend to us, Nathan. Make no mistake about that. I hope nothing was in the letter to upset you."

His grandmother was amazingly intuitive. Nathan's siblings had complained that he was hard to read. Impassive, Randolph had described him. *If you were an Indian, your name would be Stone Face*, he'd once told him. How had Mavis Waverling sensed his sadness, and how could she have known the letter was from a member of his family? But then, who else would be writing to him? Nathan did not know how much Trevor had told his grandmother of Millicent Holloway. It would have been dense of him to divulge his mother's claim that Nathan was the product of rape. That was a card no man would lay on the table before his mother, especially one prepared to believe the worst of her son.

"My mother has sold our farm to an oil producer," Nathan said. "She and my stepfather are moving into town."

"And that upsets you?"

"That upsets me. Acres could be ruined for years to come from the drilling, even if no oil is found."

"You had hoped to buy the farm someday?"

Nathan said in surprise, "Your son told you?"

"There's little he hasn't told me about you. I insisted."

His grandmother's gaze held no knowing light, so Nathan assumed Trevor had allowed her to remain ignorant of his mother's charge of rape. So far, she'd regaled him with tales of his grandfather and the early days of Dallas and introduced him to the light side of Jordan Waverling from her memories, but she had not told him the story she'd promised—or threatened—to reveal in "another private moment." *Mystery surrounds his death to this day*, he remembered her saying in speaking of her late son, but Nathan thought that perhaps Mavis Waverling had changed her mind about that private moment because she did not want her grandson to think ill of his father. Since he'd come to live among them, Nathan could detect some warming toward Trevor. All that his grandmother had told Nathan about Jordan's dark side was that his moods were subject to pendulum swings. Rebecca might have inherited a strain of her uncle's sometimes erratic behavior, she said, but he was never violent or brutal when in the grip of a bout. No, Mavis said, Jordan's emotional downturns took more the form of depression. That was why he loved the river so. The water soothed him. "It was ironical that the place where he was most at peace should claim his life," she'd said.

The statement was the closest his grandmother had ever come to opening up about Jordan's death.

Suddenly, Rebecca stood. "*I must go down to the seas again, to the lonely sea and the sky, / And all I ask is a tall ship and a star to steer her by*," she recited.

Mavis interpreted. "That's one of her favorite poems. John Masefield was Jordan's favorite poet. Rebecca means she wants to go down to the riverbank. I suppose because it holds fond memories of her and her uncle. They were very close. He'd take her swimming and fishing down at the pier, and they'd recite poetry to each other. Her love for it comes from his passion for rhyme. Would you mind going with her, Nathan? We never let her venture down there alone."

Nathan felt an eerie chill. It was as if Rebecca had been reading his thoughts about her uncle. "Zak and I will be honored," he said. He slipped the letter into the book he'd been reading and took Rebecca's hand.

"Don't be gone long, Nathan," Mavis said. "Hurry back for tea before Trevor gets home. You and I don't often have a chance to speak alone together. And, Rebecca, take care not to soil your dress."

Going down the steps, Nathan wondered at the uncanny perception these relatives of his seemed to possess. Had his grandmother read his wonderings about Jordan as well? When he returned, was he to be treated to one of those "private moments" in which she would reveal at last why she suspected her younger son of killing his brother? Had she figured out that what was once a matter of curiosity had become a state of deep concern to her grandson?

After Nathan shut the yard gate behind them, Rebecca, dark locks bouncing about her shoulders, skipped down to the bank of the wide flow of the Trinity River, Zak leaping beside her. The stretch of manicured grassland that sloped down to the water's edge was part of his grandmother's property and provided a place where Nathan could throw Zak a ball. High hedges on either side separated it from the neighbors' residences. A small dock jutted out into the water. "Watch yourself, Rebecca!" Nathan called as his half sister hopped onto the wooden planks, Zak following. "Don't get too close to the edge."

"I won't," she called back, startling Nathan. It was rare to hear a normal response from the child. She spoke in riddles and rhymes, shut tight in her own world of poetry and coloring books and dolls and make-believe friends. She seemed to desire no company but that of her grandmother, Lenora, and Benjy, and now Nathan and Zak. Occasionally, Nathan had seen her dark eyes clear of their unfocused gaze and center on what was going on around her. Such moments raised goose bumps. It was like seeing a doll suddenly spark to life.

Nathan reached Rebecca's side on the short platform, ready to catch her arm if she should topple over in one of her uncoordinated moments of enthusiasm. "There," she said, pointing.

"There?" Nathan said.

"There!" She pointed at a large rock jutting up from the water by the bank.

"What about it, Rebecca?" Nathan asked quietly.

"That's where it happened."

"What happened?"

"My uncle drowned."

Nathan's flesh crawled. He gently pulled the little girl away from the dock's edge and took her by the shoulders. "You saw your uncle drown, Rebecca? From here? What were you doing on the dock? Was anyone else here?"

She spun away from him and pointed to the rock. "*I must go down to the seas again, to the lonely sea and the sky, / And all I ask is a tall ship and a star to steer her by.*" Rebecca turned to Nathan again. "That's what he said," she declared.

Nathan strained to understand. "Who said? Your uncle?" The child's eyes were bright with hope that he would believe her—lucid, transparent, unmistakable hope. Again Nathan felt his skin move. But as suddenly, the brightness dimmed. A cast dropped over her sight, and the moment of truth was lost. Rebecca turned away to look toward the river. "*And the wheel's kick and the wind's song and the white sail's shaking, / And a grey mist on the sea's face, and a grey dawn breaking,*" she chanted.

Nathan listened in awe to the singsong cadence of the complicated lines, riveted by the sense of a hidden meaning in them. What was she saying to him? Had she truly seen Jordan Waverling drown? Had she been alone or with someone? She would have been nine years old and even more closely guarded than she was now. He offered her his hand. "Come, Rebecca. Let's go back. Your grandmother is waiting on us for tea," he said.

Rebecca refused his hand and skipped ahead, Zak bounding alongside her. Nathan shook his head in amazement as Rebecca recited in a merry voice in step with her bounce: "*Her china cup is white and thin; A thousand times her heart has been / Made merry at its scalloped brink; / And in the bottom, painted pink, / A dragon greets her with a grin.*"

Chapter Thirty

On Friday, the twenty-second day of June, Nathan boarded the train to Gainesville. The plans for his visit had been set forth in a letter from Leon. He would meet Nathan at the station and take him to the new family home into which they were now nicely settled. They would attend commencement exercises on Saturday morning, the luncheon afterward, and it would be up to him if he wanted to attend the graduates' dinner and dance that evening. Nathan was relieved that he would not have to go back to the old home place.

As expected, Leon was eagerly waiting for him outside the station house when the train pulled in. He greeted and embraced him with tears in his eyes. "Thanks for comin', Nathan. We're all mighty glad you did."

"I'm glad I came, too," Nathan said. He couldn't have said those words when he first received the invitation to Randolph's graduation. How would he feel when he saw for what his mother had sacrificed the farm? The finer house, better clothes for Lily and Randolph, maybe even one of those horseless carriages the *New York Times* called an automobile. Would it even make a difference to his family if he showed up or not? But then he'd reflected that Randolph was Leon's son, and he would be so proud to see him walk across the stage wearing the gold mantle of the class valedictorian. Randolph had earned that honor. Nathan had then decided it would make a difference to him personally to pass up this opportunity to be with his family. This was perhaps the final time they'd all be together.

"I wouldn't have missed it, for sure," Nathan said to reassure Leon that he was glad he'd come. His stepfather looked older, but the deeper creases around his eyes and across his forehead had more to do with sorrow than age, Nathan perceived. Neither was dressed as they'd last seen the other. Both wore business suits and striped shirts with tall, stiff collars turned down to form wings that anchored their neckties. Nathan had gone straight to the train station from Waverling Tools, where he wore such garb every day, and he had not had time to change into more comfortable traveling clothes. Leon wore a straw boater and Nathan a soft derby.

"Aren't we the dudes?" Leon laughed.

"We are. I brought along one of my old shirts and a pair of jeans to kick around in," Nathan said.

"I'm gettin' into my overalls the minute we walk into the house. Millicent doesn't like me to be seen runnin' around town in them. As if anybody would notice, and who in hell would care if they did? Have you had your supper?"

"A sandwich on the train."

"Millicent has apple pie and ice cream waitin'." Leon put his arm around Nathan's shoulders and gave them a squeeze. "Missed you, son."

"Same here, Dad," Nathan said. Saying his name for Leon squeezed his throat. Would he ever use it with the same feeling for Trevor Waverling?

They shared a silence thick with the sadness of irremediable loss as Leon led him to a spanking new six-seat surrey that sported a body of exquisite woods, fine leather seats, polished brass trim, and folding top. A fine-looking horse stood in its traces. "Just got the two a few days ago, or I would have warned you not to expect me to pick you up in ol' Betsy," Leon said to explain the vehicle and animal that had replaced their rickety old buckboard and aging mare. "Millicent thinks we should go about in style now that we're city folks. I said I'd never ride in the damn thing if she chucked our old Lizzy Belle. The buckboard will be sold soon, as I no longer need it to go back and forth to the farm. Naturally, Randolph hopes his mother will eventually buy him one of those expensive-as-all-get-out horseless carriages they're turning out in Detroit."

"Will she, you think?" Nathan asked, a spur of resentment nicking the pleasure of his homecoming.

Leon flicked the reins over the back of the daintily stepping filly. "She's going a little crazy with all that money she got, but I think she'll draw the line on buyin' one of them newfangled driving machines. They're too dangerous. Tell me how it's goin' in Dallas. How's Zak settlin' to the city and what about that little girl, Rebecca? She takin' to you all right? How are you gettin' along with Trevor, and are they feedin' you well?"

On the ten-minute drive, Nathan answered his stepfather's questions, embellishing his answers a bit to relieve him of his concerns for his well-being. He would always miss the country, no doubt about it, he told Leon, but he was adjusting to living with an indoor bathroom, electric lights, running water, and a telephone. He was becoming accustomed to the sights, sounds, and smells of the city, the convenience and ease of living close to where you could buy things before you ran out of them. "You will, too, Dad," Nathan assured him.

"As long as I don't get soft," Leon said.

He was afraid of that, too, Nathan said, but he saw a solution to the problem. Trevor had been an amateur pugilist and gone on the middleweight circuit for a time but now was too old for competition. He still practiced his skills religiously, though, and had finally invited Nathan to go with him to his gym where he might decide to put on the mitts if only to learn the sport.

Nathan, a boxer? Leon said. Well, he had the build for it. They'd missed his muscles during harvest, which—wouldn't you know?—was turning out to be the best in years. They still had a couple weeks of harvest left, and it looked like they'd have a bumper crop. So far, they'd gotten a better-than-fair price for the wheat sold. Leon had seen to it that some of the money was set aside for the wage Nathan had earned. They had buyers lined up for the plow, tools, tack, and livestock when it was time to let them go. Millicent would give Leon his share, which he'd add to his secret store. It would give him enough of a stake to start over if he ever needed it. He'd heard of good land going begging in Kansas.

Hearing this, Nathan regarded him in surprise. "Does that mean you'd leave Mother?" he said.

"Nah," Leon said, "but it's a comfort knowin' I could. I'm with your mother until death do us part, Nathan. I love her, always have, always will. Couldn't tell you why. I'm done tryin' to figure out what makes a person love another despite their wicked ways and why love's withheld from those deservin' of it. There is no rhyme nor reason to love, as you'll find out someday, though I hope you'll never know the confusin' side of it. And if it's a comfort to you, son, I believe that deep down your mother loves me. She wouldn't know what to do if I left her once the children are gone."

"Sounds a lot like need to me," Nathan said.

"Ah, well, yes, there's a good bit of that in her feelin' for me, too, and often it's been enough when the deeper stuff's missin'."

The minute they drew up before the handsome two-story

dormered structure of the Holloways' new home, the door flew open. *"Nathan!"* Lily shrieked dramatically and rushed joyfully down the steps to throw her arms around him. A more sedate but smiling Randolph followed and then his mother, fashionably coiffed and attired in the latest pigeon-breasted shirtwaist and floor-clearing skirt. The bun, calico dress, and apron from the farm were memories of the past.

He was touched by their warmth, but it did not dissipate the feeling of being tossed from the nest as he was embraced and led into the unfamiliar house that was now the family home. His mother brushed off a smudge of dust from his bowler before hanging it on the hat rack in the foyer, and Lily gushed compliments over his appearance, exclaiming how handsome he looked in his city clothes. Randolph's grip was strong and sincere, and he expressed genuine pleasure at Nathan's graduation gift of a Waterman fountain pen, a vast improvement over the writing quills he was accustomed to using. "I figured you'd have a hard time chasing down a goose at Columbia," Nathan joked, causing a hilarious recounting of Randolph's attempts at the farm to snare unwilling donors to satisfy his constant need for quills.

The feeling of alienation settled in the pit of his stomach all through the apple pie and ice cream as he tried to adjust to the new faces of his mother and siblings at the dining room table, their clothes and manners and speech. He'd been gone a little under two months, but they'd all changed—assimilated to this new world that money had bought. Nathan had thought he might find them shy, self-conscious, even a little ashamed of their advanced status considering how it had all come about. Within the first hour of their reunion, he judged them well suited to the station in life they assumed they shared with the well-to-do and marveled at how out of place they had been in the rural setting of a farm. His little sister had gotten prettier and knew it. She spoke and gestured with the full awareness of her beauty, telling Nathan she had several beaus "of considerable means" wrapped around her little finger—"Oil and cotton, you know"—and that she'd be finishing her last year in school at a private academy in Denton where she could mix with those of "our own kind."

The Holloways' flush of wealth had added another layer of snobbery to Randolph's self-importance, which his superior intellect and imperial good looks had already bred. He had plans to go into politics when he finished law school, he said. He was thinking of putting up his shingle in the Oklahoma Territory. It was bound to become a state, and he would be in place when it happened. In sharing this goal around the table, he had grinned at Millicent. "How would you like to become the mother of the governor of the state of Oklahoma?" he said.

Millicent had bestowed upon him a fond, proud smile. Nathan found her the most changed of all. His brother and sister had just become what they'd always hoped to be, but he realized that his mother had become more of what she'd always been. The light of her true self had been hidden by a bun and an apron over a calico dress. Nathan had always thought her a beautiful woman, neat, orderly, and feminine, but a prairie pigeon in contrast to the elegant swan she was now. She'd resumed the mien particular to her privileged class as a girl, one she'd had to surrender as the wife of a humble farmer, and in her stylish clothes with her remarkable hair done up in a fashionable pompadour, pearls at her ears and throat, she looked the society matron she was meant to become, at home in any drawing room in the state.

At bedtime, they all trooped up the stairs to their rooms, Nathan to have one of his own. "A *guest* room! Can you imagine, Nathan!" Lily had enthused, clapping her hands as if in applause. "No more putting visitors into a loft."

"Quite a bunch, ain't they?" Leon remarked when they'd all said their good nights and he saw Nathan to his assigned door.

"They are," Nathan agreed. "I wish them…everything that they expect and hope for from the sale of the farm and the move to the city."

"Spoken like you, sure enough," Leon said.

"Any chance of Mother running through the money?"

"She's too smart for that. She knows how to make a buck look like five once she establishes the impression that she's rich. She ain't, but the appearance of it is just as good. Nathan…" Leon worked his lips a moment to arrange his words. "Going back to what I was speaking of earlier…about love, that is. Whatever a prick your brother may sometimes be, or a butterfly with syrup for brains your sister is, they have love for you. Little comes with it, I'm afraid. Randolph and Lily are too self-absorbed to have interest in anyone but themselves, but your brother and sister do care for you, Nathan. I want you to know that."

"Would they, if they knew I was only their half sibling?"

"I'm hopin' they never learn that fact. It might give them the illusion they don't need you as much. No matter on what rung up the ladder their feet might land, they'll always look up to you. They'll need you in their lives for that reason alone, because they ain't goin' to be meetin' many of your caliber in the places they hope to wind up. I want 'em always to know they have a brother that stands head and shoulders above the best of 'em, a brother they can count on to stay true to the image they have of him. They're not so stuck on themselves that they can't see that."

"What do they need me for when they have you, Dad?"

A pink flush glowed through the fringe of Leon's whiskers. "Aw, to them I'm just a dumb ol' farmer."

"Their misjudgment," Nathan said, thinking his brother and sister's miscalculation of their father would probably be among the many they would make about people along the way. He understood what Leon was asking of him. "I'll be around for them if ever they need me," Nathan promised. "And speaking of love…" He cleared his throat.

Leon cuffed his shoulder. "No need to say nothin' more about it. I hear what's in your heart. You get on to bed. We all got to be smart and lively tomorrow mornin' to watch Randolph strut his stuff. Sleep good, my boy."

"You, too," Nathan said.

He watched Leon walk down the wide, electric-lighted hall to the spacious bedroom he shared with his wife. He had not changed into his overalls out of his "monkey suit," as his stepfather referred to it. *Oh, Leon, not for eating pie in the dining room!* his mother had protested when he'd expressed his intention, so husband and son had remained in their suits to eat from the china plates. A spasm of sympathy for his stepfather caught at Nathan's heart. What would Leon do with his days now that he had no land to farm? They would have little time between social events to discuss it. After the dance tomorrow night, Nathan planned to catch the midnight train to Dallas to be home in the early hours of Sunday morning. He would leave with the question unanswered. He had finally accepted the unalterable, and he would go home with his heart easy for every member of his Gainesville family but for Leon. Nathan paused with his hand on the doorknob. It struck him that twice in the last minute, he had referred to Dallas as home.

PART TWO

Chapter Thirty-One

Friday morning, four days after her return to Fort Worth from Gainesville, Mildred Swift answered the doorbell of her mistress's town house to find the farmer on the porch who weekly peddled his produce in the neighborhood. Today, a special treat. He had figs to sell—"bursting with their syrup," he said. "Sweeter than they've been in years." Mildred was in charge of the grocery budget, the larder, and the cookie jar where her monthly food allowance was stored. She thought *overripe* a better word to describe the figs and hesitated at buying a basket. They were expensive compared to other items she could get for the same money, and these figs would perish quickly, but Estelle loved them, and those she didn't eat would be made into preserves. Mildred decided on a full basket.

In the culture of her captivity, the Comanche acknowledged no divine personage, so Mildred had been brought up ignorant of the abstractions and fantasies of the invisible and had never been won to a religious faith. That morning, however, when the mail was delivered, she thanked whatever gods there might be for the postman showing up on the peddler's heels before she could return to the kitchen. A letter was put into her hand addressed to Miss Samantha Gordon. The sender was Eleanor Tolman Brewster.

Oh, my God, thought Mildred, recognizing the name and significance of *Tolman* and sure that her mistress would, too. She heard Estelle, always alert for the delivery of the mail, come down the stairs to take it from her. Quickly, Mildred stowed Samantha's letter in her apron pocket. For the rest of that day and until early Saturday afternoon, she thought hard about how to get Eleanor Tolman Brewster's message to Samantha. Her mistress's daughter was not due back to Fort Worth until the next weekend.

"Mrs. Gordon," she said after an idea had struck, "I was wondering if it would be all right to go visit my aunt for a few hours this afternoon. It's been a long time since I've seen her, and I could go on down the road and take Miss Sam some of the figs I bought yesterday before they rot. You know how she loves them."

"Why, that's thoughtful of you, Mildred," Estelle said. "I'm sure your aunt would love to see you. Take as long as you need, and while you're at the ranch, bring back those fawn boots Samantha was wearing when you all went to Gainesville, and I'll see about getting them cleaned. I declare, I don't know what that daughter of mine stepped in to stain them so. Red river mud, it looked like."

"The streets were muddy from the recent rains," Mildred said.

The aunt, the only living relative of Mildred's mother, now deceased, would not be glad to see her. To Aunt Lil, she was still a Comanche bastard. Mildred would not be stopping by to visit, but she'd had to have some excuse to deliver the basket of figs; otherwise, Estelle would have sent Jimmy. The question now was what to do with the letter to make sure Samantha received it if it could not be placed directly into her hands.

The solution was to place the letter in the bottom of a basket facedown so the flap would not be exposed to fig juice, cover it with a thick tea towel, and spread the fruit on top. By midafternoon, Mildred was on her way to Las Tres Lomas, feeling much like a courier on a secret mission behind enemy lines. Silbia answered the door of the ranch house and, as Mildred expected, informed her that Samantha was not in—"Out tinkering in her workshop," she said. The fruit was deposited in the kitchen, and the two housekeepers chatted a while over coffee, Mildred growing more nervous that perhaps she'd made a mistake in leaving Eleanor Tolman Brewster's letter under the figs. Suppose Samantha didn't find it?

The stained boots collected, Mildred said as she rose to go, "Tell Miss Sam that her mother left her a note under the napkin," and added with a wink, "for her eyes only, if you know what I mean."

Silbia sniggered. "I do. What her papa don't know can't hurt him."

In this case, truer than you know, Mildred thought as she took her leave.

But Silbia's posit proved a misfire.

Neal clomped into the kitchen a few minutes after Mildred had driven Estelle's carriage out through the entrance posts. "What did Mildred want?" he asked, his look anxious. "I just saw her leave. Is everything all right in Fort Worth?"

"*Sí, patrón*," Silbia said and gestured toward the basket of figs. "She came by to deliver those to Miss Sam and pick up her boots for cleaning."

"Ah, figs," Neal said, his eyes lighting up. He popped one into his mouth. "Juicy and sweet and sticky. Just like I like 'em."

"You best stay out of them, *patrón*. They're for Miss Sam."

"She won't miss just one."

Or two, Neal thought as he passed back through the kitchen a short while later after retrieving a rifle from the gun cabinet. Some animal suspected to be a bobcat had mauled another of their calves and several others from the Triple S, and he and

Wayne and a few of the boys from both ranches were joining up to track it while there was still daylight. The figs were already oozing their syrup, he noticed. Where in hell was Silbia? His housekeeper should have transferred the figs to another container and set it in the butter cooler before they turned to pulp. He would spoil that woman by doing her housework for her if he wasn't careful, Neal thought, setting aside his rifle to rummage under the counter for a bowl the right size to hold the fruit. Finding it, he took the napkin by its ends and dumped the lot into it, surprised to discover an envelope lying underneath. A buffer against leakage, Neal reckoned, but he saw that the flap was sealed. A letter, then. He turned it over and read that it was addressed to Samantha and wondered what in the Sam Hill his daughter's letter was doing at the bottom of a basket of runny figs. Then his gaze moved to the return address, and *Tolman* and *Marietta, Oklahoma Territory* leaped out at him. His heart froze. What in hell? Who was Eleanor Tolman Brewster? From the order of the name, she was the daughter of Dr. Donald Tolman, but why was she writing to Samantha? Was this a follow-up letter to her father's to make sure Samantha received the information he had written to Neal? Damn the woman for her interference. He slipped his thumbnail under the moist flap, separating it easily. The single sheet of paper read:

Dear Miss Gordon.

You had already gone when I happened to come across a letter in my late father's papers from the midwife we discussed. Bridget Mahoney's San Francisco address is 505 Canal Street, but be aware that the postdate was September 7, 1889. She may have moved since then, or, alas, may not even be alive. I hope this information will bring you one step closer to locating your birth parents and that the reunion will be all your heart de-sires.

Sincerely,
Eleanor Tolman Brewster

Neal recoiled from the letter, holding it away from him in dis-belief. The bullet he thought he'd dodged struck him in the heart. His greatest fear had come to pass. It had not been unfounded. Samantha wished to find her birth parents. He and Estelle were not enough for her. They had failed her somehow, but how could that be…?

Through the window, Neal saw Silbia marching from the Trail Head, face set angrily. She and Grizzly had been at it again over some domain dispute. Quickly, before he could think clearly, Neal obeyed his conscience and replaced the letter where he found it, re-covered it with the towel, and emptied the bowl of figs back into the basket. He barely managed to return the con-tainer under the counter before Silbia stormed in. "You need to have a talk with Señor Grizzly, *patrón*. He's gone and—" She stopped, her forehead drawing into a frown. "Something wrong?"

"No!" Neal growled. "And I don't have time to hear about your and Grizzly's squabbles. Work them out yourselves!" He took rifle in hand and pushed by her, seeking air and open ground. He thought he was going to be sick. He tasted a strong resurgence of fig pulp and spat into the dirt. His horse was wait-ing and saddled, ready for the hunt. Neal shoved his rifle into his saddle scabbard and climbed aboard, questions flying like darts in his mind while shock and disbelief, like a dam breaking, gave way to a raging hurt.

Silbia had followed him outside, Spanish instincts flaring. "*Pa-*

trón?" she questioned, fearful of the strange temper that had come over him when he had been his usual gruff but tolerable self only minutes ago. She had worked for the *patrón* of Las Tres Lomas de la Trinidad for many years and knew his moods, but she had never seen him like this. "Will you be back for supper? Remember the Singleton ladies are coming."

"Don't count on me."

"What shall I tell Miss Sam?"

Neal gave his horse's ribs a good jab with his spurs. "Anything you want," he called after him as he sped off. His housekeeper stared after him. *El patrón* strictly forbade abuse to ranch animals, but if his spurs' rowels had been sharp, they would have cut, and he never used that tone when speaking of his daughter.

Back in the kitchen, puzzled and worried, Silbia had reached under the counter to withdraw a bowl into which to transfer the figs when Samantha walked in. "I just saw Daddy take off like he was chasing down a dust devil," she said. "I waved, but he didn't wave back. He must not have seen me."

Silbia was studying the bowl with a perplexed frown. "Something's taken ahold of your papa," she said. "Don't ask me what. He was fine when I left to go have it out with Grizzly. He sneaked in here when I was in the garden and took most of my cornmeal I planned for the cornbread tonight. When I got back, *el patrón* was filled with blue thunder. Maybe it was the figs." Silbia indicated the basket. "Mildred brought those to you and picked up your boots for cleaning—those with the flowers that you wore to Gainesville." She stuck the bowl under the tap to wash it. "Take what you want and I'll place the rest in the butter cooler."

Samantha selected a fig. "Where was Daddy off to?"

"Hunting down that bobcat messing around out on the north range."

"He'll be back to wash up for supper and our card game with the Singleton sisters, I hope." Sloan, of course, would be with Anne Rutherford, in whose company he always spent Saturday night.

"Didn't say," Silbia said evasively. The bowl washed and dried, she lifted the corners of the napkin to pour the fruit into the bowl. "Oh, and I forgot there's a letter from your mama under the figs. For your eyes only, Mildred said," as she handed the letter to Samantha.

Chapter Thirty-Two

Neal was at the head of the pack of four men and two hounds, Sloan riding alongside him. He'd been surprised when Sloan had shown up with one of his boys. "Thought you'd be getting ready for a big time in Fort Worth with Miss Rutherford," he said.

"Not tonight," Sloan responded.

Neal didn't feel like saying much else, and Sloan seemed to sense it. Wayne and the other riders, too. He knew he looked fearsome. Few men wanted to tangle with Neal Gordon wearing the face he wore now. The men mistook his look for rage. They knew his reputation for showing no mercy to those who would try to take what was his. Cattle rustlers avoided Las Tres Lomas, and a nasty critter had come onto his range, stalking and senselessly killing livestock in a time of plenty in area habitats. Track evidence indicated a bobcat. Bobcats put their back feet in the same spots where their front feet stepped, leaving an impression of a two-footed predator, so the animal's style of locomotion, type of scat, and lack of claw marks leading away from the carcasses made its identity almost certain. The mystery was that its kind generally attacked smaller prey in their own environment: mice, rabbits, possums, badgers, skunks, and white-tailed deer. They leaped for the throat with one great spring and could kill with a single bite and afterward drag off their kill and conceal it to feast on later, but all four calves had been viciously gutted and left where they were savaged. A young two-hundred-pound calf would have been a challenge for the meanest and most daring of them. The men believed they were probably hunting a larger-than-normal rogue male that mauled for the sheer pleasure of it.

Neal wished he'd set out alone to track the bastard. If he'd seen that letter beforehand, he'd have called off the hunt and taken off by himself. Like most men of his breed, he could make better sense of his thoughts and feelings on horseback without the intrusion of company. For the first time since Seth Singleton had died, he felt like crying. He and Estelle had tried to be the best parents alive without spoiling their daughter, and she'd come through their raising pretty damn good, if Neal made the claim himself. She'd had twenty years of their love and care, protection and support. Why now would she be putting out feelers to locate the parents who hadn't wanted her and given her away? What was lacking in his and Estelle's devotion, the home they'd provided?

Betrayed... That was the word he'd use to describe his feeling right now, and it was all he could do to keep anger out of it. Samantha had gone behind their backs, kept her need, curiosity, loneliness—whatever the hell was driving her to find the remnants of her family—from him and Estelle. Well, what else could she have done? Samantha knew how they'd feel about her desire to seek out her blood family—exactly what he was feeling now, like he'd been shot in the gut, and her mother...Oh, God. Estelle might never recover from the grief of it if she learned what else their daughter had been about on that trip to Gainesville.

Neal felt the hole of memory open up and swallow him whole. Painfully, he remembered the night Samantha was placed in his arms. He had seen many unspeakable things in his life, things that could sear the humanity right out of a man. He had battled Comanche and Mexican marauders and fought in hand-to-hand combat in a grisly civil war that had marred and hardened him for life. But the night he held his daughter, every thorn, burr, barb inside him had melted away. It was weeks before he could catch his breath when he looked at her, so tiny and sweet and perfect and all his and Estelle's. Could a man feel more love for a daughter conceived from his own loins? It wasn't possible. Of all the many people surprised by his immediate and total enthrallment to this beautiful infant, none was more surprised than he. The only female he'd ever dealt with was his wife. His mother had died when he was too young to remember her, and he'd grown up in a household of tough, hard men among whom he'd been the toughest and hardest.

The first miracle of his life occurred when Estelle agreed to marry him, but understanding a woman had taken some doing, and there were so many years when she had toiled long hours beside him in men's shirts and trousers that he forgot she was a woman at all. He'd naturally hoped for sons. It never entered his mind to wish for a daughter. When neither came, he resolved himself to their childless state and tried to make it up to Estelle. She'd had enough of ranching. She would inherit Las Tres Lomas de la Trinidad upon his death but would sell it to Sloan in memory of the boy's father who had been his closest friend. Seth had saved his life by risking his in the Seven Days Battle at Gaines's Mill in Virginia in 1862. So, trying not to think of having no heir to benefit from his hard work and sacrifice, Neal had kept the ranch going, not only to fulfill his own titan dreams but to leave it to Seth's son in honor of his friend.

And then had come his second miracle, an heir, and it hadn't mattered that she was a girl. A son could not have been more competent to step into his father's shoes, and only a daughter could have given him and Estelle the tender, sweet love they'd received from Samantha.

The riders were coming upon an area of the ranch known as Windy Bluff. "There's Saved," Sloan said, dredging Neal up from the well of his long-ago recollections. The younger man pointed at the heavy-horned steer munching grass. This part of the range had become his personal grazing ground. "How old is he now?"

"Going on five years," Neal said.

"His horn tips have faded. They'll have to be repainted soon."

"If Samantha remembers," Neal growled. Though he might occasionally lose himself in the fantasy world of titans and gods, he was a literal man not given to allegorical meanings, but he saw the faded horns as symbolic.

Sloan chided in surprise, "Now, Neal, why wouldn't Samantha remember? I've often seen her ride out here to check on him. Damned steer seems to recognize her."

Neal allowed the rebuke to linger between them without comment, then suddenly said, "A piece of advice, son. When you marry, have many babies. That way when one betrays you, you won't have lost everything."

A pointing finger and a shout "*Over there!*" from one of the men cut off further conversation. The dogs, barking, leaped ahead. A long, heavy-tailed animal almost twice the size of a bobcat snarled at them from a high, rocky ledge smothered in oak and pine brush. The creature took off, men and dogs chasing it into a thickly wooded area that, along with a rocky bluff rising behind it, formed the boundary of Las Tres Lomas. Ten minutes later, like a phantom, the animal had disappeared. The dogs whined with their noses to the trail from which it had vanished. Horses spun around with their riders, the men searching the bluff in vain for a flash of sleek, tan-colored fur.

"A mountain lion." Wayne Harris stated the identity of the dreaded sight. It had been years since the area had been menaced by a member of its species. "Probably a rogue, driven out of his territory because he didn't follow the rules."

"And too arrogant to bury his prey because there's more where it came from," Neal said grimly. "Our threat won't mean a harlot's kiss to him. He's in this for the thrill. He'll be back tonight, and when he does, I'll get 'im."

There were exclamations from the men. Sloan said, "What do you mean, Neal?"

"I'm staying. You boys go on back. Enjoy your Saturday night, but I'm not leaving until I've killed the bastard or am convinced he's taken off."

Sloan lowered his voice. "That's not a good idea, Neal, and you know it."

Wayne had moved in to add his protest. "Your sight ain't as good as it used to be, boss, especially in the dark."

"But my hearing is," Neal said, "and I've got my specs. Besides, I got some thinking to do. Alone. Wayne, take the dogs. I won't need 'em. Don't worry about me, boys. I'm where I belong right now. *Estoy dentro de mi elemento.*"

In his element, Sloan interpreted. "What you said about betrayal...were you talking about Samantha?"

Neal's face closed. "Forget I said that. I misspoke. Betrayal's not in Samantha." And it wasn't. Neal recognized that truth. Samantha would never turn her back on him and Estelle. Neal's worry was for himself and the demons of jealousy and possessiveness that would not allow him to keep and to hold those he loved who loved another. It must be all for him or nothing. How could he bear to share his daughter's love with another father—her *real* father? Or hear his daughter call Millicent Holloway *mother*? Was the woman's husband, Leon, still alive? Would Samantha write to this...Bridget Mahoney in San Francisco, and would her reply lead back to the Barrows farm?

What angered him was the idea that Samantha would even *want* to write to the midwife!

Out from the hole of memory, a terrible incident surged, one like the case of the dog he'd loved as a boy, but much worse. Neal had tried to bury it because it reminded him of himself. A commander in Hood's brigade possessed a beautiful black Arabian stallion who permitted no one to ride him but his owner. Hell's Fire was the horse's name. One day, another rider got on his back, a simple boy who looked after the officers, polished their boots, cleaned their latrines. To everyone's astonishment—and applause—the horse cantered around the paddock docilely under the boy's hand, but when he dismounted, the owner put his revolver to his horse's magnificent head and shot him dead.

Neal shook himself of the offensive recollection, the rancid taste of disgust in his mouth. Animals that a man loved who turned on him were one thing, but was he the sort who could close his heart against a daughter for her sin of loving another?

Wayne gave it one last appeal. "Neal?" he said, his tone worried. "Let's call it an evening and go home. Samantha will be worried if you don't show up."

"So be it," he said tersely. "I'm staying."

Sloan raised his eyebrows to Wayne, who lifted a brow in return. Neither man had ever heard Neal take that attitude toward his daughter. "Suit yourself," Sloan said, "but if you're not back by morning, I'm coming for you."

"No need to worry, son. I'll be back by breakfast," Neal said.

Chapter Thirty-Three

Bad news?" Silbia asked when Samantha had finished reading Eleanor Brewster's note.

Samantha thought of Silbia's description of her father's sudden mood change, recalled her unacknowledged wave as he'd thundered off on the hunt. She now believed he'd pretended not to have seen her. "My father didn't see this, did he?"

Silbia, sifting flour for biscuits to be served in lieu of cornbread, said, "No, how could he? It was buried beneath the figs."

"Right," Samantha said, feeling uneasy. The moist envelope flap would have been easy to open and reclose without notice. "The basket was not disturbed?"

"Only by your papa when he snitched one or two *higos*."

Samantha wagged the letter in front of her. "Let's keep this between ourselves, Silbia."

"*Sí, querida*. As I told Mildred, what your papa don't know can't hurt him."

It was their housekeeper's favorite expression when they agreed to keep things from *el patrón*, but this time, Samantha had the niggling feeling the horse was out of the barn before the gate was closed. Her father's quick mood change suggested something *had* disturbed him. But how could he have read the letter, buried as it was under the figs? It could be that his concentration on tracking down the vicious marauder after their cattle accounted for his mood, and his eyesight had weakened in the last year. He might not have seen her coming from her workshop. Samantha helped herself to several figs. They burst sweet and succulent in her mouth, but their taste did little to allay her apprehension as she pushed open the swinging door to go upstairs to change for her guests.

The housekeeper glanced after her as Samantha left the kitchen. Silbia had no idea of the contents of the letter, only that it contained secrets *el patrón* was not to know, *secretos* that Miss Sam thought would upset him. Silbia had spoken the truth when she told her little mistress the basket of *higos* had not been disturbed, but perhaps she should have mentioned the sticky bowl she'd had to wash before pouring the figs into it. A mystery. She never put away dirty dishes. And there was the puzzle of *el patrón*'s bark when she asked him if he would be back for supper and what he was to tell his *hija*. "Anything you want," he'd snapped, and that didn't sound like *el patrón*.

She shrugged. Still…how could Señor Gordon have read the letter if he hadn't known it was there? Silbia poured buttermilk into the dry ingredients, her temper flaring once again at Grizzly's theft of her cornmeal.

Sloan sent his ranch hand on to the Triple S and rode back to Las Tres Lomas with Neal's men, as reluctant to leave their boss alone to face the mountain lion as he, but in their case, better to follow orders than disobey them. Twilight was approaching. Billie June and Millie May would be riding over shortly for supper and a game of cards. Sloan must speak to Samantha before they arrived.

"She's upstairs," Silbia told him in the foyer of Las Tres Lomas. "I'll let her know you're here."

"Don't bother," Sloan said. "I'll go up."

Aghast, Silbia said, "But, Señor Sloan, she's dressing."

Sloan flashed her a grin. "Don't worry. I've seen her in her underwear before."

But not since they were children and swam and fished nearly buck naked in the Trinity, he thought. Lately, he'd been thinking back on that carefree period when Samantha had been his only companion. Boys his age lived on ranches too far apart to build friendships. He and Samantha had been tutored together, and after lessons, they'd run wild as they damn well pleased under the not-so-watchful eyes of their doting fathers. It had been an odd pairing, a boy and a girl nearly four years younger than he, but from the time Samantha could walk, he'd taken it upon himself to look after her, not that she needed bird-dogging after a while, so when she could keep up with him, they'd become buddies. He'd thought of her as a sister, but not the motherly kind like Millie May and Billie June. She'd been a tomboyish type of sister, ready for any derring-do. She was the sort a boy could confide in, explain things to, share discoveries with, and never think of as a girl.

But then one day that changed. Sloan remembered it well. He'd been at the tail end of twenty, working eighteen-hour days struggling to fill his father's shoes. Samantha had just turned seventeen, and they hadn't seen as much of each other after she went to live in town during the week to attend school. He'd been consulting with Neal at Las Tres Lomas, and when he took his leave and walked out of the library, there was Samantha in the great room framed before a sunny window that set her hair aglow and outlined her feminine figure. He'd noticed then the purity of her skin and the color of her eyes, gray as clouds with the sun shining through them. It was like seeing the miracle of a butterfly just emerged from its chrysalis. Right then and there, he should have followed his heart and marched right up to Samantha and said, "Okay, it's time we tied the knot, don't you think?" just as when he suggested it was time for him to teach her how to swim.

But he had not. His time and energy had been consumed by the never-ending demands of the ranch. It was a period of drought, rustlers taking advantage of his youth, battles with the railroads over freight charges, declining cattle prices and profits, and a shortage of men when his father's most trusted and reliable ranch hands took off to fight in Cuba with Theodore Roosevelt's Rough Riders. By the time he had some breathing space from the pressures of work and responsibility, he'd become a hardened man and Samantha an independent woman, and their special closeness had faded, at least on her part.

Sloan reached the landing. It had been years since he'd been here, but how could he not remember the location of Samantha's room at the end of the hall? Memories flooded: checkers and card games on rainy days, a cardboard puzzle of Barnum and Bailey's circus he and Sam had put together on a tray when she was confined to bed with a broken leg, and a very special occasion when they'd sneaked a fledgling fallen from its nest into her room under the disapproving nose of Mrs. Swift. They'd cared for it in a basket until the day they released the bird together and watched it fly away. He'd been around twelve years old then. He knocked.

"Come in!"

"Are you sure? It's Sloan."

He heard a scurrying around like a mouse bolting for a hole, then the door opened a fraction, framing a sliver of Samantha's surprised face. "Sloan! What are you doing here?"

"I came to speak with you. Open up. I don't care if you're dressed. I have sisters, you know. We don't have much time."

She opened the door and backed away, barefoot, dressed in a

robe and smelling of bath soap. Her hair was thickly knotted on top of her head and secured by barrettes. "Why? Is something wrong?"

"You tell me. The boys and I just came from the north border of Las Tres Lomas where we spotted a mountain lion. It's the culprit getting our cattle. Neal thinks he'll be back for another kill tonight."

"A mountain lion," Samantha repeated, grimacing. "And you came up to my room to tell me that?"

"Your father is staying out there to take him on alone. There was no arguing with him, Sam—not in the mood he was in. Something's got his drawers in a twist, and I came up here to see if you'd talk to me about it. Maybe I can help."

Samantha reached to untie her robe. "Oh, my God! I'm getting dressed and riding out there. He shouldn't tackle that animal alone."

"No, you're not." Sloan motioned to refasten her robe. "You hightail it out there now and you'll scare that cat away if he's in the area, and you can imagine what Neal Gordon would think of that. Besides, he says he's got some thinking to do—alone, he made it clear."

"Thinking?"

"About you, if I'm not mistaken. Is there something going on between you and your daddy?" Sloan decided not to mention Neal's cryptic remark about betrayal. It would hurt Samantha terribly. Neal had been speaking of his daughter, no matter his claim that he'd misspoken, but let it come from Samantha what it was all about.

Samantha tightened the sash of her robe and dropped into a nearby chair. "Oh God..." She rubbed her forehead and closed her eyes, lashes dark against the sudden paleness of her skin.

Sloan sat down on the chair's footstool, pushed back his hat, and took her tensely balled hand in his, "Talk to me, Sam. What's happened between you two? I'd like to help if I can."

"What's made you think something is going on between Daddy and me?"

"His manner today, and here you sit wound tight as a tourniquet."

Her eyes still closed, she said, "Why would you think either has to do with my father and me?"

Sloan had no choice. He would never get Samantha to confide in him if he didn't relate Neal's bitter advice. Her pulse was racing so strong he could feel it in the heel of her hand. "He advised me to have many babies when I marry so that when one betrayed me, I wouldn't...lose everything."

Her eyes flew open, the light gone, dark clouds gathering. "He said that, did he?"

"He said that. I never thought I'd hear anything like those words pass Neal Gordon's lips. So what's happened between him and the light of his life?"

Samantha stood in the narrow space between chair and footstool and stepped to a window still holding warmth from the western sun. There was no doubt. Her father had read the letter. Cold panic gripped her. She could only imagine her father's hurt and pain and...anger—deep, dark anger. How could Samantha do this to him...to Estelle, the best mother on earth? God help her, what should she do now? Should she lay everything on the table to her father and explain how Eleanor Brewster had come to write her that letter? Would he understand her curiosity and be convinced that her visit to Marietta had satisfied her urge and settled her interest to learn more? After all, he'd been the one who recognized and stated to her mother that certain questions were normal to an adopted child. She would start at the beginning, explain how she'd only been worried about his health and gone to Grizzly...

Her plan halted midstream. Good Lord, no! Whatever happened, she could not implicate Grizzly. Letting out a moan, she dropped her face into her hands.

Sloan was up from the footstool immediately and turning her to face him. "For goodness' sakes, Sam, tell me what's happened. It can't be all that bad. Whatever it is, we'll work it out together."

Her face still covered, Samantha shook her head and murmured into her hands, "No one can help this situation, Sloan. I've committed an irredeemable act in my father's eyes, and I'll never be able to undo what I've done. That's all I'm willing to tell you."

He pulled her hands away and held them. "You could never commit an irredeemable act in Neal's eyes, Samantha."

Tonelessly, she said, "I should have listened to Grizzly and Wayne's advice and never started down this road."

"What road?"

Samantha pulled her hands from Sloan's grip and turned back to the window, kneading them before its warmth. "Please tell your sisters the party is off," she said.

"Sam, let me go down to the library and get you a glass of sherry," Sloan persisted. "That will put some color back in your cheeks, and then maybe you'll talk to me."

"No, I need to be by myself," she said. "You can't fix this, Sloan. Nobody can."

"At least let me try. What are big brothers for?"

Irrationally, the question struck Samantha's nerves like the grate of fingernails on a chalkboard. She turned from the window and gave Sloan her full, critical attention, a vibration of anger in her despair. Sloan thought he could repair the impossible as when they were children, did he? The boy-grown-man that everybody, including her, had believed that someday would take her to be his wife had chosen another woman more beautiful, more sophisticated, more willing to honor and obey, a shallow fraud. And yet here he was expecting—demanding—to be taken into her family's deepest confidences as if he had a right to be there. He had no rights other than those of friendship, and friendship carried boundaries.

She walked to her bedroom door and drew it open. "I appreciate your offer of help, Sloan, but I'll work this out myself. No need to trouble yourself over the...misunderstanding between my father and me, and I'm sure I don't have to mention that I'd like your concerns to stay private."

She stood at the wide-open door stiff as a sentry, face hard, gaze cold. Sloan stared at her, lips parted in surprise and the shock of insult. He reset his hat and said, "As if you even have to ask me to keep your confidence, Sam, but if I choose to *trouble* myself over the *misunderstanding* between you and your father, I will." He stepped by her into the hall hardly able to look at her, his hurt was so deep. He managed to say, "Well, if you change your mind and need an ear, you know where to find me. Brothers have big shoulders, you know."

"You're not my brother, Sloan," she called after him, as he started toward the stairs.

Her words were like a lasso, yanking him to a stop. He turned slowly around. "What's that?"

"You're my friend. Nothing more, nothing less. I count myself fortunate that you are, but that's all you are—a friend."

Sloan studied her, feeling a chill tunnel through his heart. If he'd ever had doubts about her true feelings for him, she'd just confirmed them. "Well, that's good to know, Sam. Thanks for clearing up the distinction," he said. "I'll be sure to keep that in mind from now on."

Chapter Thirty-Four

A full moon appeared as twilight melted into pale night along with the fading sound of horses carrying the men back to their respective ranches. Soon the April sky would darken and fill with stars, providing enough light to make out the shape of the mountain lion skulking in for his nightly kill. Neal had his men drive Saved closer in to the ranch and out of harm's way. He regretted his remark to Sloan implying that Samantha had grown indifferent to the steer. She often rode out with treats for him—bags of prime hay, sugar lumps, even pancakes with syrup. Too much paint was harmful to a grazing animal's horns because of its sensitive inner tissue, so Samantha took a brush only to the insensate tips of the steer's horn when the last coat had faded enough to put him in danger of the slaughterhouse. Self-pity had made Neal place her in a bad light to Sloan, and he knew he should be ashamed of himself, and he was.

He tethered his horse loosely to the barbed-wire fence and took up position on the ground in the black shadow of two giant, side-by-side boulders that formed a narrow tunnel through which the wind whistled continuously. The sound would cover any human noise, and the deep darkness hide his presence from the cat. Mountain lions had great night vision in low light, but they could not see in complete darkness, and while they possessed sensitive hearing, they had a weak sense of smell. The cat would emerge from the woods in front of him and see his horse, but Neal would be concealed, and the cat unaware that it was in the crosshairs of his Winchester repeater, model 1894, that allowed him to fire a number of shots before having to reload.

A lust to annihilate the threat to his land burned within him. At least Neal attributed this particular lust to that offense, but really, was he out here in substitute to his greater desire to destroy the danger to his family unit? Dr. Tolman was dead—"my *late* father's papers," Eleanor Brewster's note had read—and the doctor's daughter apparently knew nothing of Samantha's birth but for the name of the midwife who might have assisted with it. Would Samantha try to contact her? The midwife might be dead, too, and that would be the end of the road for Samantha's inquiries. He and Estelle would be safe from the competition.

But would it ever be the same for him? That was the question. And how in hell had Samantha connected the name of Dr. Tolman from the letter's return address to the doctor who'd placed her in their hands? Grizzly? Never. He would never reveal the doctor's identity to her, even if he remembered the name after all these years.

Unless…

In startled reflection, Neal thought back to the day Samantha brought him the doctor's letter. She'd been worried and anxious that it pertained to his health and had not looked at all convinced by his cockamamie story that the letter had come from a veterinarian. And then when she saw that he'd burned the letter before she could read it…

Risking movement that the cat could detect, Neal sat up straighter as mentally he tracked Samantha's possible footsteps after she left the dinner table that day. Unconvinced that he was telling the truth about his health, deeply concerned, she'd have gone to the two men who knew him best, Wayne and Grizzly. She'd have shared her worry with them, told them about the letter her father had burned, the word "Confidential" written on the envelope, asked if they knew a doctor by the name of Tolman. Wayne had no knowledge of the night Samantha had come to them, but Grizzly…

Neal could not fathom Grizzly disclosing a word of information that would lead Samantha away from him and Estelle, but in the hands of his daughter that he loved like his own, his cook and close friend would have been malleable as putty. Somehow Samantha had wriggled out of him who Dr. Tolman was. There was no other explanation. From there, it was easy to track Samantha to Marietta, a ferry ride conveniently tacked on to the train trip to Gainesville. Did Mildred know of Samantha's clandestine excursion? Had his daughter slipped secretly across the border without her knowing? No, Estelle's housekeeper had to have been in on the plot, or why would she have hidden Eleanor Brewster's letter beneath a basket of figs?

Neal's horse tossed his head, and Neal came alert. Slowly, he removed his spectacles from his pocket and slipped them on, hoping starlight and moonshine did not strike the lens and give his position away. A long, sleek shape moved stealthily out of the dense shelter of rock and woods into the light of the full moon. It paused, listening, then turned its yellow-eyed gaze to Neal's horse tethered to the barbed-wire fence. The horse whinnied softly, nervously, but with temporary trust in the protection of his master close by. The cat began a slow, feline stalk toward his prey before sinking into a moving crouch, a signal for Neal to bring the sight of the Winchester to his eyeglasses. He fired just as his horse pulled at his loose tethers and bolted away, his panicked neigh simultaneous to the sound of the gunshot. The impact of the bullet jerked the mountain lion into the air a few inches be-

fore it fell with a thud to the ground. The shot had caught the
devil in the neck, Neal saw as he approached the inert but still
breathing predator. The animal gazed at him in yellow-eyed hatred and gave a final snarl of defiance before his vanquisher raised
the rifle once more and shot him in the head.

Neal unsheathed his knife and whacked off the tail of the
mountain lion, then whistled for his horse. This evidence of victory over the enemy would be nailed to the flagpole for human
and animal to see until it dried over time in the dust and wind
and sun to an unrecognizable mangy string. The cat's carcass he
would leave for other predators. He holstered his rifle and rolled
the end of the tail tightly around its bloody stump to place in his
saddlebag, flushed with the deep satisfaction he always experienced when successfully dealing with any who would desecrate
what he held sacred. The secret was in the quiet waiting, the patience to not make a move until intent was identified. Samantha
had stumbled onto the identity of Dr. Tolman through loving
concern for her father that had then sparked her curiosity about
her birth, and Grizzly's abetment of it had been innocent and un-
intentional. Likewise, Mildred had been caught in the snare of
Samantha's curiosity. She'd probably had no idea that her mistress's daughter would be taking a ferry trip across the Red River
when they set off for Gainesville.

So Neal would wait quietly, patiently, vigilantly, to see what his
daughter would do with the new information she now possessed.
He would not question Grizzly. The man might hang himself
over what he had done, and Neal would not interrogate Mildred.
He didn't trust the woman not to leak his inquiries back to Samantha. At the moment his daughter had no inkling her father
had read Eleanor Brewster's letter or suspected her trip to Marietta, so he would let that pot simmer unstirred.

Meanwhile, what was he to do with the guilt of keeping from

his child knowledge of the whereabouts of her real mother, who would then be able to inform her of the remaining members of her family?

Samantha heard a chorus of excited male whistles and shouts and turned Pony in its direction. Her task this morning was to drive heifers and cows into lanes that fed into holding pens for pregnancy checking. She caught sight of her father, lasso whirling, as he streaked off on a cutting horse in hot pursuit of a calf making a dash for freedom from the branding pit. At just the right instant, he let go the uncoiling rope and with perfect timing, its spinning noose settled cleanly around the young steer's neck. Samantha watched as his trained quarter horse came to a full stop, braced itself, and pulled on the rope while her father, with a few quick turns, secured his end to the saddle horn. Then, with the speed of his rodeo record, he jumped to the ground, grasped the calf, threw it on its side, and tied its four legs together, trussing it for the branding iron.

Samantha shook her head, a raw ache in her throat. At fifty-five, Neal Gordon still had it, even when his skills weren't called for, but so it had been for two months now, ever since he'd read Eleanor Brewster's letter. But for that letter, he wouldn't be out here this morning. He wouldn't be working eight-hour days flushing strays from creek beds, draws, and gullies for counting, rounding up calves for market, rotating cattle to other pastures, doing the grueling work of a much younger, dollar-a-day cowhand. Tonight, as he'd done every evening since he'd discovered the letter hidden in the basket of figs, he'd drag home tired and sore in every muscle of his body, lower himself into a tub of hot water, and call for the liniment—from Silbia. Then, having taken supper from a tray brought to his room, he'd go to bed and wake at dawn to meet with the ranch hands to assume the arduous responsibilities that his age and prosperity had allowed him to turn over to Wayne Harris, the most competent foreman in the cow business.

All this unnecessary industry was a means to get away from her, Samantha painfully recognized. They were into the third week of June, and nothing had been the same between her and Neal Gordon since the late afternoon he'd streaked off to hunt the mountain lion the fourteenth of April. Its tail blew in the wind from a pole where the American flag was flown on the Fourth of July, a chilling warning to any who would threaten his domain. Samantha could not help but look upon it as a cautionary expression of her father's view of her journey across the Red River.

No longer did they end the day with a tumbler of whiskey and a glass of sherry together in the library. Neal was "off the bottle," he said. He took his morning and midday meals in the Trail Head and usually declined supper because he was "getting a paunch." He was unfailingly polite to Samantha, still tender, still kissed her cheek before calling it a day, but there was a reserve to his affection that crushed her heart. She yearned to ease his suffering and make it right between them again, but she was bound by her promise to Grizzly. She'd caught her father in attitudes of deep thought these past two months, and daily Samantha lived with the fear that he would trace her footsteps to Grizzly's kitchen office. If they could only talk about it, she would assure him that his fears of losing her to another family were groundless. She had thrown away Eleanor Brewster's letter and had no interest in contacting Bridget Mahoney or pursuing any other line of inquiry into her birth. Neal and Estelle Gordon were her parents and she wished for no other, she would make him understand, and rely on his love for her to believe her.

Pony whinnied. He wanted to get back to work. Samantha

flicked the reins to resume their task, but despite the warmth of the June day, she shuddered. For the first time in her life, in this her twentieth year, she felt alone. She'd sent her dearest friend packing and lost connection to her father. She could not go to her mother, as yet mercifully unaware of all that had transpired, or turn to Wayne and Grizzly, who must remain uninvolved. For the first time in all the years of being loved, sheltered, protected, Samantha felt herself an orphan.

Chapter Thirty-Five

A day later, Samantha pushed open the screened door of the Trail Head to hear Wayne say to her father, "Are you sure you want to go, Neal? Your backside has got to be aching from all that saddle sittin' you've been doing the last couple of months. Send me in your place. I can go and come by train and be back within a few days. Take a breather and enjoy life."

"He's right, Neal. Let's you and me go fishin'," Grizzly said. "I hear they're bitin' like crazy up at the north branch. Mornin', Samantha."

It was early morning, but the ranch hands had already set off for the day, and the dining room of the Trail Head was empty but for her father, Wayne, and Grizzly who sat at the head table with hands around coffee cups. Her father's and Wayne's backs were to the door, and only Grizzly had seen her come in. Neal whirled around. Samantha was staring at him in surprise. "You're going somewhere, Daddy?" she asked.

Neal resumed his position. "Yes, honey," he said, bringing the cup to his lips. "To La Paloma. I need to check on the boys, see how things are going up there."

Samantha walked around the table to face him. "When?"

Neal blew into the steam of his coffee. "I'm on my way in a few minutes. I was going to tell you."

"When? As you were pulling out?"

"When you came over for breakfast after I'd left instructions with my number one man here." Neal nodded to Wayne.

There was a time when those instructions would have been given to her. "How long will you be gone?"

"A week or so." Her father seemed to have trouble meeting her eyes, and the other men, caught in the uncomfortable exchange, concentrated on their coffee cups.

"Does Mother know?"

Taking a last swig from his cup, Neal got to his feet and said, "I called her yesterday from the Triple S. I gave her your love."

"I'm sure she would have been glad to see you before you left, Daddy. It's been a while since you've been in Fort Worth, almost two weeks, in fact."

Neal took down his hat from a row of pegs and positioned it on his head with a hard swipe of its brim. "Well, I've had a lot on my mind," he said. "She wouldn't have been happy to hear about it."

Warmth flooded Samantha's cheeks. It was the closest her father had ever nudged to the trouble that lay between them. Before that day in the kitchen, he would have shared every worry and concern disturbing his sleep with her. *Let's talk about it!* she longed to shout at him, then remembered the presence of Grizzly.

"You boys and girl take care of things while I'm gone," Neal said, and paused a second, holding Samantha in his gaze as if caught in sudden thought, then suddenly strode to her and embraced her. He kissed her temple and said, "I love you, daughter," then abruptly released her and spun toward the screened door.

Its slam hung in the silence along with the clatter of pots and pans and Spanish jabber coming from the kitchen, where Grizzly's crew was preparing the midday meal. Samantha stood unmoving, her throat locking as she heard her father's big paint carry him away. Tears burned her eyes. Wayne tipped back his chair on two legs and folded his arms over his chest. "All right, MG, this has been goin' on long enough. Time to tell us what's what. We've noticed a definite change in your pa these last months and not for the better, either. He's been grumpy as hell."

Grizzly gave her a long, pained look. *Is it what I think it is?*

Samantha answered with an imperceptible shake of her head. As far as she'd been able to observe—and she'd been looking—there had been no change in Neal Gordon's manner toward Grizzly, so for the time being he was safe. Seemingly satisfied with her silent assurance, Grizzly removed a battered sign from under the serving counter that read KITCHEN CLOSED. IF YORE HUNGRY, EAT GRASS. He hung the sign on a nail driven into the outside of the inner door, closed it, and threw the lock. Coming back, he poured Samantha a steaming cup of coffee and said, "Sit down and loosen your throat on that, pretty girl, and talk to us."

Samantha wrapped her fingers around the hot coffee cup. Oh, if only she could. "It's a private matter," she said.

Wayne said, "We don't mean to pry—"

"Hell yes, we do!" Grizzly interrupted hotly. "So spill it, Mornin' Glory. What in the name of God's creation is going on between you and your pa!"

"Maybe we can help," Wayne said soothingly. "Grizzly and me probably know your pa better'n you do, because we've known him longer, and we're men. Men can't express their pain. We go into deep, dark wells and stay there until we figure out what to do about what's bothering us. That's where your daddy is now—in a deep, dark well—alone. Care to tell us why?"

Samantha searched for an answer that would satisfy them and grasped the first that popped into her head, a substitute not too distant from the truth, one prompted by Sloan, never far from her thoughts. "I've disappointed Daddy," she said, "and he's having a hard time forgiving me."

Wayne's arms came apart. He lowered the chair legs to the floor. "Now, how could you possibly disappoint your pa?"

Samantha said, "He wanted me to set my cap for Sloan Singleton because he judges him the perfect husband for me and son-in-law for him. Unbeknown to Sloan and me, ever since we were children, my father and Seth had hopes that we...would marry and combine our spreads, but Sloan and I have...had a falling-out that has...put an end to that hope."

Wayne exchanged a look of understanding with Grizzly. "That explains why we haven't seen anything of Sloan for the past two months."

Grizzly nodded, and Samantha continued. "Now Daddy is worried Sloan will marry Anne Rutherford, and I will end up an old maid and produce no heir to the ranch."

Grizzly's fleshy lips twisted, and he glanced around as if looking for a place to spit and regretted his decision to forbid spittoons in the dining hall. "Anne Rutherford, a *banker's* daughter!" he snorted. "What a rancher's wife *she'll* make!"

"What Daddy fails to see is that I'm not at fault that his dream did not pan out. Sloan has no romantic interest in me. He's apparently in love with Anne Rutherford." Samantha resisted a visible breath of relief. They were buying her story, and she could see that Grizzly was greatly comforted and relieved by it. Her explanation *could* account for her father's strange withdrawal from her and grumpiness toward his men, if a little weak under examination. Neal Gordon *was* worried that she would never marry and leave an heir to Las Tres Lomas. What man was on the horizon with whom she would possibly consider spending the rest of her life?

Wayne said gently, "And what about your romantic interest in Sloan?"

She blushed at Wayne's knowing look. Good God! Could everyone but Sloan see how she felt about him? "What does it matter, since it doesn't matter to him?" she retorted. She shoved away from the table and stood. "You can take down the sign, Grizzly. There's nothing more to discuss. I can't fix what was never meant to be. In time, Daddy will accept that."

"Well, to hurry things along," Wayne said, "I'd round up that steer of yours and repaint his horns. Neal noticed they were faded the other day when we went after that mountain lion."

"Do we have any more of the red paint?"

"In the tack barn, last I noticed," Wayne said.

"I'm on my way to Windy Bluff," Samantha said.

Chapter Thirty-Six

Neal headed north, his throat throbbing at the last look he'd seen in the eyes of his little girl. He was leaving her hurt and bewildered, but there was no way around it. All would be explained in due time, and then she would understand the why and wherefore of his behavior these last two months and maybe forgive him. No telling what she'd made of the time and distance he'd put between them, but he'd needed space to figure out what to do, and he'd finally settled on a course of action. It hadn't been easy. At fifty-five, he thought he was full grown, but Neal supposed a man never really did finish with the job of growing up. He reached a certain level of adulthood, knew who he was and what he was about, and then something came along to jar him out of his state of inalterability and forced him to a new plane of maturity or, Neal liked to think, to a more exalted height—like the unexpected situation where a man must put the welfare of someone he loved above his own, no matter the personal pain.

So he was off this morning with his heart aching on the longest, most painful journey of his life. Today was Tuesday. Neal figured that at an ambling gait of four to five miles per hour, taking into account road conditions, the terrain, some deep creeks to ford, and stops for the night, he could make around thirty miles a day, a rate that should put him into Gainesville in less than three days. He'd get a room there somewhere or sleep under the stars. The Holloway farm should not be hard to find, and he could accomplish his mission in no more than a day, then spend the rest of his time at La Paloma, if not with his original purpose in mind. Why would he wish for another ranch when Las Tres Lomas might not be preserved for future generations? That concern loomed almost as large and devastating as the possibility of losing Samantha to another family with their own dreams for her. Night after night these past sleepless months, ever since reading Mrs. Brewster's letter, he'd conjured up scenarios that made him long to yank his imaginings right out of his head. He pictured Samantha unable to resist the biological pull of her real family. He visualized her embracing her brother—a twin!—and other siblings, if they existed, and imagined her yearning to live among them. He felt the pain of her loyalties split until finally she came to him, tears streaming, to say in a choked voice that ranching was not for her. She had gone along with his plans to someday take over the ranch because of all she owed him and Estelle.

He envisioned his wife shattered with grief and himself growing embittered and angry as he aged, drying up like the tail of the mountain lion strung from the flagpole. He couldn't even be comforted by his original plan before Samantha came along for Estelle to sell the ranch to Sloan after his death, not if he married that banker's daughter. How could that vain twit of a city girl ever feel the appropriate affection for his home that Las Tres Lomas deserved?

You always imagine the worst, Neal, Estelle often accused him in his preparation for disaster, whether or not it came, but he could not shake the vision of their daughter leaving them, moving away, marrying someone not of their kind. The image was even worse than the mental picture of losing her to Lasell Seminary for Young Women in Massachusetts. *Have faith in Samantha's love for us and the ranch, Neal,* Estelle would advise should he tell her of his despair. *She would never desert us.*

But in his wrestles with his nature, conscience, and feelings during the past dark months, he'd reached the conclusion that it was not Samantha's love for Neal and Estelle Gordon that mattered. It was their love for her, and so he'd made his decision. He'd thought of sharing it with Estelle to prepare her for the darkness to come, but as was his way, he'd reconsidered laying down his hand. The cards might play in their favor and Estelle be spared the pain he was now enduring. *Sufficient unto the day is the evil thereof*, the Good Word instructed, and by it he would abide.

He was on his way now to the Holloway farm to meet Millicent Holloway, Samantha's mother, and her husband, Leon, should he still be alive. He would identify himself as the adoptive father of the daughter they had given away, but he would not volunteer the location of Samantha's whereabouts or a shred of information about her until he had an answer to the question he had come to ask: Did they wish to reunite with their daughter? An eager spark in the eyes, a flare of joy upon their faces—or the absence of them—would tell him immediately if he should return home to give Samantha the news her search was over or leave her never to learn of the existence of the mother or couple who once again had foresworn her. Neal would not have his daughter rejected twice.

After leaving Grizzly and Wayne, Samantha planned to ride out to Windy Bluff and herd Saved back to give his horns a refresher coat of paint, but an unexpected visitor showed up. Silbia met her as she entered the Main House to pick up her wide-brimmed hat for the ride to one of the farthest points of the ranch. "I was just about to send one of the girls to get you, Miss Sam. You got somebody waiting for you in the great room."

"Who?"

"Miss Anne Rutherford."

Samantha heard the name in surprise. Why on earth would Anne Rutherford come to call on her? She'd seen much of the girl, Sloan at her side, at the prenuptial socials held for Todd Baker and Ginny Warner in the last two months, their wedding the last occasion where they'd met, but only to exchange pleasantries. She and Anne, though they shared the same life-long social acquaintances, had never been friends. Samantha thought that not surprising, since they had no interests in common.

"Anne! What a surprise!" she greeted her visitor, who appeared to be tenuously seated on the edge of a lounge chair as if fearful it might swallow her. "What brings you out here to Las Tres Lomas?"

"Sloan Singleton," Anne said. She rose quickly but gracefully at Samantha's entrance, a lithe figure in a filmy spring frock, its pastel flowers a complement to her ivory skin and deep black hair.

Samantha checked her move to welcome Anne with a friendly embrace. "Sloan?"

"I am sure the reason for my visit will remain confidential, between only us, Samantha. I had no one else to come to, and I thought you could be of help. You know Sloan better than anybody other than his sisters, and they don't like me. I'm aware that they don't want him to marry me."

Samantha stood speechless. Anne's blatant declaration—and that she would make it to her, given the girl's known consideration of every word she uttered and to whom she delivered it—genuinely shocked her. Samantha sat down and with a hand invited Anne to do the same. "Why not?"

Anne shrugged as if the answer was obvious. "Oh, the typical thing. They're jealous old-maid biddies who don't want to share the house they've ruled over for years, but I don't believe Sloan would listen to them. Something else seems to have...come between us in the last several months. Sloan has changed, and I don't know why. I thought maybe you could tell me. He confides in you. Don't deny it. I don't mind. Truly, I don't. Has he said anything about...us?"

For a moment, Samantha was too stumped by Anne's brazenness to reply. "No, nothing, but he would not confide such personal matters to me," she answered. "When we were children, yes, but not now."

Doubt clouded the irises of Anne's eyes, the color of dark sapphires. "The change set in around the middle of April—on Saturday, April fourteenth, as a matter of fact," she said. "I know because I keep a daily diary. It began then. Sloan was to have telephoned to set a time to call on me that evening, but he didn't. Nor did I see him the next day. We usually spend Sundays together. I heard nothing from him for an entire week and sent a note of concern out to the Triple S. Who knows but that one of his sisters intercepted it, but he did not respond. When he finally turned up, he gave the excuse that he'd been on a hunt after a mountain lion that Saturday and busy at the ranch afterward, but I could tell it was something else. Do you recall anything else that happened involving Sloan on April fourteenth?"

Samantha was not likely to forget the date, a pivotal day in her life. It was the day her father had learned of her betrayal and she'd set Sloan straight about his "brother" role, but how could those personal and private events relate in any way to Sloan's feelings for Anne? "I can verify that Sloan did go on a hunt that Saturday," she said, "and you should believe him when he says he was busy at the ranch. I've never known Sloan to lie, and the spring months on a ranch are our most demanding. Other than that, I fear I can't be of more help, Anne. Are you sure you're not imagining Sloan's change toward you?"

"Oh, *Samantha*!" Anne hopped up, the filmy skirt of her dress swirling around her. She strolled off a distance, latching her hands together, and spoke as if to an unseen audience in the room. "You've...never...well, you've never had experience with men, so you wouldn't know the signs that tell a woman her lover's affections have cooled..."

"Lovers," Samantha repeated, a sharp pain flitting through her and her face stinging from resentment at Anne's condescending assumption of her sexual naïveté.

Anne swung around in a froth of batiste and lace. "Yes, *lovers*!" she cried. "Or at least as close to lovers as one can be without...marriage. One does not have to have physical intimacy to become lovers."

"Oh," Samantha said in a tone implying she'd been rightly enlightened. She rose. The girl was imagining things. Anne Rutherford was exquisite. How could any man, for all her insipidity, resist her? Samantha had not noticed Sloan giving his soon-to-be-betrothed a lack of attention at the social gatherings in honor of Todd and Ginny's nuptials. It could be that all the wedding folderol had made him, soon to be a groom, nervous at the permanence of marriage. But she would not give Anne Rutherford the comfort of that possibility.

Her guest seemed unwilling to take Samantha's hint that the visit was over. Anne stepped farther into the cavernous space of the great room and swept her gaze over the thick-beamed ceiling, the wood-paneled walls, and the wide oak staircase to the landing that ran the circumference of the second story. Samantha's resentment flared. Anne was thinking of the ranch house of the Triple S, whose interior was built on similar lines. She stared at the girl in some shock. Anne Rutherford was purportedly the classic model of social correctness. Yet she stood in the heart of Samantha's home, swiping her critical gaze over its layout and furnishings like a dust rag, ignoring the affront her shameless inspection might be to her hostess.

"I could get used to a place like this," Anne said.

"It might take some doing." Samantha spoke through a gritted-teeth smile. The Rutherford residence in Fort Worth was a white, palatial edifice built in homage to her family's money and social prominence.

"Not if Sloan was part of the adjustment." Anne turned to see Samantha's tight expression and gave her a faint smile. "Forgive me. I'm not myself today."

"I can see that."

A handkerchief materialized from the fluffy folds of Anne's sleeves, and she dabbed at the tears pooling in her jeweled eyes. "It's just that I'm beside myself with worry over this situation. By now I thought Sloan would have proposed, and I'd have a ring on my finger. Everybody expects us to marry. How can I face people if...we don't? What would the insult do to me and my family?"

Samantha's hackles rose further. Ah, so the shame and jeers of society were Anne's real concern. "Do you love Sloan?" she asked.

The sapphire eyes scoffed at the question. "Why, of course I do. Why would I spend so much time with a man I don't love?"

"I'm afraid I can't answer that, since I've had so little experience with men," Samantha said. "I'd offer coffee and rolls, but I'm running the ranch alone since Daddy has taken off to our cattle camp in Cooke County."

This time Anne took the hint and reached for her parasol, the handkerchief tucked back into the sleeve of her dress. "I must get back anyway before the heat sets in, and I never eat between meals." She seemed suddenly to remember her manners. "I hope

I didn't interfere with"—she whisked a sapphire inspection over Samantha's work attire—"whatever you were doing."

"I was happy for the interruption," Samantha said, smiling. "We're castrating the young steers this morning."

Anne's face blanched. "I'll see myself out," she said.

Chapter Thirty-Seven

Late in the afternoon, by a rope tied loosely around his neck and his horn tips a bright red, Samantha led Saved back to his preferred grazing area at Windy Bluff. The steer, almost the size of Pony, followed along docilely as a lamb. The trek gave her time and solitude to think. What had come over Sloan? She would not flatter herself by thinking Anne's cause for concern had to do with their quarrel. They'd had many quarrels in the past, but none that had called their brother-sister relationship into question. Could Sloan indeed have had a change of heart toward Anne? "Once my brother gets a few more years on him, he'll see through Anne's artifice," Millie May had predicted. "I hope she won't snag him before that day comes."

Had that day come? In a few weeks, Sloan would turn twenty-four. Were those enough years to make his sister's prediction come true?

Samantha thought back to their quarrel that she now acknowledged had taken on a much darker, deeper cast than a mere tiff. *You're not my brother, Sloan.* She would never forget his jolt of surprise at hearing those words, then something else had swum into his eyes, another brand of surprise. But then she'd added: *You're my friend. No more, no less.* Like an idiot.

She still believed that for all Anne's "experience" with men, which Samantha doubted, the girl could be imagining the chill between her and Sloan. Ranchers' worries were never-ending, but some came like a swarm of bees, blocking the sun. Sloan may have gone through a period like that these past months. The Triple S was not as financially solid as Las Tres Lomas. Sloan had invested heavily in breeding stock to increase future production of his herds. A strange blight had attacked his hay fields. Come winter, he would have the expense of buying fodder for his cattle beyond what the Gordons could spare. Also, unlike the Gordon ranch, the Singleton ranch carried a loan against it held by the Rutherford City Bank. Samantha assumed that when Sloan and Anne married, the debt would be forgiven.

And Sloan was still disturbed by the rift between her and her father. He had left her room deeply upset that day in April, and his concern had not abated. *Sam, I told myself I'd butt out of what you've made clear is none of my business, but I can't help myself*, he'd said in an urgent whisper at Todd and Ginny's wedding reception, the first and only time they'd conversed since that fateful afternoon. *I saw Neal in town the other day, and he looks awful. I'm worried about him. Whatever is going on between you two has got to be resolved. It's clear that you two have not patched things up.*

Not clear to everybody, Samantha had thought, but then everybody wasn't looking. Not even her mother had as yet suspected anything at odds between her husband and daughter. *You're exaggerating*, she'd said, looking around to see if they'd been overheard.

Not from where I'm standing, he'd said.

Before she could answer, Anne had drawn to his side and taken his arm, and Samantha had excused herself to go to the punch table, unable to stomach Anne's adoring gaze up into Sloan's face and the return of her smile.

In the vastness of the silence around her, broken by the occasional sounds of milling cattle and the high overhead screech of hawks, Samantha allowed her imagination to fly. She would scold herself later, but right now, with the breeze pleasant on her face and the saddle warm under her and her throat tight from a permeating sadness, she imagined what it would be like for Sloan to love her, not as a brother or friend or his surrogate father's daughter, but as a woman. For a long time now, she'd thought of them together in ways that had never entered her mind when they had romped together as children. When had her memories of their innocent play as boy and girl given way to a woman's sexual fantasies of a man? They were so right for each other in every way. Even their differences complemented the other. She'd once heard a friend of her mother's complain that she wished she hadn't married a man she'd known all her life. There was nothing left to learn about the other. *We're as dull together as a pair of old boots*, she'd said. The couple was dull to begin with, Samantha had thought, but not she and Sloan. They were familiar territory to the other, but there were still peaks and valleys to be discovered, unknown terrain that made her skin tingle to imagine exploring.

Across the flat distance, the twin boulders of Windy Bluff rose up to meet them. Samantha had never understood why they were called bluffs, since they were really peaks, but so the name had been recorded in the grant document giving her great-great-grandfather ownership of the ranch. Saved tossed his heavy-horned head, recognizing home. Samantha sighed and allowed her daydream to drift away. "Okay, buddy, we're here," she said. She dismounted and slipped the rope from around the steer's neck, then released Pony's reins to amble with him to the nearby underground spring for a drink.

There had been a wind storm in the night that had resculpted the sandy bed of skimpy grass found only on this particular strip of the ranch. It was marine sand, surviving proof of the large body of water that had covered Las Tres Lomas millions of years ago. In its recession, it had left this swath of beach sand good only for producing sprigs of grass as sparse as hair on a balding head.

Her foot struck something, and Samantha looked down, expecting to have stepped on a small outcropping of caliche rock. She looked closer, then bent down for another, longer inspection. A chill swept her flesh. She knelt and carefully brushed away more of the sand and sediment. There was no doubting the impression. Exposed by last night's wind—unmistakably—was what appeared to be the petrified form of a prehistoric animal head recognizable only from pictures in newspaper articles and from drawings in her paleontology texts. Excitement mounting, holding her breath, Samantha gently scraped further. The rest of the skull, if it was there, appeared deeply imbedded, mortared to its burial site, and she dared not dig further for fear of disturbing the bed. If her preliminary inspection was accurate, she was looking at the full forehead, blunt nose, and intact jawbone of a dinosaur.

Trembling from the shock of her discovery, Samantha got to her feet and walked carefully toward Pony with an eye on the ground for other remains. Todd Baker must see this. She must contact him to come out here immediately to assess her find. If her guess was correct, Todd, with his geological background, would know what to do, who to approach for further analysis. Windy Bluff could be the site of a huge field of dinosaur skeletons like the kind discovered in the Garden Park area in Colorado and at Camp Bluff, Wyoming, in the late 1870s.

Exhilarated by her treasure, Samantha unhooked the gate separating Las Tres Lomas and the Triple S and urged Pony to a fast pace in the direction of the Singletons' sprawling Spanish-style ranch house. She would use their telephone to contact Todd in Dallas at Waverling Tools. Worrisome thoughts of her father,

Sloan, and Anne Rutherford flew out of her mind as she contemplated the possible enormity of the identity of the species she'd found. When she'd been in school, the study of dinosaurs was relatively new to the field of paleontology. The first full skeletal form of the creature that proved its existence and gave an idea of what it looked like had been unearthed in Haddonfield, New Jersey, in 1859, and the feverish hunt was on for further evidence of its actuality, a search that had ushered in what newspapers called the "golden age" of dinosaur paleontology.

An educated guess suggested the creature's snout and mandible belonged to the genera of the sauropods, the largest animals known to live on land. They possessed huge bodies, tremendously long necks and tails, and tiny heads less than two feet in size. The exciting fact Samantha recalled of the group was that the plant-eating sauropods ran in herds. That suggested the remnant at Windy Bluff could be among hundreds an archeological dig would excavate. The herds had come to drink from the huge body of water that once covered Las Tres Lomas de la Trinidad.

The smell of smoke from branding pits and the sounds of raucous male voices and bawling cattle carried across the distance. Samantha drew a breath of relief. The Triple S was working its cattle today—as always, under Sloan's supervision. *Still trying to prove himself*, was Millie May's perception of it, but Samantha knew Sloan to be a hands-on rancher who saw it as his responsibility to oversee every aspect of the Triple S's operation. *That's what trusted foremen are for*, she'd argue, one of their sundry disagreements about ranch management where they did not see eye to eye.

The red-tiled roofline of the main house, set in a dip in the topography and fanned by gardens, outbuildings, and corrals, came into view. The white stucco structure glowed in the light of the late afternoon sun, and as she neared it, Samantha caught sight of a man and a woman emerging from the kitchen side of the house. The couple walked to a horse tethered out of view of the windows, and there the man took the woman's face between his hands and kissed her long and passionately. Samantha slowed Pony. She had been in the man's presence only a few times, but she recognized Daniel Lane and the woman in his arms. She was Billie June Singleton.

The sound of an approaching rider must have carried. The man, tall enough to see over the stucco fence, turned his head to see Samantha on Pony cresting the small rise of land fronting the compound. She nodded at him and kneed Pony to the front of the house, certain the man's face had drained of color beneath his deep tan.

Millie May threw open the door before Samantha had reached the porch. "I heard you ride up," she said. "Thank God it's you."

"You were expecting someone you didn't wish to see?" Samantha inquired dryly, having a good idea of who that might be.

Millie May gave her a nervous hug. "Just not right now. Happy to see you, Sam, though surprised. What brings you our way?"

"The telephone, if I may. I have to make a call to Dallas. It's important."

"Wouldn't matter if it wasn't," Millie May said. "Of course you may use it. Sue Ann is on the switchboard today. She'll get you through quickly, since the call is from here." Millie May smiled, showing a broken tooth acquired when she got in the way of a male fist launched during a protest of a women's freedom march. "Sue Ann has a crush on Sloan."

What woman doesn't? Samantha thought.

Within a relatively short time, the operator located a telephone number for Waverling Tools, and with relief Samantha heard Todd say, "Todd Baker speaking." One of his boasts was that his office possessed its own telephone while some of his colleagues had to answer their calls at the receptionist's desk. Conscious of listening ears on the party line, Samantha resisted the urge to explain the nature of her call, and merely informed the geologist that she must see him as soon as possible about a matter that required his expertise. If she told him she'd found what she believed to be the partial skull of a dinosaur, who knew but that the news would get out and thrill seekers might show up at Las Tres Lomas to see the phenomenon and destroy the dig site. Todd caught the anxiety in her voice and without further conversation said that he wouldn't be able to get away until Saturday. He could take the 7:40 morning train to Fort Worth. Would Samantha meet him at the station, and...was Grizzly still serving up his sausage pancakes for Saturday breakfast?

As Samantha hung up the receiver, Billie June came flying through the swinging door from the kitchen into the hall where the telephone was located, her face flushed the color of her coral cameo. "You saw him, didn't you?" she demanded of Samantha.

"Who?"

"You know who."

Millie May had come to the doorway of the great room off the hall. "He took a chance coming here, sister."

"I know, but it couldn't be helped," Billie June said. "He's going down to Beaumont for a while on an assignment for Waverling Tools and wanted to see me before he left." She looked beseechingly at Samantha. "You won't tell Sloan about us, will you, Sam?"

"Of course not," Samantha said. "Your brother and I don't speak much nowadays, anyway."

"I wish you did," Millie May said, her tone sorrowful. "Then maybe we'd know what in the Sam Hill has come between him and Miss Holier-Than-Thou. Can you stay for coffee?"

Samantha removed her hat and pulled off her riding gloves, feeling a tingle of elation. So Anne wasn't imaging things, after all. "Of course I can," she said.

Chapter Thirty-Eight

Dammit to hell!" Daniel Lane swore as he rode away from the main compound of the Triple S opposite the direction where he knew the ranch hands, overlorded by Sloan Singleton, were working cattle. The Gordon girl had seen him in the clutch with Billie June. She wasn't likely to say anything to her brother, but the fewer people who knew about their continuing affair, the better. At least for now. Before Samantha Gordon had shown up, only Millie May had been aware that he and Billie June were still seeing each other. Millie May did not approve, but she'd keep her mouth shut out of love for her sister, who might do something crazy if she were prevented from being with him. Billie June was no one to fool with when her dander got up.

It was one of the things he liked about her, that made it easier to meet her twice a month on Saturday at a depot between Fort Worth and Dallas. The place had a little café with a yard and benches out back where they could take their coffee and hold hands and kiss now and then. It was the best they could arrange until they found a better meeting place. There was *so* much more Billie June wanted to do if only they could find a private place to do it, but he would wait on that until he judged the moment ripe.

Today was the first time he had chanced coming to the ranch. If caught, the three of them had concocted a story. Millie May would swear that Daniel Lane had come in a purely professional capacity. She'd known no one else to restore her father's favorite pair of spurs that she'd promised to donate to the museum erected in Fort Worth to honor the contributions local ranchers had made to the cattle industry. As a matter of fact, Millie May was in charge of acquiring the exhibits.

The set of spurs was still lying on a back porch table, untouched, and Daniel was making clean his getaway. He'd thought of taking them with him, fixing 'em up for irony's sake in preparation for the day when he'd wear the old man's spurs as a sneer in Sloan Singleton's face, but then he'd thought: Hell, it wasn't the father's strap of spiked wheels he wanted to wear, but the son's. And he would, too. He didn't know how as yet, but he was working on it, and so far everything was going according to plan.

The truth of it was that he might have continued seeing Billie June for her own sake if her little brother had stayed out of it and allowed their relationship to run its inevitable course. Daniel hadn't been after his sister's money or a stake in the ranch like Mr. High-and-Mighty Big Britches had naturally assumed. Hell no. Billie June was plain as a sack of beans and five years older than he. In time her novelty would have worn off, and he would have moved on. The day Sloan Singleton rode up on his Thoroughbred with his gun arms at the picnic grounds and made him look like a sawed-off whip handle, Daniel hadn't been after anything from his sister but social relief from the grind of his daily life.

He'd started out by feeling sorry for Billie June. She'd popped into Chandler's one day, breathless, worried, a quick and chirpy little sparrow of a woman. Her favorite horse had thrown a shoe, and she was afraid he'd cracked a hoof or worse. "Oh, Mr. Chandler, please help Bo," she'd cried. "He's gone and—"

That was when Billie June's eye had fallen on him, shirtless, chest muscles glistening, biceps bulging as he worked over the anvil, and stopped in midspeech. Mr. Chandler had caught her pop-eyed stare. "Maybe you better have a look at what Miss Singleton's talking about, Daniel," he'd said with a wink.

Daniel was no farrier by trade. He generally did not shoe horses. He was an ironmonger and a miracle worker with metals, but he'd looked over her stallion's hoof, removed a stone, and replaced its shoe. The next day Billie June was back. "I believe I dropped my glove here," she said. "Have you by any chance found it?"

"No, miss, I haven't," Daniel said and called to his boss. "Have you seen Miss Singleton's glove, Mr. Chandler?"

His boss had shaken his head, an amused glint in his eye. "Can't say I have."

"Oh," Billie June had said, pressing her cheek thoughtfully. "Perhaps I dropped it somewhere else." Daniel had asked after Bo. Billie June was driving a two-seater trap pulled by another horse. "Well…he still seems to favor that foot," she'd answered and looked at him with wide-eyed hope. "Do you think…I hate to impose…but do you think you…could come by the ranch and take another look at that hoof?"

"Will Sunday afternoon do? I'm off then."

Her homely face had lit up like the first flare of a candle flame. "That would be perfect," she'd said.

Daniel later learned that Sloan Singleton spent Sunday afternoons and evenings in town calling upon a society do-gooder named Anne Rutherford. That first Sunday afternoon when he arrived, Billie June was dressed fit to kill and smelling like a rose garden. Lemonade and freshly baked cookies awaited him on the screened back porch. After inspecting Bo's hoof, which was perfectly all right, they had sat at the porch table and talked. After her brief shyness was overcome by a natural animation, Daniel found to his surprise that she was the most engaging person he'd ever met. He completely forgot to pay attention to her little off-centered nose, brow too strong for her small face, and a somewhat lopsided jaw. He was spellbound by the way she used her shapely hands, as if conducting a chorus, and he loved the sound of her laughter, like musical bells, but most of all, he appreciated her intelligence. They were both readers—when he could get hold of books—and discussed their favorites; many of hers he'd never heard of. "Oh, but you must read them!" she declared. "I'd be happy to let you borrow mine."

She'd sent him home with a saddlebag of books, and he'd asked, "How will I get these back to you?"

"Let's meet again here, same time, in two weeks," she'd suggested. "Then we can discuss them together."

Thus their friendship began, at least that was what Daniel called it. He knew full well that Billie June hoped for something more, but he wasn't about to oblige her. He was lonely. Billie June was lonely. That was it. They had many things to talk about. She was interested in how he created objects out of iron and steel—*works of art!* she declared—and he enjoyed hearing her views on every subject from social issues to town gossip. He looked forward to their stimulating Sundays together that offered a distraction from the forge and gave him a reason to clean up. And he had to admit it was flattering as all get-out to be in the company of a lady in a fine home rather than in bed with a floozy in an upstairs saloon room.

So he'd meant their relationship to continue as such until that Fourth of July picnic, when he'd felt his insides explode like a box of firecrackers. Daniel Lane might be nothing but a sweaty smithy's helper in the eyes of the boss of the Triple S, but no man treated him like a horseshoe spike. He would make Sloan Singleton pay for his public humiliation of him. He would get even. Billie June was used to making a spectacle of herself, what with her radical ideas about the rights of animals and women, but they would no more take her down in the eyes of the town than a gnat could topple an oak tree. She was a Singleton, a member of the landed gentry, and Daniel Lane was a nobody. All he had was the modest reputation he had built up as a man who could create anything out of metals—and his dignity, and Sloan Singleton had stripped him of it. Daniel would not hang around at Chandler's Blacksmith Shop like a whipped dog. He'd read and applied to a HELP WANTED ad posted by Waverling Tools in Dallas calling for a man skilled in ironwork. His boss had given him a sterling reference, and within days he was hired. Off he went to Dallas, leaving Billie June with the promise that he was not out of the picture yet. At Waverling Tools, he found his nirvana.

The company was going places, and Daniel Lane was going with it, but not as a simple metalworker. When Trevor Waverling found out what he could forge from a piece of iron with a hammer and chisel, he put him in his department for designing oil drilling tools. Within weeks, he came up with an improved lathe chuck for drilling pipe. He was now working on the development of a stronger steel casing to prevent the wall of the borehole from caving in during the drilling process, one of the oilman's worst nightmares. His boss had applied for patents in his name, which the company paid for, the only stipulation being that Waverling Tools would receive 90 percent of all sales resulting from his inventions for five years, and then their deal would be renegotiated. Fair enough, Daniel had thought, as long as ownership of the patents was returned to him.

While the company had begun manufacturing derricks and oil drilling tools, it was not yet ready to move into the actual business of leasing mineral rights and drilling for petroleum, but it was headed in that direction. Trevor Waverling was taking his time, but he wasn't wasting it. He was learning and preparing, an approach Daniel liked because it mirrored his own style of maneuvering. Since the oil strike in 1897 in Corsicana fifty-five miles up the pike, his boss had seen too many investors jump into the oil game only to come up with dry holes and empty pockets. To prospect oil sites, he had hired a razor-sharp geologist, Todd Baker, and was training his son, Nathan Holloway, as a landman. The two made a competent team, as Daniel had discovered when he finagled an invitation to go with them on a trip to East Texas to investigate a "land disturbance" that a farmer believed was a sure sign of the presence of oil. Turned out the farmer was dreaming. Todd Baker analyzed the fissure as nothing more than a split in the earth caused by drought and not an indicator of an oil reservoir beneath the fracture zone. Given the frenzy going on among oil and gas speculators, some geologists would have jumped first and looked later at a possible find, and some landmen would have slapped a contract before the farmer at first glance at the fissure, but not Todd and Nathan. Those two were not about to risk their boss's time and money on a pig in a poke like so many others were doing.

Yessir, Daniel had hooked up with a company he could trust to stay in business. It was with Waverling Tools he intended to make his mark—become somebody—because he planned to learn everything available about the oil business and move out from the drafting table into the operation of the company. He could see it in the works plain as day. This mission the boss was sending him on Monday to the lumber town of Beaumont in southeast Texas gave proof of that. He was to meet with a man named Anthony Lucas, who had blazed a crazy trail around Texas and up east to the large oil companies to convince investors and wildcatters that oil was under a salt dome the locals called Spindletop Hill. The man's convictions had caught Trevor Waverling's attention, which had led to Daniel's assignment. He was to go to Beaumont to assess whether the man was trying to sell a pipe dream. He would investigate Lucas's background, if possible talk to the investors Lucas had approached, and check out the dome itself for evidence to support the man's stubborn belief it held something besides salt.

Daniel had dared to ask his boss why he was interested, explaining that the information might help him with the focus of his investigation.

"I might want to offer Waverling Tools' drilling equipment at no cost in exchange for a share in the well if it comes in," he'd replied. "In that case, you'll be taking periodic trips to the site for maintenance checks and to fix problems with the equipment should they arise, but I also want you to keep your eyes open and your ear to the ground and report back to me what you see and hear. You understand what I'm asking you to do?"

"Yessir, I understand," Daniel had said. He was to be troubleshooter and spy. He liked the titles. They expanded his position and importance within the company.

"Take the full week and we'll hear what you have to say in Monday's conference meeting," Trevor Waverling had said. "I'll depend on your report to determine if it's worth my going to Beaumont to offer Lucas a deal."

"You have my word that I'll look at every tooth in that horse's mouth," Daniel had assured him. "I won't let you down."

"I'm sure you won't," his boss had said.

To get even with a man, you had to beat him at his game. Sloan Singleton's game was wealth and power. Somehow, someway, Daniel Lane meant to take him down from those pinnacles. And like the oil business that he intended to learn through association with those who could advance his ambition, he would learn the business of Sloan Singleton through his sister, Billie June.

Chapter Thirty-Nine

Early Saturday morning, Todd Baker boarded the Texas Pacific for the two-hour rail trip to Fort Worth from Dallas and saw Samantha waiting for him on the station platform as the train pulled in. The first glimpse of her through the compartment window told him that something was up. She was pacing as if constant movement might hurry the train along. His bride, Ginny, who loved and missed Samantha, had begged to come and spend the day with the three of them, but Todd had gently refused her pleas. (Ginny did not like sausage pancakes anyway.) "Sam said she needed my expertise, hon. She sounded pretty urgent about it. I'm guessing she's found something she'd like me to analyze—something like a rock formation or a sea relic—out on Las Tres Lomas. You'd be stuck alone in that cavern of a ranch house for hours unless you'd like to ride along with us, and"—a smile and quick kiss—"I'm thinking you wouldn't."

He was absolutely right about that, Ginny had said. She'd hoped that after a brief consultation over a little rock or fossil fragment, the three of them would lunch together and catch up on all the town gossip.

Todd was dressed for the possibility of a long ride in the saddle to some remote spot on the ranch, and from the train window he saw that Samantha was, too. What in the world had she found?

He was a prospecting geologist. Would Samantha have called him—a good friend, yes, but not a confidant—with an urgent request to see him if she hadn't discovered something that would interest him professionally? It couldn't be something like an oil seep or a gas-leaking fracture, although he believed, along with Trevor Waverling, that the Central Plains was rich in petroleum and natural gas deposits, as evidenced by telltale signs of oil found on land surfaces and the area's number of sulfur springs. If Samantha had discovered something of the sort on Las Tres Lomas, she'd have kept quiet about it. She was keenly opposed to oil drilling on crop and grazing lands.

He had a few minutes before leaving his seat to observe his friend through the window. What would happen to Samantha Gordon now that she'd decided to walk the path her leather-bound father had chosen for her? Was she doomed to spend her life at Las Tres Lomas fulfilling a misguided obligation as a cattleman's daughter? What a tragic waste! Samantha possessed the purest scientific mind he'd so far encountered. The scientific mind called for a continual openness to new ideas, concepts, and theories that challenged the established point of view. Samantha had been notorious for that stubbornness at Simmons Preparatory School. Her reluctance to embrace a preferred conclusion was based not on obstinacy but on a sincere desire to learn the truth. Unlike some scientists Todd knew, Samantha could let go of preconceptions and old beliefs and accept new explanations when the evidence supported them. Todd would never forget the day when a lab experiment had led her to question the accepted theory that oil originates from the fossilized remains of animals and plants buried in ancient rock layers. Her microscope and beaker had revealed the possibility that while oil contains chemical elements found in living matter, the viscous liquid itself did not evolve from once-living material. Therefore, she'd hypothesized, petroleum might come from another source not yet identified. Their professor had scoffed. Could Samantha then explain why petroleum deposits were often found on or near remains of prehistoric life?

Also, Todd mused, how in the world was Samantha, stuck out on a ranch, ever to meet a man of her same intelligence and worth, someone who would love and cherish her as he did his Ginny? The only man he knew equal to her—and Todd had his doubts about him—was Sloan Singleton, and he was courting that airhead, Anne Rutherford. What Singleton saw in her besides her beauty was beyond the capability of Todd's pragmatic mind. Maybe he'd chosen Anne over Sam because she *was* an airhead, a girl he could boss around. In that case, Samantha wouldn't have suited Sloan at all. Todd sighed. As his poetry-loving Ginny would say, was their lovely and intelligent Samantha "born to blush unseen, and waste its sweetness on the desert air" like the flower in Thomas Gray's poem?

"*A sauropod!*" Todd exclaimed a short time later, when Samantha told him the reason for her summons. His vocal astonishment carried so loudly, he drew looks from others gathered on the train platform. "Are you sure?"

"No, that's why you're here, but I'm almost certain. I've brought you a saddled horse. I would have come in a wagon, but we'd have had to leave it at the barn and pick up our horses there. This way, we can cut across from the road straight to Windy Bluff."

Todd's face fell. "What? Before we have sausage pancakes?"

"Later, when you've looked at my find. I've nearly gone crazy this week waiting for you."

A little over an hour later, Todd was squatting down next to the partial skull. He brushed more of the sand away and carefully examined the ridges of the nose and jaw. "Looks like the features of a dinosaur to me, all right. This could really be something, Sam. Most of the skeletons of these animals found so far are minus the heads. Dinosaur skulls were so small and fragile that as soon as the beast died, the head was the first part of the body to disintegrate."

"So who do I contact about this?" Samantha asked. "The American Museum of Natural History in New York?"

"I think that would be your best bet, and I'll contact a friend at the Peabody Museum of Natural History at Yale. They have a vertebrate paleontologist on staff." Todd stood up, brushing the sand off his hands. "I see you brought your Kodak. Take a picture from every angle and send them to the museum with a letter describing your find. Meanwhile, this area needs to be cordoned off—" He stopped, stared. "What on God's earth is *that?*"

To take a picture with a Kodak required the photographer to hold it at waist level, aim, and turn a knob. Samantha, concentrating on focusing the camera to capture the required angles from the awkward position, said, "What's what?"

"That creature," Todd said, pointing.

Samantha followed the direction of his finger. She smiled. "Oh, that's Saved, the steer I fed from a bottle after his mama died." The steer, horn tips a fiery red, had wandered up and stood staring at them curiously from a short distance away. Todd's mare whinnied and tossed her tail skittishly. Samantha had chosen her because of her gentleness. A city fellow, her geologist friend was unaccustomed to the saddle.

"What is that paint doing on his horns?"

"To identify him from other steers rounded up for market. It's a private story."

"He looks fearsome."

"He wouldn't hurt a fly."

"Well, in that case..." Todd turned eagerly to Samantha.

"Would you mind taking a picture of me on his back for Ginny? I know it will impress her."

Samantha laughed. "If not impress, at least amuse her," she said. "Of course I'll take a picture of you. It's the least I can do for dragging you out here. Stay put while I forewarn Saved."

Todd kept his distance while Samantha stroked the steer's ears and talked to him softly. Then she beckoned the geologist over. "Don't scare him," she said. "This is a new experience for him. Very gently, ease your leg over his back. That's good. Now hold still and grin like a drunk drover while I take a shot."

As Samantha positioned the camera, the steer suddenly let out a bellow of protest, startling Todd's horse. The mare neighed and yanked at her reins, loosely secured around a gate post. The leather ties flew free, and off the saddled horse tore across the pasture toward the haven of barn and stable. Apparently inspired by the idea, Saved reacted similarly but in the opposite direction. Samantha watched, openmouthed, as the steer thundered away with Todd bouncing on his back and hanging onto his horns; long, thin legs in their black trousers stuck out like scarecrow limbs. "*Samantha!*" he screamed.

Pony turned his head and gave her a look that questioned what she wished to do. If she rode after Todd on her quarter horse, the steer might keep running or, worse, buck Todd off his back. Her friend could not keep hanging on much longer. She decided to run after them on foot, hoping Todd would simply release his hold on Saved's horns and slide off his rump.

The geologist did just that, but only after giving up faith that the steer would eventually slow down. He landed to roll face-down onto the ground, his nose going numb in the dirt, and heard the animal amble off and begin to munch grass. Thank God, Todd thought. He was not to be trampled or gored as further punishment for the insult to the beast's dignity. It was a few minutes before he felt he could move. He was at the far end of the ranch, a place where hardly a human foot had trod. Suddenly, thoughtfully, as feeling returned, Todd raised his head a fraction, studied the ground, sniffed, then pressed his nose back into the soil. Instantly, he identified the smell. *Holy Christ!* Slowly, he got to his feet, his ride on the steer and his fall forgotten. He saw Samantha hurrying toward him. She was still a good distance away, giving him time to whip out his handkerchief and scoop up a handful of dirt. Quickly, he filled the handkerchief with its potential for untold treasure and stowed it in his pocket.

"Are you all right?" Samantha called.

"I am very much all right," Todd answered. He glanced at the rock structures rising from the earth known as Windy Bluff, and his happiness increased. From the front, the formations looked simply like steep and broad twin boulders, but from where he stood, they formed a geologic "fold," a wavelike shape of layered sediment that spoke a language of its own. As Samantha hurried up, he asked with a nonchalance that belied the pain of his throbbing nose and bubble of inner excitement, "Were you able to get a picture before Saved took me on a tour?"

"I got it," she said, beginning to laugh.

"What's so funny?"

"Your nose. It's caked with dirt."

Chapter Forty

Samantha said in amazement, "You won't stay for Grizzly's sausage pancakes? That's one of your favorite foods in all the world. He made them just for you, because beef-and-egg goulash is on the menu the third Saturday of the month."

"Uh, no, Sam, I promised Ginny I'd get back as quickly as I could." He rubbed his backside. "Mind driving me to the station in a wagon?"

They embraced in brotherly fashion at the train depot, and Todd hoped Samantha did not feel his body's tension or wait to see him boarded for his return trip to Dallas. She'd told him that she would spend the rest of the day and night at her mother's and package the camera for mailing on Monday to the Eastman Kodak Company in Rochester, New York, where the film would be developed. She'd mail him copies of the photographs as soon as they were returned so that he could send them to his friend at Yale.

Todd thought quickly. Samantha's decision to remain in Fort Worth overnight suited him to the ground—literally—but he proposed another idea. In a worried voice he said, "You'll see the camera gets mailed directly from your hands, right?"

Samantha looked puzzled. "Well, no, Todd. I'll leave it for Jimmy or Mildred to get it to the post office. With Daddy gone, I have to get back to the ranch early tomorrow."

Todd pretended doubt for the camera's safety. "Would you let me take the Kodak to mail?" he suggested. "I can take it to the post office Monday morning, earlier than Jimmy and Mildred might have a chance to get away. It would go out faster that way."

With amused tolerance, Samantha handed over the camera. "If it will make you feel easier, Mr. Fussbudget, by all means take it with my thanks," she said.

Todd accepted it with feigned care, holding it close to his chest like a priceless treasure, and told her there was no need to see him off. "Go spend the time you have with your mother," he said, relieved when Samantha, with a kiss on his cheek and after calling him a great friend, took him up on his suggestion.

Todd felt the next hours were the most anxious of his life, not counting the time he'd wandered off from his parents in New York City when he was eight years old and it had taken them half a day to find him. He had been quivering with fright when he was finally reunited with his family, but this time he trembled from a barely contained excitement. He would bet his geologist's degree that oil—maybe gushers of it—was under the rangeland at the northern edge of Las Tres Lomas. Lab tests would show if the soil in his handkerchief and other samples he would gather while Samantha was at her mother's confirmed his suspicion. Windy Bluff appeared to be an anticline, the geological name for a domelike surface structure that had proved to be an odds-on location for the existence of petroleum and gas deposits. Todd couldn't believe his luck at the opportunity to return unseen to the area. With Samantha and her father gone from the ranch and no one but that stupid steer likely to have business around Windy Bluff, he would be free to explore the terrain at will without fear of discovery.

In those interminably long hours, Todd had to wait for the manager of the livery stable, where he intended to rent a horse, to return from lunch, then navigate through Fort Worth's heavy midday traffic to the road that led to Las Tres Lomas. When he was finally underway, his spotty memory of the shortcut to the ranch failed him, and he had to retrace his route, wasting precious time until a remembered fence post with an unlikely small heart carved into the wood finally turned him in the right direction. Uttering a cry of victory, off he bounced as fast as he could tolerate on the back of the apathetic horse. He must conclude his mission in time to catch the five o'clock train to Dallas or pull in too late in the evening to call on Trevor Waverling.

Todd felt a constriction of conscience at what he was about to do, but as fond as he was of Samantha, he must consider his situation first. Samantha would be opposed to drilling for oil on an archeological site. Todd had no doubt that the photographs in her Kodak would prove her relic to be the forehead, nose, and jaw of a dinosaur, but he was a prospecting geologist. His professional reputation and financial provision for his wife and future children depended upon his finding oil for his employer. So far, he had come up empty. So far, Trevor Waverling had praised him for his savvy restraint, but Waverling Tools was ready and eager to make a move into oil exploration. The money was in the bank to drill a well. His boss was waiting only for his geologist's say-so to send his landman, Nathan Holloway, to make a deal with the landowner to lease the drilling site. After today, his geologist might have found the perfect site.

Late Saturday afternoons on the Triple S were "laid-by" times. Except for the ranch's daily maintenance that permitted no weekend break, the main chores of the week were done and the rest of the day belonged to the discretion of the ranch hands. Most washed off their dirt and sweat in a rustic outdoor bath facility set up with mirrors, shaving basins, and several showers, polished their boots, and aired out their best shirt and pair of jeans for a night on the town. In the main house, Millie May and Billie June prepared for an evening out or one in, depending on their mood. There was often some party in town or a social at a neighboring ranch to which they were invited, but if they were not disposed to attend, the sisters arranged an entertainment of their own. These could range from meetings with supporters of their passionate causes to private musicals and card games. For almost a year now, their brother would return to the house in late afternoon, bathe, dress in his town clothes, and set off for an evening in the company of Anne Rutherford.

Tonight the sisters were to entertain a group for bridge. Billie June, setting out pencils, notepads, and decks of cards on three game tables in the great room, heard the clock strike five and listened for Sloan's footsteps in the hall. Before he went upstairs, she meant to waylay him with her intent to take the T&P down to Beaumont to visit a schoolmate the coming week. He held the purse strings of her trust fund, and she needed money for a train ticket. She perked her ears in vain for a good while before going to consult her sister in the kitchen. Millie May was helping the cook prepare trays of sandwiches and other delicacies for the bridge gathering.

"Millie May, have you seen Sloan?"

At the end of the day, their brother could be counted on to stop in the kitchen for a treat to take upstairs. Since his childhood days, Consuelo, their dependable old cook, a small Mexican woman who went about her duties soundlessly, always left something for *joven maestro*—the young master—on a corner of the kitchen table to make his stomach feel *contento*—happy—until supper. For answer, Millie May gestured toward the wedge of cheese and slice of bread still under the tea cloth.

Billie June glanced fretfully at the table. "Where could he be?

He's always in this time on Saturday, and I'm sure Anne is expecting him."

"They were supposed to have finished working the cattle today. Something must have come up," her sister said.

The something that had come up caused the Triple S foreman to gaze at his boss as if he hadn't heard him correctly. At the moment of the sisters' discussion, Sloan had hoisted himself onto his cutting horse, his working mount, and told his second-in-command that he was off to ride fence. If Sloan saw a need for repair, they'd get to it Monday morning.

"You're ridin' fence, boss? This late on a Saturday afternoon? I thought you'd be goin' up to the big house."

"Not tonight. I'm riding fence."

"Which section?"

"The fence between us and the Gordons. Send someone up to the house to tell my sisters that I won't be in until later, will you?"

Millie May and Billie June would make a juicy meal of that information, Sloan thought as he cantered off. They would be expecting him home to take Anne to a party tonight, but he'd begged off from the invitation, giving work as his excuse, which today was close to the truth. He was unusually tired for a short Saturday, dirty, sweaty, and reeking of smoke. He could have done with a couple of stiff shots of bourbon, a soak, and a hot supper, but he had some thinking to do, and for him, like most ranchers, the best place for that was in the saddle.

The real truth was that under the pretense of checking for loose wire and wobbly posts, he just might see Samantha over the fence. A couple of times, he'd had the nice surprise of seeing her around Windy Bluff when she'd ridden out to bring a treat to her steer. He'd hailed her, and they'd met at the barbed-wire gate. These last years, the gate had remained closed, not like in the old days of their youth when it was an open passageway between their ranches.

He rode with a sickness in his chest, put there the pivotal day Neal had killed the mountain lion. Sloan thought of that April day as a demarcation line drawn solidly between the past and present for him and Samantha, and maybe for Neal and Samantha, too. Sloan had gone over and over the bits and pieces of shocking remarks from father and daughter that awful day. He'd concluded from Neal's statement—*that way if one betrays you, you won't have lost everything*—and Samantha's remark—*I'll never be able to undo what I've done*—that their falling-out had to do with a breach of loyalty on Sam's part. Disloyalty was at the top of transgressions Neal Gordon could not forgive. *Loyalty is the one human quality that must be returned*, his mentor once told him. *You can give respect, honor, admiration, even love without return, but loyalty must be repaid in kind.*

Since when had Samantha not returned her father's loyalty? How could she have betrayed him? She'd given up a promising career out of loyalty to Neal Gordon.

Neal's and Sam's heartbreak had been palpable that April day, given off like an odor, and he'd felt as powerless to help as an armless man on shore watching his family drown. *You're not my brother, Sloan...You're my friend...nothing more and nothing less.* The hurt of that bald statement seared him still, but it had forced him on a march of self-evaluation that had prevented him from making the biggest mistake of his life. His sisters' alienation the past year had worn him down. Without them, he missed his father more, and the special brace and sustenance of family. When his sisters had frozen him out, he'd found warmth in the arms of Anne Rutherford, a girl who did not question, challenge, or argue with him, but praised and encouraged and comforted.

Compliant, his sisters called her. *You like her because you can bend her to your will, Sloan*, they said, and he'd looked askance at that. Compliant? Just because she did not offer arbitrary opinions to everything he said and did? He would call that supportive, what a man needed in a woman.

But he had come to see that his sisters were right and that he'd been a fool to fall into the trap of Anne's willingness to pamper his manhood. It had blinded him to her real nature. Little by little, like paint flecking from a forged painting, he'd discovered that Anne was a spiteful little thing, petty, and secretly jealous of Samantha. His father had drilled into him that a man's motives defined him. "It's the reason behind the deed that determines who and what a person is," he'd say. The motivation behind Anne's zealous support of noble causes was not to promote libraries, public education, food drives, and other headline-grabbing contributions to the social welfare of others but to exalt herself. No one expected the beautiful, privileged daughter of one of the richest men in town to be so devoted to the needs of the less fortunate, so mindful of the downtrodden. Sloan now saw that Anne's "selflessness" was really a jewel designed to further enhance her beauty to the public.

His sisters had tried to tell him so.

But all those insights aside, if Anne Rutherford were as sincere as a nun, Sloan still wouldn't have married her feeling as he did about Samantha, and he must tell Anne so.

He was coming upon the Windy Bluff area. Sloan scanned the range across the fence for a pair of red horn tips but saw instead a saddled horse tethered to a fence post. For a second, his heart leaped, but the spiritless horse wasn't Pony. Its rider must have heard his approach. Sloan had reined in his cutting horse for only a minute before a man appeared from behind the towering boulders misnamed for a bluff. "Todd Baker!" Sloan said in surprise. "What the hell are you doing here? And what is that thing you've got in your hand?"

Chapter Forty-One

Sloan could hear the distant ringing from the lone belfry bell of the area's small Catholic church when he set off down the road to Fort Worth early the next morning. *Vaya con Dios*—"Go with God"—it said to him, and he hoped it would be so. He had made the decision last night to break it off with Anne today. He would catch her at an awkward time. The family would likely be still at breakfast, but there was no other slot in the Rutherfords' typical Sunday schedule to speak to her. After attending church services, Anne and her family would dine at the Worth (Sloan had declined an invitation to join them), and afterward, she would meet with a ladies' group to discuss plans for an upcoming charity ball. Sunday evenings the Rutherfords gathered for supper at the home of the matriarch of the family, the mother of Noble Rutherford, Anne's father and the president of the bank that held Sloan's loan and where he served as chairman of the board. For the last few Sundays, Sloan had declined those invitations as well. He could have waited for a more appropriate time, but he wanted his business with Anne Rutherford over and done with before another sunrise. Then at least he could breathe more fully even if his heart was no easier.

It was heavier than ever this morning after his encounter with Todd Baker yesterday afternoon. Todd had never been a favorite of his. His superior attitude rankled, and Sloan had tolerated the geologist for Samantha's sake. He had known the little weasel was up to no good when he flushed him out from behind the boulders at Windy Bluff. The geologist's Adam's apple had bobbed like a puck in a fairground's ring-the-bell attraction when he'd caught him with Samantha's archeological relic. He'd gaped up at Sloan on his horse and couldn't talk fast enough in telling him how he came to be there. He'd told him about Sam's request to take a look at what she suspected might be the fossilized head of a dinosaur, the ride on Saved, and the toss into the dirt where his nose had picked up the scent of oil. He'd admitted to doubling back after Sam had let him off at the train depot to collect further soil samples for analysis. If lab tests indicated petroleum was present, it was his notion that Windy Bluff could be the site of a productive oil field. He'd not told Samantha what he suspected, because he knew how she'd feel about drilling for oil near what she believed could be a possible burial ground of prehistoric creatures. Sloan understood that, didn't he?

Sloan had ignored the question. "Then what?"

Why, then, Todd had said, he'd take his report to his boss at Waverling Tools, who'd then approach Neal Gordon for the right to drill where his nose had been.

"And that skeleton head you're holding is part of the oil samples?" Sloan had asked.

Todd had peered down at the fossil as if he did not know how it got into his hand. He'd swallowed hard, obviously caught empty of an explanation.

"You came out here to dig it up, didn't you?" Sloan said. "That's the real reason you sneaked back—to steal Sam's discovery so she'd have no proof to present as an argument against drilling."

"No—no! I—I—thought that while I was out here, I'd take it to—to keep it safe."

"Uh-huh," Sloan had said. It was plain that Todd was lying.

Sloan had gotten down from his horse and gone to the fence and held out his palm. "Give it to me."

Todd had drawn back, cradling the skull to his chest. "What?"

"You heard me. Give it to me."

Slowly, Todd had handed over the skull. "What do you intend to do with it?"

"Give it to Samantha for safekeeping."

Todd's face screwed up in protest, but somehow his backbone stiffened. His voice was stronger when he spoke. "I beg you to re-consider that, Sloan. There's oil over here, and that could mean the field spreads across the fence line to the Triple S, but we won't know how big or how much unless we drill. Just imagine…no more money worries because of drought, cattle disease, falling beef prices, high rail rates. No more concerns about losing your ranch because of failure to meet loan or mortgage payments. The discovery of oil would make you too rich to worry about the fu-ture of the Triple S."

Sloan had returned to his horse, and Todd had thrown out one last plea. "All I'm asking is that you think twice before handing over that skull to Samantha," he'd begged. "Without it, there's no evidence to support claim of her finding."

"There's her word."

"But no *physical* finding to present to the scientific community. Without it, an archeological team will never set foot on Las Tres Lomas. But no matter," Todd had said, defiantly squaring his shoulders. "If my samples prove me right, I'm taking my report to my boss, and he'll be calling upon Neal Gordon. I think we both know which side he'll favor in the matter."

"You do know you're betraying Samantha's trust, don't you?" Sloan said. He had taken off his shirt to serve as a sack for the skull that he could tie to his saddle horn. Todd's brief mettle melted as quickly as butter in a hot pan.

"Yes, I do. Much to my regret," he admitted.

Sloan had left Todd at the fence, looking as crestfallen as he'd ever seen a man, but Sloan felt as dispirited. If Todd's soil samples proved his suspicions right, Sloan saw another serious conflict widening the gulf between Neal and Samantha. Neal would want to drill. Samantha would not. Neal would see no value in forgoing a fortune that might be under his land to preserve a burial ground of extinct animals that may or may not be. Whatever the cause of the first one, another situation of loyalty would be at stake. When it came right down to it, would Samantha argue for preservation of an archeological site over securing the financial welfare of Las Tres Lomas?

Sloan was aware that he presented a strange sight to whoever was looking when he rode back to the ranch naked to the waist. Billie June came into the kitchen just as he'd finished buttoning into his shirt, and he'd hurriedly secured the fossil under his arm and didn't stop to hear what she had to discuss with him. "Later," he'd said. No point in involving anybody else in Todd's trickery until he'd spoken to Samantha. He'd carried the skull up to his room with the plan of stopping by Estelle's the next day after he'd seen Anne to tell Samantha what had happened. Because the skull looked fragile, he'd leave it in his wardrobe and maybe they would ride back together for her to collect it.

A familiar figure bounced along on a mule about thirty yards ahead, and Sloan recognized the portly shape of Grizzly on the back of his long-eared mule, Delilah. Sloan recalled Samantha's lament: *I should have listened to Grizzly and Wayne's advice and never started down this road* ...Delilah was moving at the speed of molasses poured cold. Sloan considered whether to slow down for a chat with the cook and risk appearing at the Rutherfords' too late and at Estelle's after Samantha left for Las Tres Lomas. Maybe he could get Grizzly to open up about the rift between

Sam and her father, though Sloan doubted it. Grizzly was not one to tell tales out of school.

"Morning, Grizzly," Sloan said, drawing abreast.

"Mornin', Sloan."

"On your way to church?"

"Yep. You on your way to see Miss Rutherford?"

"You could say that."

Sloan thought he heard a soft *humph* from the cook. "Everything going all right at Las Tres Lomas?" he asked.

"Well, now, that'd be a question you wouldn't have to ask if you came around more often."

"Ah, Grizzly." Sloan pitched his voice sorrowfully. "These days I have to be invited."

Grizzly cocked an eye at him. "By who?"

"Samantha."

"Since when?"

"Since she sort of kicked me out of the house two months ago, about the time she and Neal had a falling-out. At least, that's what I call it."

Grizzly eyed him in surprise. "You know about that?"

Sloan shrugged his shoulders. "Well, I don't *know* about it, but things haven't seemed the same between them since the day Neal shot the mountain lion." He lifted an eyebrow at the cook. "You know anything to shed light on the situation?"

Grizzly turned his head aside to spit into the grass. "Not for me to tell. You'd have to ask Mornin' Glory."

"She's not speaking to me much these days. She's cut me loose from her confidence. That's why I haven't been around much. A couple of months ago, Sam told me clear as a bell that I'm to stay out of her business. Fact is, I don't feel so welcome at Las Tres Lomas anymore."

Grizzly said in an explosion of temper, "Well, whose fault is that?"

"Not mine!" Sloan said in surprise.

"It damn sure is!" Grizzly said.

Sloan pulled his horse to a sudden stop. "How do you figure?"

"Whoa up, Delilah babe," Grizzly said and shifted his weight in the saddle to face Sloan. "Don't you see that Samantha is protecting her pride by cuttin' you loose, as you say?"

Dumbfounded, Sloan said, "Protecting her pride! What the hell for?"

Grizzly threw his eyes heavenward and uttered a deep sigh. "God almighty, how did you get me into this conversation, Sloan Singleton? I guess I'm goin' to have to cut out my tongue to keep myself from blabbin' so much."

Sloan kneed his Thoroughbred to block Delilah's path. "Grizzly, if you don't tell me what you're talking about, I'll cut out your tongue myself."

"Samantha is in love with you, you numbskull, but do you think she'd show it when you've gone and taken up with Miss Rutherford! Not on your life! Not our Mornin' Glory. Miss Rutherford is no more right for you than gravy on cake," Grizzly said. "There! I've got that burr out from under my saddle. Now get out of my way, or you'll make me late for church!"

Sloan drew his horse aside. "How do you know Sam's in love with me?"

"Ask her!" Grizzly said, pumping his knees to hurry Delilah along.

"I will!" Sloan cried and slapped his reins across his horse's neck to spur him to a full gallop.

Chapter Forty-Two

As he entered the residential area of Fort Worth that was home to the wealthy, Sloan was torn between riding first to Estelle's town house five streets over from the Rutherford mansion before meeting with Anne, but wisdom curbed his impatience. He must remove the obstacle of Anne to clear a path for Samantha. Hope beat frantically in his chest that Grizzly was not imagining Samantha's feelings for him, but then the Gordons' faithful old cook knew her better in some ways than anybody else in her life.

In the courtyard of the Rutherfords' palatial home, Sloan found a couple of grooms harnessing a pair of matching white stallions to the carriage that would take Anne and her parents to the Broadway Presbyterian Church. Noble Rutherford had financed the awe-inspiring brick structure and served as an elder on its governing board. The grooms were accustomed to seeing Sloan on the premises and exchanged nods with him as he ascended the broad splay of steps to push the modish buzzer that had replaced the traditional door knocker.

A maid responded to the loud, irritating *bzzzz* he could hear from within the house. "Mr. Singleton!" she said in surprise. "We weren't expecting you, sir."

"My apologies for coming unannounced, Bella, but I must see Miss Rutherford," Sloan said. "Would you let her know I'm here?"

Anne Rutherford came tearing out of the dining room, silken robe and undressed hair flying. She had obviously seen him ride up from her place at the table facing the courtyard windows. "That won't be necessary, Bella," she said, rushing to greet him with extended hands, delight at his appearance sparkling in her eyes. "I'm here, Sloan," she said, as if his search for her was finally over.

Her beauty could stop a man's heart, Sloan conceded, but he felt no twinge of sorrow at what he must do. Her hands were warm and soft when she took his. "Forgive me for not telephoning first," he said.

Her father had come out into the hall, wearing a silk smoking jacket, the corner of a napkin tucked into his collar. His lowering countenance, dominated by a pair of dark, bristly eyebrows, was considerably less welcoming than Anne's when he greeted Sloan and shook his hand. Noble Rutherford was not unaware of the grief the chairman of his board of directors had lately caused his daughter.

"Well, never mind," Anne said airily, taking his arm. "You're here now and that's all that matters. Just in time for breakfast, too. Daddy, will you have Bella set another place at table?"

Sloan laid a hand over the clasp of his arm. "I'm sorry, Anne, but I'm not staying," he said gently. "May we go somewhere to talk?"

Anne slowly withdrew her hand. "Of course," she said, her smile tensing around small, white teeth.

Sloan ignored the suspicious draw of Noble Rutherford's ominous eyebrows as he followed the banker's daughter into the morning room. In a quarter of an hour, it was over. Sloan had explained his reason for coming and had watched the shock of it drain the luminosity from Anne's face. Yet she took the news that he would no longer be calling upon her better than he'd expected and dreaded. She did not even ask who or what was responsible for the change in his affections. He gathered from the set of her shoulders and lifted chin that to do so would be beneath her dignity, and Sloan was grateful for that particular streak of pride in Anne. He even sensed that before he concluded the purpose of his visit, she'd already begun to work out how best to turn this humiliating alteration of her expectations to her public advantage.

But as he left the morning room, he felt the blaze of her bitterness warm his back like heat from a flow of lava.

Departing the house in which his welcome would forever be withdrawn, Sloan suspected that he had made an enemy of Noble Rutherford, whose hostility would last the rest of the banker's life. Noble was not a forgiving man. Sloan must make sure never to miss a loan payment and would, of course, resign from the board of directors of the Rutherford City Bank. Sloan was leaving with no regrets but for his loneliness and blindness that had led to this unfortunate situation, but that misguided spell was behind him now and in the past. Now he had to see to his future, and he had to hurry.

Sloan's heart beat like a pendulum gone awry as he bounded up the steps of the town house and made zealous use of the brass lion's head on the front door. Estelle attended the First Methodist Church on Fourth and Jones Streets, and she might have enticed Samantha to services since she never missed an opportunity to show her off. On the other hand, Estelle might elect to stay home this Sunday to enjoy her daughter's company without sharing it with the congregation. Sloan expected Mildred to answer the knocking and demand if he believed the residents to be deaf, but it was Samantha who opened the door.

"Sloan!" she said, gray eyes rounding in surprise. "What are you doing here?" She was dressed in a morning robe, her hair unfettered, falling in thick golden ropes over her shoulders to the curve of her breasts, and Sloan was stunned by a thought so shattering his eyes misted over. What if Grizzly was wrong? What if Samantha did not love him?

Samantha gave a soft "*Oh!*" of concern. Automatically, she reached out and laid a hand on his face, as she'd done when his father had died. "Sloan, what's the matter? It's not one of your sisters, is it?"

He folded his hand around hers. "No," he said and blurted out, "Samantha, I have a question to ask you. An important one."

She stepped back into the hall, a blend of relief and curiosity in her eyes, and he followed, her hand still in his clutch. "Ask me what?"

Mildred had come down the hall to answer the door and Estelle to the open doorway of her parlor, curious as to who had called. Sloan was suddenly dry-tongued. Before either woman could speak, Samantha repeated, "Ask me what, Sloan?"

"Samantha, are you in love with me?"

Estelle clapped her hand to her cheek. "Oh, my goodness!"

Mildred drew to a stop and muttered something in the Comanche language.

Over her shoulder, Samantha said, "Mother, Mildred, will you please leave us?"

Estelle backed into the parlor; Mildred headed down to the kitchen.

Samantha turned back to Sloan. "What was the question again?"

"I thought I made it pretty clear. Are you in love with me?"

Samantha jerked away her hand and stepped back as if floodwaters were lapping at her feet. "That's what I thought you said. What kind of joke is this?"

Sloan shortened the distance between them. "A simple one with a simple answer. Yes or no. Are you in love with me?" He could see her mind working with the question. She had never lied to him. She frowned and shook her head, but only from the obvious effort of trying to figure out what this was all about. He could have made it easier for her, but he had his pride, too.

"Why are you asking?" she said. "What has gotten into you?"

They could play this hedging game all day, and he hadn't the time or heart for it. The mist gone from his eyes, Sloan took another step and drew her to him. She fit into the mold of his arm and body like a custom-made glove, and he kissed her long and hard, and after a startled second's struggle, she kissed him back, looping her arms around his neck. "My God, you do love me!" he declared when she broke free of his hold.

Red-faced, mortified tears beginning to stream, Samantha sputtered, "How dare you, Sloan Singleton! What are you trying to prove?"

"*Indeed!*" Estelle said indignantly, drawn back to the parlor door, and Mildred, too, eyes popping, had veered her head around the kitchen doorway at the end of the hall.

"That Grizzly was right, thank God, because I damn sure wouldn't have guessed it from you," Sloan said.

"What are you talking about?"

"I love you, Sam. I have never not loved you any more than I have never not breathed. They're one and the same for me."

Another gasp from Estelle, a low whistle from Mildred while Samantha stared at Sloan in mute astonishment.

"I'm not betrothed to Anne, and never intended to be," he said. "She was there when you were not, that's all, and I was lonely. I just came from her house to tell her it's over between us, whatever she presumed was there. I couldn't continue seeing her, feeling the way I do about you."

Silence fell, tantamount to the held breath of a crowd watching a trapeze artist. Sloan shoved his thumbs under his belt, shifted his weight to one leg, and stuck out the other, the stance he assumed when waiting patiently for an errant cowhand to explain himself. "Now, if Grizzly is wrong about your feelings for me," he said, "all you have to do is say simply, 'I'm not in love with you, Sloan,' and I'll be on my way with no more said on the matter. Think you can do that?"

Samantha closed her eyes and shook her head. "Not in a million years," she said.

"Well, then, come here, and let's kiss on it," Sloan said, unhooking his thumbs, and Samantha flew into his arms.

Chapter Forty-Three

That Sunday morning, Todd Baker rang the doorbell of Mavis Waverling's town house. Last night, because of the delay, he had taken the last train out of Fort Worth to Dallas and arrived too late to meet with his employer. He had made an appointment to see him this morning. Trevor Waverling let him in, motioning away the new maid who'd come in answer to the bell. "Let's go into my study where we won't be disturbed," Trevor said. "My mother and daughter will be arriving from church any minute amidst a lot of flurry and flummery."

"Has Nathan arrived back from his brother's graduation in Oklahoma?" Todd asked.

"He got in late last night and accompanied the girls to church this morning. He'll join us when he returns. What's so important that it couldn't wait until Monday?"

"I believe I've found us an oil field," Todd said.

Risking his employer's ire at the late hour, Todd had telephoned his residence last night from his office at Waverling Tools. Never would he impart his message over the telephone to the listening ears of those on the party line, so he'd briefly explained that he had news of great importance that couldn't wait. Could Mr. Waverling see him in the morning?

There had been no way to get in touch with Ginny to tell her of his delay, since their apartment possessed no telephone. She was worried sick by the time Todd made it home, but he hadn't been able to resist a laboratory analysis of the soil and strata he'd collected at Windy Bluff. A simple test of mixing a portion with water proved the presence of hydrogen and carbon, the chief components of oil and natural gas. The oil floated to the top, but dissolved in carbon disulfide, further evidence that an oil seep, not yet broken through the surface, was present in the northern reaches of Las Tres Lomas de la Trinidad. Todd had nothing to wager, but if he did, he'd bet it all on his certainty that underneath that sandy soil was a reservoir of oil.

He had borrowed a small hammer and chisel from the manager of the livery stable and had just removed the skull from its base when he'd heard a horse canter up to the fence and stop where he'd tied his nag. His hairline had risen. It shot up further when he saw that the rider was Sloan Singleton. *What the hell are you doing here?* the rancher had demanded, and Todd had almost wet his trousers. What could he say? He was a miserable liar, and before someone as intimidating as Sloan Singleton, it would have been impossible to come up with a plausible explanation, and he'd not had time to get rid of the skull. He'd told him everything.

So he was now in the clutches of Sloan Singleton. Would the man betray him to Samantha? Would it matter in the long run? His goose would be cooked with Samantha anyway when she learned he'd steered a landman to lease the area for oil exploration that he, too, believed could be a dinosaur cemetery. Todd treasured his special friendship with Samantha. She accepted his persnickety ways (just because he liked things done right) and didn't mind that he thought himself superior (because he was!), and she was his wife's best friend, but those considerations paled in comparison to what was at stake. He planned to make his boss happy, the Gordons very rich, and himself a very big name in the oil business.

They moved to the back parlor, Samantha closing the door with a look at her exultant mother and Mildred, warning she'd better not catch them listening through the keyhole. She and Sloan kissed long and passionately again, then sat down on the couch and held each other like spent but happy survivors of a ship-wreck.

"How long have you known your feelings for me, Sam?" Sloan asked, smoothing her hair. It had always made him think of early maple leaves overlaid with gold. Memories of Samantha's locks flashed through his head like sun glinting off water. Samantha at three, lost at the county fair, his nearly seven-year-old heart frozen in the search for her until he spotted the glimmer of her hair among the crowd. Samantha at ten, thrown from her horse and knocked unconscious, the straw of prairie grass matted in her hair that scratched his cheek when he cradled her in his arms and begged her not to die. Samantha at sixteen, her hair shining like a bright penny under a black graduate's cap, the dive of his heart as she walked across the stage of Simmons Preparatory School to receive her diploma that he saw as her passport to a future far be-yond their ranches, Fort Worth, and him...

"Since I could walk," she said. "Until Anne came along, I'd always assumed we'd just extend our childhood together, marry, and live happily ever after together, just like everybody else in our families expected."

"I wish my dad were here to share in our news. He'd be so pleased."

"Mine will be ecstatic," Samantha said. "Now maybe he'll find it in his heart to forgive me."

Sloan lifted her chin to look at him. "Don't you think it's time you told me what's going on between you and Neal? What did you do to make him think you had betrayed him?"

Samantha blew out a sigh of deep regret. "I made an effort to locate my birth parents, and Daddy found out."

Sloan's stomach went hollow as Samantha explained. God help her! It was a breach of loyalty, after all. Neal, possessive of all that carried his brand, tolerant of no threat to home, land, and family, would regard Samantha's search as treason, much as he loved her. The grisly view of the mountain lion tail strung from the flagpole at Las Tres Lomas flashed through his mind. Sloan had never forgotten Samantha coming to him years ago with the conversation she'd overheard between Neal and Estelle after her return from the orphanage. *I'd never leave Mother and Daddy! Why would Daddy believe I would!*

She'd been ten years old and spoken as a child. Now she was twenty and had acted as an adult. Neal would view her attempt to connect to her roots as a slap in the face, a rejection of all the parental devotion he and Estelle had heaped upon her. Even if she did nothing with the information her trip across the Red River might have gleaned, he'd find her curiosity unforgivable. And now, another conflict, equally as serious, was about to rear between father and daughter.

"I threw Mrs. Brewster's letter away," Samantha said. "I had no use for the information. I don't know why I ever pursued the idea that I did."

"I do," Sloan said. He must try to mitigate at least a little of her anguish over her perceived mistake. "It's a primal thing to want to know where you were born, who birthed you, and in your case, why you were put up for adoption. It's an urge you could no more get rid of without at least an attempt to find the answers than you could escape your shadow."

Samantha drew out of his arms and looked at him wonder-ingly. "How can you possibly understand all that, since you've always known where you came from?"

"For that very reason," Sloan said. "I've grown up knowing I'm a Singleton. That knowledge explained me to myself, for better or worse. It's provided a map for my life, set goals, given me an anchor and a compass. After Dad died, I don't know how I would have survived without that ballast. So I can understand how you'd feel somewhat…undefined." Sloan fondled a rope of her hair lying across her shoulder. "I wish you'd let me in on the situation. I'd have gone to Neal and told him your search was not a matter of wanting to connect with a new family, but simply to know more about yourself. I'd have told him to remember that you're a scientist. It's natural for you to be curious, to get to the origin of things."

Samantha shook her head in awe. "I'd forgotten that about you, Sloan Singleton."

"Forgotten what?"

"How well you understood my feelings and could say just the right thing to make me feel better. Remember those long afternoons under that giant old ash tree on the Triple S by the creek where we used to tell each other everything?"

"I remember," Sloan said. The ash tree had stood in a field of dandelions. Their horses had loved to eat the pungent-smelling flowers. His father's death had put an end to the afternoons under the tree's shade—days of the dandelions, he'd thought of them in wistful moments of recalling carefree times that would never come again. Lightning had struck the tree not long after his father died, and Sloan would have had it cut down but for his memories. Samantha, with growing excitement, had begun telling him about the animal skull she'd found at Windy Bluff, and Sloan, listening in dismay, found himself thinking of the tree's charred remains. They stood as a reminder that even the strongest, most invincible relationships could topple under the right forces.

"I believe I've found evidence that might indicate a mass grave of dinosaurs out there," Samantha was saying. "The skull will at least be a start to proving my theory. Todd has volunteered to send photographs to the Museum of Natural History in New York City and contact a paleontologist friend at the Peabody Museum of Natural History at Yale for analysis."

"Photographs?"

"From my Kodak. I took pictures of the skull, and I gave my camera to Todd to mail in the morning to the factory in Rochester, New York. It will take about a month to hear back. Meanwhile I want to keep the news to myself. My interest in paleontology makes Mother uncomfortable, and..." Samantha's voice faltered. "I want to settle this trouble between Daddy and me before I tell him about my discovery. I don't think he'll object to a dig, since the Windy Bluff area is not good grazing land."

Sloan pushed up from the couch. He'd spotted a pitcher of water on the tea trolley and had suddenly developed a dry throat. By the time those photographs were returned, Neal would have signed the lease papers with Waverling Tools and digging might have already begun at Windy Bluff. Sloan was sure Todd was counting on it. It was the right moment to expose the geologist and to tell Samantha of his rescue of the skull. But Todd's cool argument resounded in his head: *If my samples prove me right, I'm taking my report to my boss, and he'll be calling upon Neal Gordon. I think we both know which side he'll favor.* And: *All I'm asking is that you think twice before handing over that skull to Samantha. Without it, there's no evidence to support claim of her finding.*

Sloan took a long draught of water. He was back to the question of loyalty as Neal would interpret it. That skull would present another test of Samantha's devotion—this time to Las Tres Lomas. Nothing was too sacred that would prevent Neal from doing what he thought vital for the land of his fathers. He had tolerated but never understood Samantha's—or any scientist's—interest in prehistoric life. He would take an outraged view to her equally fiery argument that a burial ground of old bones was more valuable than an oil field if drilling for petroleum meant preserving the homestead. The disagreement could finish tearing the family apart. Sloan couldn't bear to think of Estelle's devastation, and he mustn't forget the side he'd be forced to take in the conflict, which would be Neal's. Oil was a natural resource of the earth, as necessary to cultivate for human welfare as land for food and animals. He agreed with his mentor that damage to a part of the land was worth it to secure the whole. So, if he had a voice in the fray, he'd speak for drilling, and where would that put him with Samantha? Without the skull, like Todd said, she would have no ground to stand on. Without it, she might give up the battle, especially now that they were to be married. Marriage—and in time, motherhood—would fill her life. How could they not? He and Neal would partner to run their combined ranches while Samantha took charge of home and hearth.

Sloan stared out the parlor window unseeing of the bright summer day outside. What in hell was he to do? Whose interest should he consider first, what greater good should be served? A person's motivations defined them, like his father said, but what if a person wasn't sure of the rightness or wrongness of his decisions?

It was a long shot, but there was the chance that Neal might honor Samantha's claim until the photographs came back as proof of it one way or the other. In that case, she wouldn't need the skull. "Sloan?" Samantha called softly, concern in her voice. "What are you thinking about?"

He made up his mind. No need to make a decision now. There was time. He turned to Samantha in the sun-dappled light of the June morning, a grin breaking. "I was thinking how early we can set the date to get married," he said.

Chapter Forty-Four

They parted at the crossroads to their ranches in late afternoon after Samantha invited Sloan to ride out to Windy Bluff with her to cordon off her treasure. At Samantha's request and without Estelle's knowledge, Mildred had collected rope and pegs and a blanket to cover and secure the skull's location. To her disappointment, Sloan refused, looking uneasy. "I have to get back, Sam," he said, leaning over to kiss her before getting down from the riding board to untie his horse. They had ridden back together in her wagon, Sloan's Thoroughbred hitched to its rear frame. Samantha supposed she understood, but it was Sunday, a day of rest. Once, out of friendly curiosity, she would have questioned why the hurry to return to the Triple S, but now... With a little thrill she thought it was not her place to ask for such explanations until they were married.

"If you hear shouts drift your way, they'll only be from Millie May and Billie June hollering with joy," Sloan said. "Finally, their little brother has done something to please them."

"I can hardly wait for Daddy to get home to tell him," Samantha said. "He should be coming in from La Paloma this next week."

Sloan set his foot in the stirrup. "Send somebody to let me know and I'll come over and formally ask for your hand in marriage. One day soon, we won't have to part like this. You can come home with me, or I can go home with you. The sooner, the better for me."

Samantha, sighing, said, "I wish it were right now." They'd decided to announce their engagement at Sloan's birthday party two weeks away and to marry the first week of August.

"Me, too," Sloan said, and leaned down from the saddle to kiss her again. "Sam," he added, drawing away, "you know that I would never make a decision, do anything, that wasn't in your best interests, don't you?"

"Of course I do," she said, surprised. "Why would you ask that?"

"Just for reassurance that you understand I'd never do anything intentionally to hurt you."

"I know that," Samantha said.

"I love you, Samantha Gordon."

"I know that, too, Sloan Singleton."

Samantha thought of Sloan's parting words, the miracle of them, as the wagon rattled along. Only yesterday she'd heard them in her imagination. Today they'd been spoken in reality. She wished her father knew of Sloan's marriage proposal. Her mother had been so happy, she'd grabbed Mildred's hands and led her in a dance of ring-around-the-rosy in her parlor. Wayne and Silbia and especially Grizzly—that interfering old bear—would be thrilled, but no one was at the ranch right now that she could lead in a jig. Wayne was at his girlfriend's in town, Silbia had the day off on Sundays, and Grizzly was serving at the Masonic Widows and Orphans Home. Samantha laughed. She guessed she could tell Saved her good news.

A while later, she spotted the steer's red horn tips in the area of Todd's fall, but before she'd stopped the wagon, she spied another sight. The depression of sand where her suspected sauropod relic should have been was empty.

*   *   *

The goal of his mission led Neal like the beam of a lighthouse as within the last few days he had left the level terrain and gentle slopes of his native territory and passed the rolling, loamy grasslands of the Blackland Prairies. He'd found the creeks running high and the grass thick and green. On he'd pushed past the sandy land called Eastern Cross Timbers, a region of blackjack and post oak, pecan and white ash, sycamore, cottonwood, hackberry, elm, and willow trees that jutted down from Oklahoma to the central part of Denton County. There were short periods when his route took him alongside the Missouri-Kansas-Texas Railroad, the train that Samantha and Mildred had taken from Fort Worth to Gainesville. Some passengers waved at him, and he waved back. At night he bedded down by a creek, cooking beans and bacon over a campfire, his horse tethered close by. Lying on his back in his bedroll, an M1900 Browning pistol and Winchester rifle by his side, he looked at the stars winking at him, all knowing and inscrutable, preferring their celestial twinkle to the lights of a town. He found a semblance of peace in their infinite vastness, the soft gurgle of water nearby, the sounds of nature at night.

On the third day, arriving in Gainesville in the early afternoon, Neal asked a postman on his rounds if he knew the location of the Barrows farm. Sure do, the man said, and gave him directions. Neal considered stopping to make discreet inquiries about the Holloways at the general store he passed near the edge of town, one the family most likely would patronize for its convenience. He'd experienced that people couldn't resist an opportunity to gossip about their neighbors, and sometimes spilling their opinions to a stranger made it easier. From people who'd probably known them all their lives, Neal would learn soon enough what sort of folks the Holloways were and get an answer to the question of whether Leon Holloway was still alive.

But he preferred to draw his own conclusion of what to make of people, so he rode on by the general store, following the postman's directions until he came upon a threshing crew at work in a wheat field, and steered his paint to the fence. In the wind-blown chaff dust, a man who looked to be in charge saw him, lifted his cap, and took out a handkerchief the size of a tea towel to wipe his brow before starting toward him. A farmer, true as rain, Neal opined. It wasn't only the cloth cap and overalls that distinguished him from a rancher, but the bent of his body and particular gait that marked him a man who worked with hoe and plow rather than horse and rope.

"Excuse me," Neal called, raising his voice to be heard over the noisy whir of the threshing machine. "I don't mean to interfere with your labor, but I'm looking for the Barrows farm."

"You're lookin' at it, stranger," the man said, elevating his voice above the din as well, "but if you were lookin' to buy the place, you've made a trip for nothin'. The farm sold back in April."

"That quick?" Neal said, his note of disappointment implying that the purchase of the farm was exactly why he'd come.

The man neared the fence and nodded. " 'Fraid so."

"And the people who owned it...I suppose they're gone, too?"

"Moved the first of June."

"Mind telling me where?"

"Well, now, I'd have to ask who's askin'."

"Neal Gordon. I ranch about five miles from Fort Worth." Neal removed his hat to wipe his brow as well. The day had grown warm. "You the new owner?"

The man stepped close to the fence, scrutinizing Neal with the gaze of a man who thought they may have met before. "I'm the seller, or rather, my wife is. I'm finishin' up the last of our harvest. Name's Leon Holloway."

Neal hoped he'd caught his expression before it gave away his shock. *God have mercy!* He was staring into the eyes of Samantha's father! He put his hat back on. "That so?" he said lamely, unprepared for what to do or say next. "Pleased to meet you."

Leon acknowledged the introduction with a nod and a squint at Neal. "I believe I met your daughter a while back. She came on behalf of her father in answer to the FOR SALE ad my wife put in a Fort Worth paper. She and my wife made an appointment to meet, but somehow they missed each other. Samantha, she said her name was. She rode out here with her maid and spoke to me when she and Millicent failed to hook up. I was working in the field."

Neal passed his tongue quickly over lips that felt dry as day-old toast. For a second the oxygen left his head. Samantha had almost met her mother. "Yes, that was my daughter. Did...you introduce yourself?"

"Can't say as I did. I believe she took me for a hired hand. What made you come inquire about the place again, Mr. Gordon?"

Neal improvised quickly. "It was a long shot, but I thought maybe the sale might have fallen through and your farm still be on the market. I own the La Paloma cattle camp south of here and was interested in buying your land as a thoroughfare to the river. No harm in checking to see if it might still be available, since I was coming this way anyhow, I thought, and the editor of the paper gave me the name of your wife."

"No harm sure enough," Leon said. He took off his hat and scratched his head. "Well now, since you've come this far—from Fort Worth, is it?—you're welcome to come by the house and sit a spell." Leon pointed to a group of rooftops in the distance that

Neal could see through the yellow haze. "The well water's cold and the peaches ripe. The new owners haven't moved in yet, and there are a couple of porch chairs left that my wife reckoned not fit for our new house. Pick up the road at the end of the fence, and it'll lead you right to it. I'll meet you there."

Neal wanted to say no. He was a savvy judge of men, and even from their short acquaintance, he could tell Leon Holloway was a good and decent man. An honest, open face, a friendly, sincere manner—how could they hide the heart of a father who would willingly part with his newborn daughter unless forced to do so? Did Neal really want to "sit a spell" with a man who might take from him the joy of his life?

But this was the reason he'd come. With a feeling of impending doom, Neal said, "That's awfully good of you. That well water and peach sound mighty nice."

Chapter Forty-Five

Holy smokes! Leon thought, walking back across the pasture. Could the girl who'd stopped by the fence last April *be* Millicent's daughter—Nathan's twin!—and the rancher her father, or rather, the man who'd adopted her? Five miles from Fort Worth, he'd said his ranch was—information close enough to the tidbit Leon had gleaned from Dr. Tolman and never forgotten. That fact and the color of the girl's hair were too much to be a coincidence. Why had the man really come? If the reason was as Leon expected, how had Neal Gordon gotten hold of the information that had led him here? From Bridget Mahoney? Dr. Tolman? And why was he showing up twenty years later?

Leon sent the threshing crew back to work, then climbed on his buckboard to cut across the pasture toward his old home. His horse and wagon sent up clouds of dust and wheat residue that obscured his vision, but he thought he could make out the ghostly crown of a Stetson skimming along the tops of the hedgerows in the direction of his house. The hat got there before he did. The rancher had dismounted and was watering his horse at the trough when the buckboard pulled up.

Leon went immediately to the well and drew up a bucket of water. He filled a tin dipper and handed it to Neal. "We've got a pump but no running water in the house," Leon explained.

"When we sold the place, my wife bought a house in Gainesville, and she's happier'n a pig in mud now we've got inside plumbing."

"That stuff from a tap can't beat this," Neal said, taking a long drink of the cold, pure-tasting water.

"How about a peach?"

"Don't mind if I do."

"Have a seat on the porch, and I'll cut us a couple of Elbertas." Leon walked a few yards to the orchard fence and clipped off two large, plump peaches from branches drooping with fruit. Carrying them up to the porch, he said, "The peach is a member of the rose family, did you know that?"

"No, I didn't," Neal said.

"Yep. Cousin to apricots, plums, and almonds."

"That so?"

"Who would have ever thought any of them were related?"

"Hard to imagine," Neal agreed. He studied the farmer as he pulled up a rickety porch chair. Was there some hidden meaning behind this little lesson in horticulture? He glanced toward the orchard. "A shame for all those peaches to go to waste. Will the new owner take possession of your place before they rot?"

Leon held up the pocketknife questioningly in offer to Neal, who shook his head and withdrew his own. "Not likely. My family used to pick those trees clean. Wife could make the best peach pies you ever put in your mouth. We made ice cream out of 'em, canned a pantry full, gave the rest to neighbors. Every one of our Elbertas ended up in its proper place." Leon sliced off a piece of the peach and popped it into his mouth. "Always good for everything and everybody to end up in their proper place."

Neal felt an inner burble from an unidentified source. He couldn't quite follow the philosophical thread of what the farmer was saying to him, what he was getting at. It was almost as if he had guessed who he was and why he'd really come. Neal pulled

out the blade of his knife. "You mentioned family. How many are
there of you?"

"Four. Me and my wife and two children, a boy and a girl."

"And their ages? Of your children, that is." Neal set off the distinction with a small smile. "My wife would kill me if I told her
age."

Leon laughed. "Mine, too, believe me. Well, let's see, my son
Randolph is seventeen, and my daughter Lily is sixteen, going on
twenty, she thinks. I try to keep her reined in. She'll get there
soon enough, too soon for me."

Neal offered a chuckle to say he understood. "You've never
had any more children?"

"Nope. Two are all the good Lord blessed my wife and me
with, and we've been mighty pleased with them. I don't mind
sayin' my daughter is a beautiful little thing. She and her mother
hope she'll snag a rich man and live happily ever after, and my
son will be goin' away to Columbia University in a few months.
That's in New York City. Goin' to make himself a big-shot
lawyer, he says, and I imagine he will, too." Leon sucked on a
peach slice. "He's just graduated high school. Valedictorian of his
class. Commencement exercises are day after tomorrow, Saturday. He's thrilled about gettin' to wear the gold mantle. His
mother is pleased about that, too. She puts great stock in ap-
pearances of superiority." The twinkle in his eye assumed Neal
understood, women being women and all.

"Congratulations to him," Neal said. The peach forgotten, he
drew in a deep breath. From his honest looks, manner, and
speech, you'd never take this man for a liar—and about something as important as the children born to him, too. Unless Dr.
Tolman had lied in his letter—and why would he?—Leon Holloway had fathered twins that he and his wife had given up for
one reason or the other before his other children were born. What

had happened to the twin boy? Had he ended up in a good and loving home like his sister? Did this man ever think of them? Neal almost felt like punching him in his pleased face. His pride in the children he'd kept was almost brazen, the son and daughter he and his wife had loved and nurtured and provided for right here on this farm, the recipients of their mother's peach pies. Neal didn't sense a smidgen of pain or regret in Leon for the firstborns they'd given away, and from the shallow sound of his wife, she hadn't suffered, either.

"Too bad about only two being born to you," Neal ventured. "This place looks like a great spot to raise children."

"Two were all we wanted and could manage," Leon said. "Any others, and I'm afraid my wife might have drowned them." He grinned to indicate he was kidding, but the twinkle in his eyes had disappeared. "How about you? How many children do you have?"

"Just the one daughter," Neal answered. "We were…given only one, and she is indeed a blessing, everything we could want in a child."

"That you were given…" Leon repeated. "Now, that's a nice way of puttin' it. And how old is she?"

"She turned twenty in late March." Neal snapped shut his pocketknife and got to his feet. He had not yet cut into the peach. "I believe I'll take this with me," he said, bouncing the fruit in his hand. "It will taste good on the road back to Fort Worth."

"And the name of your ranch?"

"Las Tres Lomas de la Trinidad. Means 'the three hills of the Trinity,' a river that forks by our place."

Leon stood also. "Sounds like a fine place. Well, safe travel to you," he said. "I'd shake hands, but mine's a mess. I've enjoyed the company, but I'm sorry you had to find you wasted your time and came for nothin'."

"Oh, I didn't waste my time," Neal said. "I got what I came for."

Leon nodded. "Good to hear it."

Neal thanked him for the water and peach and rode off down the road under the farmer's watchful gaze from the porch. No, by damn, Neal thought. He hadn't wasted his time and gone away with nothing. He'd gathered everything he'd come for, if not exactly how he'd planned to use it. He'd exercised his judgment and decided not to give that man back there the choice of whether he wished to reunite with his daughter. His answer would have been plain enough. There was no room for Samantha in his family. Leon and Millicent Holloway hadn't wanted her or her brother when they were born, and they wouldn't want them now. Their twins would be an embarrassment to them. It was indeed a wonder that as babies they hadn't been drowned! The usual disgust boiled within him at the injustice of people like the Holloways to procreate more children than they wanted when he and Estelle, desperate for them, could conceive none.

At the fork in the road, out of sight of the house, Neal tossed the peach into a field. Let the buzzards have it. All that horticultural stuff about cousins and odd relationships and proper places had meant nothing. There was no double meaning to it. He heard the thud of the peach landing in the brush and paused in his review of the farmer's remarks. Now that he reflected upon it, Neal found it odd that Leon Holloway had not questioned him about what it was that he had come for and found.

Leon went to the well and washed his hands of the peach juice. He hadn't a lick of doubt that Samantha Gordon was Millicent's daughter and that he'd just met the man who'd adopted her. A good man, Neal Gordon, hard as mesquite and just as rough, but he loved Samantha Gordon with all his heart. You could see it in the look that came over his face when he spoke of her. It took a heap of guessing, but Leon would lay odds that Samantha was at an age when she was curious about her birth parents—that is, if she'd been told she was adopted. Leon would guess she was. The young woman he'd met at the fence last April hadn't a clue who he was, but Neal Gordon knew. For what other reason would he show up out of the blue except to determine for himself the sort of people who had given Samantha up for adoption? And why would he do that if not to clear the way for the girl to meet her real parents? *I got what I came for*, he'd said, and so he had. Leon Holloway, presumed father of Samantha Gordon, had been looked over and found wanting, just as Leon had intended. He'd given the rancher a pretty good idea of Millicent, too. Leon recognized a man who could love a child not his own, a father who would protect that child from knowledge that would only hurt. Neal Gordon would ride back to his ranch with the information he'd come for under his hat and there it would remain. Samantha would never know of his investigation. Of course Leon was only surmising, and it was possible that he might see her draw up to the fence one day soon, but he wouldn't look for her.

And he could be surmising all the rest of it, too, and nothing of this afternoon might be as it appeared, but he hoped not. If things were as he perceived, he was satisfied that his daughter had ended up in good hands, better than those who would have raised her. He could live out his life in peace knowing she was where she belonged. He believed Neal Gordon could, too.

In Gainesville, Neal left his paint at a livery stable to be fed and groomed and rested for the night, then took off on foot to a Harvey House hotel where he, too, could get a room and wash off the dust of the trail and change into fresh clothes. After that, he had one more duty to see to before he could return to Las Tres Lomas with a clear conscience. The hotel manager helped him out with it, and later, bathed, shaven, and cleanly attired, Neal took a seat on a bench located in a small tree-shaded park across from the new home of the Leon Holloways. *Bought one of the nicest houses in town*, the hotel manager had told him, and it was indeed an impressive-looking place. The house was a pristine, two-story white clapboard with a row of dormer windows eyeing the park from above an expansive lawn enclosed by a white picket fence. Neal had brought along a newspaper to read, but his gaze stayed fastened on the mullioned windows and double doors of the residence for a glimpse of the residents. He was prepared to wait hours.

Eventually, his patience was rewarded. A lively horse and fringe-topped surrey appeared from the back of the house, a young man driving—the seventeen-year-old son? He directed the outfit around to the gate of the picket fence, and soon two women wearing fluttery summer dresses stepped out through the double doors and came down the rose brick walk, laughing. The women, no doubt mother and daughter, were extraordinarily comely, their voices light and carefree. Neal saw his daughter's resemblance to the mother immediately. Samantha's hair was the same color as Millicent Holloway's. The son, dressed nattily in a dark suit, was tall and slim and held himself on the surrey seat with a pompous dignity that almost made Neal laugh. No one would ever mistake him for a hardworking farmer's son, nor the silly, stylish girl as his daughter. The woman, too, elegant from the top of her feathery hat and Gibson Girl hairdo to the tips of her white pointed shoes, did not fit the image of a farmer's wife. Neal wondered if wife and children were ashamed of husband and father in his sod-stained overalls and faded cloth cap. Why the hell wasn't that prissy son out helping his pa with the threshing? The answer didn't matter. He'd seen enough. Even from this distance, without knowing them, Neal could tell they were a shallow bunch, unworthy to call his daughter kin. She was better off without them.

Neal rubbed his abdomen. He had not been hungry for days—actually, for a couple of months—but now his stomach was roaring for food. A good sign. He would eat himself a hearty supper, get a good night's restful sleep, tomorrow stop in at La Paloma overnight, and then head home. He could hardly wait.

Chapter Forty-Six

It was the last week of June, and Samantha was in the library reconciling the ranch's bank statements when Silbia appeared excitedly in the open doorway. "Miss Sam, I believe *el patrón* is home. When I was hanging out the wash, I saw a man the shape of your father on horseback in a cloud of dust heading this way from the north."

Samantha threw down her pencil and jumped up from the desk. "Let's hope so!" she said and ran for the back stairs that led up to the widow's walk which gave a three-mile view of the ranch in all directions. She had been expecting her father any day now and was dressed for his return in a white silk blouse with puffy sleeves and a slim, ankle-length skirt. She had not wished to meet him in work clothes smelling like a barnyard. When he'd had a good wash and rest from the trail, she'd tell him the news that would send him over the moon, hoping it would clear some of the air of their misunderstanding. If it did not, she planned to go to Grizzly with the real cause of her father's strange behavior the past months and ask permission to talk it out with him. It was asking a lot of the cook. He'd have to pin his faith on Neal Gordon's fairness and compassion and regard for him when he heard the truth. It was all Samantha knew to do. She and her father could not go on the way they were.

From the roof, she saw that it was indeed her father jogging along on his paint kicking up a trail of dust a half mile away. There had been no rain since he'd been gone, and the summer was bearing down hard on the summer grass. She waved, and to her relief and joy, he took off his hat and waved it back at her, kicking his horse into a faster pace. Samantha ran back down the stairs and out of the house to the edge of the compound where several ranch hands who had also spotted him had gathered to welcome him home. She waited for her father's first reaction at seeing her. By that, she would judge if the time away had shortened or lengthened the distance between them.

"Daddy!" she cried and ran to him when she saw his face break into a large smile. Neal was out of the saddle before she reached him, his arms open wide.

"My girl!" he said, hugging her tightly. "How I've missed you."

In that moment Samantha knew that everything was all right between them. Somehow, some way, her father had come to an understanding out there on the trail. He'd resolved his pain and injury, forgiven her betrayal, and emerged from his deep, dark well. His whole being made clear that no more need be said on the matter, and he would not welcome a discussion of it. Samantha would let it lie as well. What was the point of restoking a fire Neal Gordon preferred to burn down. She, too, with Sloan's help, had come to a certain understanding and acceptance. Her temporary itch to learn the origin of her birth was only natural to an adopted child. Her curiosity carried no longing, and she had no reason to feel guilty of betraying the adoptive parents who had loved and raised her.

These adjustments in attitudes seemed to hang in the air between them as arm in arm they strolled to the house. Samantha laughed and said, "We have prepared the fatted calf for you, Daddy—literally! Welcome home. Sloan has missed you, too. I've sent one of the maids to invite him and his sisters over for supper. He has something to ask you."

"Are you sure?" Trevor Waverling had asked on the Sunday Todd had gone to his boss's residence to tell him of his discovery.

Well, hell no, Todd couldn't be *absolutely* sure. No geologist could. The petroleum industry was still in its infancy. Other than a few chemical analysis procedures, laboratory and field equipment to test for the existence of energy-producing sources had yet to be developed. The bible of his profession, the *First Book of Geology*, hadn't even been published until 1897, and the text had been limited to features like soils, water and air, volcanoes, the shape of sea and land. There was very little published material about the geologic branch that dealt with the origin, occurrence, and exploitation of oil and gas. Firsthand reports of drillers, wildcatters, and sheer eccentrics who for one reason or the other believed in signs that indicated oil was under their feet were all the guidelines for a geologist to go on.

So, no, Todd had said to Mr. Waverling that Sunday, he couldn't be sure, but he was sure enough to risk his boss's thirty thousand dollars on proving that he was.

"Okay," Trevor had said and looked at his son, Nathan, who'd listened quietly to Todd's report. "You ready to get your feet wet in making your first land-lease deal?" Nathan had nodded, and the three of them had set to the discussion of the price to offer for drilling rights.

Todd had been ecstatic, but he cautioned that they'd have to wait until Neal Gordon had returned from his cattle camp in Cooke County. They did not want to deal with his daughter, who would turn them down before Nathan even got his offer out of his mouth. Why? they'd wanted to know, and Todd had explained that Samantha Gordon had found the frontal portion of a fossilized animal's head that she thought might be of archeological importance, but in his opinion it wasn't. He did not tell them of the pictures she'd taken with her Kodak that he'd promised to mail. The camera was now stowed in a desk drawer in Todd's office. If Samantha never received back her camera and film from the Eastman Kodak Company in Rochester, New York... well, things often got lost in the U.S. Mail.

It was now Wednesday, June 27, an eternity since that Saturday. Todd stared at the note Agatha Beardsley had scribbled and left on his desk. *Your wife called while you were out to tell you that somebody named Samantha had asked her to come to Fort Worth Friday to help her plan her wedding now that her father—Samantha's father, that is—is back at the ranch. She said you were to mull it over and give her an answer by supper time.*

With an excited holler, Todd punched the air with his fist. He had wondered how he would learn that Neal Gordon was back from his cattle camp. He couldn't believe his luck. Both his wife and Samantha would be in Fort Worth and out of his hair when he and Nathan approached Neal Gordon about leasing his land for oil drilling—that is, if the rancher agreed to see them. By now, Samantha would have told Neal about the discovery and disappearance of her dinosaur skull. Todd believed that Old Man Gordon and his wife always felt some guilt in their daughter's decision to forgo her opportunity to attend Lasell Seminary for Young Women. Would that guilt sway him to indulge her argument against drilling?

It had already been arranged that as soon as word came of Neal's return, Trevor's connection in Fort Worth would carry a message to the rancher explaining why representatives of Waverling Tools wished to see him and propose an appointment. Todd would suggest to Trevor that their man contact Neal today to make the appointment for Friday. If the rancher wasn't interested, the sooner they knew, the better. Todd didn't think he could bear too many more days of waiting.

And waiting he'd been doing. Every day he expected to hear from a furious Samantha accusing him of theft and betrayal. Not for any reason would he then set foot on Las Tres Lomas. Neal Gordon would kill him if his boss didn't first. When Todd finally did hear from her, it was through Ginny. "I had a telegram from Samantha today," his wife said Monday when he walked into their apartment after work. "I can't believe it, Todd."

Her shocked expression told him everything, and every muscle in his body had tensed for the blow to come. "Can't believe what?" he'd said, pretending a bad cough to cover his terror.

"Samantha and Sloan are to be married. They became engaged last Sunday."

His jaw had dropped. He'd felt faint from relief. *Holy Jesus!* What had happened to Anne Rutherford? Had Sloan taken Todd's parting shot to heart and thrown aside a banker's daughter for a potential oil heiress? As an extra bonus, had Sloan considered that marriage to Samantha would eventually put him in control of the largest ranch in Texas when the Triple S and Las Tres Lomas were combined?

Todd would never have taken Sloan Singleton for that kind of man, but then you never knew a member of the male gender until a carrot was dangled before his nose. Todd should have heard from an angry and betrayed Samantha by now, but since he had not, he could safely assume Sloan had not told her of his skullduggery—an appropriate word, he thought wryly—and he didn't have to worry now about that skull showing up in her hands. The rancher might even prove an ally on the side of Waverling Tools.

Yes indeed, it had been a very tense few days, Todd thought, but the waiting was over. With a smile, he walked down the hall to his boss's office.

Chapter Forty-Seven

Daniel Lane cupped Billie June's breast and took its nipple into his mouth. Billie June moaned in pleasure and moved her hips to receive her lover's ultimate expression of passion. They had been meeting in her hotel room and making love every night since Billie June's arrival in Beaumont to spend a week, ostensibly with her boarding school friend. Her classmate had no idea that her former roommate was in town.

Billie June hadn't had the slightest notion of how to get in touch with Daniel once she arrived in Beaumont, a small coastal town built above the shoreline of the Gulf of Mexico, but such hurdles had never deterred the marching and picket-waving champion of women's and animal rights from her course. "Where might I find the best hotel in Beaumont?" she'd inquired of the station master.

"Only one we got is the Seaway," he said.

"That's what I thought," Billie June said. She turned to a woman and fellow passenger whose husband had come to pick her up in his buckboard. "I wonder if I might impose on you good people to drop me off at the Seaway Hotel?" she asked.

At the hotel, she glanced at the names on the register as she signed hers. "Oh, I see that a family friend, Daniel Lane, is staying here," she mused to the clerk. "Wonder what he's doing in town?"

"Don't rightly know, but when he arrived, he asked for directions to Spindletop. A couple of fools think oil is under the salt dome out there. It's become a sort of tourist spectacle."

"I believe I'd like to see it myself. How do I get there?"

The clerk told her she could ask Wally, the cabbie, the only one in town, to take her to the Big Hill, another name for Spindletop, among the nicer ones it was called. Make sure he didn't take her the long way to collect a bigger fare, he warned her.

Billie June, wearing a new summer frock whose pigeon-breasted bodice and slim waist showed off her ample bust to its best advantage, climbed aboard a rickety trap driven by a knavish-looking individual she wouldn't have trusted as far as she could have thrown his wretched horse. Later, she might have to have a chat with Wally about the upkeep of the poor creature.

"The Big Hill, also known as Spindletop, please," she told the cabbie, "and don't even think of divesting me of more money than the ride is worth. Believe me, if you try, you'll be divested of a great deal more than an overcharged fare. Are we clear?"

"Yes, ma'am," Wally said.

Billie June, who'd heard of mysterious disappearances of women alone in strange cities, said, "To be assured we are, the proprietor of the hotel, his clerk, and my maid"—she was not accompanied by one—"know where I have gone and who took me there. If a mishap occurs to me, you'll be the one to hang. Are we clear?"

"Yes, ma'am," Wally said.

Four miles later, they arrived at a barren, marshy point that Wally declared was Big Hill, also known as Spindletop. To Billie June it did not look like a hill at all but a fifteen-foot mound of skimpy grass topped with a crown of white sand. Billie June could see several men in knee boots at its base, one of whom she recognized as Daniel Lane. Billie June climbed down from the trap. "Stay here and wait for me," she ordered.

"You goin' down there, ma'am? Among all them menfolk? Ain't no way to get there except on them logs they got laid down for a walk."

"I'll do just fine," Billie June said. "Wait here."

Conversation among the men suspended as they grew cognizant of Billie June holding on to her wide-brimmed hat and picking up her skirt to navigate the haphazard array of log planks set down to mark the path up to the site of interest. Daniel Lane, his mouth agape, shouldered his way past the men to greet her at the boardwalk's end.

"My God, Billie June, what are you doing here?"

"I've come to see you, Daniel. Actually, I'm supposed to be seeing my school roommate. She lives here. That's what I told Sloan, anyway, but I really came to spend time with you—alone," Billie June said, her meaning imparted by a direct gaze and ducked chin. "I'm staying at the Seaway in Beaumont, same as you. Coincidences never cease to amaze me. Room 213 at the end of the hall. It's very quiet. Perhaps you'd like to drop by tonight." She nodded at the staring men, smiled at Daniel, who was speechless, and turned to pick her way back down to where Wally was watching from his cab.

"To the hotel, Wally, if you please," Billie June commanded once she was seated.

"Yes, ma'am," Wally said.

Daniel arrived at the Seaway Hotel at eight o'clock that night. Billie June was dressed in a robe over nothing underneath, her mouse-brown hair brushed from its pompadour and splayed about her shoulders. "Have you had your supper?" she asked.

"I don't want supper," Daniel said. "I want you."

Tonight was their last night together before Billie June would take the train back to Fort Worth in the morning. "My brother is getting married," she said, sprawled in euphoric exhaustion beside Daniel.

"To that do-gooder banker's daughter?"

"No. To Samantha Gordon."

Daniel rose up on an elbow to stare at her in surprise. "Samantha Gordon! I thought he was engaged to Anne Rutherford."

Billie June played with his chest hair. "Well, they were not exactly engaged, but everybody expected them to marry."

"My God! What happened?"

"I'm not exactly sure, but Millie May and I are pleased that it did. We love Samantha, and we can't stand Anne." Billie June laughed. "It happened the day after Sloan wagged home something that looked like a dried animal's skull, I imagine to give to Samantha. That may have done the trick. She's always been fascinated by fossils."

"What kind of an animal?"

"I just got a brief look at it, so I couldn't say. Sloan whisked it under his arm and took it up to his room without a word."

Interested now, Daniel propped up on his pillows, always alert for any morsel having to do with Mr. High-and-Mighty Big Britches, and reached for a cigarette. One of the indulgences his salary from Waverling Tools afforded was machine-rolled cigarettes, generally considered effete among smokers. Cigars and pipes should be a man's choice was the general opinion. Daniel liked neither and dared anyone to call him unmanly for his preference. Those who'd dared when he rolled his own had regretted it. He especially enjoyed a cigarette after having sex. "Why be so secretive about it?" he asked.

"I don't know. Maybe he meant it as a surprise for Samantha and thought I might spill the beans. I'm not good at keeping secrets." She grinned. "Unless it's you and me. Anyway, the next day, Sunday, he ended things with Anne and proposed to Samantha."

"Really?" Daniel said, filing away that information. He knew of Samantha Gordon's interest in paleontology and smothered a smirk, thinking maybe Sloan had proposed with a fossil instead of a wedding ring. He put his unlit cigarette aside for later. Billie June had moved her hand down to his groin.

"Of course I don't mind you going to Fort Worth to spend a few days with Samantha and her mother," Todd said to Ginny Friday morning at the station. "You take as much time as you need to help Samantha plan her wedding."

"I'm so thrilled that she asked me to be her matron of honor," Ginny said. "I would have thought that privilege would go to Millie May or Billie June, but I can see the diplomacy in asking me instead. How could Sam have chosen one sister over another?"

Ginny's chatter barely filtered through Todd's tense thoughts. He wondered how thrilled his wife would be over her selection as matron of honor when Samantha discovered he had engineered the possible ravage of her suspected sauropod field. Upset, puzzled, Samantha had written to him in a letter received Wednesday about the disappearance of her fossilized find, which confirmed that Sloan had not ratted on him nor shown her the confiscated skull. She had no idea how it could have disappeared, she wrote. It wasn't the kind of thing a predator or the ranch dogs would have been interested in, and she'd found no tracks.

Maybe Saved was the culprit, he'd written back. Maybe he'd butted the thing across the pasture and destroyed it.

Todd's euphoria of Wednesday had been diluted by his anxiety over how he could stay innocently out of the picture with Samantha never the wiser about his hand in the matter, but he saw no escape. Samantha was a very smart cookie. She knew of his burning desire to prove himself a great geologist. When she learned that he was responsible for the company's oil interest in the area of Windy Bluff, especially when her camera and photographs did not arrive from New York, it wouldn't take her a minute to solve the mystery of the missing skull. The only explanation was that her good friend and fellow classmate had returned to the ranch to destroy her evidence of a possible archeological phenomenon. Todd would deny the charge, of course, and defend his soil samples by saying that as a geologist and employee of Waverling Tools, he'd felt it his job to report his suspicions of oil deposits on Las Tres Lomas to his boss. But he was no fool, either. To back up his claim of innocence, he'd taken measures to ensure it.

Ginny was taking the morning T&P to Fort Worth. She did not know that her husband, along with Nathan, would follow an hour later, but they would return the same day while Ginny planned to remain through the weekend. Neal had apparently not informed Samantha of his coming visitors, or she would have mentioned the meeting to Ginny. Todd had a feeling that the rancher, aware of his daughter's views on drilling for oil on grazing land, would have kept that information and the purpose of the visit to himself, so Todd's involvement would remain secret a little longer.

Removing—stealing—that archeological find was the most god-awful sin Todd had ever committed, and he'd bet it was for Sloan Singleton, too. The rancher's transgression was more traitorous, though. Todd was betraying a friendship. Sloan was deceiving the girl he planned to marry. Samantha would naturally have shared the news of her discovery and its mysterious disappearance with Sloan. What would she think of Sloan's marriage proposal if she should learn of her fiancé's accidental meeting with Todd and the gist of their discussion at Windy Bluff the afternoon before he asked her to marry him the next day? If the man was as smart as Todd credited him, he'd get rid of that skull.

In any case, Todd cringed at the idea that he was now tongue-in-groove in a conspiracy with Sloan Singleton, which was a little like a mongoose and a snake in the same cage. All Todd could do to protect himself was to make sure he kept his distance from Samantha's betrothed.

Chapter Forty-Eight

Friday afternoon, Neal leaned back in his chair behind his library's mammoth desk and clasped his hands over the slight bulge of his stomach in delicious enjoyment of the third most perfect time of happiness he'd ever known. The first had been the day Estelle agreed to marry him, and the second had been the night Samantha was put into his arms. Other than those memories, none other could compare to his homecoming Wednesday afternoon. The joy of seeing his daughter, of their being on an even plane again, had been happiness enough. He should have suspected something more was in the works when he found Grizzly and Silbia whispering peaceably in a huddle in the kitchen. Those two fought like cats and dogs. And the dining table had been laid especially festive with flowers and extra settings of the cupboard's best dishes beyond the number expected. "Silbia must think we've invited the bunkhouse," he'd commented to Samantha after flicking an eye over the layout, but such things were her bailiwick and no business of his.

So he'd had a good soak and a little shut-eye and woken refreshed to the welcome-home aroma of beef roasting for supper. He felt light on his feet, as if he'd shed ten pounds, and he whistled as he dressed, wondering what it was that Sloan wanted to ask him. He was looking forward to an evening with him and his sisters, always good company, and of course the delight of his daughter's presence. Now if only Estelle were with them, the party would be complete.

Ready for his bourbon, and hearing voices below, he'd gone downstairs to the library, where to his surprise, he found only Samantha and Sloan, the boy looking as handsome as the golden Titans in Neal's mythology books. He and Sloan shook hands, and Neal had said, "I believe you wanted to ask me something?"

That had been a cue. Into the room had trooped Estelle with a smile as big as a breaking sun, followed by Millie May and Billie June, Silbia, Grizzly, and Wayne. They'd all been hiding outside the door. Sloan had gone directly to Samantha, put his arm around her waist, and turned to him. "Mr. Gordon," he said, "may I have your permission to marry your daughter?"

Well, now, that was about as good as it got for a father. Neal had thought of Seth Singleton when he choked out a mighty *"YES!"* and they'd all had a grand time together drinking and making merry until the early hours. Estelle had stayed the night, of course, and they'd made love for the first time since he couldn't remember when, his love gushing out for her in one of his best performances ever. "My goodness!" she'd said. "You've still got it, old man!"

Yes, sir, he still had it—all that was important, and now his daughter was soon to be married to the perfect man for her. There would be grandchildren to come with no more worries of an heir, and he would live to see his and Seth's dream come true—the ranches of Las Tres Lomas and the Triple S joined as one. He'd discussed it privately with Sloan Wednesday night, and his soon-to-be son-in-law was all right with the two of them running the ranches as a single outfit. In time, Neal would step down and leave it to Sloan to oversee the whole operation. It was as he'd intended it anyway before Samantha came along. There would still be years to take Estelle traveling. He'd gut it up and go by train. She'd always wanted to see New York City. Neal foresaw only one problem that could shadow his complete happiness. Sam would frown on drilling for oil on Las Tres Lomas.

Samantha and her mother, who'd stayed over Thursday, had left with Millie May and Billie June early this morning to spend the weekend at Estelle's and meet with Ginny Baker to discuss plans for the wedding. Neal had let his daughter and wife go without telling them about today's meeting with a landman and Todd Baker until he learned more. Where exactly did the company wish to drill? His only information had come from the messenger representing Waverling Tools of Dallas. It seemed that Todd had visited the ranch in Neal's absence and strongly believed Las Tres Lomas could be sitting on a large deposit of petroleum.

There were plenty of arguments to soften Samantha's disapproval, and he hoped to enlist his future son-in-law's support to convince her of them. Sloan would see the practicality in drilling. Never far from all Texas cattlemen's minds was the question of how they could keep their ranches going year after year if they should head into another prolonged period of drought. Only one teasing rain shower had fallen since the first of April. With oil money in the bank, Las Tres Lomas and the Triple S could keep everybody on the payroll, buy feed for their herds when their alfalfa fields dried up, and afford to hire one of those economic botanists who fooled around with food plants to work with Samantha in developing drought-resistant grasses. Considering her passion for microscopic study, she would be sure to embrace that idea.

And there was another reason why Neal wanted to drill. He was well-off now, but he wanted to be rich. Money spoke. It was like the sword in the hands of the mighty Titans that ruled the universe in his mythology books. He had a respectable say in local politics now, but he yearned to have larger sway statewide, use his influence to do what was best for Texas, the state of his birth whose independence his family had fought for and that he'd helped to protect from Northern aggression. Too many men of low character from other parts of the country—carpetbaggers— were getting into the state legislature and leadership positions with only their own interests at heart.

Silbia's rap on the library door signaled that his visitors had arrived. She stuck her head in. "They're here," she announced. "Where do you want me to put 'em?"

Neal's heart began a rapid beat. "Show them in here," he said and inhaled a chest full of air. His glance fell on his row of well-preserved books telling the stories of the mighty Titan gods and goddesses of Greek mythology. And, he had to admit it, but only to himself, that he *liked* the idea—the *image*—of himself as a powerful champion of Texas, like those Olympians featured in the tales from his mythological collection. Since he was a boy, it had been a dream of his to become one of them in reality. In whose hand would the sword of power be better wielded? And oil money—gushers of it—would make his dream come true.

"Gentlemen, welcome," he said, getting up to shake hands with the two visitors shown into the room. They were a disparate pair. Todd Baker was tall but thin as a scarecrow, nervous as a twining rod. The other stood an equal height but was of muscular build with an air of calm, patient strength about him. Neal addressed Todd first. "Todd, good to see you again. Hardly any time seems to have passed since you were no taller than the top of your daddy's boots, and now here you are, a bona fide geologist." To Nathan he said, "And you must be the landman I was told to expect." Neal noticed that the young man's extraordinary eyes were neither blue or green but a deep combination of both.

"He's the son of Trevor Waverling," Todd offered, hoping

that information might carry weight in the negotiations and that Nathan wouldn't muddle it up by correcting his last name and confuse the issue.

"Just Nathan will do for now, Mr. Gordon," Nathan said, shaking hands. "You have a good-looking place here."

Neal cast an appraising eye around the library. "Thank you. The old abode could use a little sprucing up, but it's comfortable enough."

"I was referring to your rangeland, sir. It's some of the finest I've ever seen."

Neal was conscious of a discomfited shuffle from Todd. "Oh?" he said. "You speaking from experience as a landman or from having grown up on a ranch?"

"Neither," Nathan said. "I'm new at the job, and I grew up on a wheat farm."

So the boy might have some misgivings about sinking a drill bit into good rangeland, Neal thought, divining a little conflict in that regard between landman and geologist. Samantha would find a kindred spirit in this young man, more was the pity, but Neal found he liked him, too. The boy exuded a straightforwardness he liked. That perception remained to be tested, but for the moment, Neal was inclined to trust him to lay out all the facts and to offer a fair deal.

They took chairs around a large table used for Neal's poker games. Todd spread out a map of the area of Windy Bluff drawn from another brave, clandestine visit to the site he'd managed without discovery. Employing a plotting compass, steel-ribbon tape, and other surveyor's tools, and using the rock structure of Windy Bluff as a benchmark and the fence gate as a boundary monument, Todd was able to sketch a detailed drawing of the acreage he believed most viable for striking oil.

"So that's the area where you wish to drill!" Neal exclaimed, flooded with relief. "Thank God. That patch of ground is near worthless anyway, with hardly enough grass to feed my daughter's pet steer. How in the world was it that you came to be out at Windy Bluff to make your discovery, Todd? The messenger didn't say."

Todd exchanged a look with Nathan. From Neal's question, Samantha had obviously not told Neal of her possible archeological discovery. Todd wished he could lie, say that Samantha had invited him out to see her pet steer. However, in meeting with Nathan and his father the Sunday following his discovery, Todd had presented the snag that would prevent Neal Gordon from agreeing to drill on the desired land. Todd had had to remind father and son that they had met Samantha Gordon at the paleontology lecture in Fort Worth they attended in March. They both remembered her reddish-gold hair.

"Well, sir..." Todd began and explained, leaving out the part about the theft. When he finished, Neal's rosy mood had tempered. He remained silent for a few minutes, chewing on his thoughts, patting his chin thoughtfully. "Did...Samantha not tell you about her find, sir?" Todd asked.

Neal realigned himself in his chair, his disappointment heavy. He should have expected there'd be no clear sailing in this enterprise. "I've only been home less than two days, and there were other things of importance to discuss," he said. "My daughter is getting married, as you know, Todd. Her mother was home and we had guests to celebrate the occasion. I'm sure Samantha would have gotten around to it."

"So, until you discuss our proposal with your daughter, I should hold off my land research?" Nathan asked quietly.

Neal drummed his fingers on the table. "So my daughter thinks there's a dinosaur burial ground around Windy Bluff, does she? What do you think, Todd? You saw the skull."

"It was only a fragment of one, and I couldn't be sure."

"Was?"

Todd felt a lurch of anxiety. "Yessir, *was*. It's no longer there. Samantha wrote me that it had…disappeared." Todd felt Nathan's curious eyes on him, but he could plead that he'd simply forgotten to pass on that information since he hadn't received Samantha's letter until days after his Sunday report.

"Hmm," Neal mused. "So there's no proof of the possible existence of such a burial ground around Windy Bluff?"

"Uh, actually, there might be," Todd said reluctantly, again aware of Nathan's narrowed gaze. In their early Sunday meeting, Todd had left out the information of the photographs Samantha had taken with her Kodak, which was now hidden in his desk drawer. Eventually, that lacking piece in his Sunday report would come to light. Best to insert it now.

Under Nathan's scrutiny, Todd filled in the missing part. When he'd finished, Neal asked, "Where is that camera now?"

"On the way to Rochester, New York, for the pictures to be developed, sir," Todd said, straight-faced.

"So they'll tell the tale one way or the other?"

"That's right, sir, but again, I don't think we have to worry. In my expert opinion, they'll only show the relic to belong to a more recent species of extinct life."

Neal turned to Nathan. "How many acres are we talking about, son?"

"Two, sir."

"Only two. That should present no conflict. You can just drill a little away from wherever this"—Neal twirled a finger—"*artifact* was found, right?"

Nathan and Todd exchanged a look. Nathan said, "No sir. An oil rig has to be set up where geological findings indicate oil. Off two feet either way can produce a dry hole."

"I see…" Neal mused. "That's a damn shame." He glanced at Todd. "But if you're right and Samantha's wrong about the identity of that bone, I see no problem with leasing. I have proof of my family's land grant and property deeds, plus a copy of my father's will, but I understand before you can negotiate mineral and surface rights, you have to authenticate them from courthouse records. Is that right, Nathan?"

"That's right, Mr. Gordon."

Todd sat up eagerly. "Does that mean we have a deal?"

"It means that Nathan can begin his research, Todd. Now let's go see precisely the area we're talking about."

Chapter Forty-Nine

Monday morning, the first weekday of July, Trevor Waverling trained his gaze down the conference table around which sat Nathan, Daniel Lane, the company's geologist, its plant foreman, and its bookkeeper. He had spent the weekend in the company of a lady friend and had not returned to the town house to bathe and change suits until after his son had already left for work, so he could not question him about his interview with the owner of Las Tres Lomas de la Trinidad. "Let's hear from you first, Todd. How did it go with Neal Gordon?"

Todd squirmed. "I'm not sure, but I'm encouraged. He didn't refuse us and told Nathan to go ahead and research the courthouse records. They should be pretty clear-cut. Mr. Gordon says the land in question has been in his family since 1820. There were no other owners, so we don't expect a problem with ownership of mineral rights."

"What's his holdout? I'd think the man would jump at the fair price we're offering."

"It's his daughter," Nathan volunteered. "She's opposed to oil drilling on grazing and cropland. When we met with Mr. Gordon, she hadn't been informed of the reason for our visit. She was away from the ranch for the weekend, and until she returns today, he can't give us an answer."

"Mr. Gordon says the land where we want to drill is worthless for grazing, so I don't see how she can object," Todd said.

Nathan looked at Todd skeptically. "Don't you? In addition to an underground spring near the site, Mr. Gordon's daughter believes Windy Bluff's the burial ground of a herd of dinosaurs."

Daniel Lane said with sudden interest, "Why would she think that?"

Todd waved a hand to discount the discussion. "Oh, Samantha found a fragment of a fossilized skull with features of a dinosaur, and now she believes a bunch of them may have lived and died there millions of years ago."

Nathan said, "It makes sense. The soil in that area is marine sand, suggesting that an enormous body of water once covered the place, a natural attraction for dinosaurs."

Todd said with a trace of irritation, "How do you know so much about dinosaurs?"

"I read a lot."

Trevor glanced from his geologist to his son. Was he detecting a little friction brewing between the two? He hoped not. He'd appreciated his surprising good fortune that the pair made a compatible team. Each had his own opinions uninfluenced by the other's. So far both had been in total agreement of their analysis in the reports they'd brought back, doubling his trust in their assessments.

Trevor remarked, "You examined the relic, Todd. What do you think? Does it belong to a dinosaur?"

Todd shrugged and repeated the answer he'd given to Neal Gordon. "Not in my opinion, but we'll never know for sure. It went missing before it could be analyzed by experts in the field."

"Missing?" Daniel Lane said.

"Sam couldn't find it when she made another visit to the place. She has a pet steer that hangs out in that area. It's my belief the wretched beast butted the thing to pieces. At any rate, it's disappeared."

Daniel raised an eyebrow. "Really?" he said.

Trevor said, "So then there's no evidence or witness, except you, Todd, to support her claim to her father?"

Before the geologist could reply, Nathan answered, "Miss Gordon took pictures of the fossil, so they should tell something. She entrusted her Kodak to Todd to mail off for developing. Isn't that so, Todd?"

Turning pink and unable to resist a quick glare at Nathan, noting his use of *entrusted*, Todd said, "Yes, but I didn't think the subject of the camera worth bringing up to you, Mr. Waverling. It's my professional view the photographs will dash Samantha's expectations."

"And when did the camera go into the mail?" Nathan asked.

Todd said curtly, ignoring Nathan and addressing his answer to no one in particular, "June eighteenth."

Again, Trevor caught a spark of friction between the two. Had Todd deliberately failed to mention the camera, or did he simply believe the photographs would prove meaningless? He'd bring up the subject to his geologist later. "You seem to be familiar with the family, Todd. Do the Gordons have any more children?" he asked.

"No sir. Samantha is an only child. She was adopted by the Gordons when she was just a few days old."

"So there are no other siblings to protest or agree to drilling on that site. That being the case, who do you boys believe Neal Gordon is leaning toward—Waverling Tools or his daughter?"

"In my opinion his signature is already on the lease form," Todd said.

"You agree, Nathan?"

"I'm afraid so."

"Why afraid so?"

Nathan contemplated the question with a frown between his brows that recalled to Trevor his own father's. "Because if there is a dinosaur burial ground there, oil exploration will destroy it, not to mention contaminate the underground spring that could meet Las Tres Lomas's water needs in that section of the ranch for a generation to come. That kind of water source is manna to a man who depends on his land to make a living."

"If we find oil, Gordon won't need to depend on his land in the way he does now to make a living," Todd said.

"*If* we find oil," Nathan countered.

Trevor studied his son. Was the boy cut out to be a landman after all? Who in the boy's bloodline was responsible for his respect for land and water? Nathan's maternal grandfather, of course. Millicent's old man was a son of a bitch, but he'd had boundless regard for the "blessings of nature," he liked to say. Nathan had not been one of the blessings of nature he'd held in regard.

"Yes, that's always the big question," Trevor said. "How is Neal Gordon to notify us if we have a deal?"

Todd spoke up. "His ranch doesn't possess a telephone. He'll use his neighbor's to call us here at the office."

"Sloan Singleton's ranch?" Daniel asked.

Heads turned to him curiously. "Yes, that's right," Todd answered. "You know him?"

Daniel answered, "Yeah, I know him."

"Sloan and his daughter are getting married," Todd offered. "I'm hoping he'll be on our team and convince Samantha of the wisdom of drilling. His ranch and the Gordon ranch are smack-dab side by side, so what's good for the goose is good for the gander, so to speak."

Trevor noticed his troubleshooter's secret smirk. "You have something to add on the subject, Daniel?"

"No sir," Daniel said, straightening up in his chair. "Nothing at all."

Trevor's speculation stayed on him a few seconds before he returned to the agenda. At the close of the meeting, he said, "Nathan, I'd like to see you in my office, please."

The others in the group picked up their reports with covert glances at Nathan that wondered if the boss's son was in a spot of trouble. With Trevor Waverling, you never knew. The boss's mild order in the conference room could mask an invitation to lunch or an explosive reprimand in his office. He never favored or dressed anybody down in front of other employees. Nathan could be in for a loyalty lecture. Everybody was ready to sink a drill bit into the rancher's land except the farm boy from Gainesville, Texas. Todd walked to his office to await the call from Neal Gordon with the hope his boss gave his son the boot he deserved. He and Nathan had begun to part ways. Why be a landman if he wasn't willing to sacrifice what was on the land for what was under it?

The son of a bitch! Daniel thought to himself of Sloan Singleton as he went off to the draft room. When Billie June had told him about her brother sneaking a desiccated animal head up to his room at the Triple S—Daniel pictured it bone-white, fragile as china, and sharp-edged—he had pondered what could possibly be the reason. Now he knew. Sloan had taken it to get rid of evidence that would interfere with oil exploration on Las Tres Lomas, then turned around and proposed to Miss Gordon after ditching Anne Rutherford. Like Todd had said: What was good for the goose was good for the gander. Samantha Gordon deserved better. Daniel could count on one hand the number of people who'd been kind to him, and one of them was Samantha Gordon. When he was slaving away at Chandler's, he'd come down with a hacking cough and sore throat, but he couldn't afford to take off without pay. That week, she'd stopped in to pick up a horse bit he'd repaired, paid her bill, and left, but a half hour later she was back with a box of throat lozenges she'd bought for him at the druggist. "Hope this makes you feel better, Mr. Lane," she'd said. Very few people ever called him mister, let alone bought him anything outright for nothing he'd done. She'd also stood up for him to Sloan, so Billie June told him, and as far as Daniel knew, she'd never let on to the rancher that he was seeing his sister. What would the little lady think of her fiancé's proposal now if she were to learn who'd walked off with her artifact? Now *that* information, backed up by Billie June, would present an opportunity to get even with Mr. High-and-Mighty Big Britches.

But no, he would wait his time to wreak his vengeance against Sloan Singleton. Daniel might have added two allies to his camp, though they didn't know it. What did Anne Rutherford think of Sloan Singleton now that he'd jilted her? More important, what did her *father*, Noble Rutherford, have to say of his bank's one-time chairman of the board of directors? The banker was not the sort of man who'd allow an insult to his daughter to go unavenged. That was a point Daniel Lane would keep in mind.

Chapter Fifty

Have a seat, son, this may take a while," Trevor said, closing his office door behind him.

"You got something on your mind?" Nathan said.

"Always. Want some coffee?" Without waiting for a reply, Trevor poured two cups from a pot Jeanne had just left and handed one to Nathan. After they'd taken a seat, Trevor said, "So you're a little reluctant to drill on that patch of the Gordon ranch?"

"It would be a shame if Miss Gordon is right about that dinosaur cemetery."

Trevor added sugar to his steaming cup. "You know we're not in the business of taking such considerations into account."

"I know that. Just stating the obvious."

"The Gordon girl. Do you remember her?"

"I remember her hair."

"A pretty daughter like that and an only child…she's bound to have considerable influence with her father. It'll be up to you to override her. Do you think you're capable of that?"

Nathan considered the question over his first sip of coffee. "Can't say," he said. "Seems to me the contest will be between how much Mr. Gordon wants to please his daughter and how much he loves his ranch. Ranching's a lot like farming in that a landowner never stops worrying about his financial survival. You can be rich one year and poor the next."

"But you won't let *your* personal opinions get in the way of the negotiations? That's what I want to hear from you, Nathan."

"You have my word that I'll do my best for Waverling Tools, but I wonder if you'd let me try a compromise first."

"Tell me what you have in mind."

The map of the Windy Bluff area was on Trevor's desk. Nathan moved papers and the coffeepot aside to unroll it on its surface. "If Neal Gordon allows us to drill, I'd like to take another look at the site Todd is proposing," he said, pointing to the drawing of the rock escarpment. "It will depend on the surveyors' reports, but there may be a way to set up a rig here"—he indicated a point beyond the site of Todd's fall from the steer—"far enough east to prevent us from having to invade the area where the skull was found."

Trevor leaned forward and peered at the spot. "What about the underground spring?"

"It may be compromised."

"A pity." Trevor sat back in his chair. "All right, if we get the go-ahead from Mr. Gordon, you have my permission to review the property for an alternate drill site. You'll need to make a trip to the courthouse in Fort Worth anyway, and you can kill two birds with one stone. Just don't take Todd with you. You're likely to get grief from him. Go on your mission alone, come back with your recommendation, then we'll discuss it with Todd."

"Well, that's good, then," Nathan said. "Is that all?"

"No, it is not. I have a family matter to bring up."

"A family matter?"

Trevor, astute at judging people, especially someone as patently straightforward as his son, sensed the phrase had thrummed a chord in the boy. Family meant a lot to him. He missed the family not entirely his own in Oklahoma, the house, the farm, the people, the town where he grew up. Occasionally, Trevor could feel his homesickness. Those times aside, the boy had come to care deeply about his new family in Dallas, his sister and grandmother. About his father, Trevor was not so sure. Nathan had grown more comfortable with him, even respected him, despite the question of Jordan's death hanging between them, but the boy's heart that held a son's love for his father belonged to the man who had raised him. Those twenty years were lost to the father who had not.

With a wrench of jealousy, Trevor opened a desk drawer to remove an envelope yellowed by time. Across the desk, in his usual fashion, Nathan waited patiently to be enlightened. Trevor said, "I want you to read this, Nathan, but before you do, you must promise never to reveal its contents to anyone. You'll take what's written in the enclosed letter to your grave, as will I."

Nathan sat a little straighter. "Is this the family matter you want to bring up?"

"It is. Do I have your word?"

"May I read it before I promise?"

"No."

"Why do you want me to read it?"

"Because I want you to know the truth. You're a good one for the truth. All cards on the table, remember? But I choose who sees them."

Nathan wondered if this situation wasn't akin to a priest or lawyer about to hear a confession of guilt but bound by his profession not to reveal it. It was not a burden he wished to carry, but he had come to trust his father enough to believe he wouldn't put him in that position.

"I promise," he said.

Trevor carefully pushed the envelope across the desk. Nathan opened it and withdrew a single sheet of a letter whose spiky handwriting he instantly recognized. He had seen it on numerous company documents. He began to read.

Dear brother,

I pray you will prevail upon the family to forgive me for the decision I've made to end my life. I can no longer live with the demons and shadows and voices that haunt every moment I'm awake or asleep. I can no longer continue the deception that all is well with me as the demons grow more threatening, the shadows deeper, and the voices louder. I dread the dawn of day and the fall of night. I must find peace. I am going down to the river today, the place I've always been the calmest and the happiest, to let it take me to its depths. Like the poet, I feel the lure of the water, and so "I must go down to the seas again, to the lonely sea and the sky, and all I ask is a tall ship and a star to steer her by." There my ship and star will take me home.

Please explain to my betrothed that she could not have saved me from what I am about to do. Mother will be heartbroken, I know, and Rebecca may subside into that place of darkness she probably inherited from me and remain there always. You, my brother, will feel grief that might never entirely pass, but you have Waverling Tools to comfort you. I know you will run it with devotion and efficiency, far better than I ever could even if I were wholly well. I leave you and the family my total love and devotion,

Jordan Bartholomew Waverling, July, 1887

Floored, Nathan looked up from the letter at his father, eyes stinging. "You never showed this letter to your mother? You've deliberately allowed her to suspect that you had a hand in your brother's death? Why?"

"Because the truth would have destroyed her. No matter how hard Jordan protested that he was beyond help, my mother would have believed she could have saved him from suicide. His fiancée, too. As it is, she's never married."

Aghast, Nathan said, "But, by concealing the truth, you sacrificed her feeling for you. You'd let your mother go to *her* grave thinking the worst of you?" Confused, Nathan laid the letter on the desk as if further touch might damage the evidence of his father's innocence.

Trevor sipped his coffee. "That's exactly what I intend. She'd never understand or forgive Jordan for taking himself from her, from Rebecca. My daughter idolized him. Jordan's suicide would have tarnished Mother's memory of him. His picture would never have sat on her mantel. The pain would have been too great. Letting her live with her favorite son's memory unblemished is more important than salvaging the bit of warmth and affection she has for me."

"But *you* love *her* enough to hide this from her, a mother who suspects you of…murder?" Nathan stared at his father, incredulous.

"Yes, I do. I've disappointed your grandmother's expectations more times than I can count, but I'm not keeping that letter from her out of guilt. I simply want her to live out her life with the comfort of her memories. Jordan was the sun in her sky. I've been…the dark side of the moon. It's the least I can do for her."

Nathan shook his head. *Families!* They were like seeds. They came from the same packet, but there were always one or two that sprang up in the row different from the rest. "Why does Grandmother believe you had a hand in your brother's death?" he asked.

Trevor reached for the letter and carefully returned it to its envelope, then placed the envelope in a desk drawer and re-locked it. "A hard storm hit the day Jordan drowned. That morning we'd had a terrible argument over a company issue. I told him I'd see him dead first before I let him run Waverling Tools into the ground. Our mother heard us. That afternoon I came in late from the gym, but only Lenora was home. I re-membered that Mother had gone to a tea party, and I assumed Jordan was with his fiancée, but where was Rebecca? Lenora had thought she was in her room, but she wasn't. I went looking for her outside. I had an idea where she might be. She'd gone down to the pier against orders and got caught in the rain. Sure enough, as I got near the river, Rebecca ran toward me crying, 'Save him, Daddy, save him!'

"I knew immediately what had happened—or thought I did. Jordan had fallen into the river that by then was raging. He'd ei-ther slipped, unusual for a man of his sea legs, or Rebecca had given him cause to lose his footing. She has no sense of danger, a constant worry for us, and may have gotten too close to the edge. In any case, there was no sign of Jordan. I wasn't even sure if he'd been there. I tried to question Rebecca, but all she kept chanting were those damned lines from her uncle's favorite poem."

Trevor closed his eyes and rubbed his forehead wearily, as if his strong, manicured fingers could smooth away the remembered pain of that day. "When my mother came home from her tea party, she found me soaked. I had dried off Rebecca and put her to bed, but I was still wet through and through. Jordan's body was discovered late the next morning, but the coroner concluded he'd died by accidental drowning the afternoon before. I'll never for-get the way my mother turned and looked at me when we were given the report. By then, I'd found my brother's letter on my desk at the office and knew the truth, but the possibility of suicide never entered her mind. Suspicion that I had somehow caused Jordan's death did."

Nathan felt sick. The same nausea overcame him that he'd felt when he learned the truth of his mother's feeling for him. *Oh, Millicent cares for us, son. It's just that she cares more for Randolph and Lily.* Trevor said quietly, "You know your grandmother to be a wonderful woman, Nathan. If you can still feel love for *your* mother, who'd sell the farm—your birthright—out from under you for the sake of her other children's futures, you can understand my love for mine. What I want to hear from you again is that you will never, ever, tell her what you've learned here today. It doesn't matter to me what she believes. It matters to me what you know."

"I promise," Nathan said. "Now if you'll excuse me—" It was all he could manage before he left the room. He was afraid he was about to cry.

Chapter Fifty-One

On Monday after his daughter's midmorning return to the ranch, Neal listened patiently at his desk in the library to Samantha's happy recount of the weekend in Fort Worth, during which her mother and bridesmaids ironed out the details of her forthcoming wedding. The date had been set for August fourth, one month after Samantha and Sloan's announcement of their engagement at the Independence Day party scheduled to celebrate Sloan's twenty-fourth birthday in two days' time. Neal would have been caught up in his daughter's happiness and his own if he did not have information to tell her that was sure to dampen her spirits and threaten their reconstructed harmony. He held little hope that the possibility of her dinosaur field becoming an oil drilling site would be less repellent to her seen through the daze of her euphoria.

Samantha halted her excited flow of the weekend events. "Daddy, you seem distracted," she said.

"I am, but that doesn't mean your mother and I are not the happiest parents alive over your coming marriage, honey."

"What's wrong? You look as if you're about to punch a hole in my wedding cake."

It was an apt description. Neal grunted in appreciation of it. "In a way you're right," he said. "I have something to tell you, so take a seat and let's talk about it. While you were in Fort Worth, I had two visitors. One of them was a young man named Nathan Waverling who says you two met last spring at some sort of science lecture. He's a landman for Waverling Tools, works for his father."

"I remember him," Samantha said as she warily took a seat before his desk. "A tall, muscular boy with an unusual shade of blue eyes. He was with his father. Todd Baker introduced us. What was he doing here?"

"He came with Todd to make an offer to lease some of our land."

"For what purpose?"

"To drill an oil well."

A mutinous look came over Samantha's face. She'd taken the news as Neal expected. "Why would Nathan Waverling think there's oil on Las Tres Lomas?"

"Todd Baker told him."

"Todd? How on earth could he possibly..." Samantha paused, and Neal could tell that she was recalling Todd's ride and fall off her steer, his nosedive into the dirt.

Neal said, "He told me you'd asked him to come out to examine some kind of dried critter's head and how he concluded there's a good chance a gusher is under that marine sand around Windy Bluff."

True to form, Samantha bristled. "That critter's head is what he and I believe to be the partial skull of a sauropod, a species of dinosaur that might indicate a seabed of the creatures is buried in that location," she said. "Did Todd mention that?"

"Yes, he did, and that it's disappeared."

"It doesn't matter. The skull's not necessary to prove it was there. I snapped pictures of it. Todd took my Kodak with him to mail to New York. I should receive the photographs back any day now. He didn't suggest drilling where he believes an archeological treasure trove might be found, did he?"

"Actually, he did."

Samantha uttered a cry of disbelief. "No! He couldn't have!"

Neal held up a hand. "Now don't go getting mad at Todd Baker for doing his job. Remember he's a geologist first, not a paleontologist. He has to make a living, and he's hired to find petroleum deposits. He was dutybound to report to his boss that he suspects—no, is *convinced*—there's oil under the ground at Windy Bluff."

Samantha said slowly, horror dawning in her stare, "Daddy...you can't let them dig there. It would destroy what could be the educational find of the century. I know you think there is no value in ancient fossils. They're just old bones to you, no more important than the skeletons of cattle left to bleach in the sun, but to the scientific community, to the study of our world, they are invaluable. The fossils of dinosaurs can tell us about the age of the Earth, evolution, geological and climatic changes, the breakup of the continents..." She looked at him helplessly. "I could go on and on about what scientists can learn from them." She laid her arms on his desk and fixed him with a pointed stare. "Daddy, you can't let them drill at Windy Bluff."

Neal turned his head aside, away from the penetration of his daughter's lovely gray eyes. He fought the feeling that had come over him when he'd discovered Eleanor Brewster's letter. Her first loyalty should be to Las Tres Lomas. Todd had warned him to expect this argument from Samantha, and in another round of sleepless nights since the boys' visit, he'd tried to understand her passion for old bones and detritus from the long-ago past. Why should anybody care about the age of the Earth? It was what it was. And then he'd understood that her passion to protect prehistoric relics was little different from his to preserve the ranch of Las Tres Lomas de la Trinidad his ancestors had founded, not only for the future, but because of the past. Nonetheless, that comparison noted, the land of his fathers must take precedence.

Neal said, "You know what the income from oil would do for the ranch, don't you?"

"*If* oil is found," Samantha said. "Otherwise, we just have a big hole in the ground."

"The same could be true of an archeological dig," Neal countered.

"True, but I'm convinced my hole will not be in vain."

"So is Todd convinced of his."

Samantha sat back and crossed her arms. Impasse, Neal thought. Still, his daughter knew who would win. Her father would have the final say. It was his land, after all, but he could not live through another family crisis like the one just past. Sloan would support his argument, diplomatically, of course, but Neal would not put a strain on the marriage before it even began. He leaned forward and clasped his hands together on his desk. "Here's the best I can do, Sam," he said. "It's a reasonable assumption that if Todd is sure oil is present at Windy Bluff, then why wouldn't the black stuff exist elsewhere on Las Tres Lomas and at a distance far enough away to cause no destruction to your fossil site? I'll hold off leasing that area to Waverling Tools until you get those pictures back. If they validate your claim, we won't drill there, but if they don't, we will. There will be no digging around for further evidence to support your theory, understood? Your photographs will be your only roll of the dice. That's as fair as I can be."

Samantha let out a relieved, "Oh, thank you, Daddy!" and ran around the desk to throw her arms around his neck. "That's fair enough," she said.

"All right then," Neal said, pleased. "I'll ride over to the Triple S and put in a call to Waverling Tools to give Todd my decision."

*   *   *

Todd took the call on an empty stomach. It was the first morning in his short married life that his wife had not prepared his lunch bucket (she was suffering female difficulties), and he had not dared leave the premises to satisfy his hunger in case Neal Gordon telephoned. His stomach was rumbling by the time he jumped at the ring of the instrument on his desk, a special perk— save for Trevor Waverling's, the other offices did not boast one— and put the receiver to his ear. "Yes?" he said, and heard Neal Gordon state the code arranged to throw off eavesdroppers on the party line. "What!" he exclaimed to *Sorry, the bird won't fly.* "Why not?"

An acute silence filled the line while the rancher apparently tried to whip up an explanation without giving away the nature of the call. Finally, Neal said, "The site doesn't sit well with sister."

Holy Christ! Todd thought, incredulous. Samantha had won out! Against all expectations, that leather-skinned old rancher had sided with his daughter. If he had bet his house on Neal agreeing to the lease, he and Ginny would be living on the street. "Is that it?" Todd cried. "You mean we have to look somewhere else?"

"Not necessarily. We're awaiting the results of a package you mailed to New York. If said item shows the site unfavorable to sister, we will definitely plant there. If favorable to her, there must be other places on the property to plant your trees."

If anyone was listening in and was aware of the nature of Waverling Tools' business, they'd figure out what the old fool was talking about, Todd thought, his heart in his mouth. How big was the Gordon ranch? Ten thousand acres or more? Whatever the number, it was huge, and the boss would never agree to the overwhelming task of taking soil samples and testing them from such a large area when they could prove worthless. He'd want to move on to another site of greater possibility.

The "package" was in his bottom desk drawer, locked.

"Would you mind if we went ahead and completed our record search of sister's site, just in case?" Todd asked.

"It's your time," the rancher drawled.

"I mailed the package Monday, June eighteenth," Todd lied. "It is now July second, two weeks later. You should be receiving the results by the end of the week, then we'll know."

"I'll keep you informed," Neal said and rang off.

Todd remained seated to think and calm his galloping heart. He'd hesitated about destroying the Kodak, but he must now get rid of it. A locked desk drawer invited a hairpin. It was past the lunch break, and everyone had returned to their desks and their duties in the plant. No one should be on the grounds between the building and the river. He must find something to conceal the camera, then he'd take a stroll down to the Trinity, ostensibly to smoke his pipe and to take a break from his desk. If only he had his lunch bucket!

Eventually, he decided to remove the dirt from a large planter containing a spathiphyllum, a peace lily, that his wife had given him for his low-light office when he'd been hired by Waverling Tools. Todd set the camera in the container and plopped the plant on top.

"Just going down to the river to water my plant," he sang out to Jeanne as he sailed past her open door on the way out the back of the building, peace lily wobbling. Jeanne looked up in surprise. Todd usually doused his plant from a basin pitcher in his office.

The planter was of iron, and heavy, and Todd was puffing by the time he reached the end of the pier, obscured from office and factory windows. After a hasty reconnoiter of the immediate area, he dumped the camera into the water, returned the plant to the pot, and trudged back up the slight incline to the office building. No one took notice of him as he entered.

Had he waited a little longer, he would have smelled cigarette smoke. Daniel Lane stood hidden among flora in the cool shade of a cypress tree where he often stole away for a cigarette because smoking was forbidden in the factory. He had observed the surreptitious water burial of whatever Todd Baker had dumped into the river, and when he was sure the geologist could not glance back and see him, he hurried to identify it.

He saw at once that it was a camera, caught by its strap on a little isle of seaweed, but the mild current was moving it slowly away from the pier. Quickly, Daniel waded into the shallows, grabbed the paddle from the boat tied there, and redirected the course of the seaweed patch near enough for him to pluck the camera from its watery grave. Taking out his handkerchief, he quickly wiped off the moisture and examined it. It was a Kodak, the kind that advertised itself as "You press the button—we do the rest," and it did not seem to be waterlogged. Could the film be rescued? he wondered. He sure as hell intended to find out.

Chapter Fifty-Two

Back in his office, sweating, Todd lifted the newspaper on which he'd emptied out the dirt and funneled it back into the pot, reset the plant, watered it from his lavatory pitcher, and washed his hands in the basin. All was not lost, just delayed. He figured another two weeks, and when "the results" did not arrive, he'd apply a little arm pressure. He'd tell the rancher that Waverling Tools could not commit time and effort to gather soil samples over such a vast expanse of land as his ranch. It had found another site—not as promising, but the company was ready to drill and could afford to set up only one rig. Which was it to be, Mr. Gordon?

For the moment, Todd had to report the rancher's call to his boss. What would he say? It was not entirely untrue that the company was interested in another location to drill. When Trevor Waverling learned of the reason for the delay, he would not wish to chance the Kodak proving Samantha's claim and her father siding with her. His boss wouldn't want to wait and risk losing an opportunity to lease another oil prospect that had caught his attention on the Gulf Coast. Once other investors got a whiff of the area, they'd be snapping up leases as fast as they could borrow the money. Only trust in his geologist's certainty of oil on Las Tres Lomas had held Trevor back from sending him and Nathan to investigate possibilities of strikes in West Texas. Todd must make

sure that Trevor Waverling did not take his sights off the oil bo-
nanza waiting under that outcropping of rock his geologist had
already named the Windy Bluff Field.

Todd's heart missed a beat when he entered his employer's office and saw Nathan sitting before his desk. Earlier, he'd seen
him hurry by his office door looking upset. His father had given
him a good licking, Todd had thought gleefully, but there he sat,
a little red-eyed, but with no appearance of his tail between his
legs. There was something unexpected about his boss, too. Todd
could read it in his posture. Privately, to Ginny, he referred to
Trevor Waverling as "the cougar," the tag inspired by the man's
hard-muscled body and supple grace that made Todd think that,
provoked, he could spring for the jugular like a great cat. Today
the cougar positively lolled in his chair with the loose and relaxed
ease of someone in familiar and intimate company.

These observations Todd processed immediately as presenting
difficulties for him. Nathan Holloway was no longer simply an
employee of Waverling Tools. He was the son of the owner of the
company. Boss and farm-boy son had bonded.

The light in Nathan's uniquely blue eyes faded at the sight of
him, the eyes that had rested disturbingly on him as they'd sat
across from each other in the train compartment on the return
trip to Dallas Friday afternoon. Todd's stomach muscles had
knotted, and he'd wondered if the hayseed would tattle on him to
his father for concealing the detail of Samantha's camera. It appeared he hadn't, for it would have been his boss who would have
brought up the subject in the conference meeting.

"I've heard from Neal Gordon," Todd said.

"Well, let's hear what he had to say," Trevor said.

Nathan drawled from a side of his mouth, "*All* of it this time."

Todd said with a defensive sniff, "A fellow can't remember everything."

"He should when it's his job to remember."

Trevor frowned. "What are you boys talking about?"

"Past history, Dad," Nathan said. "At least this time."

Dad? Todd noted, as well as Nathan's warning. He was glad to get off his feet. His legs still trembled from the exertion of carrying the heavy pot to the river, but more so from shaky nerves. He felt caught in an undertow with no strength to fight the current. Nathan knew how much drilling on Windy Bluff meant to him, and now, cozy with his father, the boss's son was aware that the company's geologist wasn't above withholding certain information to achieve that aim. Keeping quiet at the beginning about Samantha taking pictures of her relic and "entrusting" him to mail her camera had been a mistake. When it wasn't returned, it would take a miracle for Trevor Waverling not to believe the worst of him. Suspecting was as good as knowing to Trevor Waverling, and he'd fire him before Todd could get out a word of self-defense. Land-lease contracts between lessee and grantor were required by law to state specifically every physical feature of the tract of land the owner agreed to lease. To keep something like a possible archeological find from him would make Waverling Tools liable to a lawsuit, because it deprived the landowner of geologic information that might have prevented him from allowing the company to drill. Well, at this point, Todd thought, what was done was done. Samantha's camera was at the bottom of the Trinity River, or soon would be, and nobody could prove he hadn't mailed off her Kodak.

"Well?" Trevor demanded. "What did Neal Gordon have to say?"

"We must hold for the present. Neal Gordon is waiting for his daughter's photographs to be returned from New York. The film will show whether the Windy Bluff area becomes an oil field or an archeological dig."

"And how long will that be?"

"At the longest, two more weeks."

"About those photographs, Todd," Trevor said. "At the start, why didn't you mention that Miss Gordon had taken them of the skull as further evidence of her claim?"

Todd hoped his bony Adam's apple did not betray his nervous swallow. "Well, as I said in the meeting, sir, in my professional opinion, there is no merit to them. That skull is not the partial head of a dinosaur, no matter how much Samantha wants to believe it is. I didn't think the photographs were important to mention because they won't prove anything, and…I was under the impression you believed time of the essence to begin drilling."

"Then your impression was wrong, Todd. To me, time is never of the essence to do anything without proper investigation, and those photographs were important to mention because they'll either support your professional opinion or refute it," Trevor said, his sea-green gaze going cold. "Since that's the case, we could have already arranged a contingent deal for another site if we learn we've been sitting on an empty nest. I understand Miss Gordon has studied fossils and the like, and her opinion may be as credible as yours. Apparently, you boys misjudged the weight of Mr. Gordon's affection for his daughter."

Nathan said, "I don't think so, Dad. There's no doubt Mr. Gordon loves his daughter, but he also loves his ranch. He struck me as the kind of man who wants to have his cake and eat it, too. It's just an impression, but I feel he's the sort to figure a way to satisfy both." *Especially if we can preserve that archeological site*, his look said to Trevor.

Trevor spoke to Todd. "Tell me again how long before those photographs are due to arrive?"

"No more than two weeks is my guess, maybe sooner, but they'll be worth the wait, Mr. Waverling, I can almost promise you," Todd said eagerly, grateful that Nathan had stepped up to his defense. Passion warmed his neck. "Please don't withdraw your offer to Mr. Gordon. If the photographs don't back up Samantha—and they won't—he'll lease to us, and you will never know a moment's regret."

Trevor regarded Todd with a thoughtful purse of his lips. "All right, Todd, I'm reluctant to argue against a man's convictions if he's totally convinced he's right," he said. "I'll hold off putting my money on another site, but two weeks is my limit. If we don't have the results of those photographs by then, we'll look elsewhere."

"Thank you, sir," Todd said, rising, the muscles of his legs as weak as fruit pulp.

Trevor nodded in dismissal, and as Todd left, he heard him say, "All right, son, ready to go eat now?" suggesting that Nathan had returned to his father's office at his invitation to join him for lunch. Todd thought his feelings should be nicked at his boss putting the question to the hayseed before he was out the door, carelessly excluding him, but they weren't. As rib-gnawing as his hunger was, his stomach turned at the thought of food. The boss had never invited him to lunch anyway, and he must go back to his office and pray for a miracle.

July fourth arrived, hot and sultry. Hand fans waved before perspiring faces, and smiles beamed when Sloan drew Samantha to his side, raised a glass of champagne to his guests in double celebration of Independence Day and his twenty-fourth birthday (which was really July second), and announced that Samantha Gordon had agreed to be his wife—"Sam to you," he added, to get a laugh. Applause and a few lewd remarks from male celebrants already tipsy on the punch greeted the couple's kiss. Neal and Estelle looked on with the glowing happiness of parents whose lifelong dream for their daughter had come true. Questions of in whose house the couple would reside, how their time would be divided between households, who would be in charge of the sprawling hacienda of the Triple S, and the role Samantha would play in helping Neal manage Las Tres Lomas de la Trinidad had been discussed, and some surprising information had come to light.

Billie June disclosed that she'd like to take a room at a women's boardinghouse in Dallas to study music at the Sarah B. Morrison Academy, and Millie May said that in the fall she'd like to enroll for classes at the Houston Museum of Fine Arts to learn how to paint in oils. Both were more than happy to yield their position as joint mistresses of the house to Samantha. Neal agreed with Estelle that it was only fitting that a bride live in the house of her husband, though he declared he'd "wander around the main house like a walrus out of water"—not that Neal had ever seen a walrus, his wife reminded him.

During a prenuptial breakfast Estelle had arranged at the town house to honor the two families, Samantha discovered she'd had a change of heart about a matter she'd expected to nettle the hound out of her. Neal announced he'd like to take Estelle to Galveston to stay at the Tremont House, the finest hotel in Texas where the likes of Sam Houston, Ulysses S. Grant, Clara Barton, and Buffalo Bill had stayed.

Estelle asked, a spark of hope in her eye, "By train?"

"By coach," Neal said and peered down the table at Sloan to say, "I'm hoping you'll help Wayne run the ranch while I'm gone, Sloan."

It was as Samantha had foreseen. She would be edged out of the running operation of Las Tres Lomas. She was heir to the ranch, but as she would be a woman married to someone as capable as Sloan, her father would expect her to step aside and let her husband into the driver's seat. The high-handed presumption of it should have made her blood flame. She had sacrificed her private dream of becoming a paleontologist for the sake of Las Tres Lomas. Now that her father was to have Sloan by his side, her services would no longer be needed. The choice of whether to hand over the reins to her husband should be hers, but Samantha found she no longer cared. She had no desire to incite another conflict between herself and her father, and he had been more than fair in respecting her argument against drilling. She would continue to see after the books, but she would not mind retiring her boots and chaps for drawing room clothes, to enjoy life as a married woman and eventually—within a year, she hoped—as a mother. In the meantime, with Sloan sharing the responsibilities of running both ranches with her father, Samantha would have leisure to pursue the excavation of the archeological site she was sure was present beneath the ground at Windy Bluff.

Chapter Fifty-Three

"Okay now, is everybody ready?" Trevor Waverling asked, sticking his head into the Concord, hands on the frame. His daughter and Zak occupied one seat. Across from it, the other was piled with picnic basket, water jug, kit of geological tools, valise of books, and beige-and-red-striped canvas traveling bag designed by Louis Vuitton of France. A bisque doll of unglazed porcelain, also French, reigned atop the mound, its dark blue stare and realistic skin-like matte finish looking eerily alive in the shadows of the velvet-draped coach.

"Ready, Daddy!" Rebecca squealed, hooking her arm around the German shepherd's neck. "Aren't we, Zak?"

"Don't hold him so tightly, Rebecca," Trevor ordered sharply. "Zak's already hot enough. Can't you see his tongue hanging out? He could bite you." He turned to Nathan. They were standing in front of the town house in Turtle Creek, Mavis and Lenora watching from the porch, Benjy already ensconced on the driver's seat. "Are you sure you want to take Rebecca along, son?" he said, pitching his voice low. "You know what a handful she can be."

"This trip to Fort Worth will be good for her," Nathan said. "She needs a change of scene, something to remember and think about in that world she inhabits, and Zak will help look after her."

"Your trip shouldn't take over seven hours. Once you get to

the Worth, use their telephone to give us a call here at the house. Mother will be worried until we hear from you."

"We'll be okay. Has everything been arranged with Mr. Gordon?"

"It has. He's expecting you, and maybe by the time you get out to his ranch, his daughter will have gotten that camera back. I hope Todd's right about the photographs. Otherwise, this trip and your research will be a waste."

"Today's the ninth, twenty-three days since Todd mailed the camera," Nathan said. "We'll know something by the end of the week. Kodak is good about developing and returning film when they say they will." Nathan stuck out his hand. He had already given his grandmother a farewell hug. "See you soon, Dad."

Trevor hesitated, then, ignoring his son's hand, pulled him into a rough embrace. "Take care, boy. We'll miss you," he said, giving Nathan's back a thump. Stepping away quickly, he called up to his driver. "Benjy! You make sure to take the road carefully, you hear?"

Benjy glanced down at Trevor. His proper coachman's attire of the winter had been replaced by less formal summer wear, and he looked less picturesque in a cotton driver's jacket and cloth cap. "I hear ye, Mr. Waverling. I'll make sure to deliver yer *paistí*— children—back to ye safe and sound."

Room had been reserved the other side of Zak for Nathan should the need arise to calm Rebecca, but for the time being, he would start the journey seated next to Benjy. He climbed up to the driver's box and at the flick of the reins gave a last wave to his grandmother, and they were off.

Trevor joined his mother on the porch. "I saw that embrace," Mavis said. "You've grown to love him, haven't you?"

Trevor nodded, his gaze on the departing coach. "You could say I do."

"Thank the Almighty for that," Mavis said. "It's good for you to love somebody other than yourself."

"Yes, it is, Mother," Trevor said.

The next morning, Tuesday, Samantha found herself unable to stay away from the library window fronting the approach to the ranch. Her father had informed her that the landman who'd accompanied the geologist to do a preliminary survey of Windy Bluff would be arriving to take another look at the area.

"What for?" Samantha had demanded, a glint of suspicion in her eye. "Our agreement was that, no matter the possibility of oil at Windy Bluff, if my photographs bear out my guess, there will be no drilling in that zone."

Neal held up his hands in a conciliatory gesture. "That's the point of the young man's visit, honey, and it was not my idea. It was Nathan Waverling's. He's coming out to determine if—should your photographs prove you right—there's a chance they might still be able to drill for oil in that region without interfering with the place where you found that head. No harm in that, is there?"

No, there was no harm in it, Samantha conceded to humor him, but she could have added that the landman was wasting his time. If a dinosaur field was there, it would encompass the whole northern section of the ranch, leaving no room for a drill site. It was clear to her that her father's excitement at the prospect of oil deposits being found on Las Tres Lomas had grown like a newly planted seed since their agreement. She'd find him reading The Derrick Page, a section recently included in the *Fort Worth Gazette*, when formerly he'd been interested only in cattle news. He began subscribing to business periodicals featuring petroleum-related articles he'd discuss with Sloan when he came for supper. He'd drop snippets from them such as "It's rumored

that Henry Ford is designing a gasoline-powered auto of the kind
that everybody in America will be able to afford. Can you imagine the demand for petroleum when that happens?" And, "Did
you know that France is the world's leading auto manufacturer,
but it's predicted that by 1905, the U.S. will outdo them. Imagine
that."

Her father had been bitten by the petroleum bug. Even Grizzly and Wayne seemed resigned that oil drilling was coming to
Las Tres Lomas de la Trinidad. It was only a matter of time. Samantha, repulsed, pictured bloated cattle lying dead beside their
contaminated underground spring, black crude soaking into rich
green grass, destructive service roads cutting across flowing pastures, drilling noise and the loud passage of horses and wagons
sending their livestock fleeing.

Samantha tried not to let her dread cast a shadow over her
wedding preparations and her upcoming marriage to Sloan, but
it nibbled on her happiness. The glow of her reconciliation with
her father, at its brightest and warmest the night of the party, had
dimmed somewhat. Her trust that nothing again could ever come
between them had weakened. Neal Gordon would stick to his
word—that she believed, but could he live without resentment of
her if the only oil to be found on Las Tres Lomas was over her
dinosaur bed?

"What's gotten you by the horns, Sam?" Sloan had asked. "I
know something's going on in that pretty head."

They were standing outside one of the Triple S's corrals looking over the newly purchased bull bred in England that had made
it alive and well all the way from Liverpool, a testament to its
stamina that Sloan hoped to breed into his herd. Sloan stood
behind her, his hands on the railing and she in the space between him and the corral fence. Now and then Samantha felt
Sloan's chin nuzzle the top of her head. Regardless of how many

cowhands lined the railings, when she appeared, unabashedly, he would make room for her in this intimate impound. At such times, she could hardly endure her longing for him, and she knew he felt the same. He would nibble her ear and whisper, "Soon, sweetheart. Soon."

She'd explained, and Sloan had asked slowly, "Well, to avoid another conflict with your father, would you...reconsider your part of the agreement?"

She'd swung around, horrified. "You mean forfeit an archeological dig that could yield untold prehistoric treasure for an *oil* site? No. A deal is a deal. Daddy would expect me to abide by his side of the agreement, and I expect the same of him. He knew what was at risk when he made it."

"And you know what's at risk if he loses." Sloan's meaning was clear. Had she asked herself what Neal Gordon would feel if and when inevitable disaster struck Las Tres Lomas that oil money could fix? Samantha had indeed given thought to that crisis, and it was at the root of her worry. She'd slowly nodded yes.

"I think you'd be wise to keep that in mind if no other source of petroleum is found, Sam," Sloan had said, then tightened the enclave of his arms. "But let's not worry about eggs that might never hatch. Neal's optimism is probably well-founded. My bet is that oil is all over that ranch."

Samantha had never thought she'd agree to such a statement, but she hoped so, too.

Troubling her also was the disappearance of the skull. What had happened to it? How could it have simply disappeared without a trace? What food value could an animal have found in ancient bone? Their dogs were well fed, and predators would have been more interested in live flesh. Samantha had dug carefully in the exact spot where she'd found the fossil, but found no bone source where it would have been attached. What movement of earth had caused it to surface from its centuries-old burial ground in the first place? She burned with impatience to get an archeological team out to the ranch.

Samantha heard the rumble of a coach and team turn under the crossbars. A look out the library window confirmed their visitor had arrived. She dropped her hand just as she was about to tug the bell pull to summon Silbia to send someone to get her father from the Trail Head. In the kitchen, the housekeeper would not have heard the team drive up. That was good. Samantha wanted time to look over Nathan Waverling alone, without the meddling—and intimidating—presence of Neal Gordon. She understood that this visit was the landman's idea, that he was in sympathy with the desire of the rancher's daughter to preserve her archeological site. That bode well for a tolerable meeting. She wondered if her hair would again attract his attention.

Samantha had come out on the porch by the time the team of two horses drew up to a hitching post. She recognized Nathan Waverling from their one brief meeting last March. He sat next to the driver, an odd-looking little man who handled the team of powerful horses with expert ease. A dark-haired little girl hung her head out the coach window. "Hello," she called out. "Who are you? Are you nobody, too?"

Inside the coach a dog barked.

"Howdy," Nathan said, hopping down, seemingly taking no notice of Samantha's hair, worn in the topknot style she favored in the heat of summer. "I'm Nathan Holloway. We met once before."

Perplexed, Samantha took the proffered hand. "I remember," she said, "but Holloway? I thought you were Trevor Waverling's son."

"I am." Nathan smiled at her confusion. "It's complicated. I brought my sister and dog along. I hope you don't mind."

"No, of course not," Samantha said. She smiled at the little girl. "Hello," she said.

"This is Rebecca," Nathan said, opening the coach door, "and my dog Zak, and that fellow up there grinning like a fool is Benjy, my friend and the family driver."

"How do you do?" Samantha said, with a polite nod that included them all. "Won't you come in? I believe our cook has made some fresh lemonade."

"Thank you, but we just had breakfast at the hotel."

"Are you sure, Nathan?" Benjy called down.

"I'm sure, Benjy."

Rebecca had approached Samantha. Eyes bright with wonder, she reached up and stroked an errant strand of Samantha's hair. "*O Helen fair, beyond compare! I'll make a garland o' thy hair,*" she quoted.

Samantha looked bewilderingly at Nathan. The dog, a German shepherd, had come to sit quietly on his haunches beside the little girl. "Rebecca, honey, you mustn't touch the lady's hair. You and Zak come stand by me," Nathan ordered quietly.

"It's all right," Samantha said, quickly understanding the situation. His little sister was enchanting but suffered a mental deficiency. Samantha smiled at her and said, "I like your hair, too, especially your pretty ribbon."

"*I'll tell you how the sun rose a ribbon at a time. The steeples swam in amethyst, the news, like squirrels ran,*" Rebecca began, but Nathan stepped forward and took her hand.

"Excuse me, Rebecca," he said, his voice gentle but firm. "The nice lady and I must talk. Go sit with Zak on the porch for a little while and get out of the sun. Will you do that for me?"

"Yes, Nathan," she said. "Come, Zak. You come, too, Benjy."

"That I will, wee one," Benjy said, nimbly hopping down on his short legs from the carriage seat to take charge of Rebecca's hand.

"You impress me as a kind and patient brother," Samantha said, risking an observation the landman might take as too familiar on such short acquaintance. At first blush, it was hard not to like him.

"My sister's no trouble. She'll go with us for the inspection. Would you direct me to the spot? I can't quite remember how to get there. Also, is Mr. Gordon about? I imagine he wants to be on hand. You, too, I suspect."

"You suspect right, but my father is…indisposed. I'll lead you out to Windy Bluff myself. My horse is already saddled."

"Lead on, then," Nathan said. "We'll follow."

Chapter Fifty-Four

An hour later, Nathan's inspection had been completed. Todd's maps and tools, along with Samantha's knowledge of the huge fields of dinosaur skeletons found in Colorado and Wyoming in the late 1870s, had helped him make his geological assessment. "It was estimated that the quarry in Colorado encompassed forty acres," Samantha told Nathan. Nathan did not state what was glaringly apparent to both of them: If Samantha's theory proved correct, a cemetery of deeply buried fossils half that size would spread over Todd's proposed drill site.

Samantha asked, "If oil is present in this area of the ranch, can it be assumed to exist in another?"

"Not necessarily," Nathan said and explained that he'd seen a gusher shoot out of a well dug a half acre from its sister rig that produced nothing but sand. "Pinpointing the exact location of oil is near impossible," he said. "Even when there are indications of petroleum deposits, you can still come up empty. Wells are dug on belief and gut feelings and noses. Nothing scientific about it."

Samantha's heart fell. "I can't tell you how sorry I am to hear that, but your company will look at other possibilities on the ranch, right?"

"I couldn't say, Miss Gordon. That will be up to my father." Nathan's heart had fallen also. He scanned the surrounding rangeland, vast in scope but only a fraction of the ranch of Las Tres Lomas de la Trinidad. If Waverling Tools did not sink a well in this spot, the company would move on. "You've got a big place here. Todd might not be able to sniff every foot of it."

"I understand," Samantha said, thinking of Todd Baker's nose that had generated all this trouble. If only Todd had not gotten on the back of Saved that day...

She would not exactly call him a traitor to the cause. That would be unfair. His cause was geology. Todd's job, as her father had pointed out, was to find oil for his employer. But he was a traitor to the principles of the earth sciences he'd professed to embrace, those that called for respect and reverence for relics of the past. And he was a traitor to their friendship. That day at Windy Bluff, he should have told her of his belief that an oil field lay near where she found the skull rather than express it to her father behind her back. What was more disturbing, at his suggestion, she'd handed over her camera to Todd to mail to New York. It was a concern that only recently had come to haunt her when she learned the extent of his treachery.

Benjy stole up to Nathan's side. "Nathan, me lad, isn't it time to spread the picnic? It's been a while since breakfast. I'm sure Rebecca is hungry."

"Ah, so it's her stomach I hear growling, is it?" Nathan said, grinning. He turned to Samantha. "Won't you stay and have a bite to eat with us, Miss Gordon? There's plenty."

"*Please!*" they heard from inside the coach, as the door flew open and Rebecca jumped out. Nathan and Samantha glanced at each other in surprise that she'd been listening. During the inspection, Rebecca had been content to sit in the coach reading to her doll one of the many books brought along to keep her occupied. The little girl ran to Samantha and wrapped her arms around her waist. "Please stay," she begged.

Samantha thought a moment. Her father, finding her gone, would have deduced their visitor had arrived and she and the landman had taken off to Windy Bluff without him. Grass and dirt flying, he would be thundering up any minute in a fume that she'd not alerted him and caused him to miss out on information she'd been privy to. She was glad he wasn't with them. Neal Gordon would not want to hear what Nathan Holloway had to say. God help them if Todd's nose did not turn up another prospective place to drill. Meanwhile, this little girl's arms were around her, her upturned face as tender as a flower, her plea irresistible. "I'd love to," Samantha said.

They sat down in the shade of a large cottonwood tree near the underground spring, Nathan and Samantha with their backs against the trunk. He had ordered the picnic prepared back at the hotel, the menu suggested by Benjy, and they watched as the coachman spread a blanket and set out a basket of fried chicken, cornbread, onions, pickled okra, a crock of pinto beans, and a butter cooler of banana pudding. But for Saved, cattle did not range this far north, and they would be spared the smell and sight of "cow patties," which would have affected their appetites. Today, the steer had wandered out of sight.

"How long have you been a landman?" Samantha asked.

"Not long enough to call myself one," Nathan answered, and without going into personal detail, volunteered that he'd come to work for his father when he turned twenty. He now lived with him and his grandmother and sister in Dallas and was finally becoming weaned from the wheat farm in Gainesville where he'd grown up.

Samantha smiled. "I was in Gainesville not so long ago. Beautiful farming country. So you're becoming accustomed to city life?"

"Trying to," Nathan said.

Samantha enjoyed the sound of his voice. He was a very comfortable person to be around, she thought, peaceful as a slow-moving river. While they conversed, Rebecca and Zak splashed in the spring, the little girl holding up her skirts and squealing when the dog shook himself and showered her with droplets. A cool breeze off the water relieved the heat, and only an occasional caw from a bird or the distant low of cattle disturbed the noon stillness.

Samantha felt the tension drain from her shoulders, if only for a little while. She found herself recalling the boy's handsome father and tried to reconstruct their conversation at the paleontology lecture last March...

I could not help but notice that you seemed to believe you knew me when Barnard and I joined you, Mr. Waverling, then decided not. Am I correct?

To a degree. The color of your hair reminds me stunningly of someone I used to know.

Then I hope it evokes a pleasant memory.

Unforgettable ones.

Samantha glanced at Nathan. Did he know the woman to whom her hair reminded his father stunningly of someone he used to know, the woman whose memory he had not forgotten? It didn't matter now. She was no longer curious as to who that might be, no longer desired an incidental encounter with a stranger who might say, *You look so familiar, especially the color of your hair. Are you related to so-and-so?*

Her thoughts were interrupted by Benjy calling them to the blanket. "Nathan," he said, "ye'd best get Zak to shake himself before he joins us. Come, Rebecca, let me fix yer plate."

They arranged themselves on the blanket, the earth warm beneath it. Samantha expressed that the chicken looked delicious. On a cattle ranch, they didn't get the opportunity to eat much fowl. She had never enjoyed picnics on the ground. Gnats and ants were an irritant, and balancing a plate in her hand a challenge, but somehow today the company of the entertaining little group made the annoyances unnoticeable.

"*Benjy!*" Rebecca raised her voice authoritatively. "Pudding, please!"

"You don't want to eat your chicken first, Rebecca?" Nathan suggested.

"Pudding first, and then the chicken," Rebecca said decisively then demanded in a shriek, "*Benjy! Where's my spoon?*"

"Ah, now lass, let Uncle Benjy tell ye a thing or two about spoons," the coachman said. He ladled a scoop of pudding onto Rebecca's plate and picked up a spoon. "With a spoon, ye take too much into yer mouth all at once, see?" Benjy demonstrated and afterward took up a fork. "With a fork the food lasts longer if ye dip only the tips into it, like this."

Rebecca looked skeptical and took the fork he handed her. They all watched as she carefully dipped the tips of the utensil into the pudding and quoted, " '*Pudding and pie,' said Jane. 'Oh, my!' / 'Which would you rather?' said her father / 'Both,' cried Jane, quite bold and plain.*"

Samantha looked at Nathan, and he answered the question in her glance. "My sister responds in poetry. It is her way of communicating."

"Her way is charming," Samantha said. "She has quite a fine mind to hold all those verses."

"She's brilliant," Benjy said, savoring a nibble of his chicken leg. "Her mind just thinks differently from the rest of us."

They heard a rider approaching at a gallop from the direction of the ranch house. Samantha sighed. "My father, Neal Gordon," she said, brushing crumbs from her lap, prepared to meet his ire.

Neal noted the spread picnic fare and halted his paint a distance away to prevent soil and turf from landing on the food. He dismounted hurriedly and approached with his hand held out to Nathan. "Good afternoon," he said. "Sorry to be late to greet you, but"—he cast an annoyed glance at Samantha—"nobody came to get me when you arrived."

Samantha said in a playful tone, "I wanted my time with Nathan before you took over, Daddy. I thought it best, and I was right."

"Come join us in a picnic, Mr. Gordon," Nathan invited.

"Aw, Nathan!" Benjy muttered low in protest.

Nathan ignored him. "We have plenty," he said to Neal.

But Neal Gordon was not interested in food. "Actually, what I'd like to have is your opinion, Mr. Waverling. Can this...supposed cemetery of old bones—" he waved an arm to encompass the area around the twin boulders of Windy Bluff "—be spared if we drill for oil over there?" He pointed in the direction beyond the underground spring.

"No sir, it cannot," Nathan answered, "and, Mr. Gordon, I go by the last name of Holloway, not Waverling. Holloway is my stepfather's name. He raised me. I've just recently come to live with and work for my father."

Neal's arm fell. He stared at Nathan as though he'd suddenly pointed a gun at him.

Nathan said, "But, like I introduced myself when we met, just Nathan will do."

When Neal, stiff and unmoving, continued to stare, Samantha took his arm. "Daddy? What has happened to you?"

"I—I don't know," Neal said. He ran a hand over his face. "For a few seconds there, I...I seemed to lose my train of thought. I guess I was bowled over by...by the disappointing news." It wasn't possible, he thought, shock deafening his ears to all sound. These things didn't happen. The young man he'd invited onto his land was Samantha's twin brother and...that must mean that...Trevor Waverling was her father.

Chapter Fifty-Five

Holloway, you say?" Neal said. There was no doubt of the boy's identity. He'd said he'd grown up on a wheat farm. His stepfather was the Leon Holloway of Dr. Tolman's letter, the man he'd sat with on his porch, who'd said he and his wife had been blessed with only two children, a son and daughter. He'd spoken the truth. Vaguely Neal noted the presence of a short-legged man, a young girl, and a German shepherd, all staring up at him from their blanket as if wondering if he were about to topple over on their picnic.

Samantha still held his arm, brow knitted in concern. "Daddy?" she said. "Maybe you'd better sit down."

"Here in the coach, sir," Nathan suggested, stepping quickly to open the vehicle's door. "We'll get you some water."

"No, no, I'm all right," Neal protested, recovering. "I just felt the breath knocked out of me there for a few seconds. Don't know what got into me." He forced normalcy into his voice and put his arm around Samantha's shoulders, hoping she'd not feel his trembling. "Well, so that's that, then," he said to Nathan. "There will be no drilling in this area of the ranch." He gave Samantha's shoulder a hearty rub. "That sound good to you, honey?"

Samantha, looking startled by his sudden jovial manner, said, "I'm just surprised that it sounds so good to you."

Nathan said, "Just so I know what to put in my report, sir, am I to understand that if Miss Gordon's photographs don't show this to be a prehistoric site, Waverling Tools will have the go-ahead to drill?"

"Well…I don't know," Neal said. "I've reconsidered drilling anywhere in this vicinity. My daughter is convinced this field is sacred ground, so it doesn't matter what the pictures say. They can lie, you know, so until experts have had a chance to come out here and dig around, I'm afraid I can't sign a lease. That could take years, so my daughter tells me."

Samantha dislodged herself from Neal's arm and stared at him incredulously. "Daddy! Do you mean it?"

"I mean it," Neal said. He held out his hand to Nathan. "Young man, I'm sorry for your trouble, and I hope you'll give my apologies to your father for taking up his company's time, but I've just now realized what could be lost if your company drills here."

Nathan shook Neal's hand firmly. "My father and Todd will be disappointed, but I understand your view that an oil field would be a poor trade for what might be under the ground here." He looked down at Benjy, who had followed the conversation while continuing to eat. Rebecca was daintily pulling flesh from a chicken leg sliver by sliver and feeding it to Zak in apparent oblivion of the conversation conducted over her head. "Benjy, I believe we'd better pack up," Nathan said. "Our business here is done, and Grandmother won't stir from the front window until we're home."

"Aw, Nathan, can't we finish the food?" Benjy whined.

"You're welcome to stay as long as you like," Samantha said, "but I'd better get my father home." She gave Neal's rib a mock jab. "The sun seems to have affected his brain."

"No!" Rebecca cried suddenly, hopping up, startling her blanket companion and the two blackbirds hovering for crumbs. She bolted to Samantha and locked her arms around her. "You can't go! No, no! *Come live with me and be my love / And we will all the pleasures prove / That hills and valleys, dale and field / and all the craggy mountains yield.*"

Nathan moved to unclench Rebecca's arms, but Samantha gently took the child's face between her hands. "I have to go, Rebecca," she said, "but you're welcome to come visit me anytime, and you can recite poetry to me. Would you like that?"

Mollified, Rebecca nodded and released her hold. "Nathan can bring me."

Neal said with a trace of urgency, "We must get back to the house, Samantha. I'm afraid I don't feel all that well. Maybe the sun *has* gotten to me."

Samantha gave Nathan a look of apology as Neal strode toward his horse. "This sudden about-face is not like my father, Nathan. Only this morning, he was hoping you wouldn't find reason *not* to drill in this area, and I'm sure he's had his fingers crossed that my photographs will prove negative for a prehistoric find. Something has taken hold of him."

Nathan smiled. "Maybe a father's love for his daughter? And like he said, he's come to realize what could be lost if you're right about your find. One more question before you go?" He stroked Rebecca's hair. The little girl had run to Nathan for comfort and wrapped her arms around his hips. "When did you discover the skull missing? How many days after Todd came out here to inspect it?"

Surprised, Samantha said, "The very next day. It disappeared between noon Saturday after I left to take Todd back to the station to catch the two o'clock train to Dallas and Sunday when I stopped by here in late afternoon. Why do you ask?"

"Just curious," Nathan said.

"*Samantha!*" Neal bellowed impatiently, already in the saddle, Pony's reins in his hand. "*Come on!*"

Samantha held out her hand. "Good-bye, Nathan, but only until I see you again, I hope. I meant what I said to Rebecca."

"I know you did," Nathan said, taking her hand. "If your excavation dig turns out to be what you suspect, I'd like to come out and see it."

"I'll send a personal invitation, and you can bring Rebecca."

Nathan smiled. "Good-bye then, until we see you again."

"Daddy, you must tell me the truth," Samantha demanded when they were back at the house. "Are you feeling sick?"

Yes, yes, he did feel sick, Neal thought. Sick to the soles of his boots. "No, no," he said. "I just suffered a little dizzy spell. Maybe you're right about the sun. It's blistering out there." He yearned to be alone. An ache was swallowing him whole. He felt as if the sky had fallen upon him. He'd dodged two bullets. Now this. "The little girl..." he said vaguely. "Who is she?"

"Her name is Rebecca. She's Nathan's sister."

"Oh, so he has another sister, does he?"

"I don't know about *another* sister, Daddy." Samantha eyed him in growing concern. "I don't know if I should leave you for my dress fitting—" she began, but Neal interrupted her.

"*Yes, you will!*" he bellowed. "Your mother is dying to see you in the final fitting of your wedding dress. Silbia can look after me, and Sloan is coming over to have a bourbon with me after his workday."

Still looking worried, Samantha said, "All right, but while I'm in town, I'm making an appointment for you to see Dr. Madigan, and you will keep it if Sloan and I have to hogtie and drag you to his office, understand?"

Neal did not argue. "I understand," he said, feeling as empty as a feed sack. He allowed Samantha to see him comfortably settled in his library chair before she left, but he pushed out of it the minute the door closed. He could not think sitting still. He paced from wall to wall to clear his buzzing head, to relieve the gnats crawling beneath his skin. He was a man who did not entirely discount the possibility of divine interventions. Was the appearance of the nice young landman the work of the Almighty to correct an error of fate and to trigger Neal's conscience to take notice and do right by it? He'd heard of Trevor Waverling through Todd Baker, who'd given Neal the impression the man was an amalgam of Attila the Hun and Jesus Christ. His employer was a prominent figure in Dallas, rich, educated, influential, a member of old-city gentry, and the father of a fine son and a pretty little girl, even if she was touched in the head. After a turn or two about the room, Neal plunked down in his deep-seated chair, exhausted, bewildered, frightened. Trevor Waverling had everything that could lure his own little girl away from him.

Neal jarred his memory into sharp recall of his conversation with Leon Holloway last month. He had hardly been able to dislodge it. The farmer had realized who Neal Gordon was and why he'd come. There was no second guessing about it. Leon Holloway had known that the rancher who'd come on the pretext of inquiring whether the farm was still for sale was the adoptive father of the child he and his wife had given away, a daughter that was not Leon's but Trevor Waverling's. *Always good for everything and everybody to end up in their proper place*, the farmer had said. His statement had seemed strange and irrelevant at the time, but now it was clear as rainwater. After meeting Neal, Leon Holloway had determined that Samantha had ended up in the proper place.

Neal lit a cigar to calm himself and to figure who knew what. It was no secret that Trevor Waverling was Nathan's father, but did the tools manufacturer know that he had another daughter born a twin to Nathan? It appeared almost certain that he did not, or why wouldn't he have made himself known to her? Obviously, Nathan was unaware of Samantha's existence. The Holloways had concealed her birth from him as they had from Trevor. If Neal had to stroke in the rest of the canvas, he would guess that Millicent was probably in the family way with the twins by Waverling when Leon married her. Why else would a beautiful woman of property have married a man as lowly and plain as a haystack like Leon Holloway? Trevor may or may not have known of her pregnancy, but he hadn't hung around to make things right. Would Leon have told his wife of Neal's visit to the farm and that the girl who'd answered her ad in April was her long-lost daughter? If Neal was any judge of men and from the way their conversation had gone, he'd have said no. In any case, Neal hadn't seen or heard hide nor hair from the Holloways.

So, he was back to the same old worries and fears as before, and the same question for his conscience: What should he do with this newfound knowledge? Say nothing? Do nothing? Keep the secret that only he and Leon Holloway knew, and go on with life as it was? Who would ever know the difference? The Holloways had their family; Trevor Waverling had his. The Gordons would have no family to call exclusively their own if the truth got out. Once again, the specter rose of how it would be if the members incorporated, little different from unfamiliar cattle wandering onto a rancher's land, mixing brands, adulterating the herd. He must spare Estelle the horror of having to share the daughter she'd always called her own with another mother. To see his wife in the state she was now, riding on clouds of joy in anticipation of their daughter's marriage to the man they would have chosen for her, of becoming a grandmother…how could he shatter those clouds? *I wonder if the first child will be a boy or girl*, she'd cooed to him the other day. *Oh, Neal, my old mountain lion hunter, aren't we the luckiest parents alive?*

As for him, he no longer had to worry that his heart would grow cold toward Samantha if she should choose her birth family over him and Estelle. It would simply cease to beat.

A jab of guilt forced him from his chair. But did he have the right to keep Samantha from her twin brother? They'd cottoned to each other. He'd seen that at first glance. The boy was worthy to claim kinship to her. He'd be a fine sibling, fill that yawning void in her. But with him would come the rich Trevor Waverling and the little girl, and Nathan had mentioned a grandmother. Even Millicent and that son and daughter she doted on might horn in. You could cut so many slices from the pie before the cook was left with nothing.

Neal walked to the fireplace and stared into its empty mouth, still holding some of winter's ashes. He'd made his decision. He'd meant his word to Nathan Holloway. No matter what Samantha's photographs revealed, Waverling Tools would never set up a derrick on Windy Bluff or any other site on Las Tres Lomas. There were other oil drilling companies. No reason why his daughter and the landman should ever meet up again. Neal would keep his newly discovered information to himself. Time was like a river. Eventually, it carried the debris on its shore far from its origins and left no trace of its existence. Unless...

Neal wished he hadn't made the comparison. He recalled the rubble left behind when the ranch tributaries had dried up. Among the litter was a gun that convicted a killer of murder.

Chapter Fifty-Six

Todd stared incredulously at Trevor Waverling. "What do you mean Neal Gordon has decided not to drill at Windy Bluff! *Ever?*" It was Thursday morning, July twelfth, the day after Nathan's return to Dallas from Fort Worth.

"That's what he said," Nathan answered for his father. "Mr. Gordon doesn't care what the photographs show. His daughter believes a dinosaur burial ground is under that stretch of land, and that's good enough for him."

"But excavation could take *years!*" Todd shrieked.

"That's what I understand."

Todd pressed a balled fist to his forehead. "My God! The man's giving up a fortune!"

"Todd, sit down before you have a stroke," Trevor ordered. "Your neck veins are standing out. This isn't the end of the world. We'll find other places to drill."

Todd plopped, stunned, into a chair before Trevor Waverling's desk. Nathan occupied the other beside him. "I can't believe it. I simply can't believe it," he said. "You bear me out on this, Nathan. Neal Gordon was burning for us to set up a rig on that property, regardless of his daughter's find."

"It sure seemed so," Nathan agreed.

The trace of crow's-feet around Todd's eyes tightened. An idea had suddenly crawled into his head. "You didn't by any chance talk Mr. Gordon out of it, did you, Nathan—you with your holy feeling for God's green earth?"

Trevor creaked back in his desk chair and laced his hands over his silk vest, a subtle movement that Todd perceived could be a warning he'd stepped too close to the tail of his cub.

"No, Todd, I did not," Nathan said without taking offense. "His respect for his daughter's feelings did that. And you seem convinced her photographs will not bear out her theory. Why is that?"

"I *told* you. I saw the skull." Todd let out an anguished sigh. "I would hope you could understand *my* feelings as well, Nathan. You must know how disappointed I am." He turned imploringly to his employer. "There's oil at Windy Bluff, Mr. Waverling, barrels and barrels of it, I just *know* it, and to think that it all stays underground because of a bunch of ancient fossils that mean absolutely nothing to anybody but a handful of musty old paleontologists."

"And Samantha Gordon," Nathan said quietly.

Todd's eyes flashed. "She's going to get *married*, for heaven's sakes! To Sloan Singleton, breaker of women's hearts. Married to him, mistress of a couple of ranches the size of two small countries ought to be enough for any woman. Samantha had her chance at the field of archeology when she turned down an opportunity to study at Lasell Seminary in Massachusetts."

"You know this because you were in school together?" Trevor asked.

Todd nodded, his lips clamped in bitter chagrin. "The headmaster called me to his office to show me her acceptance letter with the hope I could talk some sense into her. One of only ten applicants was accepted. Samantha was a brilliant student and could have been a brilliant scientist. I was shocked when I learned she'd elected to stay home and help her old fart of a father run the ranch. She's his only heir."

"You believe her choice a waste," Trevor stated.

"I damn sure do, and I told her so. Now she's gone and thrown a rock into *my* plans for my career!"

Trevor drew back to his desk and reached for a sheet of paper, a signal that he'd had enough of this particular discussion. "Your career has suffered a temporary setback, Todd, that's all. I know you're disappointed, but study this report from Daniel and decide whether you think the Gulf Coast property worth a look."

Todd took the report reluctantly. "Damn it to hell," he said, "I could strangle Samantha."

"Oh, come on, take heart," Trevor said. "If those photographs come back with conclusive proof that Miss Gordon is mistaken, her father's practical side may take over, and we'll be hearing from him before we make a major move. I understand that camera is supposed to arrive by tomorrow."

"Dad may be right about Mr. Gordon, Todd," Nathan said. "You don't know which way the wind blows with him." He had described to his father the scene of the rancher riding pell-mell up to Windy Bluff upset that he had not been informed of Nathan's arrival, fired up as a steam engine to drill no matter the desecration to the supposed "cemetery of old bones." Then within minutes, he had done a 180-degree turn and was totally against drilling on what he called "sacred ground."

Todd asked, "What…if the camera doesn't arrive?"

Nathan squinted at Todd. "Why wouldn't it?"

Todd hiked his shoulders. "I don't know. Post offices lose things."

"Don't be such a pessimist, Todd," Trevor said, his tone closing the meeting. "Okay, fellas, get out of here. I've got work to do.

Nathan, remember you and I are going to the gym after work to-day."

"Looking forward to it," his son said.

Nathan walked next door to Jeanne's office, repository of the firm's accounting books. The secretary looked up at his entrance and smiled coyly. "Have you come to propose?"

Nathan grinned. He liked Jeanne. She was three years older than he and had unabashedly let it be known that if Nathan was interested, so was she. Nathan knew it to be only banter and good-humored flirtation. If he took her seriously, the fun would be over, and they both preferred the fun. "When I can afford the ring," he said and took a seat before her desk. "I've got a favor to ask."

"Ask away, handsome one."

"On the QT."

Jeanne put her hand over her heart. "Always."

"I'd like to see Todd Baker's expense sheet, one for Saturday, June sixteenth."

Jeanne's brow lifted. "May I ask why?"

"It would be a waste of breath."

"Well, in that case..." Jeanne swiveled her chair to a wooden cabinet behind her that contained drawers of lateral files. Recently acquired, the upright structure was her personal bailiwick, and she ruled over it with great pride and appreciation for an employer who recognized the importance of time-saving devices. Until the production of the vertical filing system in 1898, which gave ready access to specific information, business papers were kept in envelopes and stored in pigeonholes. Jeanne pulled open the filing drawer, flipped through the manila folders, another in-novation, and within seconds extracted one with Todd Baker's name written on the tab. "Here you go," she said, handing it to Nathan, "but I prefer it not leave this office."

"Your wish is my command," Nathan said.

He took the folder to a table with better light to peruse its contents. Waverling Tools did not balk at paying expenses in conduction of company business, even if associated with after-hours personal pleasure or objectives. It was a joke between Nathan and Jeanne that no item was too small for Todd to list for reimbursement. "He'd record a stick of gum if he chewed it on the job!" Jeanne once told him with a laugh.

Nathan found the information he expected on an expense sheet dated Saturday, June sixteenth, the date Todd went by train to check out Samantha's relic. Attached were his departure and return tickets, since on that occasion he'd brought back news and evidence of the near certainty of oil on Las Tres Lomas de la Trinidad. Samantha had said she drove Todd to the train station in Fort Worth to catch the two o'clock train back to Dallas, but his return ticket was stamped eight o'clock that night. It was as Nathan suspected: The company's geologist had ample time to return to Windy Bluff to dig up and dispose of the fossil supporting Samantha Gordon's claim. Nathan noted one expense item missing. There was no postage receipt for the camera Todd claimed he mailed on June eighteenth.

In the Worth's restaurant, Samantha took a menu from the waitress and finished her point to Sloan having to do with the question Nathan had put to her on his departure Tuesday. Sloan had met her in town this morning, two days later, to keep an appointment with a photographer to take their engagement picture for release to local newspapers.

"Why would Nathan ask me the time of the skull's disappearance if he didn't suspect Todd of making away with it?" she asked. "The more I put two and two together, I'm convinced Todd is responsible for its disappearance. At the train station, he was in a hurry to see me off to Mother's. I believe he somehow made it back to Windy Bluff and stole the skull to remove evidence that would interfere with *his* claim."

"But you will have your photographs as proof," Sloan reminded her.

"That's just it, Sloan!" Samantha said, her voice desperate. "What if Todd destroyed my camera, too?"

A muscle twitched along Sloan's jawline, a vexation caused by unease—or guilt—he'd suffered since childhood. He kept his eyes on the menu. He wouldn't put it past Todd to have gotten rid of that camera. He'd been a fool not to have anticipated it when Samantha told him of his offer to mail it from Dallas. The boy's applecart had been upset, though, by Neal's sudden decision not to lease Windy Bluff for drilling regardless of what Samantha's photographs showed. Sloan should feel relieved as now both the skull and the photographs were irrelevant, but he did not. Samantha needed physical evidence to drag a team of archeologists to Windy Bluff.

Now was the time to say he had the skull and own up to how it had come into his possession. Samantha would believe him when he explained he'd seized it from Todd and said nothing to her because he'd thought it might widen the gulf between her and Neal. But would she wonder why he hadn't returned it to her earlier to spare her so much undue worry, especially after she and her father had ironed out their differences? Could it be that Sloan had kept the fossil to clear the way for Waverling Tools to drill just over the fence from the Triple S? Would she wonder if he had known that her photographs would not show up? Had he and Todd come to some sort of agreement the day of their tête-à-tête across the fence, and had a guilty conscience prompted him to return it to her now? Samantha knew of the Triple S's tenuous financial situation and what an oil well would mean to its bottom line. And then there was the suddenness with which he'd dropped Anne and proposed to her right after the discussion with Todd.

Would Samantha believe him capable of such deceit?

"You're in deep thought behind that menu, Sloan," Samantha said. "It can't be that interesting. Have you been listening to a word I've said?"

"I've been listening," Sloan said. He gazed across the table at her. Samantha had never looked more beautiful. The photographer had been enraptured, going beyond the call of his usual professional fussiness to put together a summer background to show off her yellow lawn dress with a lace bodice that defined her feminine curves. Sloan was dressed in a new tailor-made suit, but he might as well have been a blank canvas for all the notice the photographer had taken of him.

Someday, we'll be able to take pictures in color, the man had said, obviously bemoaning that he could not capture on film the glorious color of Samantha's hair.

Sloan laid down the menu. "Actually, I'm lusting not after food, but you," he said. "We're in a hotel, and you're so beautiful. I wish I could take you upstairs right this minute."

Samantha blushed. "What a delicious thought. Hold it for twenty-four more days."

"Why twenty-four more days?"

Awed surprise filled Samantha's face. "Oh, Sloan…you're not proposing…?"

"We're going to be married, Sam. Why wait?"

"But where? There's no privacy at either of our ranches, certainly not at Mother's."

"There's a horse auction in Dallas Saturday after next, the twenty-first. Isn't Las Tres Lomas in the market for new horse flesh? The auction ads feature a wide choice."

"Umm," Samantha said, toying coyly with the ribbon at the throat of her dress. "Is there anything at the sale that might interest you?"

"There are a couple of quarter horses I'd like to take a look at."

"What if Daddy decides he'd like to join the party?"

"And leave the ranch unattended with half his staff gone? Not if I know your father."

Pressure mounted under Samantha's rib cage. "How can our families not suspect us of...being tempted to do what we're going to do if we're alone together in Dallas?"

"That's easy. We won't tell them. Why do my sisters need to be informed that you're attending the auction? Your parents certainly don't have to be told of my plans to go. But I'm guessing it wouldn't matter to either family if they learned we were together, especially not to my sisters. They couldn't care a mule's ear what we do as long as we get married. They're probably wondering how we've stayed apart so long, and as for your parents...I doubt they'd have much to say about what they themselves were guilty of before they married, if guilty is the word for it. We can meet at the train station on Friday and take the two o'clock into Dallas, then go to the Strathmore. I'll reserve two rooms, yours under Sam Gordon. We're just two ranchers from Fort Worth in Dallas for the horse auction. What could be more innocent?"

"The rooms on the same floor, of course."

"Adjoining."

Samantha's eyes danced. "Oh, Sloan, I...don't know what to say."

"*Yes* would be a good option."

"Yes," she whispered.

"Are you sure, Samantha?"

"Sloan Singleton! I've lusted after you since you strutted around in your first pair of long breeches. Of course I'm sure!" Samantha said.

Sloan stretched out his hand on the table, and she placed hers in its palm. "Then I must make sure you're not disappointed," he said.

He would wait for a more appropriate time to return the skull, Sloan decided. There might never be a need for it to come to light. A recent discovery of fossils in Utah had drawn the attention of the Carnegie Museum of Natural History by word of the finder alone. Samantha might be as fortunate. He loved the girl across the table with all his heart, in childhood his best friend, now to become his lover and wife, and he would risk nothing that would cause her to doubt it.

Chapter Fifty-Seven

Daniel Lane walked out of the Morris Keaton Brownie camera shop in downtown Dallas, a smug grin revealing a sharp bicuspid. He had not known if the owner, recommended as an expert in rescuing damaged film, but who sold and worked with a simpler and less expensive camera, would be able to salvage the roll in Samantha Gordon's Kodak. Daniel had thought he might have to mail it to the film company in New York and wait a month for the results, but the expert had lived up to his reputation.

"Not very interesting material," the man had said when he turned over the 2¼-by-3¼-inch photographs. "They're just various shots of a dried-up animal head and one of a skinny fellow on a big steer."

"Well, now, their interest depends on who's looking at them," Daniel drawled. "Thanks very much. You've been a lifesaver."

That phrase wasn't exactly true, Daniel thought as he exited the shop. In Todd's case, these pictures could be a life destroyer, a career breaker at the very least. Todd was to have mailed Samantha Gordon's Kodak to New York. Instead he'd thrown it into the Trinity River, the reason obvious. The pictures could substantiate the girl's claim of a prehistoric burial ground in the area Todd was hot to drill. His and Sloan Singleton's motive to keep quiet about the skull was the same, which meant that they could be in cahoots. All along, Daniel had wondered how Sloan had ended up in possession of the skull. He wasn't the sort to go digging around for fossils even to please Samantha. Todd must have given it to him. The geologist learned about Samantha's discovery the day he was photographed on the steer at Windy Bluff. Daniel couldn't figure when he and Sloan conspired, but he had proposed to Samantha the day after Billie June saw him wag the artifact into the kitchen, right after the date listed on these photographs.

Well…well…well…

The Gordon girl's father had backed off from leasing his land for oil drilling, a decision that made the theft of the skull pointless and scuttled Todd's first attempt to bring in a gusher. From gossip around the office, it wouldn't matter if the photographs told a tale one way or the other; the rancher would have no drilling on what his daughter believed to be hallowed ground, and the photographs seemed to bear out her conviction. Daniel was no archeologist, but the shots of the fossil remnant from every angle sure looked as if it could be the partial skull of a dinosaur.

He must find out if Sloan Singleton still possessed the skull, and that discovery might come tomorrow, Saturday. Billie June was taking the first train out of Fort Worth in the morning to be in Dallas by breakfast time. At first when she'd informed him of her plan to move to Dallas on the pretense of studying music at the Sarah B. Morrison Academy, he'd panicked. His job was going great. He had a comfortable apartment, a growing wardrobe, a reliable horse, and a two-seater trap he'd bought used and refurbished to look like new. He'd been able to stash away some sizable money, thanks to his increase in salary and his 10 percent share of the sales of his lathe invention. He'd deliberately moved slowly, living frugally, getting his bearings at Waverling Tools, studying investing, and learning his way around Dallas before spreading his wings too soon. When he was more firmly settled, he'd branch out into a grander manner of living, a style that included women.

And now into the slow, purposeful flow of his life would come the arrival of Billie June. Billie June residing in Dallas, where she would expect to see or hear from him every day, was not part of his plan at all.

But Daniel had to admit that when he would return from their midway rendezvous every other Saturday, meeting these days in a hotel where they had a standing reservation, he missed her. Daniel found thoughts of her occupying his mind for days afterward. He'd see something in a shop window and think to himself that Billie June would like that. He'd rehash in memory her wit and sense of humor, the gist of their conversations, the artistry of her lovemaking, and realize that unconsciously his gaze had strayed to the calendar to check the days remaining until he saw her again. He enjoyed her company so much that occasionally he forgot the motivation that had caused him to seek it. His thirst for revenge weakened. After all, Sloan Singleton was Billie June's brother, and, despite their differences, she loved him. He was family.

But Sloan Singleton's collusion with Todd had renewed his desire to take down Mr. High-and-Mighty Big Britches. He was sorry he had to use Billie June as a means to do it. He was fond of the woman and dreaded the inevitable day when he would simply not show up at their rendezvous spot, answer her mail, or take her telephone calls. When he had everything he needed from her, he would leave her and put his plan into action. What he hadn't counted on was Billie June showing up on his doorstep.

Samantha heard the rattle of the brass lid of the mailbox and opened the door before the blue-and-gray-uniformed postal carrier could drop in the daily mail. Two black stars on his sleeve testified that he had delivered mail for the U.S. Postal Department for ten years, all of them servicing the street of her mother's town house, and he'd become a family friend. Today was Friday, when the carrier altered his route and made his delivery in the morning rather than the afternoon, a boon for Samantha.

"No package for me, Mr. Mason?" she asked.

The mail man handed her the day's correspondence and shook his head. "You were expecting a package, Miss Gordon?"

"For days now," Samantha said. Today was July twentieth. If Todd had mailed her Kodak over a month ago, as he'd said, it should have been returned to her by now.

The man's gaze beneath the brim of his regulation military hat made popular by Teddy Roosevelt's Rough Riders expressed regret. "I'm sorry for your disappointment. Maybe it will be here by Monday."

"I doubt it, Mr. Mason, but thank you."

Samantha closed the door, nauseous from a surge of awful realizations. Her photographs would never see the light of day. There would be no team coming to Las Tres Lomas from the American Museum of Natural History in New York or from any other university's department of archeology willing to spare and financially support an excavation crew over several years' work. She could discount assistance from the Peabody Museum of Natural History at Yale, as Todd had never again mentioned contacting his friend who worked there. The cost of a private excavation would be prohibitive, even if a team of experts was available to hire. Just as important, there would be no photographs to justify the sacrifice her father had made on her behalf to forgo drilling at Windy Bluff.

Mildred came down the hall to collect the mail to take upstairs to Estelle. "I've never seen a face that long on a hound dog," she said. "What's wrong?"

"A good friend has betrayed me."

"Few knives cut deeper. Anything to be done about it?"

"Yes," Samantha said. She shouldn't jump to conclusions, accuse Todd unjustly, but she could not quiet her suspicion that her Kodak had never left Dallas. There was only one way to find out. She must confront Todd directly. No matter what his mouth said, his eyes would betray the truth. They had a way of shifting and his ears moved back when he attempted to lie, as Ginny was learning in their marriage. "I know when he's not being completely honest with me, and that's a good thing for a wife to know," she'd giggled, "but Todd would never fib about anything *big*."

Well, Samantha would see. She would not bother calling Rochester, New York, run up an enormous long-distance telephone bill to speak to a clerk who would have her wait interminably while he located and checked the paperwork, then risk being disconnected to boot. Long-distance service was sketchy at best. No, her answer would come simpler, faster, and more accurately from Todd Baker.

"Mildred, will you please go tell Jimmy to harness the carriage," Samantha said. "I want him to drive me to the train station. I'm taking the eleven o'clock to Dallas rather than the later one, and...I need a favor from you."

"You have only to ask, Miss Sam."

Samantha had to get word to Sloan that she would not be meeting him at the depot at two o'clock as planned. She could not risk leaving the message with Millie May or Billie June by telephone, because they did not know that Samantha would also be going to the auction and would be meeting their brother at the station. She would have to send Mildred with a note to give to him before he boarded the train. They would meet up at the hotel. A later train to Dallas would give Samantha little time to get to the office of Waverling Tools before it closed. She preferred to confront Todd at his desk rather than to show up on Saturday at his home with Ginny present. Her matron of honor was already aware of the cooling relationship between her husband and her best friend. "You can understand Todd's disappointment when he was told your father had changed his mind about drilling, can't you, Samantha?" she'd said, a touch of frost to her tone. "Todd was all but *promised* the opportunity to prove his expert knowledge about the presence of oil on your ranch, and then to have the rug pulled right out from under him…"

When Samantha explained, Mildred said in surprise, "Mr. Sloan is taking the two o'clock to Dallas as well?"

"Yes," Samantha said, her look level, "but my mother is not to know."

"And so she won't, not from me. I hope you packed that pretty nightgown you got for your birthday."

Samantha carried the mail to her mother's room, where she sat addressing final wedding invitations, and told her that she'd decided to take an earlier train to Dallas to meet privately with Todd at his office before it closed. She would not have time on Saturday when she would be at the auction. "I need to clear up a misunderstanding between us before the wedding," she said.

"A very good idea," her mother agreed, only vaguely aware of the strain between her daughter and the geologist. Samantha and Neal kept much of the ranch's business from her, but she did not object, since she had little interest in the day-to-day affairs of Las Tres Lomas other than its survival.

Samantha threw a few more items into her one piece of packed luggage and carried it downstairs. The pretty, unworn night-gown lay folded among her things, and she thought she ought to be excited about the night ahead rather than angry about the upcoming confrontation with Todd. She had looked forward to being with Sloan on the train, just the two of them. It was hard to find time and space and privacy on their ranches to be alone. The endless distractions of work and responsibilities and the presence of Sloan's sisters, her father, the household staffs, and cowhands made intimacy impossible. But she must put to rest this issue of her camera before she could fully relax in Sloan's arms tonight. By then, she would know the truth of its fate, and that would determine her decision to make the sacrifice for her father that he had made for her. If she learned that all evidence of her discovery was lost, she would withdraw her objection to drilling for oil at Windy Bluff.

Chapter Fifty-Eight

Samantha presented herself to the receptionist at Waverling Tools and introduced herself. A brass nameplate with the engraving AGATHA BEARDSLEY sat on her desk. "I'm here to see Todd Baker," Samantha said, "but I prefer not to be announced. We're friends. I'd like to surprise him."

The middle-aged Miss Beardsley, immaculately and professionally attired in a navy blue dress with a white collar, had worked for Trevor Waverling's father long before the introduction of the telephone switchboard behind the counter. She had been secretly in love with Edwin and had never quite recovered from Jordan Waverling's death. She was aware of the Gordon name and that it was associated with a career disappointment for the company's budding geologist. She hesitated before responding to Samantha's request but then reflected that perhaps Miss Gordon had come to extend an olive branch. She compromised.

"I'm afraid Mr. Waverling would object to that, but why don't I escort you down to Mr. Baker's office rather than ring his bell to summon him here?" she suggested.

"A fine idea," Samantha said.

Samantha followed Miss Beardsley's tall, straight back down the corridor, the fragrance of the gardenias on her desk drifting after them. Where in the world were gardenias to be found in the middle of July? she wondered. Their snow-white arrangement, spilling from a green vase on the mahogany counter, added another flourish of elegance to the order, cleanliness, and fine furnishings of the reception room. Already impressed with the exterior of the building, Samantha would not have expected to find such refinement in the office of an industrial complex. She passed a large and grand office and was surprised to find standing beyond the open door the man introduced to her last March as Trevor Waverling, Nathan Holloway's father. Her appearance drew his attention from the reading material in his hand, and their gazes held briefly, Samantha recalling the memorable blue of his eyes, so like his son's. She nodded, wondering if he recognized her, then passed on in the receptionist's wake to Todd Baker's office.

Trevor drew thoughtfully to the door and watched Samantha walk down the hall. She was wearing a light summer traveling suit with a small hat that left much of her hair exposed. He observed her pause behind his receptionist as Miss Beardsley knocked on the door of Todd's office, his attention caught by the curiously familiar shape of the young woman's nose and chin. He had recognized her. As a matter of fact, Samantha Gordon had remained like a shadow in his memory ever since they'd been introduced the evening of the paleontology lecture. He was not sure why. She was too young to stir him sexually. He preferred mature women, and this girl looked no older than Nathan. Her hair and skin reminded him of Millicent Barrows before she became Millicent Holloway, but her bearing, graceful posture, the way she held her head resembled someone else whose face and name he could not place.

Todd took his time answering the door—he could be such an arrogant little prick, Trevor thought—and then came a surprised exclamation of "*Sam! What are you doing here?*" Trevor wondered that himself. He had thought her business with his geologist finished. He had been about to leave his office to collect Nathan and leave early when he remembered a report he meant to take home. But for that delay, he would have missed seeing the girl. His mother was hosting a dinner party that evening for the sole purpose of introducing her grandson to a young woman she deemed fit to become Mrs. Nathan Holloway. Trevor approved. Reconsidering his departure, Trevor returned to his desk and sat down, remembering Millicent.

With her, he'd enjoyed the greatest sex he'd ever known. He had warned her many times of the danger of getting pregnant, but she had said she didn't care. *I want your babies, Trevor*, she'd said, *and I want them all to look like you*.

He had thought that sentiment surprising, since Millicent was so enamored with her own beauty. He had tried to break off his lust for her, because he had no intention of marrying a woman so shallow, but it proved too great until the time came when he had the excuse to leave. He didn't blame her for hating him. She'd believed she'd loved him, and Trevor was now convinced she had. Only love can breed a hatred as strong as the loathing Millicent felt for him.

If he'd known she was pregnant when he left her, their lives would have taken a different course. He would have married her and allowed their union to meet its inevitable end. Once Trevor learned of Nathan's existence, it was Leon, his stepfather, he'd kept an eye on for abuse, not his mother. It had never occurred to him that Millicent would be the one to disown the boy emotionally. Her son was the child of Trevor Waverling, the love of her life. Fool that Trevor had been not to realize that love in the heart of a narcissist like Millicent can curdle into hate, and but for the affection of his stepfather, Nathan would have been left out in the cold. Nathan had said that Samantha Gordon was a fine, intelligent young woman who had been especially tender and kind to Rebecca. No similarity to Millicent there. Nathan had liked her.

A knock on the frame of Trevor's open door interrupted his mulling. He swiveled his chair away from his view of the Trinity to find his son in the doorway. "Ready to call it a day?" Nathan asked. "Lord help us if we're late for Grandmother's party."

"Samantha Gordon is down in Todd's office," Trevor said. "I think I'll just hang around to hear why."

"Good heavens, Samantha!" Todd cried. "What an unexpected pleasure. Come in!"

Samantha glanced over her shoulder at the receptionist and nodded. The woman's eyebrows arched at her dismissal, but she took it with professional dignity and marched off down the hall. Samantha gazed piercingly at Todd. "My camera has not arrived."

"Oh, uh, well, it will soon, I'm sure."

"I'm sure not." Samantha read the truth instantly in the swerve of Todd's glance, the backward jerk of his ears. She stepped forward. "Todd, I don't have to tell you how important those photographs are to science. Where is the camera?"

Todd moved back from the pierce of Samantha's gaze. "Why—why would you think I know where it is?"

"Because you never mailed it. Where is my Kodak?"

"Samantha, I don't know what you're talking about. Honestly I don't."

"Your eyes...the wiggle of your ears say you're lying."

"My—my what?" Todd lifted his gaze to stare over her shoulder and his mouth opened wider. "Oh, my God!"

Samantha turned to see what had electrified his attention. Trevor Waverling had entered the room. "What's going on here?" he said. "May I be of assistance?"

"Perhaps," Samantha said. Todd remained speechless.

With a gracious gesture, Trevor invited Samantha to take a chair before Todd's desk while Todd flopped limply into his. Before Samantha finished explaining her suspicions and Todd denying them, Trevor had perceived that his geologist was lying. Nathan had already had his doubts about the fate of the camera as well, and with justifiable reason, it appeared. Todd had been so desperate to sink a well on the Gordon ranch that he'd eliminated the competition of the artifact that he must have believed authentic. He might have been responsible for the disappearance of the skull, too.

Trevor was torn over how to handle the situation. His first impulse was to fire the geologist for putting the company in legal jeopardy, but on what evidence? It was his word against the girl's suspicions, and Todd's scheming had come to nothing. Neal Gordon had put an end to his hope of making a name for himself at Las Tres Lomas, so Todd had been handed his just desserts. And did Trevor want to let go a truly hardworking, credentialed geologist, newly married, or allow this situation to be a lesson learned this early in his career, especially when his boss made it clear that his eyes would be upon him from now on? The camera was lost, the skull apparently vanished. What was done was done.

"Let's go straight to the horse's mouth and telephone the Eastman Kodak Company to find out when the camera was mailed from New York," he said finally.

"Or if it was ever received," Samantha said, the comment directed at Todd.

"What mailing address did you give, Todd?" Trevor asked.

Todd's Adam's apple bobbled. Trevor noticed his complexion was the color of white turnips. "I used the address of the company."

"I'll have Miss Beardsley get right on it. Miss Gordon, why don't you wait in my office? You'll be more comfortable there, and I'll have my secretary bring refreshments. Todd, you're not to leave until we get to the bottom of this. Understood?"

"Yes sir," Todd said, slumping further into his chair.

Without another word, Samantha rose and followed Trevor out of the geologist's office, where she caught a glimpse of the wedding photograph of her matron of honor smiling alongside her husband.

Trevor saw her seated in one of the sumptuous office chairs with Nathan for company before he left to give instructions to his receptionist and an order to Jeanne for iced tea and cookies. He returned and observed without interrupting the conversation between his son and the pretty daughter of one of Fort Worth's most prominent ranchers. Trevor noticed her hands, the shape of the fingers and delicate wrist structure, as she explained to Nathan that she was in Dallas to attend a horse auction and would be staying at the Strathmore. Politely, she asked about Rebecca and Zak, and Nathan inquired how her wedding plans were coming along.

"If what I suspect of Todd is true, I'll be short a matron of honor." Samantha sighed. "She is Todd's wife."

"A pity you have no sisters to step in, Miss Gordon," Trevor remarked politely. "I understand you're an only child."

"That is correct, Mr. Waverling, or at least no sisters that I know of. I was adopted at four days old."

"Really? I never ask a lady's age, but I'm allowed to guess. I put you at twenty, my son's age."

Samantha nodded. "Your guess is right. I turned twenty last March."

"Me, too," Nathan said. "March twenty-third." He shot Trevor a wry glance. "I'll never forget the day."

"That's the date of my birthday, too!" Samantha exclaimed. She smiled at Nathan. "What a coincidence!"

"Yes, quite a coincidence," Trevor mused, his gaze upon the girl intensifying. He felt the thump of his heart in his ears. It had just dawned on him. The familiar features he'd noticed reminded him of his mother. "Forgive my curiosity, Miss Gordon," he said, interrupting a question she was putting to Nathan, "but have you any knowledge about the location of your birth?"

It was a startlingly personal question that drew the appropriate reactions of surprise. "Why, I—no," Samantha stammered. "It's not a subject my adoptive parents have ever discussed with me." She paused, then volunteered, "From what little I know, I'd guess I was born up north, close to either side of the Red River."

"And…you know this how, may I ask?"

His interest—or her good manners—seemed to compel Samantha to answer. "I have reason to believe the doctor who delivered me practiced in Marietta, Oklahoma Territory, close to the border."

Trevor nodded. "I am acquainted with the place. Do you know the doctor's name?"

"Yes…" Samantha answered, visibly puzzled and a little disconcerted by his questions. "Dr. Donald Tolman."

They were interrupted by Miss Beardsley who reported that the Eastman Kodak Company of Rochester, New York, had no record of a camera received from the address of Waverling Tools in Dallas, Texas.

"Send Todd to me," Trevor ordered.

Todd arrived, nervous and pale, and flashed a look at Samantha that promised never to forgive her for her accusations.

"I'm afraid we have bad news for you, Todd," Trevor said, and nodded to his receptionist. "Tell him, Miss Beardsley."

Todd listened, growing paler until anger daubed his cheeks

with color. "Well, it's not my fault the package didn't arrive. I mailed the damned camera, and I can prove it!" he sputtered.

A swell of silent incredulity met this disclaimer. Frantically, Todd dug around in the breast pocket of his suit and removed a yellow postal receipt. His face reflecting deep injury, he handed it to Trevor. His employer read it and stared amazed at Todd. "Why the hell didn't you show this to us earlier?"

"I just now found it, Mr. Waverling. I didn't think I'd need to keep it so I carelessly misplaced it. I…I was afraid that if I said I had a postage receipt for the package, then couldn't find it, I'd look even worse in your eyes."

Nathan spoke up. "Why didn't you list the cost of the postage on your expense sheet, Todd?"

Todd blinked at him. "You've been inspecting my expense sheets?"

Trevor clapped his geologist's shoulder. "Let's not get off track here. Todd, we owe you an apology. This receipt solves the mystery, and I hope clears up any misunderstanding between you and Miss Gordon."

Samantha was standing. "I'd like to believe it does," she said, her stiff face and unyielding glare suggesting doubt to the contrary.

With wounded but charitable grace, Todd inclined his head in acceptance of the apologies. "Then if you'll excuse me, I will get back to my work," he said.

On his way to his office, Todd repulsed the urge to skip. It had worked, and he'd had the satisfaction of seeing egg on their faces in the bargain, the reason he'd delayed producing the postal slip until they were sure of his guilt. He'd figured he would have to account for the missing camera and had prepared for it. At the post office on Monday, June eighteenth, he'd dutifully handed over to the clerk the wrapped package of the Kodak addressed to the company's headquarters. He paid the eighty cents for postage and left. Minutes later, he was back at the clerk's window. "I'm sorry," he said, "but I've changed my mind. May I have back my package? I've decided not to mail it." He'd then pocketed the eighty cents along with the receipt that would clear him of what he'd inevitably be accused. His only regret was that he did not submit a voucher for the eighty cents. That would have been proof of the pudding, but unlike some employees he could name, he was not one to request reimbursement from the company for expense money he did not spend.

In Trevor's office, Samantha said, "Mr. Waverling, may I impose upon your receptionist to call a cab to take me to my hotel?"

"My dear Miss Gordon, after all we've put you through, I couldn't possibly allow you to go by cab. It will be Nathan's and my great pleasure to drop you off at your hotel."

Chapter Fifty-Nine

What's got hold of your thinking, Dad?" Nathan asked, swaying with the jostle of the carriage as it pulled away from the Strathmore Hotel.

"Nothing, or it could be everything," Trevor replied.

"You're one for the cryptic answer, aren't you?"

"I'm trying to break myself of the habit, especially with you. Are you looking forward to meeting Miss Charlotte Weatherspoon tonight?"

"Not particularly. Is she pretty?"

"You'll have to be the judge of that, but I can say she's a young woman of worth."

Ah, thought Nathan. He got the picture. A Jane Eyre type, nice and pleasant, but plain as a mutton chop. "By that, I assume she's rich."

"As God, but don't let that be a deterrent. By worth, I mean she's a young woman of character, or your grandmother wouldn't have her at her table. Her son may marry ladies of questionable virtue, but that won't do for her grandson."

Nathan felt a prickle of resentment. His grandmother meant well, but she was being presumptuous to figure it a family duty to find a mate for him. He must make clear that when it came to his social life, he would choose his companions, and in regard to his future wife, he would decide the girl right for him. He would indulge his grandmother's matchmaking tonight, but it would be the last occasion he'd be placed in such a spot.

The dining room table had been set with the finest in the china cabinets. Sterling gleamed, crystal sparkled, damask glowed, even without the benefit of the myriad of candles stuck in the arms of the candelabra to be lit later. Mirrored bowls of antique roses threw rainbow prisms about the rooms and filled the house with their fragrance. Surveying the splendor, Nathan remarked to his grandmother, "Are we entertaining the king of England?"

"No, dear boy, the girl I hope will become the queen of your heart."

Nathan had a firm grip on his resolution to avoid being pushed into a relationship not of his instigation until the entrance of Charlotte Weatherspoon and her parents into the parlor. She was tall and willowy, dark-haired, brown-eyed, and stunning, and from the get-go, totally disinterested in him. She wore the re-signed face of a kidnap victim conscripted to serve an adversarial government. Nathan presented the same expression to her but out of tongue-tied awe rather than indifference. Shaken from his expectation of a Jane Eyre, Nathan took the hand she offered and managed a greeting without stuttering. "How do you do, Miss Weatherspoon. It's nice to meet you."

"How do you know?" she queried, her dark eyes already flash-ing boredom. "We've only just been introduced."

Irrationally cut to the quick, Nathan replied, "I suppose my judgment came from anticipation, but I can see it was prema-ture."

An exquisite eyebrow spiked. She was unaccustomed to having the stone she'd thrown tossed back at her, Nathan perceived. "I much doubt the evening will improve it," she said.

Nathan bowed slightly to say she'd get no argument from him.

"Have mercy, Charlotte," her mother scolded and frowned her disapproval, but Mavis simply smiled into her sherry glass.

Trevor despised traveling long distances—by horse, coach, or train, it didn't matter. But as with the carriage trip he'd taken to collect his son back in March, this trip would be worth his valuable time and discomfort. Early the next morning, Saturday, he bought a first-class train ticket to Gainesville. His traveling valise packed the night before, he had risen before dawn and crept quietly out of the house, leaving a note for his mother saying simply that he had gone on a business trip and would return in a few days. Benjy had managed to harness the horses without waking the household, and carriage and driver were before the front gate when he was ready to leave.

A surprise awaited him at the train station. He had sent Benjy on his way and was standing with his valise on the platform prepared to board when he caught sight of Daniel Lane farther down, obviously waiting for a passenger to disembark. He had no wish to engage in conversation with an employee this early in the morning, but his curiosity was roused. He stepped behind a lamppost where he could see without being seen, and presently a small, well-dressed woman stepped down from the train and flew into Daniel's arms. They walked off holding hands toward the livery area, Daniel swinging her one piece of luggage as if he might break into a dance step any second, their laughter carrying the distance to Trevor's ears.

Hmm, he thought, then all speculation about Daniel and his girlfriend vanished as Trevor settled into his first-class compartment and concentrated on what he might discover in Marietta, Oklahoma Territory.

*   *   *

Sloan was the first to open his eyes. He gently removed Samantha's arm from around him and stole quietly out of bed, keeping
an eye on her for signs of movement. She did not stir. Pulling
on a robe, he resisted the impulse to brush away her hair from
her eyes to observe her face in sleep. How trusting and vulnera-
ble she looked. How unsuspecting and innocent. But for the guilt
raking his conscience, he would have climbed back in bed and
kissed her awake. As it was, he stepped out on the small balcony
to draw in fresh air before the sun rose and burned the life out of
it. He needed time and privacy to mull over the course of action
he should take now. Was it too late to tell Samantha of the skull
in his wardrobe? Had he passed the point of no return?

Yesterday, he was already at the hotel when Samantha arrived.
He had checked in minutes before and had his room key in hand
when a handsomely outfitted Concord coach drew under the
portico of the hotel and Samantha alighted, assisted by two gentlemen who climbed back into the coach when the doorman took
charge of his bride-to-be. She'd made eye contact with him as he
followed the porter up to his room adjoining hers. She did not explain her reason for taking an earlier train until later when they'd
finished with the purpose for which they'd booked the rooms.
Then she'd related the events of the past hours.

"I don't believe Todd mailed the camera, no matter that he had
a postal receipt," she said. "Neither does Nathan."

"How about Trevor Waverling?"

"Hard to tell. He's a difficult man to read behind all his grace
and charm."

"Yes, I saw what a handsome devil he is," Sloan said. "Also that
he had a little more of an eye on you than a man of his age should
have."

She'd arched an eyebrow. "Jealous, are we? Stay that way. I
love it."

In telling of Todd's treachery, Samantha had presented Sloan with another opportunity—and his last—to assure her that all was not lost. He had a surprise for her stored in his wardrobe. But then she had said, "So, after painful and long consideration, I've decided to let Daddy have a go at Windy Bluff."

Sloan was not sure he understood. "What does that mean, Sam?"

"It means that I saw Daddy's face the day he told Nathan Holloway there would be no drilling on my archeological site. I could almost see his heart fall at giving up a possible fortune to make his daughter happy, the way mine fell when I thought about your question, Sloan. How would I feel when the next disaster strikes and obliterates our surplus. I decided I could live without the world knowing of the scientific treasure that could lie beneath the sand at Windy Bluff, but I couldn't live with my guilt or Daddy's resentment if Las Tres Lomas—or the Triple S—was ever in financial jeopardy that an oil strike would have prevented." She'd smiled sadly. "The land is Daddy's, after all, not mine. It is the blood of *his* people in the soil, not my own. I have no right to impose my will on what was entrusted to him to hold and preserve. It's enough to know that he would have sacrificed it all on my behalf."

Sloan had listened to her little speech knowing what it cost her to arrive at her decision. He knew only the business of cattle and the hard life of ranching. He'd ridden his horse over many a creature's bones left to dry in the sun and disintegrate without ever giving a thought to their origin. But Samantha...Her eye never wavered from the ground in search of a speck that identified it as different from the ordinary graveyard scatterings found on the prairie. He'd had to make sure he understood. "Exactly what are you saying, Sam?" he'd asked.

"I'm saying I've had my shot. Now I'll let Daddy have his. I will not stand in the way of Waverling Tools setting up shop at Windy Bluff. It's not good grazing land anyway, and Mr. Waverling and his son are aware of my aversion to the destruction of oil drilling and are sensitive to it. They'll respect the rest of the ranch. Mr. Waverling will contact Daddy Monday morning. I'm to tell him to be at the Triple S at ten o'clock to take the call."

The sun was rising, casting its strong, virulent arms over the city. By midmorning, the temperature would have soared over a hundred blistering degrees. Sloan filled his lungs with another cleansing draught of air. What was the point now of saying a word to Samantha about the skull? She had made her decision, and it was for the best. It might be that Neal would turn down Trevor Waverling after all and abide by his resolution to forbid drilling at Windy Bluff. In that case, Samantha need never know about the skull at all. He could endure a guilty conscience, but not the doubts the woman he loved might have about him.

The balcony door opened and Samantha, rubbing the sleep from her eyes, stepped out in a loosely tied robe, the birthday nightgown long discarded. Sloan felt a stunning rush of desire. "Good morning," he said. "How's my girl, or rather"—he grinned—"how's my woman?"

Samantha laughed. "Your woman, my foot! How's my man?"

"Come here and I'll show you."

"This is perfect," Billie June said, casting a last glance around the apartment, the third listed in the FOR RENT section of the *Dallas Herald* that she and Daniel had inspected. "I'm going to take it."

Daniel waved his hat before his face. The room, owing to the closed windows, was suffocating. Billie June had removed her suit jacket. There was a small patch of moisture under her arms and between her shoulder blades, but her batiste blouse with its ruffled collar looked as if she'd just stepped from her dressing room. Daniel liked that about her. Always looking fresh and tidy and cool in public was Billie June, such a contrast to the hot little number she was in bed.

While she opened wardrobes and pulled out drawers, sniffing and examining their interiors, Daniel inspected Billie June. He'd dreaded this day of taking her around to rental properties, mainly because he was afraid he'd give away his disrelish for having her live full-time within shacking-up distance. She'd not wanted to live in a women's boardinghouse with its rules and curfews but in an apartment where she could come and go, entertain as she pleased. Of course, she'd told her brother that she'd come to Dallas looking for just the sort of abode he thought her trust fund was paying for. Billie June said she'd rather live in a homeless shelter than in a coop of clucking hens.

"Won't your brother find out you're not living in a boardinghouse when he gets the bill?" Daniel asked.

"He doesn't want to be bothered with writing checks from my trust fund for my expenses each month," Billie June had answered. "He will open an account for me at his bank, and I'm to draw on that to pay my bills."

"Do you intend to study music at the Sarah B. Morrison Academy?"

"Of course I do. I wouldn't deceive him about *that*."

Daniel watched her move about the room. Everything about her trim figure was perfect, from her small, perky breasts to her round little buttocks and shapely legs. The day was too hot for sex, but he found himself wanting to take her to bed when he had planned on getting rid of her as fast as he could. He had already told her that she could not stay at his apartment. There was no electricity because some idiot had shot out the generator. A pipe had sprung a leak, and he had no running water. The humidity had swollen shut some of the bedroom windows, and the house would be unbearably hot.

"That's all right," she'd said. "I'll stay at the Strathmore, but I'll have to sneak you in. The Singletons are known there. It's the hotel where members of my family stay when they're in Dallas."

So rather than wishing her gone, he was glad she would be staying until Sunday afternoon when she'd catch the four o'clock back to Fort Worth. He'd heard the Strathmore had a grand dining room, and he would treat her to a fine supper and champagne and later take her to a club where they could dance. He was looking forward to her company. Sometime during the evening he'd bring up the subject of the skull, though he had to be careful how he did it. Billie June had never said another word about the relic. Did she know of its importance to Samantha and that it had gone missing? Did she know of Samantha's worry over the fate of her camera and its significance? Wouldn't the subject have come up in girl talk? Was Billie June protecting her brother because, smart as she was, once aware of Samantha's concerns, coupled with Sloan's quick proposal to her, she'd have added it all up and arrived at the only explanation for that skull being in Sloan's hand that day? Somehow, despite family loyalty, Daniel couldn't see Billie June supporting her brother in committing what amounted to outright theft and fraud. Her sense of right and wrong was as ramrod straight as her slim little back, and Mr. High-and-Mighty Big Britches would be in big trouble with his sister if she ever learned the significance of that skull.

No, Daniel was willing to wager that it all boiled down to Samantha not trusting Billie June with her concerns simply because Billie June was sleeping with Daniel Lane, an employee of Waverling Tools, virtually the enemy, and she did not want her worries to be the topic of pillow talk and later the conference room.

Chapter Sixty

Trevor arrived in Gainesville shortly after noon, booked a room at the Harvey House without taking time for a meal, rented a horse, set it to a trot, and reached the Texas-Oklahoma border of the Red River two hours later. Luckily, the Saturday ferry traffic was light of both passengers and river rafts, and he made it across without delay. He set off for Marietta, estimating the short distance would take a half hour, getting him into town by midafternoon. He reined in before a small hotel called the Wayfarer Inn and asked the manager for the infirmary address of a Dr. Donald Tolman.

The man looked surprised. "You're the second person in the last few months asking about the doc, and I have to tell you what I told her. He ain't alive no more. Died back around the first of April."

"Her?" Trevor queried.

"A nice young lady. Anyway, we got a new doc now if you wish to see him. He took over Dr. Tolman's practice."

Trevor's heart jumped. "Do you recall the nice young lady's name?"

The manager shook his head. "Never heard it."

"Would it be in the registry?"

"She didn't take a room here. She deposited her maid in the

lobby and went off to Dr, Tolman's residence, then came back and collected her to head back to the ferry."

"What did she look like? The nice young lady, not the maid."

Trevor's question was met with a calculating gaze. "Can't recall."

Trevor extracted a large bill from his wallet. "Would this refresh your memory?"

The manager made to snatch the bill, but Trevor held it back. "Pretty, reddish hair, nice way of speaking," the man said.

"Did you learn where she was from?"

"No."

Trevor handed over the bill. "Where can I find the late Dr. Tolman's infirmary?"

Ten minutes later, Trevor walked into the rustic log facility that served the medical needs of the surrounding territory and introduced himself to a stout, happy-faced woman behind the reception desk. "I may have come on an impossible mission," he said at his most charming, "but I'm attempting to find information about an infant girl born around March twenty-third, 1880, who was given to Dr. Tolman to be put up for adoption. She may be a relative of mine. I understand he's deceased, but would there be a record on hand of her birth and circumstances?"

The woman had listened as if starstruck. Trevor understood. It wasn't every day that someone of his sartorial appearance walked through the planked door of the infirmary. "Why, I declare," she said, composure returned, "you're the second person who's asked after a little girl born about that time."

Once again, Trevor's heartbeat quickened. "A pretty young woman with reddish hair, and do you remember her name and the date she called?"

"I didn't meet her. I was in Ardmore that day visiting my nephew, but yes, that sounds like the young woman Dr. Tolman's daughter described to me. I served as Dr. Tolman's midwife until his death. Eleanor was in town at the time to settle her father's affairs. Last April that was. I don't believe she mentioned the young woman's name."

"I'd appreciate hearing every word you may recall," Trevor said. "I assume Dr. Tolman's daughter does not live here?"

The midwife shook her head. "In Oklahoma City, and Eleanor told me that the young woman was trying to find information about her birth parents and siblings. She believed she'd been born around here or across the river in Texas. I was not Dr. Tolman's midwife at the time she was inquiring about. She and Eleanor looked through his files but could find no record of a little girl's birth date that would have fit hers." The midwife's gaze sharpened, her expression wondering if she'd given out too much information. "You say you are a relative of hers?"

"I could be her father."

The midwife pressed her hand to her throat. "Oh, my goodness."

"Did...Eleanor say what the young woman looked like?"

Flustered, the woman answered, "Only that she was very pretty, with a nice manner to her, and she had the most glorious shade of hair. Not red, not gold, but a combination of both, Eleanor said. Does that description ring any bells?"

"It certainly does," Trevor said. "And does the name Samantha Gordon ring any bells for you?"

"I'm afraid not," the woman said, looking sorrowful.

"Did she tell Eleanor where she was from, where she lived?"

"I asked her that question, and she said that she assumed Fort Worth, Texas. The girl left a postal address in that city in case Eleanor came across any other information. I doubt she did."

Trevor drew a quick breath. "Is there anything else you remember that Eleanor said?"

"Well, yes." The midwife looked about to cry. "Eleanor said the young woman—I wish I could verify her name for you—looked so disappointed that she couldn't help her. She felt sorry for her. As pretty and well dressed as she was, she made Eleanor think of a little waif. I'm sorry I can't be of more assistance to you, sir, but I so hope you find each other."

Once more, Trevor removed his wallet and extracted several bills that he dunked into a tin can on her desk marked FOR THE CHICKA-SAW ORPHANS. "You've been more help than you know," he said.

The sun had not yet begun to set when Trevor made it back to the livery stable in Gainesville to turn in his horse. He was tired, hot, and hungry. At the Harvey House, before going up to his room for a bath, he asked for the address of the Leon Holloways.

"Ah, yes, our newcomers," the clerk said. "They bought the Billings place. Nice man, Mr. Holloway."

"And Mrs. Holloway?" he asked.

The clerk thought over his answer. "Pretty as a rose but a bit…prickly. No offense if she's family."

"She's not and none taken."

After a bath and a sustaining meal in the hotel dining room, Trevor wrote a note and asked the clerk if there was anyone around who would deliver it. He'd be paid when he returned with an answer. The offer was snatched up by a schoolboy named Jeeper hired on Saturdays to clean toilets and swab floors. He set aside his mop and bucket to sprint down the street and across the town common to an avenue bordered by a park. There he pressed the newfangled doorbell of the house belonging to the Leon Hol-loways. The man to whom he'd been instructed to deliver the note—"Only to him, no one else"—answered the door, a napkin tucked into his collar. He'd been called from his supper. He read the note, removed the napkin, and reached for his cloth cap hang-ing from a hall tree in the foyer.

"Leon?" A woman's voice called from the dining room. "Who is it?"

"Nobody," her husband answered, winking an apology at the messenger. He stepped outside, closed the door softly behind him, and followed the boy to the hotel.

Trevor, sitting outside on a bench to await Jeeper's return, was surprised to see Leon Holloway in the boy's wake. The note had asked that the man meet him in the morning in the lounge of the hotel. Trevor was standing when they hurried up. He put a quarter in Jeeper's palm and held out his other hand to Leon. "Thank you for coming," he said.

"Is it about Nathan?" Leon huffed. "Is he all right?"

"He's fine," Trevor said. "He doesn't know I've come."

"Then why have you?"

"Shall we go into the bar, Mr. Holloway?" Trevor invited. "We will both need fortification for me to answer that."

They had ordered room service during the day, but as evening fell, Samantha and Sloan dressed to have supper in the hotel dining room. They would go down separately, Sloan first, and book a table. Samantha would follow a little later, and as the maître d' led her in, Sloan Singleton, an old family friend from home in town for the horse auction, would spot her, rise from his table in pleased surprise, and ask her to join him.

Sloan asked for a table by a window giving a view of the wide portico. He expected to see no guest coming and going that he knew, but since his arrival, he'd kept an eye out for anyone of his acquaintance staying at the hotel. Those attending the horse sale usually stayed in lodging closer to the auction grounds.

Glancing out the window, he then thought he was hallucinating when he saw the doorman assist his sister, Billie June, down from a two-seater trap. Sloan was so engaged that for a moment, he did not register the identity of the driver who came around to offer his arm, leaving his trap and horse to the care of a hotel groomsman. When his vision cleared, Sloan stood abruptly, knocking over his water glass, and threw his napkin on the table.

A waiter rushed over. "Mr. Singleton, sir? Is something wrong?"

"There damn sure is!" Sloan growled and strode toward the dining room entrance. He was standing, tall and menacing, directly in front of the rotating hotel door when it swung open and disgorged his sister and Daniel Lane.

"Oh, God," moaned Billie June.

Leon took a sip of his scotch and water. He drank only beer, but rarely and never after supper, but Trevor Waverling was right. This situation called for fortification. Leon had remained quiet, listening without expression, showing no physical reaction while Trevor Waverling laid out his reasons for suspecting that Samantha Gordon was his daughter and Millicent her mother. First of all, Millicent was Millicent, Trevor said, so that point explained a lot. She had given birth to a pair of boy and girl twins. She had kept her son and given her daughter away. She'd hated the man by whom she'd conceived them enough to get rid of both, but she had to keep one because she was known to be pregnant.

Leon felt the hair rise on his neck. With every pitch, Trevor Waverling had hit the stake squarely. If Leon were of a mind to, all he could tell the man was that Millicent had indeed birthed a pair of girl and boy twins. He, too, was convinced Samantha Gordon was her daughter, a conviction of which Millicent was blithely unaware, and Leon wanted to keep it that way. But the tools manufacturer could stew in his theories without a yea or nay confirmation from him. Samantha Gordon already had a loving father and mother, a good home. Trevor Waverling had made his bed, knowingly or innocently, when he went off and left Millicent pregnant. Whether the twins were the result of rape or mutual consent had no bearing on the other issue at hand, and that was Leon's promise to Millicent never to reveal that she'd given birth to an infant she'd given away. Furthermore, Leon knew what it was like to have the boy he loved like his own torn away from him—and by this man. Trevor Waverling was proposing to inflict the same hurt to Neal Gordon, a man who couldn't love a daughter he'd sired more than that sweet girl who'd come to check out the farm. Trevor Waverling was not owed the truth. Let sleeping dogs lie. If Leon felt any sorrow in taking the truth to his grave, it was from denying Nathan the sister with whom he'd shared a womb.

"I can appreciate that it's asking a lot of you to tell me, Mr. Holloway," Trevor said when Leon did not speak, "but as a father, surely you understand why I must know. Are my son and Samantha Gordon twins? Is she my daughter?"

Leon had sensed immediately that here was a man quick to divine the truth by astute observance. He must be very careful to give nothing away by so much as the quiver of an eyelid. Later, Leon would not know how he did it, but he met Trevor Waverling's gaze, incisive as a scalpel's, with his own. "Mr. Waverling, is that your first drink?" he asked.

For the hold of a heartbeat, Trevor looked confused by the question, then he leaned forward, powerful shoulders straining the fabric of his expensive frock coat. "I assure you I'm not drunk, Mr. Holloway, and you did not answer my question."

"My right," Leon said. He should get up and go, he thought, but this man might confront Millicent, and her hate would get the better of her. She'd hurl the truth in his face out of pure spite. Somehow, he had to prevent that from happening. Leon pulled out his pipe, then his tobacco pouch. Meticulously, he filled the bowl with its mixture, tamped it down with his forefinger, set the pipe stem between his teeth, and struck a match to the powerful blend, made by an old Comanche chief who sold the concoction for a living. Leon drew on the stem and, when the tobacco was glowing to his satisfaction, said casually, "Millicent delivered when I wasn't there. I was in Oklahoma City. When I got home, there was Nathan."

"Delivered by a Dr. Tolman."

Leon bit down hard on the pipe stem to avoid showing his surprise that the man knew of Dr. Tolman. "Nope," he said. "A midwife delivered her."

"What was her name?"

"Can't remember if I ever knew. It was a long time ago."

"Do you suppose she took the other twin?"

Leon removed his pipe. "What other twin? If Millicent was pregnant with twins, it was news to her and would have been a hell of a shock. All I can tell you is that she never said a word to me about expectin' or havin' twins. I might've had somethin' to say about that, you know."

Trevor eyed him keenly. Leon's gaze behind the smoke held steady. "Well, if the midwife was there when you arrived, wouldn't you have seen if she made off with a baby?"

"Couldn't say. She was in her buggy, ready to leave, when I showed up. Millicent was nursin' Nathan."

Trevor Waverling sat back and pulled at the lapels of his coat—striving for patience, Leon judged. "I have reason to believe the midwife was associated with a doctor from Marietta, a Donald Tolman."

"Wouldn't know about that," Leon said.

"What *do* you know?" Trevor demanded with a flash of irritation. "What doctor attended Millicent when she had her other children?" He leaned over the table, the glass of his barely touched scotch and water forming a puddle around its base.

Leon relit his pipe and blew the smoke across the table. "A Dr. Bledsoe. Came to Gainesville the summer my son was born."

"The midwife was acting on her own, with no affiliation with a doctor?"

"Couldn't say."

With an exasperated sigh, Trevor took a quick sip of his drink. "You certainly didn't take much interest in the credentials of the woman who delivered Nathan, did you? I find that hard to believe."

"Up to you."

Trevor got to his feet and held out his hand. "Well, thanks for meeting me, Mr. Holloway. Hope I didn't take you from your supper."

"You did," Leon said, unwinding his legs, "but I'd had enough." He knocked the ashes from his pipe, stowed it in his shirt pocket with the bowl peeping out, and accepted Trevor's hand. "Glad to oblige. Safe trip home." He slapped on his cloth hat and turned to go when he asked suddenly, "Don't you have a daughter, Mr. Waverling?"

It was as if a match had struck behind Trevor Waverling's disappointed scowl, but from surprise, not joy. "Why, yes."

"Name's Rebecca, right? Nathan told us. He's quite taken with her, his half sister. Pretty as a peach, he says."

The implication was clear: *You have one daughter. Be satisfied with that blessing.* Leon shuffled off, lifting his hand in a little wave of farewell over his shoulder. "Tell Nathan hello for us and to keep the letters comin'," he said.

For the first seconds, Sloan, Billie June, and Daniel Lane remained frozen in a staring standoff. Billie June was the first to thaw. "Now, Sloan, it's not what you think," she said, her hands raised in surrender. "Daniel has kindly been taking me around to appropriate places for lodging while I go to music school."

"What's he doing in Dallas?" Sloan demanded.

"I work here," Daniel said.

Sloan ignored him. "What are both of you doing in this hotel?"

Daniel answered. "She's booking a room for the night. Or would you rather she bunk with me?"

Sloan took a step toward Daniel, who did not budge. At that moment, Billie June pointed toward the staircase. "Why, there's Samantha! What's *she* doing here?"

"Talk about the pot calling the kettle black," Daniel said out of the side of his mouth, eye level with Sloan.

Sloan turned to his sister. "We're in town for the horse auction."

"Uh-huh. And I'm a fiddler's monkey," Daniel said.

Samantha, having spotted them from the stairs, hurried the distance to where they were clustered, smile flickering like a lamp with a faulty connection. "Hello everybody," she said. "Billie June, what a nice surprise. So good to see you. You, too, Mr. Lane. How are you liking your new position?"

"Very well, Miss Gordon. Thanks for asking. It suits me to the ground."

"That's lovely to hear. Billie June, whatever are you in town for?"

"To find lodging for the semester I'm attending the Sarah B. Morrison Academy to study music. Daniel has been driving me around in answer to the rent ads." She tossed a defiant glance at Sloan. "I just may like Dallas so much, I'll move here permanently when you and Sloan marry."

"We'll discuss that privately, Billie June," Sloan said through tightly clenched teeth.

Samantha hurriedly interposed, "We were just going in for

supper. Why don't you join us if you don't find the conversation boring. Sloan and I are going to compare notes of the auction."

Eyeball to eyeball, tight jaw to tight jaw, Sloan said to Daniel, "That invitation is extended to Billie June only, Lane."

Returning Sloan's glare without a flinch, Daniel said, "Mr. Singleton, could we step aside so that I might have a word with you privately?"

"You have nothing to say to me."

"Oh, but I do. Trust me."

"Please, Sloan," Billie June begged.

With grim-faced reluctance, Sloan followed Daniel to an enclosure of palm trees. "What is it?"

"I know about the skull."

"What?"

"That fossil you stole from your fiancée's dinosaur site to eliminate proof of her claim. *That* one, Mr. High-and-Mighty Big Britches. Billie June saw you take it up to your room, but she has no idea of its significance, at least I don't think she does, and you better hope she never finds out."

"What are you getting at, Lane?"

"Oh, I think you know."

"Relieve me of my ignorance."

"I know why you took the skull."

"You know nothing."

"Oh, well now, yes I do. So will Miss Gordon if I should tell her. The pieces won't take long to fit into place. You and Todd Baker colluded to destroy evidence that would prevent her daddy from drilling on land Todd is convinced is over a gusher. You take the skull. Todd destroys Miss Gordon's Kodak." Daniel snapped his fingers. "Just like that all obstacles to drilling are removed. Then you dump Miss Rutherford to propose to Miss Gordon. I don't blame you for not waiting to put a ring on her

finger until after the oil comes in. That would have been *too* obvious." When Sloan kept his stony silence, Daniel said, wide-eyed,
"What? No denial?"

Sloan's jaw clenched tighter. "What do you want, Lane?"

"I'm not sure yet, but for the time being, I want you to remember that I can destroy you with Miss Gordon, her father, and
your sisters. It doesn't matter that Old Man Gordon changed his
mind about drilling out of respect for his daughter's wishes. That
may make the skull and photographs inconsequential, but not
your part in the matter. That's what I want from you—for you
to remember. Also, I want you to stay out of your sister's business. She's a grown woman with every right to step out with any
man she damn well pleases without interference from her little
brother."

"Her money is in a trust fund of which I'm the trustee and
have the power to suspend at my discretion," Sloan said. "The
ranch is entirely in my name, and my sisters have no title to so
much as a blade of grass on it. So, mister, if your game is to marry
Billie June and pick up a share of the Triple S, you better look
elsewhere for your bread and butter."

Daniel's eyes narrowed to pin points. "I see your opinion of me
hasn't changed. That's good. Makes my pursuit a whole lot easier
with no regrets."

"What pursuit? What are you talking about?"

"What I've determined is now my life's mission." Daniel
smiled smoothly. "Now, shall we go join the ladies?"

PART THREE

The Titans

Chapter Sixty-One

On Las Tres Lomas and the Triple S, all talk of any other subject but the August fourth nuptials of Samantha and Sloan was put aside in the rush to finalize details. Though never involved in the folderol, Neal quietly removed himself from the frenetic activity to work out a plan to set up an oil rig on Las Tres Lomas without involving Waverling Tools now that Samantha had sadly but graciously withdrawn her opposition to drilling. He believed he'd found a solution that would preserve the "integrity" of the ranch, as his daughter would voice it, while accessing the untold wealth that might lie under its grasslands. His new peace of mind allowed him to savor the vanquish of a longtime worry. His daughter was to be wed to a man of their breed from a family that was like an extension of his own. No competition there. She would produce heirs. Finally he could apprise Estelle of what had been going on these past months—selectively, of course. Meanwhile, her patience had grown thin and her temper sharp in preparing for a wedding "so memorable" that it would leave a lasting impression on Fort Worth society.

As events turned out, Estelle's prophecy would come true, and the extravagant ceremony provide Fort Worth residents relief from the usual summer talk of the dire heat, cattle prices, and the heated presidential campaign in which three political parties were running candidates hoping to unseat the Republican incumbent, William McKinley.

The anticipated soaring temperatures of August had dictated that the Gordon-Singleton nuptials should take place midmorning when guests, packed into the pews of the First Methodist Church of Fort Worth, could still breathe normally and the white amaryllis remain perky above their stately stems. A lobster salad and champagne luncheon would follow in the ballroom of the Worth Hotel. To thwart the effects of the heat, Estelle had recruited a slew of elementary school students to line the walls of the church and wave large white feather fans over the assemblage. "It will be a courtesy unprecedented, original, and elegant," she declared, on pins and needles that the box of feathered fans, ordered from a specialty shop in Florida, would not arrive in time. She had led practice sessions with the children to make sure the fans were waved in unison and endured long, tact-straining meetings with their mothers to assure uniformity of their offsprings' dress and grooming.

It all seemed the height of lunacy to Samantha and Mildred. Why not provide each guest with a fan decorated in the green-and-white wedding colors? the housekeeper suggested, and Samantha agreed. Because, sillywonkins, Estelle chastised them irritably with her fond name for fools, all that waving in the pews would distract from the ceremony. Also, as crowded as they'd be, somebody could get poked in the eye.

Thus it was that the guests arrived, the women in large, flower-bedecked hats, the men in suits with shirt collars starched stiff, to find a regiment of ten-year-olds hugging the walls in their pressed white shirts, black pants, and polished shoes, feather fans at the ready to await the signal to spring into action.

When it came, particles of the white plumes, loosened during practice sessions, descended over the guests like floating snowflakes, eliciting a number of sneezes and not a few giggles, the sounds of which drifted with the feathers down to Estelle seated in the front row. As the ceremony wore on, small arms grew tired and faltered, losing their rhythm, and finally, one by one, the fans came to rest like weary birds by the sides of their young custodians. Out from the ladies' handbags came the waving fans the mother of the bride had meant to avoid. Estelle was mortified. At the altar, Samantha and Sloan exchanged marriage vows unaware of the cause for embarrassment, eyes and ears only for each other.

In the receiving line at the luncheon, Estelle saw her hope to leave Fort Worth with a lasting memory of her daughter's wedding further assured by the entrance of Anne Rutherford. She was the last to arrive, and all guests, flutes of champagne already in hand, turned at her appearance. An audible murmur of awed surprise and admiration went up, and members of the small orchestra dropped a bar or two of music. Invited for the sake of decorum, the one-time love interest of Sloan Singleton had been expected to decline for the same reason. Anne's parents had been invited as well, but they had sent regrets. Stunning in a dress of sapphire blue that intensified the color of her remarkable eyes, Anne glided toward the bride and groom, hand outstretched, smile dazzling.

"Sloan, I can't tell you how happy I am to congratulate you on your marriage to Samantha and to wish you, Samantha, dear, *every* marital blessing. It thrills my heart to have the occasion to say it."

"Believe me, it thrills our hearts for you to have the occasion to say it," Millie May said, her smile glinting like the tip of a hat pin.

"Thank you for sharing in the joy of our day," Samantha said, pressing a satin-shod foot upon the black patent toe of her older sister-in-law, but the bride's thunder had been stolen. For the rest

of the celebration, except for the groom's wedding toast in trib-
ute to his bride, guests' eyes were mainly on Anne. It was as if the
event had been arranged exclusively to pay her homage. The men
gathered around, exuding compliments, making a fuss over who
would have the privilege of getting her a glass of champagne,
whose table she would grace, whose invitation she would accept
to take her home. There were whispers praising her for harbor-
ing no ill will toward the man to whom she had every reason to
feel it, but that was Anne for you—a girl with a heart as big as a
dance floor, so went the consensus around the room.

Estelle was furious.

Throughout it all, Neal Gordon's feet barely touched the
ground. Estelle resented his chirpy mood, especially after Samantha and Sloan departed on their honeymoon to Galveston to cool
off in the waters of the Gulf of Mexico. Weary, disappointed,
still smarting from the blights on her daughter's perfect wedding, she was also feeling the maternal emptiness inherent to
the occasion of her only child marrying and leaving the family
nest. Feeling lonely, she moved back to Las Tres Lomas to await
the newlyweds' return, welcoming the breezes that blew in from
the tributaries and the more comfortable temperature the ranch
house's thick walls provided.

"Trevor, what's come over you?" Mavis asked. "You haven't been
yourself lately. Is business bad?"

"No, no, Mother," Trevor protested rigorously to reassure her.
"Business has never been better. As a matter of fact, I'm looking
at a new location to extend our plant facilities. I've hired some
extra people, and we've got a large shipment of steel coming in
without office or storage space for either one."

"Then what is it, son? And don't tell me it's nothing. I always
know when something is going on with you," Mavis said.

Really? Trevor thought. It was Sunday afternoon, the day after nuptials were exchanged between Samantha Gordon and Sloan Singleton. Nathan had taken Rebecca and Zak for a walk down by the river.

"Are you worried about Rebecca?" Mavis asked, waving her fan before her moist face. She and Trevor sat under the shade of a maple tree in her backyard to catch a breeze from the Trinity, a table between them set with glasses and a pitcher of cold lemonade. "I am, too," she admitted. "I know Nathan and Zak will look after her, but it's so difficult to keep her safe. Rebecca has such an obsession for the river, not so strange since she inherited it from her uncle. That ditty she keeps repeating...'I must go down to the seas again...' That was a favorite of Jordan's."

Trevor swirled the ice cubes in his lemonade. "Yes, I know, and yes, I've got my daughter on my mind," he said, thinking of Samantha Gordon.

"I've never seen Rebecca happier, however, and we should be glad of that. Nathan and that dog of his have made all the difference in her life."

"Indeed they have," Trevor said absently.

"Then whatever is wrong, Trevor?" His mother's voice rose insistently. "You look sad when you should be happy."

Trevor poured another glass of lemonade. "Don't read too much into my expression, Mother. I don't take the heat as well as I used to, and it was late when I got in last night. I didn't get much sleep."

"Poppycock!" Mavis said. "You're used to foundry heat twice as hot, and you can go days without sleep after spending nights with your harlots. So what's wrong? I can't believe it all has to do with Rebecca. I'm your mother. You must tell me."

Trevor took a sip of lemonade. "I love someone who will never be mine," he said.

"Oh, Trevor, not again! She's married, I suppose."

"Yes, she is."

"Then you must forget her, son. Haven't you learned your lesson by now?"

"Yes, I have. That's why I'm going to let her go."

Oh, God, Nathan moaned to himself as he saw Charlotte Weatherspoon step from a carriage before a house he and Rebecca and Zak must pass on the way home. He had forgotten that she lived on this street, or rather, didn't wish to remember the fact. He was returning to his grandmother's town house the long way around with hope the heat would partially dry Rebecca's skirt and his pants by the time they arrived. His stepsister had waded too far into the river before he could snag her. Nathan was fairly certain his grandmother would not have approved his allowing her to take off her socks and shoes to dip her toes into the water, abetted by Nathan removing his and rolling up his pants legs to accompany her. The cautionary measure had made little difference, because by the time he'd pulled Rebecca back to the bank, his trousers were soaked. Zak was wet, too.

Charlotte halted abruptly at the sight of them, eyes enlarging and expressive eyebrows rising beneath the wide brim of her hat. "Nathan, is that you?" she called from the shade of her parasol.

"None other," Nathan said, surprised she remembered his name. He thought her breathtaking but bossy and snobby as hell. Like an imbedded thorn too deep to cut out, he'd not been able to get her out of his mind, and he could make no sense of it. She was not the type of girl he could go for at all, even if she'd thought him her sort, which she'd made clear he wasn't. In her eyes he was the bastard son of Trevor Waverling, no matter the eminence of the family name. His grandmother had misjudged the probability of anything developing between them. Nathan intended to wish Charlotte good day and step by her without pausing for further conversation.

He tipped his hat and made to move by the obstruction of the parasol, but Charlotte said, "Rebecca! Is that you, darling? I haven't seen you in ages! My goodness, you've grown so. Remember me? I'm Charlotte."

Rebecca looked blank, clearly not remembering, but politely extended her hand. "Charlotte...Like Charlotte Brontë?"

"The very same," Charlotte said with a laugh. "Is this your dog?"

"My brother's," Rebecca said. "His name is Zak. My brother's name is Nathan."

"We've met," Nathan said. "Let's go, Rebecca. Good day, Miss Weatherspoon."

As if she were a sentry and the parasol a weapon to bar illicit passage, Charlotte lowered its tip to Nathan's waistcoat. "Just a moment." Her gaze dropped to Nathan's wet pants, then to the hem of Rebecca's dress. "You can't go home and meet Mavis looking like that. I think you'd best come inside and dry off." She smiled down at Rebecca and offered the little girl her hand to take. "And I'll bet we can rustle up some lemonade, too."

Rustle up? thought Nathan. Did she really say that? It was one of Leon's favorite folksy expressions. He followed, finding himself powerless to disobey.

Chapter Sixty-Two

Neal had gathered Estelle, Samantha, and Sloan for his much-anticipated confab in the library at Las Tres Lomas. He had delayed calling it until certain objectives were reached and obstacles removed before informing them of the news they'd been collected to hear. Today's conference was not to be a committee meeting. He had the final say and the only vote, but Neal recognized that tact and sensitivity were called for to prevent ill will, qualities for which he was not noted. Estelle had little interest in ranch activities but bristled when she felt excluded, and Neal must take into account Samantha's distaste for what was about to transpire on Las Tres Lomas and not nail it home with too heavy a hammer. His stomach clenched at weakening their carefully mended fences, but he would hold firm. It was still his ranch, by God. An invigorating cool front had moved in during the night, ushering in the first day of September 1900, and bringing relief from the August heat. Mildred had prophesied to Estelle: *We are in for an early and cold autumn. There will be no Indian summer this year.*

It was late Saturday afternoon. Chores were done, and the ranch was at rest. In the big house, naps were over after a heavy meal in the Trail Head, where the three members of the Gordon family and Sloan had sat down at the center table to the delight of

TITANS   445

Grizzly and the surprise of the cowhands. It had been a long time since Estelle had set foot in the Trail Head, and since returning from her honeymoon, Samantha had moved into the hacienda on the Triple S and taken her meals with Sloan. Billie June had moved to Dallas to study music and Millie May to Houston to attend art classes.

"What in heaven's name is this all about, Neal?" Estelle asked. "You've been about to burst out of your britches to tell us something for weeks now."

Neal cleared his throat. He'd had everybody take seats around the fireplace, and he stood in its center, his back to the dead embers of the fire laid against the early morning chill. "Family," he began formally, as if calling to order the annual meeting of the Cattlemen's Association. "I've called you here today to inform you of several coming developments that will affect Las Tres Lomas. Honeybee," he said, turning to his wife, "there have been some recent happenings here at the ranch that I've not discussed with you."

Estelle cocked an eyebrow. "And there is news in that?"

"By your own choice, my dear," Neal reminded her dryly and went on. "Last June while I was gone to La Paloma, Todd Baker visited the ranch and found signs of oil deposits in the area of Windy Bluff."

"Really?" Estelle said, her interest sharpened. "How exciting."

"I'm glad you think so," Neal said with a brief assessing glance at Samantha. He was counting on Estelle's support. She would want to lease. The money would alleviate her constant concern about finances, and the idea of an oil well on Las Tres Lomas would appeal to her. "So I have been in negotiations to lease that area to a drilling company for oil exploration," he said. "It is there that I wish to begin drilling."

"*Begin* drilling?" Samantha repeated.

Neal hesitated and exchanged a look with Sloan that Samantha intercepted. She glanced from one to the other. "What's going on?" she said.

"You explain, Sloan," Neal said.

Sloan, sitting next to his wife on the couch, placed a conciliatory hand over hers. "Your father and I have discussed how to take advantage of the oil deposits that might be on Las Tres Lomas without affecting its core, Sam. Neal has come up with a plan to protect the main business of Las Tres Lomas while at the same time unplug its other assets."

Neal's enthusiasm compelled him to butt in. "Sloan has agreed to my proposal that we remove the fence between our ranches and combine them as one," he said. "Once drilling starts, we'll run our displaced cattle on the spare range of the Triple S and continue our ranching operations like always." He was prepared for Samantha's resentment at being left out of the agreement and grinned. "Knowing that you'd like the idea of the fence coming down, we saved this information until today as a surprise to you, honey."

Samantha's face tightened with suspicion, and she withdrew her hand from under Sloan's. "Explain what you mean by 'begin drilling.' Why do we need to run our cattle across the boundary line since only Saved feeds at Windy Bluff?"

Neal drew in a chestful of air. "I've been told that other areas look hopeful as well, enough to set up other rigs if the field at Windy Bluff comes in."

Samantha looked baffled. "Really? I understood from Nathan that Waverling Tools was interested in only that one area. Did Todd come out here and take other soil samples while Sloan and I were on our honeymoon?"

The dreaded moment had arrived. Neal steeled himself to meet Samantha's disapproval, but he was ready with his defense.

"After the skullduggery you suspect Todd of?" he exclaimed. "Not on your life! It's my view the boy's a reflection of the man he works for, and that makes me trust Trevor Waverling about as far as I could throw one of his rigs." Neal turned away from Samantha's astonished stare to select a thinly shaped cigar from a humidor on the mantel. In certain situations, a good panatela served a man better than Jim Beam, and it was too early for his evening bourbon.

"What skullduggery?" Estelle demanded. "What did Todd do?"

Sloan spoke up. "Sam suspects Todd destroyed her Kodak that contained pictures of her dinosaur site."

"What dinosaur site?" Confusedly, Estelle looked from her husband to her daughter. "What else has been going on out here?"

While Samantha remained silent, Sloan answered, chronologically filling Estelle in on the series of happenings that had led to the question of Todd's integrity and the conflict of interests over the site.

Estelle's glance lit on Samantha. "And you didn't think to tell your mother about finding a dinosaur?"

Samantha answered curtly, "I didn't find a dinosaur, Mother, only a partial head of what I suspect is one, and I mentioned nothing to you because you don't like to hear anything having to do with paleontology."

Estelle's flat cheeks darkened guiltily. "So now that your proof of the pudding has mysteriously disappeared, you've given your blessing to lease that section of land in return for the sacrifice your father was willing to make for you? Well, I think that's very noble of you, darling, but it's also the right thing to do. I mean, after all, to trade the prospect of oil for a burial ground of old bones…"

Samantha dismissed the view with a tired shake of her head and pointed her gaze at her father. "You're not leasing the land to Waverling Tools?"

Neal had found a match and struck it to the tip of the cigar. "No, I plan to lease to the Corsicana Oil Development Company. Those folks have a proven success record and are more experienced in the oil business than Waverling Tools. That's why I've decided to go with them."

Anger, dismay, disappointment, and a bitter sense of betrayal washed through Samantha, revolting as bilge water. She'd seen newspaper pictures of the cotton fields laid to waste in Navarro County by the drilling company her father had selected. "Daddy, you're not being fair," she said, unable to keep her voice from trembling. "It was Nathan Holloway who has done the title search and Waverling Tools that you originally promised the lease to. Todd's sins are his own. Mr. Waverling is a good and decent man, and so is his son. They'll respect our grasslands, and Billie June says that Daniel is working on a device that will prevent oil from spewing out the top of the derrick. It's a first and only of its kind that the Corsicana company won't have."

Neal removed his cigar, tensing at the familiarity with which Samantha praised Trevor Waverling. Everyone was looking at him. Estelle, clearly bewildered by the discussion, squinted at him in the way she had when she knew he was up to something. Sloan, too, was giving him an odd look. He'd also assumed that the company Todd worked for would be doing the drilling. "How do you know Trevor Waverling?" he asked.

"I met him at a paleontology lecture in the spring and spent time with him the day I confronted Todd at Waverling Tools. I found him kind and considerate, and my instincts tell me he's honorable." Samantha paused. "And regardless of my personal view of Todd, the fact is that he could have gone to work for any number of oil companies up East, but he chose Waverling Tools. That says something about his faith in the company."

"That says only that Todd Baker wished to land a job close to home," Neal countered. He felt he'd taken an unguarded blow behind the knees. In telling him of her suspicions of Todd, his daughter had not mentioned meeting Trevor Waverling.

"Why would you object, Neal?" Estelle said, her look at her husband wary. She turned to Samantha. "Tell me again why it's necessary for Waverling Tools to drill, darling."

"Because I trust them to prevent wanton desecration of our pastureland."

"Hmm," Estelle said. She looked again at her husband. "You haven't signed any lease agreement yet, have you, Neal?"

"No...not yet, but I intend to," Neal said, puffing fiercely on his cigar. "I believe the Corsicana people are right for the job, and I gave them my word they'd get the go-ahead—"

Estelle motioned away those grounds as of no consequence. "Well, then, you'll just have to break it and sign the agreement with Waverling Tools. There seems to be absolutely no reason not to."

Neal had the feeling he was about to be thrown from the bull he'd been confident he could ride. He pointed his cigar at his wife. "Now see here, Estelle, that's for no one but me to decide, and I've decided. The concrete's been poured on this deal. I've given my word to the Corsicana Oil Development Company, and that's that!"

"No, it isn't," Sloan said, his quiet contradiction falling like a crack of thunder in the room. "Waverling Tools does the drilling, Neal, or the fence between our ranches does not come down, and that's that." He took his wife's hand again. "Allowing the oil company of Samantha's choice to drill is the least we can do to make up for the sacrifice of her archeological field."

Neal felt his face turn as gray as the ashes fallen on the front of his shirt. "But...Sloan...Estelle, you don't understand..."

"What's there to understand?" Estelle said. "Honestly, Neal, you mystify me sometimes. You're getting the dream you've always wanted. The only difference is the oil company that will make it come true."

"Estelle, you don't know..." Neal started to say, but panic choked his throat.

Monday morning, Trevor Waverling was stunned to hear from Miss Beardsley that Mrs. Sloan Singleton was on the line. Could Mr. Waverling take the call? He most certainly could, Trevor told his receptionist.

She was calling on behalf of Las Tres Lomas, Samantha explained. Her father had reconsidered drilling in the Windy Bluff area of the ranch and would like to reopen discussions. Could Mr. Waverling send Todd Baker and Nathan Holloway to meet with her and her father and husband?

All Mrs. Singleton had to do was to tell him when and where, Trevor said, and he'd like to come along, too. He wanted to look over this area that had caused such a fuss.

By all means, his caller said. Would tomorrow be too early, and would he mind meeting them at the ranch? There would be a driver and coach at the train station to pick them up and take them back. Otherwise, they could gather in Fort Worth later in the week at a place of his choosing.

The ranch would be fine, Trevor said, and tomorrow perfect. What time?

Las Tres Lomas possessed the best ranch cook in Texas, Samantha informed him with a smile in her voice. Could she entice him to arrive by noon?

He and the boys would be there with bells on, he said.

Trevor hung up the receiver and sat back in his desk chair flushed with surprise and pleasure. He had never expected to see or hear from his daughter again. He had thought he would have to make do with his few memories of her and the keepsake of a small white feather he'd discovered caught in the nap of his suit coat. But it looked as if fate might have intervened on his behalf. He had never been a favorite of fate, but he would be open to whatever it had in mind, wherever path it led. Trevor glanced at his black metal desk calendar, the month and day displayed in numbers in round yellow sockets. Today's showed 9-3—September third. He wondered if tomorrow, when he turned the knob to roll 9-4 into place, he would remember the date as an omen of ill or a harbinger of good to come.

Chapter Sixty-Three

Neal looked down the long table in the Trail Head and wondered how in the bloody hell it had happened that his worst nightmare had come to life and sat at his table as a dinner guest. The world was an infinite place. Damn, Texas was as big as a *country*! How was it possible that in all the space in the universe, the child he'd adopted and raised as his own would be dining with her father and twin brother at the same table in her home without any of them having a clue to the other's identity? What force had collected and driven them into this one chute? He could not shake the gut-emptying feeling that a divine power had herded them here today.

"Here you go, folks," Grizzly said, setting down a huge serving bowl of steaming stew on the table. "Hope you enjoy."

"We always do, Grizzly," Samantha said, hoping the savory hot meal would thaw the atmosphere. All those gathered had issues with someone at the table. Tacit truces had been declared between the combatants, but there was still a bite of hard frost in the air between Sloan and Daniel, she and Todd, and Neal Gordon and Trevor Waverling. For some inexplicable reason, unless her father was a poor loser, he had taken a dislike to the owner of Waverling Tools. Even Nathan Holloway, easy with everybody, treated Todd with reserve. Samantha stood up from her place at the table. "I'll serve," she said.

There were a few murmurs professing hungry appetites as Samantha ladled the beef stew into bowls. At the news that there would be visitors arriving for the noonday meal today, Grizzly had ordered the main table moved to a side of the room away from the noise and flurry of the chow line. He had personally covered it with a tablecloth and set out cutlery and napkins, salt and pepper shakers, glassware, and pitchers of iced tea.

"I'll bring more butter for the cornbread if you need it," the cook said, hovering in his clean apron. It wasn't every day he was called upon to feed men wearing business suits in the Trail Head. Thank God for that, but still he was flattered. The important entertaining was always done in the main house.

"We have plenty for the time being," Samantha said. "Thank you, Grizzly."

"Holler when you want your pie," Grizzly said. "It's pecan today."

That announcement sat well with all faces but Neal's, sitting in gloomy silence at one end of the table.

Trevor said as they lifted their forks, "I asked Daniel, my troubleshooter, to join us today because he will be overseeing the site Todd believes best to place the rig. He will ensure the drilling crew will do what they can to respect your archeological field, Mrs. Singleton."

Samantha smiled down the table at him. "I'd be pleased if you called me Samantha, Mr. Waverling. Mrs. Singleton is such a mouthful."

"It would be my pleasure," Trevor said, returning her smile. "And perhaps you could call me Trevor."

Neal grunted rudely. "Pass the butter to this end of the table, if you please. My cornbread is getting cold."

But by the conclusion of the visit, the visitors' mission had been accomplished to the satisfaction of all concerned. Trevor had offered Neal a better financial arrangement than the Corsicana Oil Exploration Company, but that was nobody's business but his. If the well came in, his percentage of the revenue, called royalties, would dwarf the generous lease payment. The contract included clauses that restricted willy-nilly damage to property, livestock, and water, and promised minimum interference in the ranch's operations. To assuage Samantha's horror of a deluge of oil spreading over acres beyond the drill site, Daniel confirmed that he was working on a blowout preventer that might be up and going by the time the well came in. He explained that it was a series of control valves and pressure gauges designed to constrain the flow of oil and keep it from blowing out the drill hole up through the derrick. In other words, prevent a gusher. Samantha noticed that Sloan, despite himself, looked impressed. How could he not deduce that if the device worked, Waverling Tools—and Daniel—would make a great deal of money?

By late afternoon, their business concluded, a host's manners dictated that Neal invite the male contingent to stay for something to "wet their whiskers" before Jimmy drove them to the station, but instead he saw his guests to the door immediately and wished them a safe journey back to Dallas. Samantha was ashamed of her father's inhospitality, but she was no longer the mistress of the house in her mother's absence. Her home was now at the Triple S. Leaving Sloan with her father, she walked the men to the waiting carriage and shook hands with each of them. When she offered hers to Nathan, she said, "I'll keep you in my thoughts with Charlotte. Good luck to you."

"I'll need it," Nathan said, "and thank you for your advice. I plan to follow it."

Earlier, when Samantha and Nathan were reexamining the area where she had found the skull, she'd said, "Forgive me if I'm presuming on our short acquaintance, Nathan, but I must say you seem awfully quiet today."

"Well, I'm a quiet person."

"But unusually so today, I've observed." She felt drawn to Nathan, as if they'd been friends all their lives.

"That obvious, is it?"

"Perhaps only to me."

"Well...since you asked, I've got my mind on a girl I've met recently who's given me no reason at all to occupy it."

"Oh," Samantha said. "Why doesn't she deserve to be in your head?"

"She's stuck up and opinionated and thinks too much of herself."

"But beautiful and you're attracted to her," Samantha said, grinning.

He'd blushed sheepishly. "That obvious as well?"

She'd chuckled. "How did you meet?"

Nathan had related the awkward circumstances of the night of his first meeting with Charlotte and the impression she'd left, then their chance encounter on the sidewalk in front of her house when she'd invited him and Rebecca and Zak inside. Charlotte had given Rebecca poetry books to read and allowed Zak to dry off on the rug in the morning room while she put Nathan to work. He could make himself useful while his pants dried, she said, and instructed him to form his hand into the shape of a gun. Then she wrapped knitting yarn in a figure 8 around his thumb and forefinger so that the strands would stay neat and not become tangled. "We formed these balls," Nathan said, "and by the time I left, we had a whole basket full of them at her feet."

"Center-pull balls," Samantha identified them.

"Is that what they are called? My mother never knitted."

"You all had to talk about something. How did the conversation go?"

"It was mostly about me. I learned very little about her, oddly enough. I'd have expected her to talk about nothing but herself, but she wanted to know about my job, my rescue of Zak, my opinion of Dallas." Nathan wagged his head. "She got me to talking about growing wheat, of all things."

Samantha said, "Umm..."

"What does that mean?"

"Could it be you may be mistaken in your impression of her? Perhaps Charlotte resents, as you did, the effort of her family and your grandmother to pair you two up. Perhaps her appearance of snobbery and superiority is really a form of independence."

"Oh, she's independent all right!" Nathan declared. "You have only to see her walk and hear her speak to suspect that."

"She can't be too indifferent to you to invite you in to dry off your pants," Samantha said with a smile. "Will you have an opportunity to see her again?"

"She's invited me to a party at her house," Nathan said, uncertainty in his tone. "Do you think I ought to attend?"

Samantha popped his shoulder playfully. "Of course! Why not? The party will give you a better view of her."

"What if she just wishes to embarrass me?"

"I imagine you can handle yourself pretty well in a situation like that," Samantha said. "Think of the evening as a means to confirm your opinion of her one way or the other."

After a second's consideration, Nathan had said, "By gum, you're right. Why not?"

They became aware that Trevor Waverling had come upon them and been standing there for some time. "Time to go, son," he said quietly when they noticed him. "Our business for the day is finished."

*   *   *

From his upstairs bedroom, Neal Gordon watched the family coach driven by Jimmy trundle out through the twin posts of the entrance to his ranch. He turned away sick at heart. He should be feeling over the moon. Instead, he felt only a fraction of the joy, relief, and enthusiasm he'd hardly been able to contain when the Corsicana people had inspected the area. Neal had never seen a man as deliriously happy as Todd Baker when they reached the spot where he'd taken a tumble off Samantha's pet steer. Neal would not have been surprised to see the geologist leap up and down on his skinny legs like a jumping frog. To suffice, Todd had thrown back his head, opened his arms wide, and cried, "It's here! It's here! It's here! As sure as God's in His heaven, it's here!"

That should have been enough to make any rancher's heart soar right out of him, especially when the talk turned to America's insatiable future needs for petroleum. "Once ol' Henry Ford's Model T catches on," Daniel Lane had predicted, "there won't be a family who won't want to retire ol' Dobbin for a motor car!" The men from Waverling Tools had not had time to check out the other areas of the ranch that the Corsicana geologist had taken a look at for potential petroleum deposits, but Todd had winked and said, "Don't worry, Mr. Gordon. We'll have plenty of opportunity to inspect other possible sites on your ranch. I wouldn't be surprised if Las Tres Lomas is over one of the biggest oil fields in the country."

Downstairs, Neal had excused himself to Sloan and Samantha and told his son-in-law to help himself to the bourbon, that he'd be down directly. Before he went up, Sloan had drawn him aside and said, "I hope there are no hard feelings between us, Neal, and that you understand that I couldn't go against my wife to take your side against Waverling Tools."

"Of course I understand," Neal had said. "I would expect no less from Seth Singleton's son or the man who married my daughter. I'll be down in a bit."

The climb up the stairs had made him feel that he'd lifted something too heavy for his age and condition. He'd have liked a shot of bourbon himself, but he'd needed to be alone to think. The Waverling Tools men were coming back next Monday to stake out the drilling site and set up the platform. Then a service road would be cleared for hauling equipment, and after that the rig would be erected. It would be a number of weeks before the actual drilling could begin.

"What will be your job in the operation, Mr. Waverling?" Neal had asked.

"A limited one. The driller will be in charge of the site, but Daniel Lane and Todd and Nathan will be here until everything is well underway. I'll make only periodic visits."

"That so?" Neal had said, relieved. "You must let us know when to expect you so Grizzly can make some of that stew you enjoyed."

He spoke more sincerely and less graciously in making it clear that La Tres Lomas had no extra bunks to lodge the drilling and supervising crew, and he could not ask his cook to provide additional meals and serve them in the crowded space of the dining room. The men would have to bring their own sleeping tents, food, and drinking water. He hoped Trevor Waverling understood that included Nathan and Todd and Daniel Lane. Trevor had countered with an understanding smile. He wouldn't for the world impose on Mr. Gordon's staff or expect accommodations of any sort. His men would be instructed to eat and sleep within the compound of the work area.

Neal threw water on his face. Now that he had been in the company of Trevor Waverling and Nathan, the lump of guilt and fear was back wreaking havoc to his peace. He could raise objections against Samantha's natural mother and her silly stepsiblings back in Gainesville, but Neal could find none to lift against her real father and twin—none to justify keeping knowledge of their identities a secret. The Waverling men appeared deserving and Trevor irresistible to a daughter's affection. He was charming, suave, sophisticated, smart, and as fit for his age as any man Neal had ever known—a fine grandfather figure. Once again, Neal sensed destiny's hand behind the events of today. Would fate's quirky humor lead Samantha to discover the identities of Trevor Waverling and Nathan Holloway and expose Neal Gordon's crime in keeping them from her? Todd's deceit would be a molehill compared to the mountain range of his deception.

Neal dried his face and contemplated himself in the mirror. Of course, he could be dragging around his ball and chain for nothing. Most worries never came to pass. But to be sure, he must prevent any interaction between Samantha and the Waverling men. In the meantime, he would do some digging into Trevor Waverling's background. The man might not be as pure as he appeared, and Neal's findings might loosen the tight squeeze on his conscience. He ran a brush through his hair and hitched up his pants. Going down the stairs to where Samantha and Sloan waited, he plastered a smile on his face and rubbed his hands together as if he were the happiest man in all the world.

Chapter Sixty-Four

That night, Nathan wrote his usual twice-a-month letter to Leon. He always included his mother in the salutation, but it was to his stepfather that he addressed his thoughts and shared the details of his life. That evening he hardly knew where to start, he was so full of news. He decided to write of events that had occurred since his last correspondence the middle of August. He dated his letter September fourth, 1900.

> *I have met an unusual and very attractive young lady by the name of Charlotte Weatherspoon. She's from a prominent Dallas family long and well acquainted with the Waverlings. We met at my grandmother's house at a dinner party she arranged to intro-duce us. I was quite taken with her at first sight but then taken aback by her at the second. I thought her a snob, still do, but I may have reason to change my mind.*

Nathan described the circumstances of his second meeting with Charlotte Weatherspoon, how she hadn't minded that Zak lay on a Wilton rug or that Rebecca immediately ran to her bookcase and took down several volumes without asking per-mission. To him she'd been less cordial, bossy even. He wrote of the task she'd set him to while his pants dried, appalled at his ignorance of the technique involved in preventing snarls and snags of yarn: *She asked me if you knitted, Mother, and I said no, so the whole experience was new to me. It made for a very pleasant two hours.*

Nathan went on to write that on the advice of another new acquaintance, he had accepted an invitation to a party at Charlotte's home the coming Sunday, September ninth, and that his grandmother had insisted on having him fitted for a new suit for the occasion—*"a tuxedo!"* Nathan described the satin lapels and tailless (*"thank God!"*) formal evening suit his grandmother had in mind, smiling to himself as he mentally heard his mother say in annoyance, "Oh, for goodness' sakes! Doesn't Nathan know that we know what a tuxedo is?"

Nathan cited other tidbits he thought might interest Leon, and perhaps his mother, mixing news of his boxing lessons with social events he'd attended. He kept for last the mention that Waverling Tools would soon drill its first oil well on a ranch near Fort Worth in Tarrant County called Las Tres Lomas de la Trinidad, translated as "the Three Hills of the Trinity." He would be busy and away from Dallas for a few months as part of the supervising crew.

I've had occasion to meet the rancher's daughter, the acquaintance I mentioned earlier. Her name is Samantha Gordon—or rather, Mrs. Sloan Singleton now. I met her back in July when the company geologist and I made a visit to the ranch to check out a spot where Todd Baker believes oil is to be found. There is quite a story associated with that site inspection, but it can wait until my next visit. At any rate, Samantha seems the sort you can tell anything to. I told her about the conflict of my feelings toward Charlotte Weatherspoon—how on one hand I find her enthralling and on the other . . . well, put-offish, and she ex-

*plained that perhaps Charlotte resented my being rammed down
her throat as a suitable prospect for marriage. Imagine that! Me,
Nathan Holloway, considered a suitable marriage prospect for a
debutante!*

Nathan reread his letter, confident he'd left nothing out that
he'd remember later and wish he'd put in. Leon looked forward
to his letters. His stepfather would answer this one right away,
commenting on each item since there was so little in his own life
to write about. Leon's last correspondence had stated that Randolph had left for Columbia, and Lily was getting ready to enter
the girls' academy in Denton. He played checkers every Wednesday afternoon on the courthouse lawn with some new cronies:
the courthouse janitor, a retired railroad man who ferried across
the Red River from Marietta to join them, and a Spanish-American War veteran who'd lost his leg in Cuba. The "Courthouse
boys," he called them, the only friends he'd made in town. He and
Millicent had joined a spanking new modern church, but Leon
couldn't stand the preacher. They had begun drilling out at the
farm. He'd let Nathan know if they struck it out there, but he'd
never see it for himself. Millicent was finding they needed more
money to keep up the lifestyle they were living, and Leon had
offered to go to work for any number of farmers around who'd
be glad to have him, but Millicent wouldn't have it. Gentlemen
of means do not do physical labor, she told him. Well, as Nathan
knew, he was no gentleman and he had no means, but he would
allow Millicent her illusion. Anytime Nathan felt like paying
them a visit, he knew he was more than welcome.

Nathan addressed the envelope and slipped his letter inside.
He would mail it the next day.

*   *   *

In his room, Trevor Waverling undressed slowly, thoughtfully, sadly. He'd brought up a scotch and soda to mellow his mood, but the alcohol had not yet taken effect. His mission was now completed. He'd observed his daughter in her natural habitat and found it not wanting. She was loved, protected, cared for. He could offer her nothing she did not have already. If he imposed himself further on her in any way, he'd have Neal Gordon to deal with. The rancher's eyes had been on him the entire visit, as if he suspected that given the opportunity, Trevor Waverling would take advantage of his daughter. Well, let the man think he was a lecher. He wasn't afraid of Neal Gordon but afraid of the truth that was bound to come out if he pressed his luck.

Now if only he could do something about this...gut-deep ache of paternal loss. Trevor already had a daughter, as Leon Holloway had reminded him. He also had a son, a wonderful boy who, though he didn't know it, looked likely in time to be snared by Charlotte Weatherspoon, a splendid girl. They would have children and he would become a grandfather, a pleasure he looked forward to. Family had not mattered so much to him before the advent of Nathan. In fact, he'd tried to distance himself from the need for family. Family caused pain. It had taken him years to get over the sudden death of his father, the suicide of his brother. His mother did not like him, and his marriages had ended in disaster and divorce, one leaving him with a retarded child, his biggest heartache of all.

What was so great about family?

But then, into his life had come Nathan, who had taught him what it was like to feel—*be*—a father. His mother's house was now a home, not a place where he simply hung his hat. His mother and daughter were not merely tenants with whom he lodged. They had become family.

And a vital member was missing.

Trevor pulled a chair to a window and sat down to look out into the starry night. It was a spot he often occupied in the late hours to consider a pending business deal. It was his custom to separate its components from the whole and examine them individually. He made no decision based on an overall, general picture. If all the parts, or at least a significant number, matched its sum, he was ready to make his move. In likewise fashion, he placed his impressions of people as he came to know them into mental pigeonholes to be inspected separately before he came to a conclusion about them.

So it had been with Samantha.

He'd had the opportunity to study her on only four occasions, if briefly: at the paleontology lecture in Fort Worth, in his office at Waverling Tools, at her wedding ceremony (as he sat in the far-corner seat of the back row), and on her own turf at Las Tres Lomas today. From these short associations—these quick peeks into her life—he had determined her happy and fulfilled, her situation close to ideal. She lived in an impressive, comfortable home surrounded by people who loved her—doting parents, an adoring husband, and a ranch staff who would have killed for her. Why would he declare himself and muck up Samantha Gordon's life, cause pain to the loving but jealously possessive people who'd given her a good home? What would the information do to Nathan, to his affection for his mother that he held on to despite her indifference, but more important, to his feeling for Leon, if Trevor Waverling were to reveal that they had given away his twin sister at their birth?

If he had not heard from the midwife that Samantha had made a visit to Dr. Tolman's office with questions about her birth— seeking her kin—he would not be sitting here tonight feeling every breath like the jab of a hot poker. He would have left the late doctor's office without definite proof but with almost certain knowledge that Samantha Gordon was his daughter and Nathan's twin, and that would have been the end of it. He would have let matters lie as he had when he learned of Nathan's existence, keeping an eye on her from afar and feeling the loss of a child he would never know, but he would have been comforted by the knowledge that all was well with her life. But then he'd discovered that all was not well with her life. Samantha had gone looking for her birth family—for Millicent, God spare the child—for Nathan...for him. His heart would not let go the description Dr. Tolman's daughter had given the midwife: *Eleanor said the young woman looked so disappointed that she couldn't help her. She felt sorry for her. As pretty and well dressed as she was, she made Eleanor think of a little waif.*

So here he sat picturing Samantha heartsick with disappointment before the midwife's desk and her father unable to go to her and say, *Here I am, my darling daughter,* like today when he came upon Nathan in conference with Samantha and he was powerless to announce, *You are speaking to your sister, son. Samantha is your twin.*

Trevor took a large swallow of the scotch, feeling the burn of tears. But what was, was, and he must let it be. Samantha was happily settled into her life. The longing that had sent her to Marietta would lessen and fade over the years. Nathan would have his own family in time, never knowing and therefore never missing the link that tied him to the girl with the hair like his mother's. As for him, their father, he would hope that after the company's business with Las Tres Lomas de la Trinidad was done, he could glean reports of his daughter's welfare through Daniel now and then. Trevor understood that the woman he'd observed fling herself into his draftsman's arms at the train station was Sloan Singleton's sister.

Trevor took another belt of his drink. And as Samantha's father, he could draw some satisfaction from knowing that his lovely, intelligent, and kindhearted daughter would never learn that Millicent Holloway was her mother.

"You are *not* going to spend your nights in a tent and eat canned beans and jerky for supper when bed and board are available at the Triple S!" Billie June declared to Daniel that night.

"I'm afraid I am, cupcake," Daniel said. "Your brother isn't about to have me under his roof."

"He'll have no say about it. My father's will stated that I can live in the house at the Triple S as long as I live."

Daniel stared agog at her. "What are you saying, Billie June? Are you going back to the Triple S to live?"

Billie June swirled before her mirror. She had purchased a new frock and had tried it on for Daniel to admire. "I propose to go home for the duration of the drilling and take you with me. As my guest, Sloan can't possibly kick you out any more than he could me."

Daniel scraped his hand over his bristly chin. "Oh, Billie June, I don't know. Your brother would have every right to object to our sleeping together in the family home."

Billie June unbuttoned the fitted bodice of her dress. "You weren't listening. I'm not talking about sleeping together. I'm talking about your taking up residence in one of the spare rooms as my guest." She grinned at him impishly. "Of course you can always slip down the hall to my room when the house is asleep."

"As if your brother wouldn't figure that out," Daniel said.

Billie June slipped out of the dress. "Let him," she said. "He's not liable to come barging in on us. How embarrassing that would be for everybody! Samantha would not allow it anyway."

"What about your music lessons?"

"I can always resume them. Besides, I'm homesick for Sloan and Samantha and the ranch. This time of year the Triple S is at its most glorious, and it's fall calving season. I love to feed the orphaned calves their bottles. Also," Billie June said, with a jiggling of her eyebrows, "I'd miss you here all by myself."

Daniel gazed at her. He ought to feel nettled at this feeling of hers that they could not be apart. When she first came to live in Dallas, he'd vowed to make it clear to her that he had other demands on his time, other people in his life, and she would have to seek other interests besides him to fill her time, but he had not gotten around to it. Billie June's apartment building had a telephone in the hall, and he would contact her there from the office around five o'clock. The other tenants had learned that a ring at that time was probably for Billie June and left it for her to answer. He had not wanted to make a habit of that, so for a few afternoons each week at the beginning, he'd deliberately not telephoned. He'd gone to a bar, the races, treated himself to a fine dinner or to a cabaret show, always with an eye for the girls, but there had been a hollow feeling where his pleasure should have been. He realized he missed Billie June. He would also miss her the weeks he'd be away spent only in the company of men, eating out of a tin plate around a campfire and falling asleep in a cold tent while listening to the bay of coyotes. On the other hand, he wouldn't enjoy the awkwardness of living in the same house with Sloan Singleton watching his sister thumb her nose at him. And he had to consider the discomfort the situation might cause Samantha.

Billie June was now in her corset and stockings, and he thought she'd never looked more fetching. Now that he thought about it, her idea wasn't such a bad one. The barb of Sloan Singleton's archenemy living in his grand house, sitting at his dinner table, and lolling about in his fine chairs would be a pleasure he wouldn't mind experiencing. Daniel had never stepped foot beyond the screened back porch of the Triple S.

"All right, cupcake," he said. "If you can manage the frowns and growls of your brother, it's okay with me. Now let me help you with those ties."

Chapter Sixty-Five

Three days later, September seventh, Leon Holloway collected Nathan's letter from his post office box in Gainesville. He slipped a fingernail under the envelope's flap, thrilled to see two full pages enclosed—*two!*—and began to read even before he got outside the building. There was one from Randolph, too, mailed from New York City, but he would wait until he got home to give it to Millicent to read aloud to both of them. His house was within walking distance, and he enjoyed the daily trek to and from the post office, especially on sunny, brisk days like today.

By the time he reached the park, Leon had finished the letter and was forced to sit down on the bench he often occupied when the house became too confining. Dropping his head back, he stared horror-stricken up into the canopy of the turning maple tree that afforded shade in summer, two items in the script dancing before his stark gaze: *Samantha Gordon* and *Las Tres Lomas de la Trinidad*. Lord have mercy! Nathan had met his twin sister! The shock of it had knocked his pins right out from under him, but as his heart rate slowed and his legs steadied, Leon wondered why he should feel so blown off his feet. There had been times when he had worried that the hand that had made the universe would somehow, some way, throw the twins together. Dallas and Fort Worth were not that far apart. He'd known of such strange, far-fetched things happening. He'd heard of a soldier in the war who, when rifling through a dead Yankee's pockets for a souvenir of his kill, had pulled out a photograph of his own parents. The Yankee had killed the man's brother.

Another time, a member of Millicent's sewing circle was visiting a sick neighbor and noticed a birthmark on the back of the woman's leg in the same spot and identical in appearance as that of her baby sister, who had been adopted. Comparing notes, the two women discovered they were siblings. They had lived two blocks apart in Gainesville for over twenty years.

So why should Leon Holloway doubt that a divine wind had not blown the twins together? Already there had been warnings that the chickens were coming home to roost when Neal Gordon and Trevor Waverling had unexpectedly turned up on his doorstep. Leon had been concerned that should Nathan and Samantha ever meet, there might be a romantic spark between them, and his blood would go cold at what could come of that. But no, thank goodness, Samantha Gordon was married, and it sounded like Nathan was smitten with Charlotte Weatherspoon, somebody who sounded right up Millicent's alley.

So what should he do now, if anything? He must think. He alone held the box lid showing the full picture of the puzzle of which each player held a piece. Neal Gordon had learned of Samantha's parentage and believed Leon to be her father, a secret the rancher had apparently kept to himself. Somehow Trevor Waverling had come to suspect that Samantha was his daughter and twin sister to his son, but he had said nothing to Nathan or declared himself to Samantha, or the boy most certainly would have written of it in his letter. Nathan knew nothing about his birth other than he'd been begotten by another man than the one he'd thought was his father. Millicent, of course, knew she had a daughter born a twin but had no idea of who or where she was.

Samantha had no knowledge of the father and twin brother living right under her nose, at least not yet.

What a jumble!

Leon would keep his counsel, allow the powers that be their sway with no interference from him. He slipped the letter in its envelope into his overalls' pocket, mentally hearing Millicent chirp when he arrived with the mail: *I see you've read Nathan's letter, so let's open Randolph's.* It was always the way. Nathan was forever last with his mother. Ah, Millie girl, Leon thought, heaven help you if you ever have to answer for what you did to your firstborns, but maybe the eye that had kept Nathan and Samantha in its sight was behind that, too. The twins were better off abandoned to the folks who'd taken them in, sure enough. Leon wished only that he could share in the lives they had made.

Stretching to his full height, Sloan carefully pushed the skull in its burlap wrapping far back behind a box of painted wooden balls that annually adorned the Christmas tree. It was early Friday afternoon and hay-baling season. His foreman would be wondering where in blazes he was. His boss was needed to inspect and decide which areas of his hay fields to bale. A blight had wiped out at least half of his fodder crop, and it was essential that the rest be collected and baled before it became too dry or inclement weather set in and ruined the first cutting. Rain was expected on the coast and could move inland, but Sloan had had to hang around after lunch until Samantha left for Las Tres Lomas and Millie May had gone to exercise her mare. His older sister had come in from Houston for the weekend but would extend her stay now that Billie June was moving back—"for as long as Daniel's services are needed at the drill site," she'd informed them by telephone. Samantha had taken the message.

The news that Billie June would be bringing Daniel Lane

home with her on Sunday to occupy the best guest room had been as hard to swallow as a patch of cockleburs. The shock had been delivered at lunch, the women surprised that Sloan had not risen from the table like an enraged stallion to declare that he would absolutely forbid it, but he was in no position to protest the impudence of the man to push the proposal on Billie June. Daniel Lane's threat—*I want you to remember that I can destroy you with Miss Gordon, her father, and your sisters*—still buzzed in his head like a swarm of gnats. Sloan had yet to figure out how to handle the threat and turn the table on the upstart.

"And before you accuse Daniel of the idea," Samantha had said at lunch as if reading his thoughts, "the notion was all Billie June's."

"According to the dictates of Dad's will, I'm afraid you can't refuse her, Sloan," Millie May had reminded him.

"Dad's dictates never included his daughter using a guest room for sexual trysts with a smithy's helper!" he'd snapped.

Samantha had inserted quietly, "A prince would be more suitable?"

It was the first marital dispute between them. Sloan had felt a flush of shame. He was no snob. He respected all men who worked hard at their jobs. None stood more exalted in his estimation, and Daniel Lane had been known around Fort Worth as a hard and conscientious worker. Also, the solid fact was that Daniel no longer earned his living over a fire and anvil. To hear Billie June tell it, he had become indispensable to Waverling Tools. But what Samantha and his sisters did not know was that Daniel Lane was out to get him, and Billie June was his tool to do it.

Makes my pursuit a whole lot easier with no regrets, the man had said.

What pursuit?

What I've determined is now my life's mission.

The memory of that cryptic exchange still raised his flesh a little, whatever it meant, but Sloan forced himself to close his mind to it. He had too much to do to worry about Daniel Lane's "life's mission." He had thrown his napkin on the table and pushed back his chair. "You're twisting my words, Samantha. Snobbery has nothing to do with it. Intentions do. Daniel Lane is up to no good with my younger sister."

"By now, don't you think Billie June would have determined that for herself?" Millie May had asked.

"She's so besotted she can't see she's setting herself up for a waterfall of heartbreak," Sloan had said. "I can't prevent it in Dallas, but I can in my own house."

"It's her heart, Sloan," Samantha had said, again in that quiet, unflinching tone of reason.

The long and short of it was that Daniel Lane was to plunk his bedroll in the main house of the Triple S Sunday, and that had forced Sloan to find another place to store the skull. With the women about, Sloan would have had a hard time explaining his reason for rummaging through the upstairs closet when he had supposedly stayed behind to write checks to pay the monthly bills. Their absence from the house was the first opportunity he'd had to sneak into the guest room where he'd hidden the relic. After his marriage, he'd moved it there from the master suite he'd taken over when his father died. Tomorrow, the maids would be cleaning the guest room Daniel was to occupy, airing out drawers and wardrobes, and Sloan had had little time to think of a place where the skull would be kept dry, safe from damage, and unlikely to be discovered. There had never been a need for locks inside the house at the Triple S, not even in the study. No building outside would do. Try as he might, despite the space available in his home, Sloan could think of no other place to hide the albatross around his neck but in a storage cabinet of Christmas items never opened until the holidays. It was across from the guest room, but even considering that liability, Sloan thought it the best hiding place temporarily available. A warped jamb made the door difficult to open, and when pried loose it grated like the lid of an ancient crypt. If Daniel went on the prowl to ferret out the skull—supposing he thought the owner of the Triple S dumb enough to keep it—Sloan could depend on the noise alone to alert the whole upper floor, but he must make sure not to sleep too soundly or ever to leave Daniel alone in the house.

If only he could get rid of the damn thing, but his conscience shook a finger at him. The relic belonged to Sam. It could be an archeological treasure. If destroyed, the likes of it might never surface again.

His wife and sister had pleaded with him to behave to Daniel. Samantha was already disturbed by her father's refusal to allow Nathan Holloway and Todd Baker, pariah that he was, to stay in the house at Las Tres Lomas while they mapped out the drill site. The men would have to set up a tent and cook over a campfire. They would be arriving Monday by train, and at least Neal had agreed to send a wagon to pick them up at the station.

"I don't understand how Daddy can be so unreasonable and inhospitable," Samantha had complained. "With me gone from the house, you'd think he'd welcome those men's company and be eager to hear all about the preliminary work they're doing at Windy Bluff." Sloan didn't understand Neal's stand, either. The Gordon house could accommodate any number of guests, and Daniel could have been shuffled off over there.

Samantha had said, "If things get too tense, we can always move over to Las Tres Lomas for the week. Daddy would love it."

And leave Daniel Lane with the run of the house, Sloan had thought. Never! "I'm not about to allow a man I suspect of dishonorable intentions toward my sister to drive me out of my house, Samantha, so we're staying put," he'd said, closing the discussion.

As he put a shoulder to the cabinet door to push it closed when his task was completed, Sloan realized an advantage of having his sister's lover under his roof. Daniel Lane's presence would give him the opportunity to size up the man who claimed him to be his life's mission.

"Nobody better light a match," Jeanne announced as she took her designated place with notepad and pencil in hand at the conference table of Waverling Tools. "The excitement in here is ignitable."

"That's one way of putting it," Todd said, grinning widely. "I'd describe it as electric." He gave the table a smack. "By God, we're moving into the oil business, folks! Next to the day I married, this is the happiest day of my life." He winked at Nathan. "Right, buddy?"

"How would I know?" Nathan said, once again evading Todd's attempt to give the impression they were as close as riders on a tandem bike.

"I hope we're not getting excited for nothing," Jamie Foster said, shaking his head. An extremely competent and loyal carry-over from the days of the company's founding, the plant foreman was a taciturn fellow noted for resisting change. "Digging for oil is a whole lot riskier than digging for salt and water."

"We can always count on you to provide drag, can't we?" his assistant said, good-humoredly clapping the foreman's shoulder. He grinned around the table. "What would we do without our doubting Thomas?"

"You'd be doin' a whole hell of a lotta leapin' without lookin', that's what, son," Jamie said.

"I like *ignitable* better," Jeanne said, the defense of her choice of diction cast irritably at the company geologist.

"I'd call it gaseous," Daniel said, teasingly poking the ribs of the accountant next to him. "Did you eat beans for supper last night, Norman?"

The accountant observed Daniel as if he were a roach found in his teacup. Spidery thin, his flesh as papery as the pages upon which he meticulously recorded the company's expenses and manner as starched as his prim white shirts, the entrenched bachelor was often the secret butt of office jokes. "I *never* eat beans at any time, Mr. Lane. Whatever *gas* is floating around must surely be emitted from your own mouth. And may I remind you a lady is present."

"Yes, indeed," Jeanne said huffily, feigning offense. "Thank you, Norman, for reminding that fact to the man sitting next to you who most certainly is *not* a gentleman."

Daniel grinned and blew her a kiss.

At the head of the table, Trevor rapped a pen against his water glass to gain their attention. He'd been studying sheets of estimated drilling expenses and had barely listened to his employees' banter. He was used to what an outsider might observe as squabbling among his department chiefs. It was nothing new to him that Todd Baker had become persona non grata to Nathan and an irritant to Jeanne. His accountant's prissy fussiness about financial reports invited ribbing, Daniel Lane's coarse humor grated, and even Trevor found his faithful foreman's incorrigible naysaying beyond endurance at times. But despite their differences, they all worked exceptionally well together, even fondly, and were eager to head into the company's new direction regardless of the risk to the employee profit-sharing plan Trevor had instated last year. Trevor had learned early in his business career that a company's solvency went a long way to guaranteeing an employee's output and loyalty, and to that end he made no secret of the robust financial health of Waverling Tools. Now he was about to reduce some of the fat from its bottom line.

"Never had no such thing before. Don't expect to have no such thing afterward," his pessimistic foreman had grumbled in the meeting Trevor had called to apprise his team of the risky waters into which the company was headed, and all the others had nodded their approval. Trevor had explained that while Waverling Tools would be manufacturing much of the equipment used in the drilling process, there would be the major costs of labor, pipeline and road construction, storage tank rental, and wagon and rail transportation from the drill site to the refinery in Corsicana, not to mention ancillary expenses like feeding and sheltering the dozen or so men required to work a rig.

And then there was no guarantee the well would come in.

But all had hopped eagerly on board with faith in Todd's analysis for this first sortie into deep waters and hope that come December there might be an extra bonus in their company Christmas stockings. Trevor hoped that none around the table had seen his gulp when he looked at the new table of expenses his accountant had prepared. Railroad transport fees had gone up. The Texas and Pacific was charging more for oil tankers, since they were in short supply. The teamster company Trevor had hired to haul the oil to its destination insisted on placing a clause in the contract calling for compensation for animal injury. The manufacturer of storage tubs had increased its prices. For the time being, these particular cost hikes were a moot point if no oil was discovered at Windy Bluff, but he, too, shared in his employees' highly charged expectations for the company's future. How much of it had to do with his daughter living on the land he was set to drill—the opportunity it would provide to see her again—he could not have said, but there was an extra note of optimism in his voice when he addressed the now-attentive group.

"Gentlemen and lady," he said, nodding at Jeanne, "I know it's late to call a meeting on a Friday afternoon, but I believe today, September seventh, 1900, marks the end of Waverling Tools as we've known it, and Monday will begin the company as it will come to be known. As Todd says, we're going into the oil business, not only to manufacture the tools and equipment essential to the industry, but to dig for the stuff ourselves. I believe we are on the eve of an unprecedented experience in Texas, one that will change our state as we know it, maybe even our lives. At the end of your reports, I will have Miss Beardsley haul out the champagne to toast our new beginnings. We have much to raise our glasses to."

Good to his promise, after the last item of business was concluded, Miss Beardsley appeared with a tray laden with tall flutes of champagne. Trevor lifted his glass, never again to drink the sparkling wine without remembering the prophecy he uttered that would soon come to pass.

Chapter Sixty-Six

On Saturday morning, September eighth, Nathan woke to a disquietude whose source eluded him. When he lived on the farm, he could blame this kind of disturbance on his farmer's extra sense of perception. Something was coming. It was in the atmosphere. Hail, wind, flood? Locusts? Fire? An accident to human or animal? At such times, with his thumbs hooked in the straps of his overalls, he went outside to smell the air and listen to the wind, scrutinize the skies, and inspect the ground. His presentiments sometimes proved to be tricksters. They were not always true to him, but he never dismissed their warnings as unfounded. The calamities that failed to materialize did not mean they had not been of a mind to strike. They had simply diverted course, like the unseen rattlesnake that slithers off into the bush before an unsuspecting foot can feel its fangs.

It's a sort of sixth sense that comes from the farmer's honed mistrust of Mother Nature, son, especially when the old girl has been exceptionally kind, Leon once explained. *The wavin' fields of wheat we see today might lie flattened by her hand tomorrow.*

There were no fields of wheat to rouse his instincts here in this house in the city with the sounds of Saturday traffic floating in through his open window, Nathan thought. To shake free of his uneasy mood, he thought of Charlotte—he'd see her at her party tomorrow night—and the sparring match he'd have later this morning with his father. Nathan chuckled. He didn't know Charlotte well at all, but if she should be privy to his thoughts, he imagined her putting her pretty hands on her slim hips and saying in mock horror, *Nathan Holloway! You mean to say you thought of me in the same category as smelly old boxing gloves?* And he fantasized drawing her into his arms and saying, *Only because you both connect with the same punch.*

Zak licked his face. Time to get up. Nathan let the dog outside through a hall door opening to an exterior set of stairs and heard the raucous cry of birds. Stepping onto the landing, he looked up and saw a large formation of seagulls heading north. Benjy, in an undershirt, his suspenders down about his hips and his face lathered in shaving cream, had come out onto his apartment's small balcony on top of the carriage house, apparently attracted by the noise. He saw Nathan and hollered, "They must have come from the coast. Wonder what's up down there?"

"I think a tropical storm must be headed that way," Nathan hollered back. "Telegraph and telephone lines were down in Florida and Louisiana last week."

So his farmer's instincts weren't wrong, Nathan thought as he returned to his room. September was hurricane season in the Gulf, sometimes sending a backlash of rain and wind as far into Texas as the Panhandle and up into the Oklahoma Territory. He remembered that Sloan Singleton had begun baling his hay last week. Nathan hoped he'd gotten it into his barns in case rain was on the way. If it held off and the cutting wasn't finished, on Monday he'd pop over the fence from Las Tres Lomas and lend a hand to his men.

He hurried to wash and dress. He'd gotten his gym gear together last night: lightly padded gloves the old-timers still called "mufflers," high-top lace shoes, boxer's shorts, and the leather helmet used for sparring just introduced to the sport. His father was a stickler for safety in the ring, despite his grandmother's expressed doubt there could be any protection "for two men bent on knocking out each other."

"That's not the point of what we do, Mother," Trevor tried to assure her. "I'm not training Nathan for competition. I'm teaching him to spar."

"What's the difference?"

"The intent."

His grandmother did not approve of the Saturday morning boxing sessions. They laid another bone of contention between her and her son. The tragedy of their relationship continued to sadden Nathan. His grandmother's days were numbered. He did not want her to die without knowing of her son's sacrifice to preserve her image of the son she'd preferred. And Nathan did not want his father to live without having known the expressed love of his mother. Nathan understood that pain. Trevor Waverling was a good man and a devoted son. A little shy of a father's attention to his daughter, maybe, but only because he hadn't the temperament to handle her. Did his grandmother not see that deficiency as a great burden to him? It was the saddest heartbreak of all to love deeply and not possess the right nature to express it. At times, Nathan could hardly keep quiet about the knowledge he possessed. The tragedy of his grandmother going to her grave with the suspicion that his father had killed her son burned in him like a lump of coal.

Trevor, I went along with your insane participation in that barbaric sport, but must you infect my grandson with your lust to hurt and be hurt? she'd said in outrage when she first learned her son had invited Nathan to his boxing gym. His father had argued that inflicting bodily injury was not the goal of sparring. Its object was to develop proper head movement and footwork, evasive techniques like slipping and dodging, to build skills in bobbing, countering, and angling. Sparring trained a man to improvise, to think under pressure, and to keep his emotions in check.

His grandmother had told him to quit his jargon blabber. She hadn't the foggiest notion what he was talking about. Just tell her for what purpose was her grandson to be trained to "improvise, think under pressure, and keep his emotions in check."

It was always good for a man to know how to deal with a fast, powerful, and determined attacker, his father had told her.

Nathan reduced her ire somewhat by explaining that sparring was really the *practice* of boxing and safe as long as the partners were friendly and no emotional tension was involved. He enjoyed exchanging punches, or better yet, learning the skills to avoid them, and the physical benefits of the ring were showing on him. He'd always thought himself a rather clumsy fellow, lacking grace. The training had improved his balance and coordination, strengthened and toned his muscles, slimmed his waist, and increased his energy. Nathan did not tell his grandmother that ringside observers agreed with his father's opinion that he was made for the sport. He had the big upper-body strength and strong legs boxing called for. Powerful punches and explosive movements all came from the calves, thighs, hams, and hips, the likes of which he possessed.

His painting of the brighter side of the Saturday sessions earned only an unconvinced *humph!* from Mavis Waverling, but she quit her harping with a final shot. *You're the mirror image of your grandfather in every way, Nathan, and thank goodness HIS father saw no need to subject him to "footwork in the ring" to improve himself*, she said.

Dressed, his bed made, Nathan grabbed his gym satchel. Maybe he and his father would get down to the breakfast table and be gone before his grandmother got up to see them off with her usual tight-lipped frown of disapproval. Lenora would let Zak in and feed him. His dog was getting old and was perfectly content to spend the morning curled up with Scat while Rebecca read poetry to them.

Along with the enjoyment of the sport, Nathan looked forward to these Saturday mornings spent with his father. They took the coach because Benjy liked to have breakfast in a little Irish café down from the boxing gym where they sparred. The waitress was sweet on him, he declared, and she'd add an extra potato pancake to his stack and slip him more applesauce without charge when his bowl was empty. *Best boxty this side of Cork County*, he would say, his brogue thick from the anticipated pleasure to his palate. The time alone with his father in the coach had become special to Nathan, because it gave him an opportunity to learn more about Trevor Waverling. On one ride, the thought occurred to Nathan that perhaps his father enjoyed their Saturday trips together because they gave him the chance to learn more about his son.

When they were underway, Trevor asked suddenly, "Are you happy with us, Nathan?"

Surprised by the question, Nathan could not immediately answer. A mood had come over his father. He'd seemed thoughtful and distracted at breakfast. How did Nathan reply to his question? Happiness was something he'd never thought too much about. Contentment, yes. He knew what it was to be contented.

"I would have to say I am," Nathan said.

"Do you miss your half brother and sister?"

"I don't know that I miss them," Nathan said, puzzled by the question. "I think about them often, wonder how they're getting along without me. I was always there to look out for them."

"Do you suppose they miss you?"

"I wouldn't doubt it. That is, until somebody else comes along and gives them a shoulder to lean on." Nathan smiled to say that he did not hold their fickleness against them.

"It takes a special man to always be a brother, Nathan. For most men, other loves and responsibilities come along to take the space siblings fill when they are growing up. Wives, children, jobs, interests, not to mention the separation of distance, can make strangers of brothers and sisters. But with a man like you, I sense that once a brother, always a brother, and that's a comfort to me."

"Oh, I'll always be around for Rebecca, Dad. Have no fear of that."

"I have no fear of that. It's simply that I wish—"

His father bit off whatever he had meant to say and turned his head to stare out the window. What was going on with him this morning? Nathan wondered. He'd been in a mild blue funk since their inspection visit to Las Tres Lomas. "Wish what, Dad?"

His father shook his head. "Nothing, son. Just an old father's wish that things could have been different, that's all."

He's referring to Rebecca, Nathan thought, feeling sympathy for him. He must wonder what would happen to Rebecca once her grandmother and father were gone. Who would take care of her? Was it fair to impose her on Nathan, burden the son he never knew until six months ago and his eventual wife with a retarded half sister? Nathan leaned forward and tapped his father on the knee. "You're worrying about Rebecca's future welfare for nothing, Dad. I give you my word that no matter what, I'll see after Rebecca as long as she lives."

Trevor stared at him, and Nathan, shocked, glimpsed a shimmer of tears in his father's eyes, quickly blinked away. "Thank you for that assurance, Nathan," he said. "I've come to believe I can expect no less from my son."

*   *   *

Rain began falling Sunday morning as the Waverling family was seated in their pews at church services. A strong wind latched on to the ringer of the church bell just as the choir was finishing "Fairest Lord Jesus," ruining the ancient anthem's blissful conclusion and the results of a week's rehearsals. The bell continued its erratic clanging during the distribution of the offering plates, and murmurs of dismay rose from those who had walked to services and those whose carriages leaked. The citizens of Dallas had not been warned of a rainstorm coming. The Waverlings' Concord was weatherproof, but Mavis and Trevor and Nathan cast worried eyes on Rebecca and hoped someone was sent to silence the bell's crazed tongue before it jangled her from her absorption in a new book of poetry Charlotte had sent over with a note to Nathan that had thrilled his heart: *Looking forward to seeing you tonight.* Rebecca could not abide certain kinds of storms. Easy, gentle rainfall did not disturb her, but those that shook the heavens sent her into a state of great agitation. Her adored uncle had died during a day of frenzied wind and rain.

Whispered concerns strengthened when a deacon quietly slipped from a side door to the altar and spoke into the ear of the minister who had been about to rise to take the pulpit. The reverend nodded grimly in apparent understanding and approached the lectern.

"My dear friends," he said, "word has just now reached us that a huge hurricane struck Galveston yesterday, causing enormous damage and loss of life. Telegraph and telephone lines are down, and train service no longer exists in that area. The storm's aftermath has arrived here. I propose we immediately conclude with the benediction and adjourn to secure our homes and the safety of our animals. As we pray, let us remember the devastated city of Galveston and its citizens."

The benediction was brief. When eyes opened, the congregation hurriedly stood to depart, all but Rebecca. Her family stared at her. The book of poetry lay open in her lap and she had covered her ears against the bell's clangor and the sound of the slashing wind and rain. "*Lord of the winds!*" she chanted, rocking back and forth. "*I feel thee nigh / I know thy breath in the burning sky! / And I wait, with a thrill in every vein / For the coming of the hurricane!*"

"Good God!" Trevor muttered.

"I didn't think she was listening," Mavis said, quickly folding Rebecca's cape around her granddaughter's shoulders.

"She was," Nathan said. "Let's get her home to Zak."

Chapter Sixty-Seven

For the occupants of the Concord, the ride to the town house in Turtle Creek was tense. All had gotten soaked in their dash to the carriage—Nathan and Trevor especially, since they had to help Benjy quiet the horses—and Rebecca would not be shushed. The brim of her sailor hat dripped water as she rocked back and forth reciting the opening lines of John Masefield's poem interminably until Nathan could hardly resist the urge to put his hands over his ears. At one point, Trevor could stand no more and snapped at Rebecca to stop her infernal chanting. Mavis scolded him, demanding why he thought it necessary to prevent the child from quoting poetry that had been dear to her uncle. "Days like this remind her of him," she said.

"They do me, too, Mother. That's why those particular lines are unbearable to hear," Trevor had said, silencing his mother.

Once home, the men went to their rooms to change out of their tailored suits and handmade shoes, while Mavis and Lenora tried to divest Rebecca of her wet clothing and wrap a blanket around her. Wild-eyed, she fought their efforts, continuing her chant until her father appeared in the kitchen with Nathan to hang their sodden clothes in the mud room. *"Rebecca! Stop that this instant!"* Trevor commanded. "You're driving everybody mad with that jingle."

Rebecca, stripped down to her chemise and bloomers, halted midline and blinked at her father as if having to think who he was. Suddenly she sprang toward him crying, "Daddy, Daddy, save him!" and seized Trevor around his waist.

Stricken silence gripped the kitchen. All were aware of whom she spoke. Nathan dropped his eyes, and Lenora and Mavis exchanged helpless glances. Even Zak, sitting on his haunches, sank to the floor with a soulful whine. After a minute's surprise, Trevor wrapped his arms protectively around his daughter's delicate shoulders. "I wish I could have, kitten," he said softly. Mavis turned abruptly to shake out Rebecca's suit jacket with great force over the sink, but Nathan couldn't tell if the loud snap was from contempt or to free the garment of water.

Lenora bent to Rebecca's ear. "Poor little baby," she crooned. "Come, let's have a cup of hot chocolate Lenora made for her angel."

But Rebecca would not be enticed from her father's waist. She had buried her head into his midriff and begun to cry, sobbing into his freshly donned shirt. "There now, it's all right," Trevor said, extricating himself from Rebecca's vise to scoop her up in his arms. "Let's go to your room and see your dolls."

"I'll be right there soon as I change clothes," Mavis called, as Trevor carried his daughter from the kitchen, Zak trotting after them.

Nathan touched her arm. "Maybe they need to be alone for a while, just the two of them," he said, a little aggravated with his grandmother for wishing to butt in on this private time between his father and Rebecca when she complained often enough that he made no room for her in his daily life. "Rebecca seemed to want only her father just now."

Mavis turned to him with surprise in her gaze. Nathan expected to be put soundly in his place. It was not his business to suggest when or if his grandmother should look in on her granddaughter, but Mavis with a softly breaking smile reached up and patted his cheek. "You dear boy," she said. "So very wise beyond your years. It must have been growing up in the country that made you a sage before your time. Yes, they should be alone. Trevor loves Rebecca...in his own way. I forget that sometimes. Lenora, I'm going up to change, then Nathan and I could use a cup of chocolate in the parlor."

Nathan had a fire going in the grate when she returned. The rain had brought a drop in temperature, and his grandmother drew her shawl around her and sighed deeply as she took her seat in her designated chair. "That heat feels good to these old bones," she said. "Thank you, Nathan. Thank you for everything, as a matter of fact. You've brought so much warmth into our lives in ways you're too modest to realize."

Nathan sat down opposite her, feeling inadequate to comment. It looked as if this stormy day had unearthed sad memories. "It all has to do with Jordan, you know," Mavis said. "It's been three years, but Rebecca never has gotten over her uncle's death. He was her best friend. They were two of a kind, I'm sad to say, and she misses him so. Rain like this"—she motioned toward the streaming parlor windows—"brings back the day he died." Her lips tightened from the memory. Firelight caught in her bluish-green irises, faded by time, and Nathan saw the bitterness in them that the years had not faded in kind. Sadness filled him for the facts she did not know, information that might relieve the pain of her memories if only his father would trust her with the truth. She might surprise him. It might be that rather than tarnish his grandmother's memory of her first son, the truth would revive her love for her last. But Nathan had given his word, and he would stick to it.

Lenora brought in the hot chocolate and Nathan gratefully accepted a cup, glad of the heat to soothe his tight larynx. Mavis fixed him with her piercing gaze. "You're choking on your thoughts over there, Nathan. I can tell. Your grandfather had the same faculty of saying absolutely nothing when he had too much to say. So spit it out. What's stuck in your gullet?"

Nathan set his cup in its saucer. There was no getting around that sharp, intuitive beam once it lit. A fellow would have a better chance diverting a shooting comet. He cleared his throat and avoided the thrust of her stare by gazing into the fire. Actually, it was Leon who had taught him the wisdom of saying absolutely nothing when he had too much to say. "I prefer to keep private what's not my place to mention, Grandmother," Nathan said.

"Oh, fiddlesticks!" Mavis tapped the floor with her cane. "This is your home. You are family. In this house, nobody has 'a place' the way you mean it. There should be no secrets of true feelings. You don't want to be like your father."

Nathan glanced at her sharply. "I don't know why not. I see nothing about him that would put me off."

Surprise, close to shock, struck her porcelain face, translucent and finely lined as ancient china. "Ah, I see he's won you to him. That's good. You and Trevor have created a father-and-son bond. It's what I hoped would happen. Trevor will not be left without family when I die."

Which implied that Rebecca was not family to her son, not by his definition, and Nathan had to yield to his grandmother's point. Nathan didn't doubt his father loved his daughter, but Rebecca could no more fill that role to a man like Trevor Waverling, a worshipper of health and fitness and wholeness, than could a family pet.

"I meant only that your father keeps his feelings under lock and key," Mavis explained. "Always has, ever since he was a little boy. I wish he hadn't. I could have known him better. Jordan, now, he opened up about everything."

"No, he didn't," Nathan disputed, the contradiction out before he thought. He felt his face glow red. "I mean—" He bit his lip.

Mavis's little laugh made light of his embarrassment. "I know what you mean, dear. My elder son couldn't have told his mother *everything*. Jordan was a male, after all."

They heard Trevor come down the stairs and say to Lenora that Rebecca would take that cup of cocoa now. "She's settled down with Zak," he reported to his mother and Nathan. "I gave her a small dose of laudanum, and in a little while, she'll be asleep. When she wakes up, the storm may have passed, and she'll have forgotten all about the scene in the kitchen. Nathan, come join me in the study. I have a couple of business items I want to discuss with you before lunch."

Nathan rose with relief at the interruption but felt his grandmother's forlorn disappointment to be left alone in the parlor with only the sound of the storm and the fire to keep her company on a day like the kind in which her son had died.

The telephone rang on and off the rest of the day with callers sharing trickles of information from friends and relatives of the devastation in Galveston. There would be no full reports of the damage until communication lines were reestablished. Trevor was sure that Beaumont, forty miles up the coast from Galveston, had been hit and thanked fate that the cargo of steel casings, boxed and supposed to have been already shipped by rail to Spindletop, had been delayed by a lack of boxcar space. The salt dome lay virtually in the lap of the Gulf of Mexico. With every ring of the telephone, Nathan expected to hear that Charlotte had canceled her party.

Each member of the household took turns checking on Rebecca. Zak lay vigilant on the floor by her bed, and after lunch, Mavis took a nap lying beside her. The rain continued its pummeling, and Nathan was relieved that Rebecca slept on. After lunch, he managed to contact Charlotte, whose family, too, had been drenched hurrying to their carriage after Sunday worship. It was as Nathan had feared and expected. The party must be canceled, but Charlotte suggested they get together for a game of cards when the weather cleared. Cheered by that proposal, he and Trevor spent the rest of the day in the study discussing business-related topics. As the afternoon wore on, the wind gradually died, and the pounding rain turned to a soft drizzle. Talk ranged from Trevor's design plans for the new plant complex to his interview with the veteran water-well driller he had engaged to dig his first oil well. The man's name was Jarvis Putnam, and Nathan and Todd and Daniel had been invited to sit in on the preliminary meeting at Waverling Tools. Todd had asked him if he thought there was a lot of oil in Texas.

"Hell, yes!" the salty old veteran had answered. "There's oceans of oil in Texas, just like there is water. Been here for thousands and thousands of years way down deep just wait'n to be tapped. Fact of the matter, the whole history of the Earth is down there, trapped in strata older than the first man born to Earth. First trick is to find the experts and develop the tools to dig it out. Second trick is not to destroy one to suit the other."

Trevor and Nathan had exchanged glances expressing the same thought. Samantha would like this man. Trevor had signed him on the spot.

As the sun began to set, they were about to adjourn to the parlor for Trevor's evening scotch and soda when they heard a frantic pawing and yelping at the closed study door. Nathan hurried to open it and was greeted by the lunge of a pair of wet paws to his chest. "What is it, Zak?" he said, ruffling the German shepherd's sodden neck, but the answer came like a dart to his heart. The dog jumped down and took off barking toward the stairs. "We'd better go," Nathan said to Trevor. "I think it's Rebecca."

With a panicked scrape of his desk chair, Trevor was right behind him as they chased after the dog to the upper story. On the landing, the men would have headed toward the open door of Rebecca's room, but Zak, barking, bounded down the corridor in the opposite direction. By then, Mavis had come sleepily out into the hall. "What's going on?" she called. "Why is Zak barking? Where's Rebecca?"

Trevor paused long enough to yell, "She's not with you?"

"No. She was on the other side of me, fast asleep."

Trevor, eyes strained from thinking the unthinkable, looked at Nathan. "She's gone to the river."

They sped off after Zak, who had waited yelping by the outer door that stood wide open. As the men rounded the corner, water puddles on the floor told the horror of what had happened. Rebecca had let herself out into the rain with Zak following and had come to some sort of grief that had caused the dog to run back to raise the alarm. Seeing the men, the German shepherd took off down the outside stairs and sprinted toward the pier. Nathan and Trevor splashed in pursuit, Trevor yelling *"Rebecca!"* from panic-stricken lungs. Nathan joined in the cry, but in his pounding heart he knew it was no use. Rebecca had gone to find her uncle. In the rain-drenched afternoon that was slowly fading to dusk, he could almost hear the chant of her last words: *I must go down to the seas again, to the lonely sea and the sky, / And all I ask is a tall ship and a star to steer her by.*

Benjy had heard the commotion and come running, reaching them as their feet hit the flooded pier. Nathan feared that Zak would leap into the churning current, and there would be no saving him, but the dog circled in a whining frenzy at the dock's edge, then raced by them to the ground again, setting off up the riverbank. "I think we should follow Zak," Nathan yelled to Trevor, who nodded, his face the color of the gathering dusk.

It was Zak who found her. The current had not borne her downstream to be swallowed into the mouth of the Trinity River. She lay facedown, wedged between two large rocks by the water's edge, her long, dark hair and napping gown billowing around her. The dog pawed at her and whined until Nathan pulled him away so that Trevor could wade into the water and lift his daughter into his arms. Benjy moved to help him, but he said, "I've got her. I've got my little girl."

Mavis, thin and fragile, her shawl drawn around her, stood waiting and watching on the crest of the slope leading down to the pier. From her vantage point, her white hair and pale gown water-soaked, she looked like an ancient ghost risen from the river. Her face showed no emotion through the film of drizzle when the silent men, Trevor carrying his streaming burden, gained the ground where she stood. Not even her eyes blinked from the weight of the moisture on her lashes.

"Come inside, Mother, before you catch your death," Trevor ordered gently.

Mavis followed dutifully, wordlessly. They entered the house through the door to the back stairs where Lenora hovered anxiously in the hall, and Mavis spoke for the first time. "I knew the river would get her one day. Lay her on her bed, Trevor, and I'll get blankets."

The family doctor was on his way to Galveston with his nurse to offer his services, Nathan was told when he was instructed to telephone the physician's office. It would be best to contact the police, who would notify the coroner.

They all waited in various modes of shock and grief in the parlor for the police to arrive. Dry-eyed, Mavis sat in her wingback like one grieving the long-ago loss of a loved one for whom all her tears had been spent, face pale, lips pressed firmly together, Scat curled in a ball in her lap. Lenora cried quietly in a corner, and in another Benjy fingered his Catholic rosary, his lips moving in a requiem for the dead. Trevor brooded in his customary chair by the window, his profile rigid as a Roman bust. Nathan sprawled, sickened, in the wingback across from his grandmother, Zak at his feet with his head on his paws, the door to Rebecca's room closed against him.

"Why?" Mavis asked vaguely of no one in particular. "Why? I knew the child was fascinated by the river, but she'd been warned so many times about going down there without someone being with her. Why of all days did she go down there?"

Nathan glanced at his father. Only he and Trevor knew the answer. Rebecca had witnessed her uncle drown. Today, because of the storm, her mind had become trapped in the memory of that day, and she'd gone down to the pier to rescue him. His little half sister had tried to tell them, but none had listened. He remembered the promise he'd made to his father: *I'll see after Rebecca for as long as she lives.* Nathan turned his gaze to his grandmother, and to his utter astonishment, before he could put a clamp on his tongue, no more able to prevent himself from speaking than he could keep a boil from rupturing, he heard himself answer, "Rebecca saw her uncle drown himself and went down to the river to save him."

Chapter Sixty-Eight

Billie June and Daniel caught the first afternoon train to Fort Worth and managed to arrive at the Triple S just as the rain and wind laid siege to Dallas. On his round to punch tickets, the conductor had told his passengers of a rumor that Galveston had been struck by a terrible storm coming from the Gulf of Mexico, and the Central Plains would probably get its share of it. "I hope Sloan got his hay in," Billie June said. "Winter feeding will be awfully slight if he didn't, and of course if it floods, he'll be worried sick about his cattle. Neal Gordon, too. Livestock have a natural instinct to move away from floodwaters, but there's only so much high ground on both ranches, and of course, there's always danger of crowded animals stampeding if lightning strikes."

"What happens if they can't make it to high ground or there's not enough room?" Daniel asked.

Billie June had looked bleak for a moment. "It means they lose some of their herds and a sizable chunk of income. Raising cattle is an awful hard way to earn a living, because so much of successful ranching depends on the weather. If this storm is bad and lasts long, the Triple S may be in trouble."

Daniel heard Billie June in surprise. He'd assumed a ranch the size and prosperity of the Triple S could weather any storm. "The Triple S in trouble? How so?"

Billie June looked as if she regretted divulging the information. Daniel encouraged her to share family news, hoping for a
morsel about Sloan that might be useful, but Billie June had become closemouthed about her brother in the last months except
to say something favorable. Daniel half suspected that Billie June
may have had another reason other than his comfort in insisting
that he lodge at the Triple S during his assignment at Windy
Bluff. She might hold the hope that once her brother and Daniel
got to know each other, they might sheathe their swords. Not a
chance. Sloan Singleton represented the type of man Daniel most
despised, the ones who thought themselves better than anybody
simply by the luck of their birth. Daniel had been born in the gut-
ter, no say about where he'd popped out, but he'd climbed out
of it almost from the minute he'd shed his nappies. He hadn't
much to show for it until now, and in a way, he owed the upward
direction in his life to Sloan Singleton. If Mr. High-and-Mighty
Big Britches hadn't humiliated him that day, Daniel might not
be where he was now, but that didn't mean he had reason to forgive and forget. The man was still a condescending, self-serving
snob. If for no other reason, he'd get even with Sloan for the pain
Samantha would suffer when she learned the real reason he had
married her.

Billie June's worry was as raw and exposed as an open
wound, and Daniel suspected she could not keep it to herself
long. He wondered how she hadn't yet figured out his motive
in continuing to see her. He had never spoken of love. He
had drawn a line at that deception. That he desired her, admired her, enjoyed her company more than any other woman
he'd ever known—those were endearments he could truthfully
shower upon her, but love, no.

"Why would the Triple S be in trouble if the storm is bad?" he
prodded.

Billie June pulled nervously at the sleeve end of her jacket. "Let's just say that every cow is needed right now to pay the bills," she said, and after a moment, as if forced by anxiety, volunteered, "especially Sloan's loan from the Rutherford City Bank."

Daniel could hardly keep his jaw from dropping. *Sloan Singleton in hock to the Rutherford City Bank?* After his ditch of his daughter, Noble Rutherford would not hesitate to call in the loan if Sloan failed to meet his obligation to the bank. "Surely your brother's debt is not enough to be too big a worry," Daniel said.

Billie June's mournful nod disputed the feigned certainty of his statement. Shocked, Daniel said, "Your brother wouldn't have been d—" he caught himself before he said *dumb*, and said instead "desperate enough to put the ranch up for collateral, would he?"

Again the sorrowful fall of Billie June's face. "I'm afraid he did. We didn't ride out the drought like the Gordons, and Sloan needed money to buy breeding stock more suitable to our climate and grasslands when another dry spell hits. He expected our herds to increase twofold within a few years, and it was happening, too. Sloan would never have pledged the ranch if he'd thought it at risk."

Of course it wasn't at risk when he made the deal, Daniel thought. He'd planned to marry Anne Rutherford, whose daddy wouldn't allow his daughter to suffer the stigma of foreclosure, so the ranch would never be in jeopardy. When his daughter married Sloan, Noble Rutherford would most likely forgive the debt—probably as a wedding present. But then Sloan had taken a gamble and cast his lot with Samantha, a potential oil heiress and a far more suitable wife to a rancher, with the same idea in mind that Neal Gordon, for the exact reason as Noble Rutherford, would never allow the Triple S to go under. What a scheming bastard! Sloan Singleton was turning out to be no better than any other man and a whole lot dumber than most. He hadn't even had the foresight to anticipate a catastrophe beyond drought that could wipe him out before the Gordon well came in—*if* it came in—and now the banker had him by the short hairs. It couldn't happen to a more deserving guy. Daniel had heard the *we* and *our* in Billie June's explanation. She was still very much tied to the ranch. "So now I guess he'll rely on your and your sister's trust fund money to bail him out," he suggested.

Billie June turned to him with a look that could have fried bacon. Daniel realized he'd overstepped. No doubt about it. Blood was thicker than water. They were sitting together on the Pullman seat holding hands, and Billie June snatched hers away.

"For your information, Sloan would *never* take a dime of my or my sister's trust fund money for any reason," she declared. "We offered him a loan when we learned he needed money, but he adamantly refused. He would never risk Dad's provision in the will that represents our own livelihoods in case we do not marry."

Any other woman might have arched a look conveying a hint at the end of that statement, but Billie June turned her withering glare to the compartment window. Daniel felt a sudden, unexpected dip of his heart at her rebuff and tried to take her hand again. "I'm sorry if I sounded like I was maligning your brother," he apologized.

"You don't know him," Billie June said.

Yes I do, Daniel contradicted silently. Why would Sloan borrow from his sisters if he planned to marry a bank vault's daughter or an oil-rich rancher's pride and joy? Mr. High-and-Mighty Big Britches hadn't counted on a hurricane getting in the way of his strategy. It was going to be interesting to see how he got out of this fix—*if* he did. He smiled to himself and settled against the leather-padded back of his seat. He missed Billie June's soft hand and her trim little shoulder turned from him, but he was warmed by the speculation that the storm might accomplish his life's mission for him.

Millie May, Samantha anxiously standing behind her, had the front door open to greet her sister and Daniel before they could be completely drenched in the dash from the coach sent to collect them from the train station. Sloan ran out in the rain to help unload the luggage, grumbling that his sister must have brought everything but the icebox from her Dallas apartment. Along with Daniel's large satchel of tools, the entrance to the house was soon filled with several suitcases, valises, hatboxes, and a steamer trunk pooling the floor. The men did not shake hands. Daniel might have been a spool on the staircase banister for all the notice Sloan took of him. "For God's sakes, Billie June, this is more than you left home with!" her brother complained. "Where are we going to store all this luggage?"

"There's the upstairs hall cabinet where we keep Christmas decorations," Billie June said. "We can put some things in there."

"*No!*" Sloan protested, his outburst so explosive it startled him as much as his wife and sisters and—dammit!—Daniel Lane. One of the ironmonger's eyelids lowered thoughtfully while the women gazed at him in surprise. "I mean...that's not a good idea, Billie June. That cabinet is full to the gills already, and there are some fragile decorations in there of our mother's."

"Oh, that's right," his sister agreed. "We'll make room in the storage compartment behind the stairs, and there's room under the beds for our valises."

Luggage arrangements over, Billie June imparted news of the Galveston hurricane and that its aftermath was headed inland. "That will mean a delay of your drilling schedule, then," Sloan said to Daniel, hoping the man would take the hint and go back to Dallas. He could not have him free to roam his house while he and his men were out trying to avert the damage the storm would inflict.

"I'll have to see what Monday's weather looks like. I expect my boss to telephone today or tomorrow with new orders. Mr. Waverling might send me down to the coast to check for damage on a drilling operation. Meanwhile, maybe I could be of help to you on the ranch," Daniel offered.

Billie June patted Daniel's arm, her miff over, and said with pride, "Daniel cannot sit still unless he's reading. He's always got to be doing something productive. Surely you can find something for him to do, Sloan?"

Surprised at the offer, Sloan leaped at it. His stomach had knotted within seconds of hearing of the hurricane. The rain had caught the last of his hay to be baled, an unexpected and possibly crippling financial loss. If the storm was as far-reaching and long-lasting as Sloan suspected, every rancher's hay in the North Central plains would be hit. Little would be for sale and sold at sky-high prices, but he would worry about that bridge when he came to it. More pressing were his fears of blackleg, especially to his breeding stock. It was a highly fatal disease resulting from a soil-borne bacteria released after flooding. Then there were the infectious diseases like foot rot and pneumonia, caused by long-term exposure to wet weather and pastures standing in water. Somehow he had to get his cattle to higher ground. Also, the wind had gotten up, the strongest in years, which meant that for the next few days, a detail would have to ride fence to check for damage, and, when the weather cleared, comb the pastures for metal objects like nails and bits of wire that could be ingested and cause damage to intestinal tracts. Brush and debris, especially the poisonous leaves and branches of the black cherry trees, impossible to root out from the land, had to be cleared from the pastures and drowned animals hauled off to a lime pit and burned. There was

plenty of work to be done, not even counting the care and maintenance of thousands of head of cattle if a fraction survived.

"You know anything about herding livestock in inclement
weather?" Sloan asked.

Of all his sundry drifter jobs, Daniel had never worked on a
ranch in any kind of weather. "I can ride a horse and use a rope
as good as any man," he said.

Sloan thought it didn't matter whether the ironmonger knew
the difference between either one as long as the man stayed away
from his house. "Follow me," he said.

By the time the men and horses set out, premature darkness
had fallen and the rain and wind increased in velocity. Through
the sheets of water and blast of wind, they strained to see where
the noises were coming from that cattle make in distress: calves
bawling for their mothers, cows mooing for their young, bulls
bellowing. All these and other sounds of snorting and grunting
could be heard over the fury of the storm, but sight was useless.
Sloan and his men, Daniel among them, had started out riding
abreast in rain slickers, their trouser legs over their boots, to better
find stray or imperiled cows, but the wall of rain prevailed over
the wall of men and made it impossible for them to judge the animals' location. Sloan and his crew headed by knowledge toward
the draws—the cattleman's name for deep, narrow gorges with
steep sides—to search by hearing and experience for cows that
in their panic had tumbled into them. They found to their dismay that their instincts were right, the most disheartening sight a
cow mooing from the rim of the ravine for her fallen calf bawling from knee-deep water. The rescue procedure involved ranch
hands dropping into the ditch and positioning a lariat under the
forelegs of the hapless animals, then putting their shoulders to
their rumps while other cowboys astride horses on the rim tugged
them up and out by the ropes.

Daniel was the first to volunteer for ravine duty, but the wind played havoc with his rope. Its force tried to tear it from his grip, and on such slippery ground, the horse at the top of the ravine could not sustain its footing bearing the calf's weight. As hard as he tried, Daniel's first rescue effort to save the calf proved futile.

"We can't just let the little fellow drown," Daniel hollered up to Sloan on the lip of the draw when the rancher let go the rope to preserve his horse.

"I'm afraid we have to," Sloan shouted down to him, surprised at the anguish he saw on Daniel's rainwashed face. "There's nothing to be done, and we have others to see to. I'm sorry, Lane."

Defeated, the men called it a day. Sloan and Daniel returned to the main house and the cowhands to the ranch dining hall to disrobe, wrap in blankets, and dry their work clothes before the room's gigantic fireplace. By orders of their boss, if the rain did not let up, they would spend the rest of the day and sleep that night on the hard floor rather than get another drenching in a sprint to the bunkhouse. Sloan did not need influenza sweeping the ranks of his crew on top of everything else.

Samantha fussed over him, getting him into dry clothes, tugging off his muddy, water-swollen boots, pouring hot coffee into him, but without the words of consolation with which other wives might comfort their men. She was a ranch woman. Samantha knew too well the heart-numbing devastation such a storm could wreak and no loving reassurances soothe. Both ranches had suffered floodwaters before, but in summer when ground and grass dried quickly. They were now into an early and chilly autumn, and the pastures had already given up their stored heat. Mildred's prediction was correct. There would be no Indian summer this year. The ground would stay damp for a long time, a breeding ground for the horrible diseases that could wipe out a herd within twelve to forty-eight hours of infection.

Mutely, in their room, Samantha and Sloan held each other in their only expression of mutual condolence for the economic loss and property destruction that awaited them. When the skies cleared, they would ride out to pastures littered and draws and drainage ditches filled with the swollen carcasses of drowned cattle. They could only guess at the numbers. They would find their rangeland a rubbish field of shredded tree branches and debris, roofs ripped off sheds, fences blown down or their wire entangled with the prairie's refuse, hay fields ruined, and paddock railings and pens splintered by panic-stricken livestock that had freed themselves at risk to life and limb—all requiring long, back-breaking hours of labor to clear and money to replenish and repair.

"We may be ruined," Sloan said.

"Don't say that. I have some money of my own, and Daddy will help us."

Sloan had not told Samantha the full and embarrassing extent of his debt. Confession was coming, but not now as long as there was a shred of hope he could get out of this financial mess. "*No!*" he said roughly. "That money is yours, and I will not let your father bail me out. I made my own bed and will have to lie in it. He'll have expenses enough as it is."

"You can get a loan from our bank if need be. Daddy will vouch for you at Cattleman's."

"Absolutely not." Not until the final bitter end would he disclose to Neal Gordon how he happened to get in this hole, which he'd have to do if his father-in-law stood behind him, Sloan thought.

"You can try another bank."

"Noble Rutherford would use his influence to blackball me."

Samantha let out a sound between a chortle and a scoff. "And how would that set with his daughter's altruistic reputation? If we can hold out until the well comes in, neither ranch will have to worry about money. Half the royalties will be mine, you know." It had been an agreement Neal had insisted upon when he signed the drilling contract with Waverling Tools. The lease payment was to go into the till of Las Tres Lomas, but if oil was found, the royalties would be split between him and his daughter—"It all goes into the same pot anyway," he'd said with a wink at his daughter and son-in-law.

Sloan said, "That well coming in—if it does—is a long way off, honey."

Samantha combed her fingers through his damp hair and said wistfully, "I wish a kiss could make it all go away."

"Try it anyway," Sloan said.

A weary tension compounded by the assault of wind and rain at the dining room windows eliminated all efforts to make conversation around the table during supper. To relieve the anxiety and gloom, Millie May suggested a game of bridge, but only four could play. "Oh, count me out anyway," Daniel said. "I've never been much of a card player."

"No, take my place, Lane," Sloan said. "I insist." He could not have his sister's lover wandering around his house while he was engaged at the card table.

"Insist away, but I say no thanks," Daniel said and turned to Samantha. "Would you happen to have anything in the house you'd like me to put my hand to? My assistance to your husband proved worthless today, but if you need any repairs that need to be done before I have to get to work, I'd be glad to do them. I'm pretty good with tools."

Before Samantha could speak, Billie June spoke up proudly. "You should see how Daniel maintains my apartment, Sam. There's not a hinge that squeaks, a doorknob loose, or a cupboard door off-kilter like we have here."

Ignoring Sloan's glare at Daniel, Samantha said, "Why, that's very good of you, Daniel. As a matter of fact, we have a number of things around here that could use your tool kit, don't we, girls?"

Sloan said pointedly, "I believe you asked me if *I* could use your help, Lane, and believe me, I can. If the rain lets up, we can mend fences tomorrow. How about giving me and the boys a hand?" *Dammit!* He could not have the man run around his house with hammer and saw while he was out at the ranch.

"Be happy to," Daniel said, smiling equably. "Soon's I get to your wife's list."

Chapter Sixty-Nine

Lenora, leave the room, please, and close the door—tight," Trevor ordered, his jaw barely moving. "Benjy, ride over to Todd Baker's house and tell him that he and Nathan will not be catching the train to Fort Worth tomorrow. Preliminaries for the drilling site at Las Tres Lomas have been postponed."

"Should I tell him why, boss?" The coachman's voice, scratchy with grief, could hardly be heard.

"Yes."

Mavis was staring at Nathan, shocked from her former trance. "What did you say, Nathan?"

Trevor had gotten to his feet, hands balled at his sides. "That's enough, Nathan. You leave the room, too. Go call the Triple S and tell Daniel what's happened. He's to stay there until I call for him."

Nathan swallowed hard, his heart pounding. It was out now. He could not put the bird back into its cage. He noticed his father's powerful fists that could send him sprawling into tomorrow—if he could land a punch. "Not until I tell Grandmother the truth she needs to hear, Dad. Zak and I will be out of here by morning, but I'm not leaving without your mother knowing the truth about her sons—both of them. It will be the only way you and she can bear Rebecca's death."

Mavis's puzzled stare swept from grandson to son. "What truth is he talking about, Trevor? What haven't you told me? What have you kept from me this time? And why is Nathan talking of leaving?"

The ridges of Trevor's cheeks burned with a white heat. "Because he broke his word."

"Broke his word?" Mavis pushed up unsteadily from her chair, dumping Scat to the floor, the cane wobbling under her hand. She teetered toward Nathan, suspicious eyes probing his face. "What truth, Nathan? Tell your grandmother."

"Nathan, I'm telling you—" Trevor threatened, but Mavis motioned with her cane for him to remain silent.

"My father didn't cause the death of his brother, Grandmother," Nathan said. "Your son Jordan committed suicide by drowning. The proof is in a letter he wrote to my father. I've read it. Rebecca witnessed her uncle's suicide. She must have. It explains the ditty she was always repeating, the same lines she heard her uncle often quote and wrote in his letter. She saw him walk down to the pier—down to the seas again—with no idea, even if she'd been capable of thinking it, that he meant to take his own life. By the time she realized he was drowning, it was too late to rescue him. Today's storm brought it all back to her, locked her in that scene, and she must have run down to the river with the intent that this time..." Nathan's voice faltered from a sudden clog of grief "...that this time she would save him."

The thin red capillaries in Mavis's eyes stood out starkly against their white background. Stiffly, she turned her attention to Trevor, standing still as a portrait subject before the window where the rain pattered with playful indifference to the drama unfolding inside.

"Is this true, Trevor?"

A muscle pulsed along Trevor's jawline. "Yes, Mother, it's true."

Mavis tapped closer, peering at her son as if to make out the shape of a shadow in the dark. "Why? Why didn't you tell me?"

"Tell you? Oh, Mother, must you ask?" Trevor's guffaw sounded dredged from the bitterest depths of his soul. "How could I not have kept it from you? The son you loved, idolized, the fulfillment of all your maternal dreams, had committed suicide. He had denied you the future you'd counted on—Jordan running the company the way you thought Dad would have wished, marrying the girl you approved of, giving you the sane and whole grandchildren your heart yearned for." Trevor paused and closed his eyes briefly as if drained of words. "Most importantly," he said, with less force when he gazed at her again, "he left you with the lasting grief of knowing that all your mother's love was not enough to save him from himself. Now you tell me. Could you have lived with that?"

Silence, save for the cheerily crackling flames, held the room in thrall. Nathan saw his grandmother attempt to speak. Her delicately lined lips formed words that did not come. Spittle formed at the corners of her mouth. Finally, she rasped, "I loved you both, only differently, Trevor, and you permitted me to believe…Dear God, why ever did you do such a thing?"

"I just told you, Mother. And as usual you didn't hear me. But you know why. I had always been a disappointment to you. I could at least leave you with an untainted memory of Jordan."

"And you…spared me the truth because…"

"Give it a guess. What other reason could there be but one?"

"I want to hear it from you."

"Very well, then. Because I love you."

"Not because it's what your father would have wanted?"

"My father would never have allowed you to suspect for a second that I was responsible for my brother's death."

Mavis weaved as if struck, and Nathan moved to catch her if she toppled, but with trembling effort, she held herself steady with the cane. When she spoke, her voice sounded like dry wheat rustled by the wind. "And you thought living with that suspicion would be easier for me to bear than the suicide of your brother? You couldn't have been more wrong, son. Good Lord, no." Tears filled her eyes. "What paltry knowledge you have of me and I of you. How little we know of the love we have for each other."

Trevor's rigid countenance softened, and there was the movement of a hard knot pass down his throat. "You suppose it's too late for us to learn?"

"Never for a mother, no matter how old she is, nor the need for forgiveness, no matter how long overdue the realization."

Trevor stepped toward his mother, arms held out, and Nathan said, "Come, Zak."

"Where do you think you're going?" Trevor asked from the doorway of Nathan's room. The police had come and gone and taken everybody's statements. Night had fallen. Mavis was resting. Funeral arrangements could be left for tomorrow.

"I'm heading out to California first thing in the morning," Nathan said, folding his shirts. "I believe the worst of the storm is over." He hoped his father would not make the parting hard. Their hearts were all heavy enough. "I've always wanted to take a look at the place," he added.

"What about Charlotte?"

Nathan looked up in surprise. "What about her? I hardly know her."

Trevor handed him an envelope, somewhat damp. "She sent this by way of the Weatherspoons' butler. The poor man almost drowned delivering it, but that would have been better for him than if he hadn't."

Nathan chuckled dryly and opened the envelope bearing his name in fine script. *Mr. Nathan Holloway.*

My dear Nathan,

I have learned of your sister's death, and I yearn to be with you at this tragic time to be of what comfort you would allow on the basis of our limited friendship.

Selfishly, I feel you would be a comfort to me. I knew Rebecca only slightly, but I feel I could no more forget her than I could not recall the fragrance of roses. May I await your call?

Sincerely,
Your devoted friend, Charlotte

Trevor's eyebrow was hitched when Nathan finished reading the note. "Well?"

"Well," Nathan repeated, feeling tears rush to his eyes on a surge of gratitude. He tucked the note inside his shirt pocket.

"Nathan, you're not going anywhere. Put those things back where they belong."

Nathan looked at Trevor questioningly. "I'm not fired?"

"As my son or my landman? Well, a father can't very well fire his own son from being his flesh and blood, now can he, and you've given me no reason to fire you as my landman."

Nathan continued packing. He would leave his suits and dress shoes behind. They'd make his duffel too heavy for the road. "But I did as your son. I gave you my word, and I broke it."

"You did what you thought was right, and as things have turned out, you were right and I was wrong. A man can't hold to a promise that makes it wrong to keep."

"You sound like Leon."

"He's a good man to emulate. I'll have to do more of it." Trevor came around to the side of the bed where Nathan continued packing his duffel and curbed his hand. His eyes were as red-shot as Nathan's own. "Don't go, Nathan," he pleaded. "I could not bear to lose my son when I've already lost my two..." His voice broke. Trevor let go his hold and shook a handkerchief from his coat pocket.

Nathan said, "Two what?"

Trevor blew his nose. "A misnomer. Forget I said that. I spoke from the memory of losing another child I thought of as mine. Her loss was a long time ago, before Rebecca. She was the daughter of a friend."

"I'm sorry," Nathan said. For a moment he experienced a jolt of déjà vu. *Forget I said that.* The exact words he'd heard from Leon in the barn the day his world fell apart, the time his stepfather had declared he wasn't about to keep another secret from him. When Nathan had asked what secret, Leon had said, *Ah, forget I said that. It don't pertain to you, so don't pester me about it.*

They had not returned to that exchange, but Nathan recalled how Leon's eyes had shifted and his face closed, a sure giveaway more was to the story than he let on. Nathan had that same sense of evasion now.

"You've no cause to leave, Nathan," Trevor said. "No father could be prouder of his son than I was of you today. You have no idea what you did for your grandmother and me."

Actually, he did, Nathan thought, but it was a reconciliation that he himself would probably never know. "I'd be much obliged to stay," he said, forcing his voice to remain steady. "It would have been awfully hard for Zak and me to leave another home."

"Harder on us if you'd left." Trevor put his arm around Nathan's shoulders to lead him from the room. "Leave those things for Lenora to put away, and let's go see if we can entice your grandmother to eat a bite of supper. Also," he said, "I'd be grateful if you telephoned the Triple S to get word to Neal Gordon that drilling will be delayed."

It was Samantha who answered the telephone when Nathan called and asked to speak to Daniel. Oddly, for no reason she could name, the landman had been on her mind on and off since early afternoon, lighting unexpectedly like a butterfly as she helped Billie June unpack, cut the bread for supper, counted her points at the card table. "I hope you all are not drowning there in Dallas," she said. "We're on the verge of it here." From the pause, Samantha sensed she'd said something inappropriate. "Nathan? Is everything all right?"

"No, it isn't," Nathan said after another short lull. "It's...Rebecca...She drowned this afternoon."

A minute of silence went by while the telephone line hummed with static and perhaps the suspended breaths of those listening on the party line. "Samantha?" Nathan said. "Are you there? I know this comes as a shock."

Samantha said, "I'm...here, Nathan." *I'll tell you how the sun rose / A ribbon at a time...* "How?" she asked.

"She...wandered too far from us when we weren't looking and...drowned in the Trinity River behind my grandmother's house. I've called to leave word for your father that drilling plans have been suspended for a while. Nothing can be done until the ground dries enough to lay pipe and set up tents and the rig platform. This rain is the aftermath of a hurricane that struck Galveston yesterday, and Daniel is to stay with you until he hears from us, probably not until after the funeral later in the week."

Samantha heard the instructions, recited mechanically as if Nathan were reading them from a list, through a fog of stunned disbelief. "Nathan," she said, "is there anything I can do for you and your family?"

"Just...remember her."

"I will remember her in every line of poetry I read from now on."

"Thank you. She would like that."

Samantha hung up the receiver quietly and sat a while at the table below the wall telephone. She hardly knew Nathan Holloway and had met his little sister only once, yet she felt as shattered as if she'd known them all her life. She sat so long that Sloan came in search of her and found her staring listlessly, tears flooding her eyes, running silently down her face. With a grunt of dismay, he drew her up into his arms. "Sam, honey, what's happened? Who was that on the phone?"

"Nathan Holloway. His little sister drowned today."

Chapter Seventy

Samantha finished writing a note of condolence to Nathan Holloway and his family and withdrew her address book from a desk drawer. The book did not contain the address of his residence, but she'd recorded the mailing information of Waverling Tools. The note was so little to offer at a time like this, but at least it satisfied her need to do *something* to express her sympathy. She would have liked to attend Rebecca's funeral, but unlike Galveston, where the skies cleared on Sunday morning as the hurricane's forces pressed northward, the rain had continued on and off. The roads were still muddy and unsafe for travel, and Samantha had no details of the time or place where Rebecca would be laid to rest. She didn't even know when the weather would be dry enough to allow her to mail her letter.

Melancholia pressed around her, smothering as a blanket, gray as this fourth day of dwindling rain, with no good news on the horizon to relieve her depression. Over the telephone, the lines miraculously having survived the storm, her mother had read to her the *Fort Worth Gazette*'s articles about the horrific death toll, property destruction, and reprehensible behavior of looters in Galveston. Friends' relatives and friends had been lost, their homes destroyed, the hotel where Samantha and Sloan had honeymooned washed away. Anne Rutherford had spearheaded a disaster relief campaign in which Estelle had participated, and volunteers had sent a train car loaded with collected food, clothing, blankets, and medicines to the devastated city.

The losses of the Triple S were as dire as expected, and the ranch hands were working round the clock to salvage and repair what could be saved. Las Tres Lomas had suffered higher losses. The Triple S was on a greater elevation, and in times of floods, water flowed downhill rather than stood stationary until it soaked into the ground. Sloan had aged five years in less than a week's period. His Thoroughbred had broken a leg and had to be put down, and Saved was missing.

One weak light shone through the darkness. Sloan's animosity toward Daniel had dissipated somewhat, at least temporarily, owing to the shoulder that Daniel had willingly put to the wheel in assisting him and the ranch hands in the brutal and endless hours of cleanup and restoration. He had put his smithy, carpenter, and ironmonger's skills to work, and within a few days had repaired several faulty pulleys necessary to haul bales of hay into the barn loft, hewn fence posts, and reconstructed two lean-tos over feeding bins. He'd addressed a number of items on Samantha's household list and adjusted the hinges on the oven door, hammered out a collar for a leaky pipe in the kitchen, and built a new shelf for the pantry.

"Not a lazy bone in his body, I'll give him that," Sloan had said.

Daniel was not bad company at the end of the day, either, though Sloan would not go so far as to admit it. A couple of nights the five of them simply sat around the fire in the great room, the women mending or knitting, the men, their legs stretched out before them, too tired from the day's work to concentrate on a card game. Of all of them, Daniel was the better read and more informed on current affairs, but he did not trip out his knowledge like many men with less education and refinement would have in the company of those supposedly having more of both. It was from Daniel they learned that two brothers from North Carolina had designed a man-carrying glider they planned to test soon to prove their theory that man could fly and control an air craft that defied gravity.

"I'm convinced they'll do it," Daniel said. "Maybe not this go-round, but in time I'm positive we'll see flying machines manned by men."

Samantha had held her breath that Sloan would ridicule the idea as absurd, but he'd leaned forward interestedly. "When is this test supposed to take place?"

"Sometime in October at a place in North Carolina called Kitty Hawk. The Wright brothers—Orville and Wilbur—have been experimenting with their idea of an airship for years."

"We'll have to keep a lookout for news of it," Sloan said. "Wouldn't that be something—a manned flying machine. What gave those brothers the idea for their glider?"

Daniel launched into the history of the brothers' attempts to put a craft into the air by observing buzzards in flight, then designing kites to simulate birds' wing movements—gliding, soaring, banking, flapping—in relation to air currents that enabled them to stay airborne. It was called wing warping, Daniel said. Samantha could not follow Daniel's aeronautical explanation for the distraction of worries over the fate of the ranch, but she and Billie June, pleased that their men were getting along, winked at each other over their needlework.

Samantha turned to the page where she'd listed Trevor Waverling's company address. It was the last to be recorded. Above it was the imprint of Bridget Mahoney's name and address in San Francisco, the information still vaguely discernible because of the failure of her India gum "plug" to erase it completely. She had forgotten that she'd written down the address, then tried to rub it out after throwing away Eleanor Brewster's letter. Last April fourteenth seemed so long ago in light of all that had happened since. She heard the weary boot tread of Sloan coming up the stairs, then his tired sigh as he entered the bedroom and bent down to kiss her neck. "Nice to touch something clean and fresh," he said. He had refused to let her participate in the field cleanup. "Men's work," he said, and Samantha had not over-ridden him. Her job, along with Sloan's sisters, had been the daily and constant bottle-feeding of motherless calves. Consuela and the domestic staff had been allowed to stay with their families during the rain, and the household work had fallen to the women. Samantha reached up and drew Sloan's head down to press her cheek to his. He smelled of mud and rain.

"Who are you writing?" he asked.

Samantha told him, and he said, "A sad business, but I've got some good news for a change."

"Finally. Let's hear it."

Sloan unbuttoned his shirt. "I talked to Wayne today. Neal's boys found Saved. Guess where?"

"No idea," Samantha said with a thrill of relief. She had imagined the worst.

"First crack of thunder, the boy must have hightailed it back to the ranch and got himself a nice little berth in one of the hay barns. They found him sound and dry. Had all the feed he could eat."

Samantha laughed. "Sounds like him, the big spoiled baby. Did you ask Wayne how Daddy is getting along?"

"He's worried like everybody else. Their damages are far worse than at first thought, honey. Neal is really counting on that well coming in."

The tone of Sloan's voice told Samantha to prepare for even more dire news than their own when she would see her father the next day, her first opportunity to visit him since the storm. The distance had been too wet and muddy for safety, and she'd been needed at the Triple S. At least there was money in the bank to cover the ranch's losses, but they would wipe out the surplus and put Las Tres Lomas back on the teetering line between the red and the black, a position her father loathed.

Out of his soiled clothes, Sloan tugged the long plait of her hair trailing down her back. "I'm hitting the tub. Feel free to come scrub my back if the spirit moves you."

Samantha said something about flying pigs and finished addressing the envelope to Nathan Holloway at Waverling Tools. Maybe tomorrow one of the boys could run it to the post office in Fort Worth. She capped the ink bottle and put pen and paper away. It was time to help her sisters-in-law prepare supper. Samantha started to close the address book, but the faint trace of Bridget Mahoney's name held her eye. Samantha thought of Rebecca and the suddenness of her death. Had there been things her family meant to say to her, do for her, but delayed, thinking there was always time for words and deeds tomorrow for one so young? Would they regret the opportunities allowed to slip away? Samantha's throat closed. The midwife was the very last connection she would ever have to learn the truth about her birth. Was the woman still alive? She would be elderly now. Did she still live in San Francisco at this address or had she moved on? Or had time run out on Bridget Mahoney? Would Samantha one day regret letting the opportunity go by to contact the midwife while there might still be time?

Spurred by a sense of urgency, she drew out pen and paper again. She could now write to the woman without fear that her reply would be intercepted by her father or mother. Bridget Mahoney's letter would be placed in the Singleton post office box, not in the Gordons' or delivered to her mother's town house. Her parents need never know of her correspondence to the woman who'd assisted in her delivery. What were the chances that her letter would reach her anyway? Or that she would respond? Quickly, before she changed her mind, Samantha uncapped the ink bottle and dipped the point of her pen into the black liquid. "Dear Mrs. Mahoney," she began.

She had finished the letter and folded it when she heard a hammering down the hall. Sloan came out of the bathroom dripping water and fastening a towel around his waist. "What in blazes is that noise?"

Licking the envelope, Samantha said carelessly, "Oh, that's just Daniel, replacing the doorjamb of the Christmas closet. Now maybe we can open it without using a crowbar."

"What?!"

Before Samantha could register his outburst, Sloan had flung open their bedroom door and stomped off down the hall in his bare feet yelling, "Lane, what the hell do you think you're doing?"

Samantha heard Daniel's calm reply. "What does it look like I'm doing?"

Samantha jumped up to defuse the situation before it got out of hand. What on earth had gotten into Sloan? She rushed out into the hall to see that Billie June, too, had come out of her room, expression bewildered. Millie May had already gone down to start the evening meal, but in the kitchen Samantha was sure she could hear her brother shouting in what sounded like the beginning of a ruckus. When Samantha reached them, the two men looked as if they were about to square off at each other.

"Who gave you permission to fix that door?" Sloan demanded.

Daniel stepped away from his task, hammer in hand. "Your wife. It's on her repair list."

Billie June put her hands on her hips, her face tight and angry.

"For goodness' sakes, Sloan," she said. "You ought to be thanking Daniel rather than dressing him down. That door has needed fixing for years, a job *you've* never taken the time to do! And speaking of dressing down, what are you doing out here in a bath towel?"

Millie May had come to the foot of the stairs. "What's going on up there?" she called.

Samantha eyed Sloan. "Yes, Sloan, what's going on?"

Sloan suddenly looked like a man knocked unconscious who'd had cold water splashed into his face. Dazedly, he shook his head. "I—I'm sorry," he said. "I...overreacted."

"I'll say you did," Billie June snapped.

"It's just that...Billie June, you know we have that angel Mother made for me one Christmas stored in there and...some other breakable things of hers. I was afraid of what the hammering might do to them. Look, I'm...sorry, Daniel." Sloan offered his hand. "Thank you...for fixing the door. It...was good of you."

"No apology necessary," Daniel said, accepting Sloan's hand. "I just fixed the jamb. I don't think the hammering would have damaged your mother's things."

"But you're finished now, right?"

"Yes, I've finished."

"That's that, then." For good measure, in demonstration, Sloan opened and closed the door. It swung easily both ways with no sticking or sound of squeaking. "Very good. Fine job. Now let's go down and have a drink before supper, shall we?"

"Fine with me, but...uh, like that?" Daniel glanced down at the towel.

Sloan peered down. "Right. Later then." With embarrassed dignity, he struck off down the hall, leaving wet footprints, and sailed without word or nod to Millie May, who'd reached the top of the stairs. She stared after him in astonishment.

"What just happened?" she asked the trio at the hall closet.

Billie June explained and Samantha said, "Tell me about this angel. I don't ever recall seeing it on your Christmas tree."

"That's because we haven't taken it out of the cupboard in years. It's made of papier-mâché and probably almost dust by now. Our mother made it for Sloan, her baby boy, the last year of her life when he was four years old. It's very special to him."

"Is there a chance I could see it before it completely disintegrates?"

"Of course," Millie May said. "We'll need to clean out this storage cabinet anyway, see what all we can keep and what must be thrown away in case..." Her voice dropped. Silence fell, the meaning of *in case* hanging heavy in the void. Millie May said, "We'll sort through things tomorrow morning after we feed the calves. No telling what's in there." She turned to Daniel. "It was awfully good of you to fix the doorjamb, Daniel. Thank you so much."

"My pleasure," Daniel said with a thoughtful glance at the storage cabinet before packing up his tools.

Chapter Seventy-One

In the great room where all had gathered after an almost silent supper, the gloom of worry, sadness, and lingering embarrassment of the scene at the Christmas closet was brightened by an unexpected ray of sunshine stealing into the room before it was swiftly extinguished by nightfall. Billie June dropped her head back against her tall chair and closed her eyes. Brown smudges darkened the flesh beneath them. Visibly, she was taking the threat of foreclosure harder than the rest of them. "Oh, thank God. I hope that sliver of sunlight means the rain is finally over," she said with a sigh of relief.

"I never thought I'd say it about rain, but I hope so, too, Billie June," Samantha said.

Daniel entered the room from the hall after taking a telephone call from Trevor Waverling. "You missed the promise of a sunny tomorrow, Daniel," Billie June said.

"That's what my boss called to tell me. The weather forecast calls for clearing rain, and I'm to get out to the drill site tomorrow and check out conditions, then report back to him. If it looks like the area will be dry enough by Monday, the crew can get started on the platform." He clasped his hands together and shook them high like a victorious boxer before a cheering crowd. "The sooner we get that rig up and running, the better."

His meaning was clear. The quicker the well started producing, the sooner the chance for all their financial worries to be over, but his attempt to inspire a little faith failed. No hope flickered on the faces of the others in the room. Slumped in his deep personal chair, crushed by an overwhelming sadness, Sloan was surprised that Daniel cared one way or the other whether the Triple S survived, but then he admitted that Daniel had surprised him in lots of ways. This chair, for instance. Out of sheer insolence, Sloan had expected the upstart to take possession of it as well as help himself without permission to his expensive cigars—to attempt to, that is—but he'd done neither. Simply to rub his nose into the physical intimacy going on between him and Billie June, Sloan had anticipated Daniel's behavior toward his sister no better than a randy cowboy taking liberties with a saloon call girl, but he'd fooled him there, too. In the presence of the household, Daniel had shown Billie June nothing but courtly respect. And Sloan had to recognize that he didn't know what the Triple S would have done without Daniel's help and expertise in these past days.

But it could all be a ruse. It could be a ploy to throw Mr. High-and-Mighty Big Britches off, get him to forget his threat to ruin him. Wearily, Sloan rubbed his forehead. The storm might have accomplished that goal for Daniel. Noble Rutherford would want his money in full, an impossible amount to pay right now. Sloan could expect no extension, no mercy. He'd struck a deal with the banker to repay the loan with interest quarterly. If the ranch's cash flow was slim one month, the next would make up for it and average out by the end of the three months, but this quarter, with the loss of so many of his market calves and the cost of feeding the ones that had survived, he would not have the money unless he let go half his workforce, the bitterest pill of all to swallow. Some of the men had worked for his father, and the measure would only forestall the inevitable. Without giving him time to regroup financially, Anne's father would call in the loan, and the Triple S would belong to the bank.

Sloan cursed himself for his haste to buy so many of his imported breeding animals at one stroke. It had shown poor judgment. The transportation costs alone had been staggering, but the time and price had seemed right. Now he was on the verge of losing the ranch that had been in his family for seventy years because of his foolhardiness to use it as collateral against a loan far less in value. His father would be holding his head in the grave. The next payment was due the first of October, but it would take a miracle to gather the money by then. Tomorrow, he must lay out the full stark truth to Samantha, then his sisters. The tragedy and shame of it sickened him to the pith of his soul. He and Samantha would have to live on Las Tres Lomas. He would be working for Neal Gordon, no matter what face his father-in-law put on their partnership. As fond as they were of each other, no ship could abide two captains, especially when one of them had sunk his own.

More immediate, though, was the necessity of getting rid of that blasted relic before the women cleaned out the Christmas closet tomorrow. If he didn't, he might lose Samantha, too. He had almost swallowed his fork when they brought up their intention at the supper table. Why had he made such a fuss over that door? Fatigue, anxiety, and lack of sleep had caused him to lose control of himself. If sly Daniel had suspected before that something was hidden behind that door that Sloan didn't want discovered, he would be sure of it now. Sloan hoped he'd bought his story of the angel, but to make sure, tonight when everybody was asleep, he'd remove the skull. Several problems faced him. Somehow he had to leave his bed without waking Samantha, take the skull from the cabinet without alerting Daniel in his room across the hall, steal down to the main floor without the stairs creaking, and where in blazes could he store the skull once he'd collected it?

Daniel Lane lay awake. It was past midnight. He wished he was in bed with Billie June, not for any reason but to keep watch over her. He missed her. He was worried about her. She was taking the likely foreclosure of the ranch harder than he would have thought. Little that she ate stayed down, and she'd become very quiet, reflective. Tonight he'd noticed the faint beginning of a wrinkle on her cheek, and rather than repulse him, he'd wished he could trace it with his finger. She was thirty-three, five years older than he, but sometimes he thought that if she'd been any younger, she'd have been too young for him. She was intelligent, sensible, and self-assured, but in some ways—innocent ways that were not his—she was still childlike. She could still find wonder in wonders, feel joy, believe, trust, love. He'd mortared over those dangers to human survival long ago, like concreting over an abandoned well for safety's sake. But Billie June, braver than he, opened herself to such foibles of the heart with full understanding of their perils, as she'd surely understood and accepted when she fell in love with him.

Daniel arranged his pillows behind his back and sat up against the headboard, listening for the strike of the clock downstairs. It would be only a matter of time before Sloan Singleton would be at the door across the hall. The skull was in there. Daniel was sure of it, the proof that would have won his wife's argument against drilling. It was almost too preposterous to think Sloan Singleton would have kept that skull—why would he?—but for whatever reason, it was a good thing he was getting rid of it. If Samantha should come across it tomorrow...Christ almighty, it represented the kind of betrayal that could end their marriage.

Daniel did not desire that for either of them. He could now plainly see that Sloan genuinely loved his wife—was insane about her. Daniel had come to know the rancher better, and—not taking into account the boy's feelings for Samantha—he didn't seem of the moral fiber to destroy evidence of her dinosaur field to ensure drilling on Las Tres Lomas. Daniel was now willing to believe that Sloan had a more vaulted reason for spiriting away the skull than the motive he'd accused him of, but would it outweigh the most obvious and less scrupulous one to Samantha? It would depend on their trust in each other, but Daniel was well experienced with the fragility of trust, and he'd have no part in breaking up a marriage meant to be. Mr. High-and-Mighty Big Britches could rest easy. Daniel Lane had no intention of exposing him to his wife.

Daniel had come around to another shocking realization as well. He didn't want Sloan Singleton's ranch. God, no! Four days ago, he arrived at the Triple S still obsessed with the aim of making it his life's mission to wrest it from Mr. High-and-Mighty Big Britches, impossible though his dream was. Nothing was impossible if you had enough hate and will to make it happen. He'd thrived on the image of taking over the ranch, wearing Sloan's spurs, riding his big stallion about the thousands of acres that were once Sloan Singleton's. In the darkness, Daniel could feel himself blush from the infantilism of the idea.

Now Daniel couldn't give a tinker's dam about getting his own back from Sloan Singleton. What a waste of time and energy, and for what? Ranching had to be in your blood to make it work, or even if it didn't work, and this past week of muscle-aching, gut-wrenching, never-ending toil had proved to him that it damn sure wasn't in his. Sloan Singleton was welcome to the Triple S with his blessing and no threat from him, not that it might belong to the rancher much longer, and the tragedy of it was tearing

Billie June up inside, the main reason—he had to admit it—his obsession had lost its fire.

A soft shuffling sound in the hall made Daniel sit up. He wouldn't have heard it if he hadn't been listening. He fastened his eyes on the narrow gap at the foot of his door, and sure enough, a shadow fell across the light cast by a hall sconce. Soundlessly, Daniel swung his legs off the bed, tiptoed to the door, and pressed his ear against it. All was quiet, but Daniel could almost feel a human presence on the other side of the wood. Sloan had stolen to the door to listen for a sound from Daniel's room. Daniel held his breath. After a few seconds the shadow moved away. Daniel resisted confirming his suspicion, for if Sloan was at the closet, the slightest sound might startle him. It might cause him to drop something—the skull, probably—that would fall to the floor and shatter, and then all hell would break loose. He figured Sloan would have hidden the fossil far back and out of reach of the girls. By Daniel's estimation, Sloan's quest would be over in less than a minute. After another three, Daniel cracked the door slightly to catch sight of the sconce light shining on Sloan's blond head as he hurried silently down the stairs carrying a wrapped bundle.

Good boy! thought Daniel. At least one concern was off his worried mind.

The next day, Friday, the skies cleared and the sun came out to shed its light upon the sodden pastures of Las Tres Lomas and the Triple S and grew hotter as the day progressed. It seemed like summer again. No clouds threatened the horizon, giving promise of a drying trend with high temperatures, not unprecedented in Central Texas. The owners and cowhands of both ranches, despite the work they knew awaited them, cheered in joy and relief. They'd anticipated cold, moist days following the departure of the rain to their northern neighbors that would delay the drying process. Daniel met his inspection of the drill site with less enthusiasm.

"Looks like the area will take part of next week to dry before we can get to work," he told his boss, and felt disheartened when he was ordered back to Dallas and his draftsman table by Monday. Further disappointment awaited when Billie June told him she'd not return with him. He was to have no say in her decision, having no ground on which to argue.

"My place is here," she told Daniel. "I have to help my brother and sister prepare to dismantle the house."

That afternoon, with Samantha, Billie June, and Daniel gathered round, Millie May carefully drew out from the decorations closet a wrapped item and removed the covering of a small papier-mâché angel. An awed silence greeted the unveiling of the exquisite western figure. A cowboy hat of Lilliputian dimensions sat rakishly on its little halo, a tiny bandanna encircled its neck, and a coiled miniature rope hung from a wing. "There were little boots, too, but they disintegrated long ago," Billie June explained, her choked voice echoing the sadness of Christmas holidays that would never be celebrated in the house again. That morning, Sloan had called his wife and sisters into his study. They'd gone in with eyes hollow but dry. They came out crying, and Daniel had felt a queer heaviness in his chest.

Chapter Seventy-Two

On Thursday, September twentieth, Nathan appeared at the thick, iron-hinged front door of Las Tres Lomas with Zak and Todd Baker beside him. They'd ridden the train to Fort Worth and rented a horse and wagon, onto which they unloaded from a railcar the equipment necessary to map out the location of the oil rig to be erected at Windy Bluff. A telephone message, received at the Triple S, had been relayed to alert Neal of their arrival, and Samantha was waiting to greet them when the men alighted.

Todd's obvious surprise made it clear that he'd expected Neal Gordon to open the door to them. In an officious tone to hide his discomfort at the strain that had come between them, he announced, "We're here to begin, Sam. We'll be heading out to Windy Bluff to set up camp."

"Not before you have a cup of coffee and one of Silbia's cinnamon rolls, I hope," she said, the invitation directed at Nathan.

"Well, I don't know that we have time," Todd said. "We're eleven days behind schedule already."

"Ah, well, delays are bound to happen when little things like a death in your employer's family and a hurricane occur, Todd," Samantha said tartly. "In that light, surely a half hour's more delay for coffee and rolls can have little consequence."

Nathan cleared his throat diplomatically and removed his hat.

"That sounds awfully tempting, Samantha. It's been a long morning. We accept with pleasure, don't we, Todd?"

"I suppose," Todd said.

"Then come on into the house," Samantha invited. "You too, Zak."

The men stamped the mud from their boots and followed her inside to the great room. "Thank you for your kind note," Nathan said to Samantha. "It meant much to my grandmother and especially to my father. He read it over and over."

"Would it be inane to ask how they are?" Samantha asked, leading them to the lounging area.

"Not at all. They're better than you'd expect," Nathan said. "The tragedy has brought them closer, and they've drawn comfort from each other."

"And you? How are you, Nathan?" Samantha asked gently.

"We miss her, Zak and I." He looked down at his dog. "That's why I brought him along. He's…lost without her and I couldn't go off and leave him."

"Certainly not," Samantha said, patting the shepherd's head. "You men have a seat while I tell Silbia you're here."

They'd had time for a full cup of coffee, and Todd had made appreciable work of the cinnamon rolls before Neal arrived, summoned by Silbia, who'd had to go to the barn to fetch him after she'd served her guests. "You were to come get me the minute they showed up, not a second less," Neal scolded his housekeeper.

"I'm sorry, *patrón*. I didn't see the harm in serving your guests first."

Well, he did, Neal thought irritably, his annoyance increased, which had begun when Samantha insisted on being on hand when the men arrived. He'd hoped to forestall needless conversation between Nathan and his daughter.

At the door to the great room, Neal paused when he saw Samantha and Nathan quietly talking, a dog lying at their feet.

Todd sat stiffly apart, excluded, his posture shouting *Let's get on with it!* Again, like buzzards returning to feast once more on long-dead carrion, guilt tore at Neal's conscience. Samantha had told him of Nathan's recent loss, and Neal had seen how deeply the little girl's death had affected her. She'd ridden over to Las Tres Lomas the morning after she'd heard the news—how glad he'd been to see her!—but almost immediately, in relating the tragedy, she'd begun to cry. "Sweetheart," he'd said, "you hardly knew the child. Why are you carrying on so?"

"I don't know...I can't account for it, but I feel so sorry for Nathan and his family, as if their loss is mine, too."

Of course she'd feel that way, Neal had thought. The little girl was her half sister, Nathan her twin. Sam and Nathan had gestated in the same womb. Once again, seeing the pair together, Neal wondered at the hand that had brought them here today. But for Dr. Tolman's letter—but for Samantha collecting the mail that day—Neal Gordon would have had no idea that the young man sitting in his house drinking coffee with his daughter was her brother or that the man who'd be drilling his oil well was her father. Daily, he would not have suffered the mouth-drying fear that Samantha would find him out and despise him for what he knew and had kept from her. What divine bliss that ignorance would have been. He made himself known.

Todd leaped up, his happy smile beaming *An ally!* Neal extended his hand to the men, warmly to Nathan, coolly to Todd. "Well, boys, are you ready to get out to Windy Bluff?"

"Yessir!" Todd said. "Can't wait."

Samantha smiled at Nathan and indicated the basket of cinnamon rolls. "I'll have Silbia package those and bring them along."

Startled, Neal said, "Bring them along?"

Samantha said, "I'm coming, too. I want to see where the platform will be laid."

"Why?"

"Because I want to make sure the boundary is set up as promised and does not encroach farther on the site where I discovered my dinosaur skull," Samantha explained. "Any objection?"

Neal said, tone innocent, "None. None at all, daughter." *Damn*, he thought.

Daniel fretted. He was mad at his boss. Rather than being sweet back to the Triple S with Nathan and Todd, he'd been ordered to accompany a load of drilling material to Beaumont in the morning to replace Spindletop's equipment lost during the hurricane. Damn it all to hell! He'd already been away from Billie June four days, having left her to return to Dallas last Sunday. He was bewildered at himself. In the past, he would have welcomed her absence from the city. He'd then be free to enjoy its more lascivious pleasures, but now he hadn't the taste for them. He missed Billie June, and the evenings spent before the fireside within the Singleton enclave. Her house gave him the only experience of family and home he'd ever known. Besides, Billie June looked unwell, and he was concerned about her. He'd telephoned every day, encouraging her to see a doctor, and she'd assured him there was nothing wrong with her but anxiety over the future of the Triple S. "I don't know what we'll do, where we'll go," she said.

The calamity of that ancestral ranch, Billie June's birthplace, passing out of family hands had begun to rub him raw. Singleton had nine more days to come up with the money, or the Triple S was gone. He and his family would be practically homeless. He and Samantha would move into the house on Las Tres Lomas—Old Man Gordon would love that!—but where would Millie May and Billie June go? What would happen to their household goods, their family treasures?

So, too sunken in spirit to go home to his empty apartment the last three nights, he'd worked late at his drafting table, putting the final touches on the blowout preventer designed to cap the flow of oil before it could shoot out the top of the derrick. The patent for it had already been granted, and he hoped it would be manufactured in time to be in use when the Windy Bluff well came in. That would please Samantha. Daniel was as convinced as Todd that it would be a gusher.

Tidying his draftsman table before he went home to pack, Daniel's glance fell on his drawings. A sudden idea struck like a hammer blow. He stared at the design of the blowout preventer, and sheer joy, like an electrical charge, surged through him. *By damn!* He believed he'd just figured a way to save the Triple S! He left his workroom and hurried back to his boss's office.

That afternoon, a box on which was printed LIBBY'S STRING BEANS was delivered to the curator of the American Museum of Natural History in New York City. There was no return address. Opening the box, the curator removed an object swaddled in cup towels and inspected it in drop-jawed surprise. He held a relic that he immediately identified as the snout and jawbone of a dinosaur head. "Where did this come from?" he demanded of the staff member who'd set it on his desk.

"I can't say, sir," he replied, "but it's a rare find, isn't it?"

In San Francisco, California, at 505 Canal Street, the postman inserted the occupant's letters in the opening of the metal mailbox and deliberately let the lid bang shut. The racket was enough to have startled the widow next door from her afternoon nap, but she was used to it. The postman smelled freshly baked cookies. He paused on the stoop before moving on down the steps, ostensibly to organize the collection of correspondence in his hand for delivery at other houses down the street. Immediately, he heard footsteps approaching from inside the house and smiled. As usual, his strategy had worked. The lady of the house opened the door.

"Good afternoon, Mr. Kilburn," she greeted him, the roll of her r's declaring her of Irish descent. "You're just in time for my chocolate cookies, Mr. Mahoney's favorite."

Bridget Mahoney always mentioned her husband's name when she fed him treats on his rounds lest he forget she was a married woman. She baked around this time every other afternoon, and the postman made a point of timing his delivery just when he thought the pan would be coming out of the oven.

"Oh, now, I don't want to be a bother," he demurred, as usual.

"Nonsense. Wait right here, and I'll fetch you a few."

"Then allow me to retrieve your mail for you," the postman said, like always. "Wouldn't want you to scrape your hand on the metal, now would we?"

When Mrs. Mahoney returned, they exchanged their offerings. "I see you have a letter from Texas, postmarked September thirteenth, seven days ago," the postman said, chewing the cookie. "Amazing it got delivered with all the destruction to the rail system from that awful hurricane."

"I don't know anyone from Texas who'd be writing to me," Bridget Mahoney mused, studying the return address.

"Nice handwriting, I'd say. Well, I'll be on my rounds," the postman said. "Thank you for the cookies. Delicious as always."

Bridget did not acknowledge the compliment. Her attention still on the return address, she lowered herself onto the porch swing of her trim little two-story house, proudly purchased and paid for with the earnings from her husband's ferry business, begun when the Mahoneys first arrived in San Francisco in 1885. The postman was stepping up to the porch of the widow's house next door when he heard Mrs. Mahoney cry, "May the merciful heavens be praised!"

Chapter Seventy-Three

It was the end of a long day. The brief reappearance of summer was over. The sun withdrew its warmth as it began to sink, leaving a threat that tomorrow it would rise on the return of a cold and blustery autumn. None who had ridden out to the drill site in the morning—Samantha, Neal, Nathan, Todd—had broken for a meal or rest. First they had unloaded the wagon of the tools and equipment to be used for the start of the drilling operation, then the Waverling contingent had set about plotting the various areas for the mud pit, latrines, and ditches to imbed pipelines to the underground spring.

Samantha had kept a wary eye on the proposed placement of the oil storage tanks and portable steam engine and boiler, the service road, and the crewmen's camp, sometimes offering her opinion of better locations.

"For holy sakes, Sam, let the men do their job!" Neal wailed.

"I'm not interfering with their jobs, Daddy. I'm seeing they abide by the contract to preserve as much of our land as possible."

Samantha had wanted to know everything about the drilling operation from boring the hole in which the rig was to be set (which she understood would first be cemented in "surface casing") to the working of each part of the machinery used to penetrate the Earth's crust for the purpose of drawing up oil. No foreign term uttered between Nathan and Todd escaped without her asking for a definition.

"What is a marmon board?"

"It's a five-foot-long board pulled by a team of draft animals to scrape dirt over a pipeline in a ditch."

"What does 'spudded in' mean?"

"The very first date the drill bit hits the ground. In other words, the day the drilling begins."

At long last, it was time to call it a day. Nathan called to Todd, "We'd better get the tents up."

"Be right there," Todd called back.

Samantha, standing nearby, heard the summons. "It's too late to pitch your tents tonight, Nathan. You and Todd can stay at the Triple S. We've got room to put you up, Zak, too."

Nathan's eye strayed to Todd, surveying the plot they'd set off with wire strung between pegs to cordon off a one-hundred-yard area for a platform that would support the derrick. Nathan had not expressed his suspicion to anyone that Todd was responsible for the theft of Samantha's prehistoric find, and he never would unless the geologist gave him further cause. Todd had remained under a cloud with his boss over doubt that the failure of Samantha's camera to arrive at the Kodak Company in New York was the fault of the U.S. Postal Service. He would be under Trevor Waverling's scrutiny for the rest of his employ. And Todd's reversal of his initial belief in the authenticity of Samantha's dinosaur skull—her betrayal for his own gain—had severed their lifelong friendship, a break that Nathan sensed the geologist deeply regretted. So, in Nathan's mind, to a degree, justice had been done without his having to put a hand in it. However, he did not have to subject Samantha to Todd's company in order to offer her hospitality to him and Zak. He opened his mouth to respond when a loud "No!" came from Neal, so startling that it caught Todd's attention.

Neal, weary to his spurs, had overheard the invitation as he was coming to break up the confab between Nathan and his daughter. Already exasperated that she had hung around the entire day when she should have been back at the Triple S so that he could return to his duties at Las Tres Lomas, he had bellowed out before he thought. "I mean—I was just coming over to invite you and Todd to bunk with me tonight, Nathan. It's been damn lonely cut off from everybody this past week, and I was sort of looking forward to the pleasure of some company. We could have a bite of supper, drink a little bourbon, play some cards."

"That's most kind of you, Mr. Gordon, but as you can see, I've got my dog with me, and, uh, well, he stays with me at night."

Neal flapped a hand. "Hell, he's welcome, too. I don't mind a dog in the house."

Samantha heard her father in disbelief. He *never* allowed dogs in the house. She'd feared he would rudely banish Zak when he found him in the great room that morning, and during contract negotiations, he'd adamantly refused to feed and house Nathan and Todd and Daniel as the supervising crew. These baffling spells of sudden mind changes were becoming a deep concern. Todd had drawn up to the conversation, his face brightening at Neal's offer of overnight room and board, and said eagerly, "I say it beats the cold ground and colder beans, Nathan."

"Well, all right then, it's settled," Neal said. "Pack up what gear you'll need and come on to the house."

Samantha said, "Daddy, we were planning on having you for supper tonight. It's been a while since the girls have seen you."

"Thanks, hon, but it would be too late to ride home in the dark. Come on, boys."

Samantha received his usual kiss on her cheek in further bewilderment. No matter how late, her father had never before appeared afraid to ride home from the Triple S in the dark.

*   *   *

The next morning, dressed in his Sunday best, his legs crossed and bowler hat resting on his knee, Daniel Lane waited in the reception area for Noble Rutherford to receive him. He had scrubbed his nails cleaner than usual (Billie June had a fetish about clean fingernails) and knew he had caught the admiration of the receptionist—herself an eyeful—trying primly not to show it. Daniel had to admit it. He was one handsome dude, a commonly held opinion among the ladies that never seemed to faze Billie June. Other plain women, courted by a younger man of his masculine appeal, would feel threatened and insecure in the presence of her lover under the eye of a beautiful woman, but not Billie June. If she were sitting beside him, she would take up a magazine and allow the woman her look without a heartbeat's flutter of apprehension. Or at least not one she'd ever show. No one in the world had more pride than Billie June, and that was why he was here.

A bell on the wall behind her pinged. "Mr. Rutherford will see you now," the receptionist announced.

Daniel followed the curve of her hips into the banker's luxurious office, overpowering in its ostentatious elegance. With obvious reluctance, Noble rose from behind a desk of gigantic proportions and offered a lackadaisical hand without bothering to button his coat. His barely civil greeting raised Daniel's ire. Noble Rutherford topped the list of the breed of man he most despised. How could he have ever thought Sloan Singleton one of his kind?

Noble sat down again and gestured that Daniel do the same. "I must say I'm puzzled, Lane. Why ask for a private audience? If you're seeking a loan, surely one of my clerks could assist you?"

"They couldn't with the loan I'm seeking, Mr. Rutherford."

"Oh? And what kind is that?"

"Not kind. Whose."

"I beg your pardon?"

"I'm not here to seek a loan, but to buy one that your bank is carrying, Mr. Rutherford. It's in your best interest to sell it to me, no pun intended."

Noble Rutherford observed Daniel in surprise. "And whose loan do you wish to buy?"

"Sloan Singleton's."

That afternoon, on a rented horse, Daniel rode out to the Triple S. He did not go to the main house, but asked one of the cowhands where he might find his boss. The dining hall, the man said.

He found the target of his former vengeance seated with the ranch cook over cups of coffee, Sloan looking drawn and worried, years older than his age. Daniel entered the dining room quietly and allowed the cook to finish his fuming before announcing his presence. Apparently the cook was still stewing about a mystery that had occurred a week ago. Somebody had stolen into the pantry during the night and confiscated a cardboard box that had held cans of string beans. "Who in the crew would feel he had to steal a box, leave the cans on the floor and make off with half my drying towels?" the cook fussed. "At first, I thought the box and towels might be for a litter of kittens or pups, but we ain't had any of those about for years now. Besides, all any of our boys would have had to do was ask."

"It's a mystery all right," Sloan agreed. He glanced over his shoulder and saw Daniel behind him. "What are you doing here? Billie June said you were headed down to the coast today."

"I had some business to attend here in Fort Worth," Daniel said, chuckling inwardly, "and it included you. May we speak privately?"

Sloan glanced at his cook, who immediately got up from the table and made himself scarce. "Have a seat, Lane. Included me? How so?"

"Well, first read this," Daniel said and handed Sloan an envelope from which he extracted a sheet of paper. As Sloan read it, his jaw slowly sagged. He looked at Daniel in disbelief. "What is this? It says my loan at the Rutherford City Bank has been paid in full."

"That's right."

"But...I don't understand. How did that happen? And what are you doing with the notification?"

"This will explain it."

Daniel withdrew a legal document from another envelope and pushed it across the table to Sloan. Sloan read it, and his eyelids momentarily sank. He shook his head and pressed his lips together in the clear and painful expression of a man who should have seen it coming but hadn't, and now it was too late. He opened his eyes to stare at Daniel and said in a voice weary with resignation, "You've paid off the loan. You now own the Triple S."

Daniel reached forward to take back the conveyance of title to personal property. "Sure looks like it."

Sloan's face had become the color of granite. "It's what you've been after all along, isn't it—to get your hands on my ranch."

"Well, yes...that was my intent at first. However"—Daniel scratched the back of his neck thoughtfully—"I changed my mind. There's something else of yours I'd rather have instead. In exchange for it, I'm willing to sign your ranch back over to you right now, free and clear, no conditions attached, and nothing need ever be said on the matter again."

"And what in the world is that?"

"Your blessing when I propose marriage to your sister Billie June."

Chapter Seventy-Four

Ｈow did you manage it?" Billie June asked, enfolded in Daniel's arms.

"I offered my boss lifetime patent rights to my blowout preventer if he would give me the money to pay off your brother's loan," Daniel answered. He chuckled. "That vengeful bastard Noble Rutherford was only too happy to oblige. He believed I was out to get Sloan Singleton even more than he was." Daniel mimicked the banker's pompous voice. " 'Lane, I'm going to deny myself the pleasure of foreclosure and give it to you. That way, it can't be said that I took possession of the Triple S out of revenge for Sloan's insult to my daughter. What the hell do I want with a ranch anyway, especially one on the verge of ruin.' "

Billie June chuckled. "You know what you forfeited, don't you?" she said, her cheek wet against Daniel's shirt front.

"I'll make it back. I've got a rotary drill design up my sleeve as well as some other ideas for revolutionary tools, and I've got enough money left to buy you a nice ring." Setting her away from him, Daniel pleaded, "Now will you go see a doctor?"

Billie June sighed and settled back into his arms. "I will, but I know what's wrong with me."

"You do? What?"

"I'm pregnant," Billie June said.

Two weeks later, October sixth, Billie June and Daniel were married in a civil ceremony conducted by a judge and longtime family friend of the Singletons in the county courthouse. The proceedings, attended only by Samantha and Millie May and Sloan, who stood as Daniel's best man, were simple, but his new brother-in-law emptied the ranch coffers to pay for an extravagant party afterward, arranged by Millie May and Samantha. It was held in the reception room of the Opera House, a monument to Fort Worth's transition from cattle town to modern city that proved an ideal venue to accommodate the rousing guest list. Grizzly and Wayne, Claude Chandler, the cowhands of the Triple S, Billie June and Millie May's activist cohorts, and Daniel's new friends at Waverling Tools, including his employer, were invited along with many who had attended Sloan and Samantha's wedding. Anne Rutherford's name was excluded, and Todd Baker declined the invitation.

On the park bench, Leon searched Randolph's letter for information hidden between the lines. The letter was dated October tenth, written seventeen days earlier but postmarked October twenty-third. It was as if, after writing the letter, Randolph had a change of mind about mailing it but held on to it until something prompted him to send it. His usual precise, upright script leaned a little, and the periods looked inexact. Some of the *i*'s had tails, as if his hand had slipped. The contents had very little to do with his school courses, grades, professors, and friends, news Millicent lived to read from letter to letter. This latest was mostly about Randolph's plea for more money.

Leon couldn't understand it. As parents of a first-year student in Columbia University, they had received a list of school expenses and their estimated cost from the school's Office of the Exchequer. In Randolph's name, Millicent had opened an account at a campus bank for the amount as well as a sum for his personal expenses to which she'd add each month. When Randolph wrote his letter asking for additional funds, October was only ten days into the month. How could he have been out of money so soon?

"I want to join a fraternity, and I have to pay the entrance fee up front," he wrote. "I've received bids from several of the top Greeks on campus without even rushing their houses, and that says a lot about what they think of me. Mother, you'd be so pleased because the members are sons of tycoons and diplomats and high political leaders and the like. A fellow can't go wrong brushing shoulders with them. Who knows what future influence they might mean to me? Right?"

Pompous little ass, Leon thought. Uneducated that his son's father was, he was ignorant of college jargon like *fraternities*, *bids*, *Greeks*, *rushing*, and *houses*, but he could figure out their meaning from the letter's context, and it all smelled fishy. Randolph had not been popular among his classmates throughout his school years in Gainesville. How could the pretentious son of a modest farmer from a little town in Texas suddenly become in demand to join a fraternity whose members were the offspring of tycoons and diplomats? With brains had to go an engaging personality, which Randolph sorely lacked.

"Oh, Leon, this is what we've hoped for our son!" Millicent raved when she read the letter. "Of course we have to send him the money!"

Leon wondered where she got the *we*. His wife might consult him about expenditures, but the final say was hers. It was her money she spoke of, and only her name on the bank checks. Unknown to her, he still maintained an account in a bank in town, to which he added from his spending money now and then.

"Millicent, you've got to watch your pennies," he advised. "The money from the sale of the farm isn't endless. What will you do if you run out?"

"We won't run out," she snapped. "By the time it's…low, Randolph will be in a position to help us."

Leon worried also about his daughter disappointing Millicent's expectations. She had entered the girls' academy in Denton and had no dearth of suitors pleasing to her mother's calculations. Lately, however, her letters had given her parents the impression she'd foresworn her interest in them to put her attention to her schoolwork.

"What's gotten into her?" Millicent asked of him. "She's never given a fig about her studies."

Leon could have given her an answer, but he didn't. He had an idea of what was up. On a recent solo trip to Denton to cart Lily some items from home, the two of them had had a chance to talk. His daughter had always been able to share with him confidences she wouldn't with her mother. Over ice cream sodas in a local drugstore, she'd told him of her admiration for the head of the history department whom Leon and Millicent had met when Lily enrolled. "So inspiring, so learned," Lily gushed. He was also unmarried, handsome, not too many years older than she, and very eligible, if a girl was inclined to seek the attentions of a member of a profession who would keep her in genteel poverty. Lily's infatuation with the man was probably shared by every other history student at the academy and was nothing more than a schoolgirl crush that would fade by the arrival of the new moon. Leon thought there was no point in worrying her mother with this latest distraction that had improved their daughter's grades.

Leon sighed. How he missed the days of his farming. For all its uncertainties, crops were a mighty lot easier to raise than children.

*   *   *

Bridget Mahoney reread her response, dated October twenty-seventh, 1900, to Samantha Gordon's letter. It had taken her over a month to decide whether to answer it. The poor girl had expressed doubt that her letter would reach her and had probably given up hope of a reply. Bridget had agonized over the issue of her moral obligation to the newborn infant she'd taken to her nipple over twenty years ago, now a grown woman. Should she let the circumstances of her birth lie undisturbed and allow Samantha Gordon's questions to go unanswered?

According to the young woman's letter, she'd landed in a bed of roses. She'd been raised by a couple who loved her with all their hearts and that she loved with hers. They had seen to her every need, and she'd wanted for nothing in their care. She was now happily married to a man she'd loved all her life. She lived in a comfortable home on her husband's ranch and enjoyed the companionship of his two sisters, whom she regarded as her kin. She was writing her letter not because she felt her life incomplete, but because she'd like to put her curiosity to rest, and Bridget Mahoney was her last link to satisfying it. Did Bridget know who were her parents and if they were still alive? Did she know if she'd been born a sibling? Could she shed light on why she had been given up for adoption? Any details Bridget could give her about her birth, Samantha would most appreciate. Bridget was not to worry that she was telling tales out of school or that her information would be detrimental to anyone concerned. She must trust Samantha on that.

But could she? Bridget wondered. What sort of applecart would she upset if she imparted the information she knew? She'd discussed it with Mr. Mahoney, who'd said, as she'd known he would, "Do what you think best, darlin'."

In the end, what she thought best was to respond truthfully to Samantha Gordon's letter and let the apples fall where they would. Bridget was rather proud of her composition.

Dear Miss Gordon,

I am in receipt of your inquiry of September 13 and send hope that you and your family were spared mishap from the Galveston hurricane. You were born March 23, 1880, of parents Leon and Millicent Holloway. They lived on a wheat farm in Gainesville, Texas. I do not know if they are still alive. You were born with a twin brother. I do not know his name or if he is still living. For some reason, your mother refused to keep both of you and ordered your father to give one twin away. Unable to choose, Mr. Holloway turned his back to the table where you babies lay and pointed over his shoulder. On whoever the finger "landed," that was the twin to be kept. His finger pointed to your brother. Your daddy then turned you over to me to take to my employer, Dr. Tolman, a fine physician in Marietta, Oklahoma Territory. Within days he had placed you with a childless couple he'd heard of in Fort Worth, Texas, the people who are now your parents. That's all I know. I have often wondered about the little girl I nursed at my breast because her mother refused to feed her, and I can't tell you how happy I am for your survival and happiness. May God bless you and your loved ones always.

Sincerely,
Bridget Mahoney

Yes, Bridget thought, a very good letter indeed. Straight and to the point and truthful. She'd refrained from passing judgment on the child's mother. Let that be for her daughter to do.

Chapter Seventy-Five

On the morning of October twenty-seventh, Daniel received a call at the Triple S from Trevor Waverling directing him to take a train to Beaumont, Texas. The Hamill brothers were spudding in their well on Spindletop that day, and Daniel was to make sure the company's equipment was working properly. "You have a feeling about this one, Mr. Waverling?" Daniel asked.

"I've got a feeling about this one," his boss replied.

"And I have a feeling about the one at Windy Bluff," Daniel said.

"Let's hope we have a double winner."

In sharing this information at the breakfast table, Samantha listened with some sorrow to the household changes the last of autumn would bring. Daniel's frequent stays at the Triple S, and consequently Billie June's, were at an end. Drilling was well underway at Windy Bluff and in the competent hands of a crusty old driller named Jarvis Putnam. The rig was up and all the machinery humming along in fine order. After his return from Beaumont, Daniel would assume his drafting duties at Waverling Tools. His boss had come up with an idea for a new sand pump he wanted Daniel to take to the drawing board.

Billie June was far enough along in her pregnancy to raise the question of whether she would be better off staying at the Triple

S rather than to be alone in Daniel's apartment while he was away for the day. The parents-to-be decided that husband and wife could not be separated, and so Billie June, too, would be leaving within the week. Millie May had qualified to study advance watercolor painting at the Houston Museum of Fine Arts and would soon be off to begin the second leg of her lifelong dream to become a working artist. Nathan Holloway and Todd Baker had long since left the scene for their new assignments.

Sensing her pensive mood, Millie May asked, "When will Sloan be back, Samantha?"

"By the first of next week," she said. "I'll know when I see a dust cloud on the horizon."

The terrain was now dry and dusty. As the vagaries of Mother Nature would have it, not a spatter of rain had touched the ground since the middle of September, when the storm blew off to wreak its destruction farther north along the Red River, where the La Paloma herd was pastured. A flu epidemic had sent all but a few of the ranch crew to the hospital in Gainesville, and Sloan had gone with Neal by horseback to round up and drive his surviving cattle across the river to be transferred by railcars to market. Neal was contemplating selling La Paloma. For some reason, he'd taken against the place and would look for prospective buyers while in the area. Billie June pressed Samantha's arm commiseratively. "We're sorry to leave you lonesome."

"Well, at least there's one streak of sunlight in this gloomy cloud," Samantha said. "Monday, the Bell system will be laying a telephone line to Las Tres Lomas. At least now I will be in touch with my father as well as my mother."

My father . . . my mother. Samantha was glad she'd said nothing to Sloan of the letter she'd written to Bridget Mahoney near the middle of September. It had not been returned to her, but it had not been answered, either. Sloan would have worried at the resurrection of her curiosity. Hadn't she all the family she needed? They were soon to be an aunt and uncle. There would be a baby in the family. Weren't they all number enough for her? By the time Sloan had pulled out with her father, she'd already accepted that the last slim path that might lead to answers about her birth had disappeared.

Samantha spent the first part of the next week helping Billie June and Millie May pack. The sisters would go by train to Dallas together on Thursday, the first day of November, before Millie May traveled on to Houston. To make a going-away party of it, they'd drive into Fort Worth a day early to be with Estelle, have lunch together the next day, then Samantha would drop her sisters-in-law off at the station on her way home. During luncheon at the Worth, Estelle begged her daughter to stay another night. "You look tired, darling. You could use a good night's sleep and your mother's loving care."

Samantha considered it, but she expected Sloan home today or tomorrow, and duty called back at the ranch. There was a calf that would take a bottle only from her, and she must pop over to Las Tres Lomas to check on how things were going there. Waving the sisters off from the depot, their handkerchiefs flapping in farewell from the train window, Samantha almost decided not to go by the post office. She *was* tired, uncommonly so, she allowed, and did not look forward to the drain of driving a horse and wagon through city traffic. At Las Tres Lomas, she would ask Silbia to check her mailbox when she made a run into town later in the day to collect her father's correspondence. He would want it on his desk and current when he arrived. But just as she made the decision to turn toward home, Samantha changed her mind. Today the Sears and Roebuck catalog would likely arrive, and she was eager to see what items were offered for Christmas and write an order while there was still time.

A half hour later, the first emotion to break through her shock was relief that she had decided to collect the mail, for in her box was a letter postmarked California and bearing the return address of Bridget Mahoney. If she'd not come to the post office today, the letter in her hand would have been intercepted by her father.

"Nathan, you have a telephone call from a relative of yours named Leon Holloway. He's calling collect," Miss Beardsley said. Her frown and emphasis on *collect* voiced her disapproval of employees expecting company money to pay for personal expenses.

Nathan felt a hitch of apprehension. Leon would never call here except for an emergency. "That's my stepfather. Put him through and deduct the charges from my paycheck," he said.

Leon began with apologies for disturbing Nathan at his place of work and for foisting the charges off on him, but Nathan cut him off. "Not to worry about that," he said. "What's the matter?"

"It's your brother Randolph. He's in trouble at Columbia."

"What sort of trouble?"

"He's…fallen into a bad habit, I'm afraid. He's…hanging out in opium dens. Hasn't been to his classes for over a month. We received a letter from his school yesterday notifying us of his absences and that he's lost his scholarship. Also, a girl he's met wrote to tell us that maybe we ought to come get him before he gets too far gone. Want me to read the letter to you? I don't want to run up your long-distance bill."

"Read it," Nathan instructed.

At the letter's conclusion, Leon said, "Your mother is frantic. I didn't know what to do but call to ask if…maybe you could…go to New York City and bring him home."

"I'm on my way soon as I make arrangements here," Nathan

said. "Do you have any information that will give me an idea where to start looking for him?"

Nathan wrote as Leon recited Randolph's dormitory address and the names of his roommate, his counselor, the girl from whom they'd received the letter, and the café where she worked. Nathan assured Leon it was enough to go on to track down his brother.

"I suspected something was wrong when he kept asking his mother for more and more money," Leon said. "She's given him all she can. She has to think of Lily. If he's become addicted to dope and has no more money to buy it, God knows what will happen to him." Nathan heard Leon's voice sag, weighed down by disappointment and sorrow. "I'm sorry we have to impose on you like this, Nathan. With Thanksgiving coming, I'm sure you had other things in mind but to go gallivanting off to the opium dens of New York City."

"It's no imposition. Tell Mother I'll have Randolph home in plenty of time to help her pluck the turkey." Not that Randolph had ever plucked a turkey in his life. That had always been big brother's job, Nathan thought, feeling a strange lack of shock at Leon's revelations as he went to inform his father of the turn of events that would require a trip to New York City.

Trevor heard him out without saying a word. When Nathan finished, he said, "What shall I tell Charlotte?"

"The truth," Nathan said. "She'll understand."

Trevor sighed. "She'll be so disappointed that you won't be taking her to the Chrysanthemum Ball, but of course you must go." He unlocked a desk drawer to withdraw a small break-top revolver with a snub barrel and handed it to Nathan. "That's easy to carry concealed," he said, "and you'll need some money."

"No sir, I can manage, but I'll take along the pistol," Nathan said, slipping it into his coat pocket.

"I insist," Trevor said, pushing a packet of bills across his desk. "Take the money for my sake and make sure you stay safe. I want to hear from you when you arrive and when you leave to return home. Promise?"

"I promise," Nathan said. "Todd and I were going to pay a visit to the Windy Bluff site tomorrow, and Daniel is down in Beaumont. Who will you send in my place?"

"Me," Trevor said. "Now you better get going. The sooner you go, the sooner you'll get back and the less time your grandmother and I and Charlotte will miss you."

Nathan acknowledged the comment with a little salute of the packet in his hand. "Tell Charlotte I'll make it up to her and thanks for the extra cash."

"What are dads for?"

Indeed, if not to love their children, Trevor thought as his office door closed, a soft sound but carrying the loud echo of the loneliness already pinching his heart. So Millicent's fair-haired son, the one she'd bypassed Nathan for, the son she'd placed all her high hopes on, had become a dope addict, had he? As Nathan's father, he could say it served her right, but as a father he hadn't the heart. For a parent, there were no more painful hurts than disappointment in a child unless it was a parent's disappointment in himself. He'd failed Rebecca. He would not fail Nathan or Samantha, but the question of how to best serve that determination kept him awake at nights. Was he failing his children in not revealing his near certainty that they were brother and sister? Nathan could go to Leon for confirmation. His stepfather would not keep the truth from him. Or was it better to keep silent about their kinship and allow their lives to play out unknown to the other? Which course was best for them? The right course was not always the wisest. Trevor gazed out his window at the Trinity River now flowing peacefully and felt a wave of resentment at its indifference to the life it had claimed. But with rivers, as with some people, there was always the implicit warning that grief could come to those who stepped too close to its banks. Would he be taking that risk tomorrow when he took Nathan's place and stepped foot into his daughter's domain?

Chapter Seventy-Six

The shock at seeing the return address had stunned the breath from her, and a man at his mailbox glanced over at her. "Are you all right, ma'am? May I assist you to a bench?"

Samantha turned to speak to him, but the weight of the Sears and Roebuck catalog and the rest of her correspondence proved too much for the strength of her suddenly weak arms and cascaded to the floor. "*Oh!*" she gasped.

"Here, let me help you," the man said, bending down to scoop up the mail. "Maybe you'd better sit down. If you don't mind my saying so, you're as white as these envelopes."

The man's face spun as he placed the restored correspondence into Samantha's arms. Several quick blinks cleared her vision. "Thank you, but I'm perfectly fine," she said.

Once outside, she realized that she was not fine and sank onto a bench rather than risk the climb to the seat of her wagon. The wind had picked up, and late-afternoon shadows were gathering. Darkness would fall before she arrived at the ranch if she did not get underway soon, and she'd promised Sloan not to be out after sundown. She craved to rip open the letter right there and then, but a bench on the post office lawn was no place to be enlightened of the truth it might contain. She would wait until she got back to the Triple S, where only the walls of the house stood witness to her reaction.

*   *   *

The walls of the empty great room at first heard no outcry and could testify to no sign of emotion from the mistress of the house. Samantha sat motionless in her chair before the fireplace, the letter open in her still hand, the only intrusion into the silence the swish of the pendulum in the stately grandfather clock. Several minutes passed before she could grasp the disclosures in Bridget Mahoney's reply. The facts rolled slowly into her brain like a fragmentation bomb and exploded in order of revelation. Millicent Holloway was her mother...Nathan Holloway was her brother, a twin...and Trevor Waverling was her father...

Samantha let out a cry.

"Señora, what is the matter?"

The gentle voice had come from Consuela, the Singletons' ancient cook. She had caught Samantha with a balled fist pressed to her mouth.

"Have you seen a ghost, señora, a *fantasma*?"

Samantha turned her fraught stare to her. She realized that she had left her chair and wandered away from fire and lamplight into the dusky shadows of the room. "What? Yes, yes, I have, Consuela."

The woman made the sign of the cross. "God protect you," she said in Spanish. "Señora, you are the color of milk." She reached for Samantha's hand, her touch light and cool against her skin. "Let me get you something. A little brandy, no?"

"Yes, that would be good," Samantha said, dazed, and allowed the small woman to lead her back to her seat.

"A little food on a tray, as well. No?"

"Yes, that, too," Samantha said to appease her, but she accepted the brandy gratefully. When Consuela had soundlessly disappeared, Samantha reread the letter. She must approach their revelations as she would a science project, as if they were under a microscope, to draw a hypothesis from the facts. Samantha saw no reason to doubt the veracity of Bridget Mahoney's statements. She would begin with the most wonderful disclosure of all: Nathan Holloway, that fine and honorable young man, was her brother...a twin, no less, and she was—the wonder of it!— a *sister*! Nathan had never given a single indication that he had knowledge of their relationship, so from their friendly but impartial dealings and the midwife's description of their separation, Samantha could deduce the Holloways had kept that information from him. The cruelty of it was astounding.

Was Trevor Waverling aware that Samantha Gordon Singleton was his daughter? Nathan had said he'd not known Trevor Waverling existed until last March when his father suddenly appeared on his birthday at the Holloway farm swearing he'd been unaware of his son's birth until a few years before. If Trevor Waverling had made himself known to his son, did it not make sense he would have revealed himself to his daughter?

Yet...

Samantha drank deeply of the brandy and tried to recall the times they'd met, every detail she could remember. She had noticed his strange interest in her at the paleontology lecture back in April, and each time since, she'd been reminded of his comment: *The color of your hair reminds me stunningly of someone I used to know.* Had he a sense that Samantha Gordon was of Millicent Holloway's blood?

Samantha had been in his presence only on three occasions beyond their first meeting. She recalled the afternoon she'd sat with Nathan in Trevor Waverling's office while waiting for the report on her camera. They'd been speaking of the coincidence of their same birth date, now fully understood, when Trevor startled them by asking questions of her adoption. Why would he be interested? The second time they'd met had been at Las Tres Lomas, where Samantha had been aware of Trevor Waverling's discreet but intense scrutiny. Her father had noticed it and seethed.

And finally, their last encounter had been at Billie June and Daniel's marriage reception, Daniel shocked but ecstatic that his employer had accepted his invitation. He had hardly been able to believe it. *I invited him, never dreaming he'd attend,* he'd said. *You'd expect Trevor Waverling to have more highfalutin engagements on his calendar than the wedding reception of an employee who hasn't been on the payroll long.*

Billie June had gazed up at him dewy-eyed, and said, *He came because he knows how important you are to the company, Daniel. I keep telling you.*

Was Trevor Waverling's interest untoward as her father suspected? Samantha had not recognized it as such. Rather, during the short occasions they'd shared company, she'd found Trevor Waverling charming but bracingly friendly, courteous but not overly attentive. Yet there had been Billie June's remark in the discussion following her and Sloan's wedding. *I do declare I thought I caught a glimpse of Daniel's boss in a back pew.* And Nathan had said that his father had read her note of condolence over and over.

Was it possible that Trevor Waverling had discovered who she was and chosen to keep quiet about it? Could Samantha's conjectures be based on mistaken impressions? But more important was the question of how she felt about the fact that Trevor Waverling was her father.

Samantha rose from her chair to warm her hands before the fire. What did it matter in the long run? If her real father knew she was his daughter and kept the information his secret, he had his reasons, and if he didn't know her identity, then what would be the point of revealing the truth to him now? She'd learned what she'd longed to know. The questions of her birth had been answered. What advantage would come from disclosing the revelations of Mrs. Mahoney's letter to anyone concerned? Samantha did not wish even to put a thought again to the reaction of her adoptive parents. She had no desire to know her real mother or her stepsiblings. Bridget Mahoney's letter clearly implied that if she had not nursed her, Millicent Holloway might have allowed her to die. Nathan, Samantha would love from afar. She would make a point of becoming an everlasting friend. He need never learn the reason for the birth date they shared in common or of the fact they'd been born of the same set of parents. He'd never hear of his friend's relationship to their half sister, whose death Samantha mourned as deeply as he, or of her legitimate claim to the same grandmother who walked the earth only thirty miles away she'd likely never meet.

Samantha slipped the letter into her skirt pocket. Its disclosures would remain her secret, even from Sloan. He would prefer she let go of what might have been. They were happy as they were. Their family unit was complete. Nothing was gained at the loss of something of equal value, Sloan would say, quoting his father, and in this instance that wisdom most assuredly applied.

Emotionally drained, Samantha sat down again and laid her head back against the ridge of the chair, and it was there that Consuela, bearing in a supper tray, found her later with tears washing down her face.

Chapter Seventy-Seven

New York City was ankle deep in snow when Nathan finally located his half brother three days after his arrival. He had weighed the information Leon had given him and decided to try his luck on his first day in the city with Randolph's girlfriend, who was employed as a waitress in a café on the fringes of the Columbia University campus. "Leticia Draper don't work here no more," he was told by her churlish employer when Nathan walked in on his squabble with a college student over an unpaid bill. When Nathan inquired if he knew where he might find her, the café owner looked at him askance and asked if he looked like a goddamn address book. Accepting that as an answer of no, Nathan left but was chased after by another waitress hurriedly pulling on the coat she'd grabbed to run after him.

"What do you want with Leticia?" she demanded, drawing her coat tight.

Nathan told her of the letter she'd sent his parents.

"So you're Randolph's brother?"

"I am," Nathan said without explaining the exact relationship. "You know Randolph?"

"Yeah. Leticia lost her job over him."

"Why?"

"The boss is an ugly bastard to work for. He caught her giving food to your brother when he couldn't pay. Leticia went home to her folks after the boss fired her. They live on a farm outside Albany, but I don't know where it's located." The girl began to hop on one foot then the other, hugging herself against the cold.

Nathan held out his gloved hand. "I'm mighty grateful to you, miss. You'd better go inside before you get too cold and your boss fires you."

She gave him a weak smile and shook his hand. "You're nicer than your brother. Frankly, no offense, but I don't know what Leticia sees in him."

"I'll ask," Nathan said, offering a grin.

It was too late to take a train to Albany, and he might avoid the trip altogether if Randolph's roommate could help him, so to make the most of the rest of his first full day in New York City, Nathan had hailed a horse-drawn cab to drive him ten blocks to Morningside Heights, an area in upper Manhattan where Columbia University was located. Dropped off at John Jay dormitory, Nathan felt immediately drenched in the august atmosphere of the place. He looked around at the majestic, ivy-draped campus, now shrouded in snow and mist, the book-laden students rushing to class and the professors in their flapping black robes, and he wondered how his brother could have blown it. This was Randolph's element for sure. He had the brass and intelligence to fit in here despite his shame of having no pedigree to boast of. Or at least that was what his family had thought.

"Randolph? Haven't seen him in a week," his roommate informed him hurriedly, his distracted air suggesting he didn't care. It was Friday, and Nathan had interrupted him as he was packing to leave for the weekend, probably to catch one of the vehicles pulled up outside to take students to the train station.

"I understand he's frequenting opium dens. You have an idea which one?"

The roommate, a slim young man with a lofty air—the perfect bookend for Randolph, Nathan judged—gave him the same look as the owner of the café. *Do I, the son of so-and-so, look like I know the location of opium dens?* The roommate hoisted his suitcase. "Sorry, no. Now if you'll excuse me, I've a train to catch to my parents' place in Connecticut."

Nathan stepped aside. "Sure," he said.

The next day, after an abnormally long train ride because of numerous stops and an avalanche of snow that had to be cleared from the track, Nathan made it to Albany, New York, then began the trudge over muddy streets to inquire from shop owners if they knew the whereabouts of the Draper farm. Eventually, in late afternoon, Nathan's cab drew up before a run-down farmhouse with a sagging roof and snow-blown front porch piled with wood and squalid castoffs from the house. An assortment of dogs lying about like rugs stirred themselves to bark at Nathan's approach but were too gripped by the cold to threaten him further. To his relief, Leticia answered his knock, every detail about her unsurprising given her living conditions and the illiterate letter Leon had read to him over the telephone. She was splinter thin, bedraggled, and plain as a broom, clearly enraptured with Randolph, who, it was painfully obvious to Nathan, had taken her for a ride. She told him to look on Mott and Pell Streets in Chinatown and said shyly as he bade her good-bye to return to the cab, "Tell Randy I love him."

He would, Nathan assured her, not that it would mean a cold bean to his brother.

Late the next afternoon, Nathan found him in the third hot, dank, and foul-smelling den he plowed through, a basement in a Chinese-run laundry tightly sealed to prevent the escape of telltale fumes and to keep drafts away from the lamps that vaporized the opium drug. He'd expected the distilled poppy extract to have a sickly sweet smell like incense, but in every gloomy "joint," so he'd learned the grubby holes were called, he was assailed by a thick brown smoke like burning tar. He discovered Randolph sleeping off the effects of his binge among other opium smokers lying about in grimy beds attached to the walls like bunks in a slave ship. Beside them were tables spread with the paraphernalia of the opium smoker. At the sound of Nathan's voice, Randolph opened his drug-glazed eyes.

"Oh, God," he moaned.

"No, just your brother, come to take you home," Nathan said.

Leon said, "Millicent, I'm going to advertise for a job that calls for overalls. It's the only kind of work I know."

"I will die from embarrassment if you do," Millicent said.

"Better than starvation."

Millicent wrung her hands. "What will our friends think?"

"What will *your* friends think? Mine will think I've finally gone and done the sensible thing. Listen to reason, Millicent. I'm guessing you're nearly broke. To live in the way we do, to pay for Lily's schooling and Randolph's treatment, I've got to go to work."

"Nathan said he'd pay for Randolph's treatment."

Leon stared at his wife. Sometimes he couldn't understand why he still loved and needed her, but he felt those feelings growing thin. "Listen to yourself," he said in disgust. "You say that as if it's no consequence to Nathan, the son you ignored and cast aside, to pay to fix up the son you'd counted on to 'be in a position to help us.' Isn't that what you said? Well"—Leon rejected that fallacy with a backward wave of his hand—"some *position* he's in!"

Millicent clamped her hands over her ears. "Don't say that. He'll be a new person when he gets out of that place in Dallas."

"So say you," Leon said, his lips twisting scornfully, "but *I* say

I'm not countin' on Randolph for anything. I'm puttin' that ad in the paper, and *we're* going to pay to jack our son into shape, startin' by sellin' that silly-looking surrey of yours."

His JOB WANTED ad was answered by letter five days into the New Year, 1901. On his park bench, Leon reread it in disbelief, then with tears in his eyes. He had been reading about the new agribusiness conglomerates springing up in the East and wasn't sure he approved of them, but they were the answer to many a down-on-his-luck farmer willing to sell his place to a group of businessmen seeking to buy up vast croplands in order to control farm prices, food processing, and seed production. Leon had received an offer for employment from just such a corporation. It seemed that it had bought a once-upon-a-time wheat farm five miles from Gainesville from the Standard Oil Company. The land had been drilled unsuccessfully for petroleum, and the corporation wished to restore it to wheat production. Was Leon interested in overseeing its revival and serving as land manager of the property? A house was on the premises for his use. The letter included a contact name and address by which to send a telegram if he was interested.

Leon pocketed the letter lest the prankish wind snatch it from his cold fingers before he could reach the Western Union office on Main. Afterward, Leon stopped in for a celebratory soda at the drugstore next door, lips smiling around the straw. Then he walked to the house he occupied with his wife, mindless of the blowing snow that blinded his way. Sometimes, he thought, a man couldn't do better than to wind up where he started.

Millicent was peeling potatoes at the kitchen counter when he blew in the back door. They'd had to let their cook go along with the maid. "You look happy," she said, the observation sounding resentful. "What has you smiling?"

"I've got a job," he said.

Her face hardened. "Oh. Doing what?"

"Managin' a wheat farm."

"You'd stoop to growing someone else's wheat?"

"Haven't I always?"

Millicent fell silent, peeling the potatoes with vigorous strokes. "Where then?"

"Back at our old farm. Standard Oil came up empty. I'm goin' home."

Chapter Seventy-Eight

As the New Year got underway, they were all worried about Samantha—Sloan, his sisters and Daniel, Neal and Estelle, the household staffs and crews of both ranches. Since the first of November, they had noticed a change in her. She seemed distracted, pensive, sad. "Sam, honey, we're going to be all right. The ranch has ridden out the worst," Sloan said. "Let's be thankful for no blackleg and that we got to the pneumonic cows in time to quarantine them from the rest of the herd." He went on to point out several other silver linings. It looked like, come spring, they were going to have a better-than-expected crop of calves. The floods had revived sections of grassland formerly too dry for grazing. The heir to a ranch in Bexar County—a lawyer who had no interest in raising cattle—was selling off his father's property and had agreed to sell the Triple S its silos of hay for a fair price. They would have enough feed to last the winter.

Samantha forced herself to smile and to carry on as always, but she would be caught in still moments of absorbed thought and sometimes with tears in her eyes. She had lost weight and become forgetful. She misplaced things and had only a listless interest in reading, card games, needlework, diversions that had once brought her quiet pleasure at the end of the day before the fire with her husband. Sometimes she would lift her eyes and find Sloan watching her over his newspaper, worry deep in his gaze. When he reached for her in bed, she was unresponsive. "Honey, have I done something wrong?" he'd ask. No, never, she assured him. It wasn't him; it was her. She was feeling depressed these days. She couldn't tell him why. Be patient with her a little longer. She loved him so. He had no idea how much she loved him. Maybe she should go to a doctor, he suggested. Give it a little while longer, Samantha said, and she'd make an appointment with Dr. Madigan if her mood did not improve.

Sloan was her husband. They were one. There should be no closed doors between them, and at times, Samantha was almost swayed to bare her secrets to him, but what would that achieve? There was no solution to her distress that lay low during the day but ballooned in the small hours of the night. She thought that by now, the first week of January, she would have put the revelations of Bridget Mahoney's letter behind her. She had no curiosity or interest in the unconscionable woman who had given her birth and would have allowed her to die—why should she?—but then she'd wonder what kind of woman would refuse to nurse her baby, would willingly give her up for others to raise, and why? If Leon Holloway's finger had pointed another way, Nathan would have been the twin placed with the Gordons. Did her mother know her whereabouts, the names of the people who had taken her in? Did she care? What was the story between her and Trevor Waverling?

Samantha had thought of him constantly. She was now convinced that he knew she was his daughter. Why would he have come to her wedding if not to see his flesh and blood get married? Samantha had made inquiries and heard from guests that indeed there had been a handsome older man, a stranger with bluish-green eyes, seated among them in the back pew of the church. Samantha had been moved to tears at his imagined retreat before she spotted him during the recessional, her real father living like a shadow at the fringe of her life. She pictured him and Nathan and his grandmother mourning the loss of Rebecca in their house in Dallas while she, like a waif staring in at the family scene through a window from outside, remained in the cold.

Uninformed that a telephone had been installed at Las Tres Lomas, Trevor Waverling had called in November to leave a message for Neal Gordon that he would be paying a visit to Windy Bluff in lieu of his landman the next day. Samantha had taken the call, and for a concerned, daughterly moment, she had considered inviting him to stop by for coffee to warm him before starting the cold trek to the drill site and before going back to Fort Worth to catch the train, but her resolve to let the whole matter go checked the offer. How did a daughter pretend not to know that the man come to take coffee with her was not her father? If *he* knew, how did he fake his ignorance of her identity?

She'd asked Nathan to tell her about his grandmother, and he'd been happy to do so with no overt indication he suspected the reason for her interest. He spoke of Mavis Waverling in terms he never mentioned his mother, whose name never passed his lips at all and of whom she never inquired. He adored the woman in whose home he lived with his father and dog and cat, and Samantha had suppressed a surge of longing that had made her think again of the little waif with her nose pressed against the window looking in.

One day when idly listening to Nathan discuss grain varieties with Sloan, Samantha had learned some shocking information. The Barrows farm was really the Holloway homestead. Millicent Holloway was the owner of the farm near Gainesville whose FOR SALE advertisement Samantha had answered. Her mother was the haughty woman covered from hat to skirt hem who had popped in and out of the train depot coffee shop while she and Mildred waited for the man representing the Barrows farm to show up. She was the wife of the man at the fence post who declared himself a hired hand—Leon Holloway. Samantha had felt the blood leave her head. She had come within ten feet of her birth mother and not known it.

So as time passed, the need to know everything about her birth and adoption would not go away. The strange yearning persisted. Samantha could not shake it from every distraction she put her mind to. Why had her mother not wanted her? Did her rejection of her daughter have something to do with Trevor Waverling? Was it morally wrong of Samantha to keep her identity secret from a brother, father, and grandmother who lived within miles of her home?

Finally, she decided she must have answers. She had to know. She could not live without knowing. She had to find peace.

Samantha said that evening, January sixth, "Sloan, how would you feel about my taking a trip alone to Gainesville tomorrow?"

Sloan peered at her over the top of his *Fort Worth Gazette*. "Say what?"

"You heard me. It's important that I meet someone there."

Sloan slowly lowered the newspaper. "Who?" he said.

"My mother."

"Where's Sam off to?" Neal asked. "One of the oil field crew saw her board a train when he went by the station to pick up some equipment from Waverling Tools."

Sloan finished unbuckling the cinch straps of his saddle and turned away from Neal to lift it high over his horse's head so that his father-in-law could not read his face. Avoiding a direct answer was not in his nature and easily detectable when he tried it. "Gone on a little trip," he said, throwing the saddle over a beam constructed the length of the tack room for that purpose.

"She never said anything about a trip to her mother or me. Has she gone to Dallas or Houston to see one of the girls?"

"Nope," Sloan said. He took a towel from a shelf and began to dry and clean his horse's sweaty back. He was not a ranch owner who turned his horse over to someone else to groom and feed after a hard day's work.

"Dammit, Sloan, don't make me beg. Where to?"

Sloan paused with a hand on his horse's withers. "Neal, not to be rude, but that's none of your business."

Neal said anxiously, "Has she gone to see a doctor?"

"No. I can assure you of that. She wanted to get away for a while. Now that's all I can say." Sloan continued with the grooming, running the towel around the horse's mouth and over the poll.

"All you know or won't say?" Neal persisted.

"Now don't fence me in, Neal. I'm telling you like it is."

"Samantha? Wanted to get away for a while?" Neal's tone was incredulous. "That's not like her. Are you two…having trouble? I'm only butting in because her mother and I are worried about her, Sloan. She's not been herself lately. You've seen it. We just want to make sure she's not sick, but if…" He shrugged and shoved his hands into his pockets. "Well, every man and his wife have a little marital spat now and then."

Sloan tossed the towel into a bin and took a brush to the horse's flanks. "I can assure you that's not the case either, Neal. Sam and I have never been better."

Angrily, Neal grabbed the brush from Sloan's hand. "Then for God's sake, boy, I'm her father. Tell me what's wrong with her and where she's gone and for how long—*please*!"

Quietly, Sloan said, "Neal, you're closer to me than needles on a cactus, but give me back that brush. I won't tell you because I promised your daughter I wouldn't."

Slowly, embarrassment reddening his cheeks, Neal handed

back the brush. "I'm sorry, son. I forgot myself. But...you can understand how I feel, can't you?"

"Yes, Neal, I can. Go home now and be patient. She'll be back soon and all will be well. I'm sure of it."

Neal nodded, doubt in his eyes, and slumped out, hands in his jacket pockets. Sloan watched him go, not sure of the truth of the comfort he'd offered. Neal may have noticed that he did not extend an invitation to stay for a round of bourbon and a meal since they were without their womenfolk, but he couldn't face being in Neal's company tonight. His heart had jumped when his father-in-law had walked into the tack barn, questions burning in his gaze. Sloan was still not over the shock of Bridget Mahoney's letter giving the facts of Samantha's birth. He'd held his wife trembling in his arms, hate for the woman who'd brought her into the world scorching a hole in his belly. He couldn't understand why Samantha wanted to confront her. Let the bitch fry in hell without ever knowing what a great daughter she'd birthed, he'd thought, but once Samantha had explained that she thought her mother's rejection of her and Nathan had to do with Trevor Waverling, he understood.

"I have to know, Sloan. Trevor is here among us. He knows and cares about me. What did he do to make my mother give me away and treat Nathan like a stepchild?"

"And the answer will depend on whether you acknowledge him as your father? What about Neal? You know how he feels about losing you to your natural parents, especially to Trevor. He's already got his back up against that man."

"He's not going to lose me. I will have to make him understand that. My parents are Neal and Estelle Gordon. They are the parents I love and that I will call Mother and Daddy for the rest of my life. But I'll cross that creek when I come to it. Now I have to learn the full story of my birth."

He'd begged to go with her. He was afraid for her to go alone because of what she might find. She'd refused adamantly, and there was no bucking Samantha once her mind was made up. She had to do this by herself, she said, and she would be fine. Besides, he couldn't go off and leave the ranch. To hell with the ranch, he'd argued. She was all that mattered. She was his life. She'd caressed his cheek. "I know," she'd said. "That's why I'll come back to you safely." She'd left this morning and would return by the late train. It was January seventh. He had twelve more hours to suffer before she was in his arms again.

Chapter Seventy-Nine

Neal did not ride back to Las Tres Lomas to his fire and nightly bourbon and supper. He set off for the train station in Fort Worth. The T&P people kept a record of tickets sold and destinations of passengers who had boarded that day. He would spend the night with Estelle and take her back to the ranch with him tomorrow. He wanted her with him to await their daughter's return if what he suspected and long feared had come to pass. He had seen a look in Sloan's eyes when he'd yelled *For God's sake, boy, I'm her father!* But the station record would confirm or deny his fears.

"Yes, Mr. Gordon, it looks like we sold three tickets to Gainesville today."

"Have you been at the window all day?"

"Just came on, but Marvin was here. You need to speak with him? He hasn't left yet."

Neal let out a breath of relief. "Yes, please."

Marvin said, "Yes, Mr. Gordon, your daughter boarded the early morning train for Gainesville," the ticket seller told him. "Going to visit relatives there, is she?"

Neal went weak in his legs. "You could say that," he said.

White-faced, Millicent handed the telegram to Leon, then fell heavily into the nearest chair in the foyer. "I don't believe it. I simply can't believe it. How could she do this to us?"

Leon read the telegram: MOTHER/DADDY. STOP. JUST MARRIED. STOP. NOW MRS. JOSEPH HAYMAKER. STOP. HOME SOON. STOP. LOVE, LILY. STOP.

"Who is Joseph Haymaker?" Millicent asked, staring at Leon with the empty sight of a blind person aware of an intruder in the room.

"Her history teacher at the academy," Leon said. With great effort, he quelled an odd compulsion to laugh. "We met him at the parents' reception when we enrolled Lily. Seemed like a nice fellow."

Millicent focused her blank gaze upon him. "A history teacher...at the academy. Oh, Leon—" She sprang up, clutching the telegram to her chest as if coaxing air into her lungs. "My daughter married a *history teacher*?"

"Don't shriek, Millicent," Leon said. "It's bad for your vocal cords."

Millicent crushed the telegram and shook it in Leon's face. "How *dare* she go against our hopes and dreams for her happiness? How *could* she go against all we've sacrificed to guarantee her a good future?"

"Uh, well, apparently Lily had her own ideas about her happiness and future," Leon said, deciding not to correct the *our* and *we*. "Let's be happy for her, Millicent."

Rage flared, oddly heightening his wife's beauty. "Never, never, *never*!" she screamed. "How can I be happy for her? That girl has betrayed me—us! Both our children have betrayed us!" She dropped back into the chair, beginning to cry. She jerked a square of lace-edged lawn from the pocket of her dress and stabbed it to her eyes. "Look at all the work we put into raising them so that they could have what we never did. You worked hard to make the farm pay, and..." Millicent's voice faded on a wave of incredulity "...our daughter went and married a history teacher who'll never have a penny to his name." She lowered her face into the inadequate receptacle of her heartbreak and began to cry.

Sadly, Leon looked down at the bowed head of his wife, sobbing brokenly into her patch of handkerchief. Poor Millicent. She'd bet on the wrong horses in her stable and now the race was over, and she was left with nothing but the stubs of her losing tickets. Now was not the time to remind her that there were other races their son and daughter might yet win, just not to the fanfare she'd counted on.

He reached down and pulled her up into his arms. "Ah, Millie girl," he said, "now will you sell this house and come live with me back at the farm?"

"Might as well," she sniffed into his shoulder. "I have no use for the place anymore."

Samantha reached Gainesville midday. She stopped first in the Harvey House Hotel where she and Mildred had stayed in April of last year, a lifetime ago. The clerk recognized her. "Miss Gordon, isn't it?" he said.

Surprised, Samantha smiled. "You remember me?"

"I never forget the name of a pretty woman."

"It's Mrs. Singleton now," she said.

"Lucky fellow, Mr. Singleton. Welcome back to the Harvey House, Mrs. Singleton. Will you be wanting a room?"

"Only some information and a cup of coffee in your restaurant—my form of Dutch courage. Do you know the address of the Holloway family?"

Warmed by the coffee and armed with the information from the desk clerk, Samantha set off for the Holloway residence. The morning was cold but sunny and clear, the wind calm. She was dressed warmly for the walk, and it gave her a chance to go over in her mind what she would say when she met Millicent

Holloway. *Mrs. Holloway? I am Samantha Singleton, formerly Samantha Gordon. Our paths crossed once, but we had no idea who the other was. I am your daughter. You are my mother.*

Beyond that simple introduction, Samantha could not guess the direction their discourse would take. She had come for only one purpose—to learn the details associated with her birth and abandonment. She had absolutely no wish to become a part of the life of the woman who had refused nourishment to her baby girl. Samantha would make that clear. She had a mother, one who had always fulfilled her every maternal need. *So, Mrs. Holloway, if you will simply answer the questions I've come to ask, I will be on my way.*

The walk to the park was pleasant. Avoiding mud puddles from the recent snow was easy. The sun sparkled. The day was dry. Birds that had remained for the winter chirped from the branches of bare trees. She found the house easily enough and noticed a small park across the way that offered a bench upon which to sit and catch her breath, steel her will, and steady her nerves for the truth she'd come to hear. Meanwhile, she would study the house for a sign of life within, perhaps catch a glimpse of a woman with reddish-gold hair.

A man came out the front door with a newspaper tucked under his arm. He paused a moment, squinting up at the sky, assessing the day's potential, then took a pair of reading glasses from his pocket and hooked the earpieces in place. Samantha watched him walk with a familiar gait across the street toward the park. He wore a cloth cap, denim jacket, and overalls. He was so engrossed in scanning the headlines that he was almost at the bench before he saw that it was occupied. He stopped, startled.

"Hello, Mr. Holloway," Samantha said.

The man's eyes widened in shocked recognition. He whipped off his cap. "Miss Gordon! What are you doing here?"

"I've come to meet my mother—again," she said.

Chapter Eighty

Leon did not move for several blinks behind his eyeglasses before he availed himself of the space Samantha moved over to offer. He put his cap back on and laid the newspaper beside him. "That so?" he said. "How did you find her?"

Samantha had liked him the day she'd met him, and Nathan loved and trusted him. She'd go by Nathan's judgment any day. Samantha opened her purse and took out Bridget Mahoney's letter. "This is how."

After reading the letter, Leon handed it back. "It's as it happened, sure enough, I'm ashamed to say," he said.

"Fill out the rest of the picture," Samantha said. "Why did my mother not want my twin brother and me?"

Leon rubbed his knee. "It had to do with the man who got her pregnant with you. I am not your father, Samantha."

"I know that. Trevor Waverling is my father and Nathan Holloway is my twin. Neither one knows I'm aware of those facts. Never mind how I know."

Leon's eyebrow shot up above the rim of his glasses. "So you know most of the truth already."

"Not the part I need to know."

"All right, then, here it is. Millicent despises your father—your real father," Leon corrected. "She claims he raped her. I don't believe that myself, not even doin' my best to give her the benefit of the argument. He *rejected* her. That's more like it. Knowin' your mother like I do, you should believe that, too. He was her first love, and she gave him her all—heart, body, and soul—and he walked off and left it all behind."

"When my father…*rejected* her, did he know she was pregnant?"

"I'll go to my end believin' he didn't. He's admitted to us that he knew of Nathan before he showed up to claim him, but that was years later. I'd bet my last pair of overalls he didn't know about you. Until now, that is. You might as well know that, too."

Samantha's heartbeat held. "What do you mean?"

"He came here one Saturday last July and arranged to meet with me, unbeknown to Millicent. He was full of speculations about you and your birth that he wanted me to confirm as truth. I didn't. I promised my wife I'd never tell a soul that Nathan had been born a twin—"

"But she had to keep one of us because it was known she was pregnant," Samantha interrupted, fury warming her cheeks. "Otherwise, Nathan would have been given away, too."

"That's what Trevor Waverling figured out based on facts and observations regarding you."

"What sort of facts and observations?"

Leon related them as best he remembered. There was the rare color of Samantha's hair, the coincidences of her and Nathan's birth dates, the similarity of her features and gestures to Trevor's mother. Somehow he'd discovered the name of the doctor he thought had delivered her. Actually, as Samantha now knew, it was Bridget Mahoney who'd had the honor, but Dr. Tolman arranged her adoption. Leon said that later he learned that Trevor Waverling had made a trip across the Red River to Marietta in the Oklahoma Territory and called at Dr. Tolman's office. There he spoke to a midwife who'd told him that a young woman of Samantha's description had been by to inquire about her birth family. Trevor had told the woman that he might be the girl's father. She didn't have an address to give him but remembered that the young lady lived in Fort Worth. The midwife had been quite proud that she might have helped to reunite the handsome man from Dallas, Texas, with the pretty girl from Fort Worth.

"I learned all that from the midwife's husband," Leon explained. "He ferries across the river every Wednesday for a game of checkers." He peered at Samantha over his reading glasses. " 'Course I never imparted that information to my wife." Leon paused a moment to cross and recross his legs. "I'm afraid I can't bring myself around to likin' Trevor Waverling, but that's just resentment talkin'. He'll always have a part of my wife that'll never belong to me, and now he has the boy I raised, but I can sympathize with him. Can't think of nothin' worse than lovin' a child from a distance you cannot acknowledge."

Samantha took a deep breath to relieve the painful pressure under her ribs. "So my father is guilty of nothing but a questionable accusation?" she said.

"That's how I see it from here. He's tried to make it up to Nathan."

"He cares for him," Samantha said, eyes straining to remain dry. "It's evident that Nathan cares for him, too."

"As it was meant to be, sure enough." Leon removed his glasses and reached into his overalls' back pocket to withdraw a large handkerchief, its first unfolding of the day. It had been ironed, Samantha noticed irrelevantly. *By his wife's hand?* She hoped so. The man who'd put up with Millicent Holloway and obviously loved her all these years deserved at least that much mindfulness from the woman. Leon applied the cloth to the lens. "Your other father came to see me, too. You ought to know that as well."

Samantha coughed from the force of the shock. "My adoptive father, Neal Gordon? When?"

"During harvest, back in June. There he was at the fence one day, almost the spot where you'd stopped, this tough Texas rancher sittin' on his horse. I knew immediately who he was and why he'd come, even 'fore he'd given his name. I recognized it from when you came in answer to the ad, same as I recognized, or at least suspected, right then that you were Millicent's daughter."

Goosebumps rose on Samantha's flesh. "*You didn't!*"

"I shore did, missy. Think back on it, and you'll see. Anyway, returnin' to your pa. He said he'd come to see if the farm was still for sale, but I knew different. He'd come to check out us Holloways—the people who'd let strangers take their baby girl." The polishing of his glasses completed, Leon rehooked the earpieces. "I'm thinkin' he had a reason for comin' to look us over?"

"Yes...yes, he did," Samantha admitted, a lump forming in her throat. "He had plenty reason. I was the young woman from Fort Worth who questioned the midwife about her birth family. I...had reached a point when I wanted to know where I came from, who my people were. I...began a sort of secret investigation, and my father found out about it. The hurt of it just about broke his heart. The trip he made to see you...I guess he'd decided to let me go if...you met with his approval, no matter the cost to him and my mother."

Leon nodded and slipped back the pipe he'd drawn from his jacket pocket as if deciding against lighting up. "That was my notion, sure enough. I had a feelin' that's what it was all about. If the folks who'd birthed you had panned out, he'd 'a stepped back." Leon chuckled. "I turned him from that direction soon enough. You were with the folks who deserved and loved you. Wadn't no guarantee of that for you at the Holloway farm." Leon grinned at her. "I got the impression when your pa left that he'd 'a wrestled a band of Comanche 'fore he'd let us get our hands on you. 'Course he left thinkin' I was your father."

Tears pressed and Samantha fought against their release. She had not come here to cry. Emotion must not be allowed to cloud clear thinking. At the moment hers was as hazy as feathers unleashed in a pillow fight. She concentrated on placing in order the events that had led her here. Logic said that Dr. Tolman, ill and dying, had sent a letter to Neal Gordon containing information of Samantha's birth. From it, her father had learned she'd been born a twin and the name and whereabouts of the couple who'd given her away, facts he did not wish his daughter to know and the reason for destroying the letter before she could read it. He sent her to the Barrows farm in response to the classified ad with no idea that the seller was Millicent Holloway. Somehow in her absence, Neal Gordon recognized his mistake and immediately dropped interest in the property.

But then Neal Gordon discovered Eleanor Brewster's letter in the basket of figs that alerted him to the inquiries his daughter had made into her birth. The discovery accounted for the hellish months that followed and her father's decision to go to La Paloma as a ruse to check out the Holloways. Samantha's throat burned as she remembered how he'd left her the day he rode off from the Trail Head on his mission of love and sacrifice. *I love you, Samantha*, he'd said with the last look of a warrior leaving for a war from which he knew he'd never return. And then there came the day of the picnic at Windy Bluff when Neal learned that Nathan went by the last name of Holloway, a revelation that declared the landman to be his daughter's twin brother and Trevor Waverling her father.

Nearly all was clear now. Samantha had the answers she'd come for and the key to the mystery of her father's puzzling animosity toward Trevor Waverling and his clumsy attempts to keep her and Nathan apart. What a web he had spun for himself! How trapped in a net of guilt and fear. Samantha knew she should hate him, but she did not. He'd suffered enough. She understood his motives and forgave them. *A man is defined by his motives*—the mantra that Seth Singleton and now Sloan lived by. Neal Gordon's had not been pure, but they'd resulted from a father's love for his daughter and the fear of her loss. Samantha regretted only that he'd not trusted the depth of a daughter's love for her father.

Tears finally clouded her vision, and Leon laid a rough hand over hers. " 'Course if I hadn't made us sound so bad, you would have been reunited with your twin brother and that would have been a very good thing, but I had to do what I thought best."

"Have no regrets, Mr. Holloway," Samantha said. "Nathan and I have many years to make up for lost time."

Leon said without apparent surprise, "So you plan on identifying yourself to him?"

"I do."

"And Trevor Waverling?"

"To him, as well." A squirrel scampered up a tree branch and perched there eyeing them inquisitively, providing a distraction for her wet eyes. "But to my mother…no. I came here to meet her, but I don't find that necessary now. Can we keep this meeting between you and me? I'd prefer she never knew I was here."

"I promise you this meeting will be a pleasure I'll keep to myself. It's wise of you to decide not to meet her. Best for both of you. As Millicent would say, 'What good would come of it?' Nothin' that I can see. You must believe me on that. Go home to all those who love and want you, Samantha, and forget about the mother who didn't."

"My maternal grandparents? Where are they?"

"Dead. Both of 'em contemptible. Nathan knows. You're better off never havin' known 'em."

Samantha nodded and stood. Leon unwound his legs and hefted himself off the bench also. "Well, that all said, Mr. Holloway, I will take your advice and go home." She held out her hand.

Leon sandwiched it between his. "So when you go home, what do you plan to do with all these cats let out of the bag?"

"Let 'em roam free," Samantha answered. "No more keeping secrets. No more sweeping dust under the rug. We're all family. Regardless of our misguided steps, our hearts have been in the right place. There's room in them for everybody. Also"—she withdrew her hand to cup her abdomen—"I want that bag empty when my child is born."

Chapter Eighty-One

Sloan met her at the train station and held her fast and long. "Your mother is with Neal at the Triple S," he said. "He's drilling a hole through the front window watching for you."

"You didn't tell him anything, did you?"

"No, but they know, Sam. Your father figured out where you went and why. From the looks of your mother, he's told her everything. Her eyes are fiery red, and your daddy has on his wooden face, the kind he wears when he's playing poker and has a losing hand."

"If I know him, he won't play a card until he sees all of mine," Samantha said.

The Neal Gordons were standing to await her arrival when Samantha walked into the great room, her father stiff as a plank, her mother limp as a pillow with the feathers removed. Estelle's eyes did indeed look sandblasted and fastened on her in mute, heart-rending appeal. Neal's thoughts were indiscernible behind the hard screen of his gaze, but they were as easy to read as the days he'd surveyed the endless brown acres of his ranch that threatened the demise of his domain.

She held out her hands to them. "Mother, Daddy, let's sit down together," she said. "We have something to discuss."

She started at the beginning.

When it was all over and the truth exposed, feelings expressed, misperceptions and false impressions set right, transgressions forgiven, and eyes dried, Samantha left the room and stepped out onto the front porch to breathe in fresh air. She had left Neal and Estelle in the great room, her mother revitalized, thrilled over the coming grandchild, her father looking washed-out but like a draw cleaned of debris to receive fresh water in the spring. He would always be wary of Trevor Waverling. Samantha was prepared for that. Neal Gordon would keep an eye out for Trevor's encroachment on his territory as he had for Mexican marauders and the Comanche years after peace was made between country and nation and posed no threat to his land. It was his way.

"What...will you call him...Trevor Waverling?" he had asked.

Samantha had thought a moment. "Whatever the name my child chooses for him," she'd said.

The night was dark and cold. Samantha shivered and suddenly felt the warmth of her woolen shawl draped about her shoulders. From behind, Sloan wrapped his arms around her, drew her tightly against him, and laid his chin upon her head. "Since it's a night of confessions, will you hear mine?"

At last it was coming. In October an article had appeared in the monthly magazine *The Archaeologist* under the title "Dinosaur Relic Discovered in Box of Libby String Beans." The mysterious and amusing appearance of the fossil had made national news in the country's scientific community. In shock, Samantha had recognized the accompanying photo. A coldness had seized her bones. Without the description of the box and cup towels, she would have thought Todd responsible for the theft and shipment of the skull to the American Museum of Natural History in New York, but the culprit had been Sloan. Paleontologists had identified the partial skull of the dinosaur as a sauropod.

Her heart pumping, Samantha had retreated to her makeshift

laboratory where she could count on clarity and reason to prevail. Surrounded by relics and compounds, she traveled back in her mind to the day she found the skull missing. She and Sloan had parted at the crossroads to their ranches after his proposal that Sunday morning. To her disappointment, looking uneasy, he had refused to go with her to the site of her discovery and had posed a strange question. *Sam, you know that I would never make a decision, do anything, that wasn't in your best interests, don't you?*

When she'd asked the reason for the question, he'd answered: *Just for reassurance that you understand I'd never do anything intentionally to hurt you.*

I know that, she'd said.

I love you, Samantha Gordon.

I know that, too.

And she did know that, then and now, and for all the days of her life. Sloan had already taken the skull by then, ostensibly from Todd the afternoon before when he doubled back to the site. From that point of recollection, Samantha could only hypothesize, but she believed Sloan had interrupted Todd's theft of the skull and taken it to prevent him from destroying it as surely as the traitor had destroyed her Kodak. Samantha had figured out how Todd had feigned his innocence of the charge. Possibly Trevor Waverling had worked it out as well but couldn't prove it and was waiting to catch Todd in another false step.

Sloan had meant to return the skull to her, but then Samantha had confided the cause of the conflict between her and her father. Already deeply concerned about the breach between them, Sloan had realized the relic would widen it, perhaps irreparably. Neal Gordon would insist on his oil field; she would fight for her burial ground. The man who loved them both had decided the wisest course was to keep the skull in his care until he could decide what to do with it.

Samantha examined every opportunity for Sloan to have confessed his possession of the fossil but found none that he did not believe would jeopardize first their engagement and then their marriage. He did not know of Anne's visit to pump Samantha for an explanation of Sloan's waning interest. The girl's concern had been justified. Sloan Singleton was in love with Samantha Gordon and always had been. Anne's visit was proof enough that he'd had only her best interests at heart in taking and keeping the skull. Again, as with her father, he had not trusted her love for him not to believe the obvious—that he had married her with expectation of cashing in on the evidence that oil, barrels of it, was under the ground beyond the fence of the Triple S.

The skull had been in the Christmas cabinet. All the evidence pointed to it. Sloan's reaction when Billie June suggested it as storage space for her luggage, his efforts to keep Daniel out of the house, and the bath towel episode over Daniel's repair of the doorjamb made it clear. Sloan had spirited the skull away during the night when he learned the cabinet was to be sorted out the next morning. He stole out of the house to the ranch kitchen, removed the cans of string beans, and used the box and cup towels for packaging material. The address he'd taken from *The Archeologist*. He hadn't had the heart to deny the skull to posterity. *A man's motives define him.* Indeed they did. Sloan's had not been self-serving. He had acted out of love for his wife and a needless desperation to preserve their marriage, but Samantha had to hear the admission from his own lips.

"The confessional is still open," she said.

Once again she left Sloan behind. She must do this herself, she told him. Samantha boarded the train to Dallas the next morning, Thursday, January tenth. In Dallas from the train station, she took a cab to the office of Waverling Tools and was greeted by

Agatha Beardsley, who regarded her appearance with annoyance. "Does Mr. Waverling know to expect you?" the receptionist asked.

"No, he doesn't. I came with the hope I'd find him in and that he'll not view my unannounced visit as an intrusion."

"He's in, but I'm afraid I can't guarantee the latter. Mr. Waverling is very busy and has a train to catch in an hour, but I'll see if he will receive you." Miss Beardsley's crisp disapproval of the threat to her employer's schedule made clear, she said, "Please be seated until I come to fetch you."

"Of course," Samantha said and obediently took a seat.

She disappeared and within seconds, Trevor, strides ahead of Miss Beardsley, swung through the door to the reception room. "Mrs. Singleton—Samantha! What an unexpected pleasure! I hope all is well." He searched her face for signs that justified his remark and extended his hand.

Samantha rose to accept it and felt the warmth of paternal feeling through her glove. "All is well but soon to be even better, I believe," she said, smiling. "Should I return later? I understand you're very busy and have a train to catch."

Trevor shook his head adamantly to disavow the notion and shot a glare at Miss Beardsley. "Neither is absolutely of any consequence, I can assure you. I can grab a later train. I'm only going to Beaumont on the coast. Come into my office. And Miss Beardsley, will you see that we're not disturbed?"

A little over an hour later, Trevor summoned his receptionist. She was shocked to see signs he'd had a good cry, but she had never seen him look so happy. Mrs. Singleton had her handkerchief out and appeared as if she, too, had recovered from some deep emotion that had left her eyes puffy and pink-rimmed, but her lips were smiling also. *What in the world?*

"Miss Beardsley, where is my son?" Trevor asked.

"At the Loving Convalescent Home, sir. He went over there this morning to visit his brother."

"Call the place and have somebody tell Nathan he's to meet his father at his grandmother's house. It's very important. He's to come as quickly as he can. Have Benjy bring the Concord around, then call my residence and tell my mother to expect us."

"Uh, Mr. Waverling, what about your trip to the coast? Mr. Lane called from Beaumont to say they've struck a gusher at Spindletop. He's very excited, and he's wondering when you will be arriving. He says the sight is something to see." Miss Beardsley, herself excited at the news, consulted a lapel watch she pulled from its moorings on her shoulder. "It's twelve o'clock. I took the liberty of checking the next train to the coast, and if you hurry, you can make the one o'clock." She looked expectantly at Trevor, ignoring the intruder who would keep her employer from his appointed course.

"That's all very exciting news, Miss Beardsley, but I have my own to tell my family. Now if you'll hold down the fort for the rest of the day, my daughter and I will leave you to it."

"I beg your pardon?"

"You heard me correctly. Miss Beardsley, meet my daughter, Samantha Gordon Singleton. She's Nathan's twin sister."

Miss Beardsley's jaw still hung slack when Trevor escorted Samantha through the reception room to the waiting carriage.

Epilogue

In April 1901, Nathan Holloway married Charlotte Weather-spoon two weeks after his twenty-first birthday. It was the wedding of the year for Dallas society. The ceremony was conducted in the First Baptist Church of Dallas and officiated by the highly esteemed George W. Truett, the leading clergyman of his day. Over five hundred guests attended. Trevor Waverling served as Nathan's best man; Nathan's brother, Randolph, and Daniel Lane as groomsmen. Mavis, Samantha, and Sloan, along with Neal and Estelle Gordon, and Leon and Lily, accompanied by her husband, were escorted to pews reserved for the groom's family. Millicent was not among them. Nathan had cut ties with his mother.

"April is such a perfect time for a wedding," Mavis stated. "It's a period of new beginnings and should be the month that starts the New Year, not January, for heaven's sake. What were the Gregorians thinking?"

For the ranches of Las Tres Lomas de la Trinidad and the Triple S, April was indeed the start of new beginnings. Midmorning of the third week in April, Jarvis Putnam, driller of Derrick One, so the well at Windy Bluff was identified, knocked on the front door of the ranch house at Las Tres Lomas de la Trinidad. Silbia answered and immediately stepped back.

Jarvis jerked off his oil-covered driller's hat, a steel-plated affair, and swiped a large bandanna handkerchief over his black-speckled face. "I beg your pardon, ma'am. I'm sure I look a fright, but I must see Mr. Gordon and use your telephone, if you please."

Silbia had never met Jarvis Putnam, but from the looks of him, he was part of the rough crowd of men that had been digging around out at Windy Bluff. She was wary of letting him into the house, dripping black goop all over her clean floors. "What for?" she demanded.

"To let Mr. Gordon and my boss know we've struck oil."

Derrick Number One was to be the forerunner of many more successful wells drilled over the one thousand square miles of the combined ranches that would produce millions of barrels of oil from the sandstone and carbonate reservoirs under its properties. For easy reference, the Triple S and Las Tres Lomas de la Trinidad did not change their names but operated under one brand that symbolized their consolidation. The brand of the biggest cattle ranch of contiguous acreage in Texas was a simple S/S/S/. It was Samantha's idea to use the slash marks to represent the three tributaries of the Trinity River. Despite the physical evidence of vast oil production that came to dot its acres, Las Tres Lomas and the Triple S maintained their inherent character. Cattle was their business, and to that end, as Texas roared into the new century propelled by the discovery of petroleum throughout the state, new breeds were introduced to achieve better beef quality and easier adaptation to the environment of Central Texas. Experimentation with grasses led to improved rangelands where eventually healthy Santa Gertrudis and Herefords and Beefmasters grazed on green pastures teeth to jaw with oil derricks and pumping jacks.

Of those family members and associates who sat on the groom's side of the aisle or who stood with Nathan during his marriage ceremony, financial fortune smiled on most. Within a few years, Waverling Tools patented a roller cutter bit enabling oil drillers to bore through hard rock with amazing speed. Daniel Lane was the designer. The two-cone bit revolutionized the industry, poured millions of dollars into the company's coffers and Daniel's pockets, and set the company on its way to becoming a world leader in the design and manufacture of petroleum equipment.

Nathan continued in his role as the landman of the company and teammate of Todd Baker while quietly slipping into the seat of Waverling Tools as heir apparent, and the geologist rose to prominence in his profession's ranks. Todd found the oil, and Nathan negotiated the drilling rights in Texas counties whose field names would make petroleum history: Sour Lake and Batson-Old in Hardin County, Humble and Goose Creek in Harris, Mission in Bexar, Piedras Pintas in Duval, Panhandle Osborne in Wheeler. Early in his career, Todd had been paid a visit by Daniel carrying into his office a business envelope bearing the name Morris Keaton Brownie Shop. When he left Todd's office still in possession of the envelope and the photographs within, the company geologist was never again to engage in a nefarious scheme such as the one that had prompted Daniel's visit and for which he had no aptitude anyway. But as a result of it, Todd was never to belong to the private inner ring of Waverling Tools, nor were he and Ginny ever included in the intertwined social circles of the Singletons, Waverlings, and Lanes. Much to Ginny's chagrin, fueled by suspicion that her husband's somehow wrongdoing at the company was responsible, the Baker names never appeared among those in attendance at the families' social soirees reported in the society columns of Fort Worth and Dallas newspapers.

Randolph lived out his working life as a bank teller in Ardmore, Oklahoma, and was eventually promoted to vice president, a figurehead title shared by five others in the bank. He married a local girl who reminded Nathan of the waitress his brother had left behind in New York City. She bore him two sons in whom Randolph tried to instill a lust for the wealth and prominence for which he'd prepared diligently and destroyed his chance of achieving. Lily lived merrily ever after with her three daughters and history-teacher husband in a house four streets over from her brother. The Haymaker and Randolph Holloway families met every Sunday after church for a fried chicken dinner in the modest home of one or the other. The Leon Holloways were always invited, but generally, only their father came.

But there were other good fortunes that carried no dollar signs. Samantha and Sloan's first child was a boy they christened Seth Gordon Singleton. Their son's name for Neal was Granddaddy; for Trevor, Pop, by which Samantha affectionately referred to him from then on. A daughter and son followed. Billie June and Daniel, expecting a son and playmate for S.G., as the Singletons' firstborn would soon be called, became the proud parents of three daughters. Charlotte gave birth to two sons and one daughter. Millie May never married but enjoyed the role of aunt to her nieces and nephews. The Gordon, Singleton, Waverling, and Lane families melded and became as one. The automobile allowed frequent reunions at one or the other's abodes that in time grew to huge estates where there was much laughter, bounteous food, boisterous play, and general noise-making among the nine children and ten adults.

"I feel like a piñata," Neal said to Estelle after one such occasion held at Las Tres Lomas.

"A piñata, Neal?"

"Uh-huh. There I was living my life like one of those papier-mâché party animals, strung up out of reach, afraid to share, keeping my toys locked inside all to myself, when—wham! I got hit by a big stick. I'm mighty glad I did. You know what I'm tryin' to say, honeybee?"

"I do, Neal. Love is always better when it's shared."

At the end of the decade, *The Forum*, one of the most respected magazines in America, featured within its covers a three-page article and related photographs under the title *TITANS*. Neal Gordon was listed among them along with Trevor Waverling. Samantha said, "Well, Daddy, you're a titan at last. How does it feel?"

Neal frowned. "Not as good as I would have thought," he said. Samantha looked at him with understanding. Estelle had died the year before. But her death was not responsible for Neal's lack of excitement. Yesterday afternoon, his grandson, S.G., had brought him part of a long, strange-looking leg bone he'd found sticking up out of the ground in the deeply cratered area over which Derrick One had once stood. For some reason, the place held a mesmeric fascination for his grandchildren. "Granddaddy, what animal does this belong to?" he'd asked.

ACKNOWLEDGMENTS

I'd like to express my gratitude to those who, as always, made this book happen: my literary representative, David McCormick of McCormick Literary Agency; Deb Futter, editor in chief of Grand Central Publishing; and the friends and fans whose enthusiasm for and enjoyment of my former books inspired me to keep writing. There were losses along the way, and I'd like to bid a fond but sad farewell with my thanks for his help to Clint Rodgers, who for years answered every SOS call to cure my computer of its many ills. Bless you always, Clint. You were the best doctor in the house. A sorrowful good-bye to Dr. Charles Melenyzer, cyberspace whiz who came to the rescue if only briefly, but what a godsend. Charles, you'll never know how much I appreciate your timely appearance on the scene. Because of you, I managed to continue my work on this manuscript.

In addition, I owe more gratitude than can be enumerated to Dr. Beverly Alcot, neighbor and friend, whose electronic expertise met electronic illiteracy with grace and patience the many times she was frantically called from across the street to render assistance. Bev, bottom-of-the-heart thanks for being there when I needed you.

In some instances, words are useless to express the inexpressible. I will simply say thank you, Arthur Richard Meacham III, beloved husband, and Ann Ferguson Zeigler, beloved friend, for once again daily, week in and week out, making the journey with me. And posthumous gratitude goes to Sara Lynn Robbins for her expert guidance in leading me through the mountains of scientific research for *Titans*. I thank her most of all for the memories of our sixty-six years of friendship. Rest in peace, Sara Lynn.

READING GROUP GUIDE

Contains Spoilers

DISCUSSION QUESTIONS

1. Do you agree with Neal Gordon's statement: "Loyalty is the one human quality that must be returned. You can give respect, honor, admiration, even love without return, but loyalty must be repaid in kind"?

2. Grizzly says on page 148: "Just remember this, young lady. Your daddy loves you more than life, but there's no such thing as an unbreakable connection. There are some things in this world that unconditional...love can't stand up to, and the biggest is betrayal." What are your thoughts on this viewpoint?

3. After Sloan publicly puts a stop to Daniel's courtship of Billie June, Mildred claims that "nothing sets deeper or burns longer in the human gut than the shame of public humiliation." Do you agree?

4. In the early 1900s, "All over the nation, the 'new woman' was replacing the 'ideal woman,' challenging male dominance." Where do you see examples of these types of women in the

novel? Where do Samantha, Millie May, Billie June, and Anne fall on the spectrum? Do you see similar changes or divisions in concepts of womanhood today?

5. Throughout the novel, many characters—from Leon to Nathan to Grizzly—are bound by their word to keep vital information a secret. Do you think issues would have been resolved more quickly if all these secrets had been out in the open from the beginning—or was the passage of time necessary? Do you believe that it's best to stick to your word, or is it sometimes important to exercise your best judgment regardless of promises made?

6. Despite Samantha and Nathan's love for and devotion to Neal, Estelle, and Leon, these parents all fear losing their child. Do their concerns prove valid? Do you think nature or nurture plays a greater role in forming someone's character?

7. What sacrifices were the three fathers willing to make for their children: Leon for Nathan, Neal for Samantha, and Trevor for Samantha? What do they say about the men's character?

8. If you were in Samantha's shoes, would you have acted differently when faced with the big decisions of: pursuing a career in archeology or helping run her father's ranch, drilling for oil or preserving the fossil grounds, and finding her birth family or respecting her adoptive parents' wishes?

9. Examine the major spousal relationships in *Titans*: Millicent and Leon, Neal and Estelle, Daniel and Billie June, Samantha

and Sloan. Despite any differences, resentments, or betrayals, all of these marriages presumably last a lifetime. What binds each of these couples together? How are their relationships similar to or different from one another?

10. How does class play a role in informing characters' world-views and pivotal decisions? What aspect of class is most important to Neal, Daniel, and Millicent, and what are these characters willing to sacrifice to achieve their goals?

11. Who are the titans in this novel and why? Is the title fitting to the story? When Samantha asks her father how it feels to finally be a titan, Neal responds, "Not as good as I would have thought." What do you think he means by this?

A CONVERSATION WITH
LEILA MEACHAM

Q: Throughout *Titans*, the reader gains a strong sense of the zeitgeist of Texas in the early 1900s: its landscape, citizens, social structure, and the changes that were happening at that time. What about this setting appealed to you?

A: The period and locale of Central Texas best suited the spinning of the tale and the cast of characters. I wanted to confine the narrative to a short but dramatic span of time, in comparison to my other novels that unfold over many decades and truly qualify as sagas. No other time or setting was more appealing to me than the nine months prior to Texas's explosive entry into the petroleum industry on January 10, 1901, when a lonely little salt mound outside Beaumont, Texas, spewed a geyser of black gold.

Q: What was your writing process like for this book? Did it change much from your initial conception to its final creation?

A: I'll say it did! As a matter of fact, I almost completely revised my final draft after it went to the publisher. Truth told, the whole writing experience of *Titans* was different from the comparatively smooth composition of my other novels. For starters, I began and finished the original draft during a dark year in my life. A heart condition, side-saddled with all the accompanying annoyances and frustrations of endless doctors' appointments, mind-numbing medications, tests, procedures, and the two surgeries required to fix it, plagued the writing process. Then, as I was finishing the final chapter of the novel, my husband, the love of my life, was diagnosed with laryngeal cancer. In that week as well, the electronics guru who'd looked after my computer needs for ten years fired me as a client, the printer and backup system to my computer both failed, and the technician called in to repair them lost three chapters of the novel that were never reclaimed and had to be rewritten. It all constituted the perfect storm. Nonetheless, from the get-go, all through the writing of the 635 manuscript pages, my writer's instinct, whether the result of the confluence of events or not, whispered that something was amiss with the book. Something wasn't right. It was "off." My astute and wonderful editor agreed and made some suggestions for revision, but I knew the problems went deeper. So, having once more a healthy heart, a clear head, and a husband with a restored larynx, I drew in a deep breath, stepped back, took a closer look at the manuscript, and began again. The rewrite was an arduous but invaluable learning experience from which I believe I created the novel as it was meant to be.

Q: It's interesting to examine the different family dynamics in *Titans*, from Millicent's detachment from her own firstborns, to Nathan's acclimation to the Waverling household, to Samantha's instinctual attachment to Nathan and Rebecca. What draws you to write about such complicated family structures?

A: I wish I knew. It's been a surprise to me that family dynamics play a dominant role in my novels. I really don't know much about family, being childless and having come from a small unit of four, my parents and brother and me. In those days, brothers occupied one world with their buddies, and sisters occupied another with theirs, so brothers and sisters were most likely to be acquaintances rather than friends. I never knew my grandparents on either side, and aunts and uncles and cousins were few and far away. I grew up in a generation before Dr. Spock. Generally, fathers made the living, mothers made the life, and children were to be seen and not heard. While our corporeal needs were seen to, there was very little sharing of feelings, dreams, and ambitions, either from parent to child or child to parent, not from indifference but from custom. It simply wasn't done. It was enough to know that we all loved one another. So my experience with parents and sibling offers little background from which to generate the stories I write and should elicit even less interest to me as the subject of them, one would think. Drama, however, is the mainstay of fiction, and from what better source to draw drama than family relationships, the starting point of human behavior and interaction?

Q: *Titans* has an incredibly large cast of characters, all of whom have distinct personalities and paths in life. Do you have a favorite character?

A: Leon Holloway, hands down. Like all my characters, I don't know where he came from. He was simply there on the page one day, bringing in a load of firewood, responsible, kind, caring, tolerant, and wise in the way of men who've learned their lessons of life at the knee of nature. We should all be so fortunate to have a Leon Holloway in our lives.

Q: At the end of _Titans_, you manage to rather neatly tie together all the different plot threads and themes that were running through the book. Did this ending come about naturally, or did it take careful planning and outlining?

A: _Titans_ is the most complicated novel I've written because of all the balls I had to keep in the air. Keeping two lives running simultaneously in two different places was my greatest challenge yet. I hope more so for the author than the reader. To prevent confusion for the reader, several times in the story I had a character—first Leon, then Neal—organize in his head the facts as he knew them. This technique of allowing the character to list for himself who knew what and when came about in the natural flow of the narrative. The conclusion evolved naturally as well. I relied on the "character" of the characters to guide the ending. Samantha could not have denied her curiosity to learn the details of her abandonment; Neal, his love for his adopted daughter; Sloan, the skull to posterity; Daniel, his newfound self-worth and love for Billie June to exact revenge. In the end, none of the characters could deny the people they were.

Q: Many of your characters seem to be constrained by secrets and the silence surrounding them, and oftentimes shared knowledge is not spoken out loud—either due to petty reasons or well-intentioned ones. Does this theme stem from real-life observations?

A: Not from particular observation but from a general view that secrets can spawn good stories. Their revelations can be a character's undoing, or—as in _Titans_—an unexpected salvation. Secrets are a distant cousin to deception, and we all know what Walter Scott said about deceit: "Oh, what a tangled web we weave when first we practice to deceive." Family secrets lend themselves to great stories of human dilemma because their very nature creates suspense.

Q: What kinds of books did you enjoy reading as a child? As an adult? Are your own books at all reflective of past favorites?

A: As a child, I was especially fond of books that featured animals. I must have read Kenneth Grahame's *Wind in the Willows* a dozen times. Anna Sewell's *Black Beauty* sparked a lifelong admiration of horses, and the characters of Beatrice Potter's books— *Peter Rabbit*, *Mrs. Tiggy-Winkle*, and *Mrs. Tittlemouse*—make me smile from their memories still. A love of and respect for animals no doubt have prompted inclusion of pets in my books. As an adult, I enjoy any nonfiction or fiction book that is well written and researched, and features a subject or characters I can care about.

Q: Over the course of your now four books— *Roses*, *Tumbleweeds*, *Somerset*, and *Titans*—do you feel yourself revisiting certain themes or ideas? If so, what attracts you to them?

A: I don't know that a recurring thematic thread runs through my novels, but I can say that in all of them, key players make wrong decisions based on what they believe to be the right reasons. These always result in life changes, often tragic. The character must then either deal with the consequences or find his way out of the dilemma. I remember reading, "Crises define us. In them we discover who we are." I suppose that if there is a repeated element in my books, it is that revelation for a character. In real life I have never observed or been privy to a situation where a person must suffer the consequences of a wrong choice based on noble motivations. I have, however, witnessed numerous times the truth of that age-old adage: "Everything that goes around comes around." But I do not care to write of those folks who eventually get snagged in the trap of their devious designs. I like to write about characters caught in their web of good intentions.

ABOUT THE AUTHOR

Leila Meacham is a writer and former teacher who lives in San Antonio, Texas. She is the author of the bestselling novels *Roses*, *Somerset*, and *Tumbleweeds*. For more information, you can visit LeilaMeacham.com.